A CALL to EVIL

P.A. RUSSELL

This is a work of fiction. Names, characters, places, and incidents either are the
product of the author's imagination or are used fictitiously, and any resemblance
to actual persons, living or dead, businesses, companies, events, or locales is
entirely coincidental.
Cover design by Geraldine Russell.
ISBN: 979-8-35094-479-2 paperback

PROLOGUE

July 1963 Long Island, New York

Stanley Bolton, self-proclaimed juvenile delinquent at the age of 14, sat in his room carefully cutting an order form from the back page of a current pulp fiction magazine. Restless and already bored even though summer vacation had just begun, he needed some action, which usually meant getting into trouble. Stanley's motto, "who cares?" was his justification for past, dubious exploits. So, who would care if he ordered something that might be fun from this magazine?

He had swiped the Amazing Stories magazine from his father's nightstand and finished reading the featured H.P. Lovecraft story when he spotted a related item for sale on the ad page. He got a kick out of browsing these pages in previous issues and would often order joke items like hand buzzers and whoopie cushions, but this item was different: a curious piece of merchandise, a book of spells, that intrigued him and led him to thinking about possible summer pranks. The price: $1.99 plus shipping and handling came to a total of $2.50 which could be easily managed. Delivery: a week to ten days. Perfect!

As Stanley slipped the completed order form, plus two one-dollar bills and a fifty-cent piece scotched taped to a square of cardboard (

money won from playing craps before school ended) into the stamped envelope, his excitement grew. Who could he try this new scheme on?

There was only one person. The kid across the street, Tim Ryan, seemed like a friend. He was the only boy his age who would actually hang around with him and not call him "monkey boy" like all the others did. Stanley's protruding ears, fat lips and a dark single eyebrow that grew across his forehead and hung over his eyes, had earned him this hurtful moniker. He knew he could tempt this kid because Tim Ryan loved all things science fiction and horror. He smiled to himself. This could turn out to be great fun.

Stanley ran down the stairs and out the front door, ignoring his mother's call from the kitchen. He jumped on his bike, lit a cigarette, and sped off down Cabel Street heading toward downtown Hillsville and the first public mailbox he could find. Experience taught him that mailing this type of item from the house mailbox could be troublesome; especially if his father found it.

Little did he know that this escapade would turn out to be more *troublesome* than anything he could ever imagine.

PART ONE

CHAPTER 1

One week later

Stanley Bolton leaned against his mother's faded, black 54 Ford Crestline parked in front of his house. Waiting. Trying to decide if he should cross the street and ring Tim Ryan's doorbell or not. It felt childish or wimpy. *Can Timmy come out to play?*

Regardless of the July heat he had an image to maintain. His tough guy look: black tee shirt with rolled up sleeves, dungarees with rolled up cuffs and black high-top sneakers. A lit Camel cigarette hanging from the corner of his mouth to complete the look.

Just then Tim Ryan came sauntering down his driveway to retrieve the empty trash cans from the morning pickup. Stan straightened.

"Hey Ryan," he called. "You doin anythin'?"

Tim Ryan looked up and gave a quick wave.

"I have chores to do before I go deliver my papers," he said. And I want to get an early start on the route in case it rains.

They both looked skyward at the same time. Heavy gray clouds were moving in. The 90-degree temperature plus high humidity were just right for a summer thunderstorm, Long Island style.

"Forget the chores," Stan said. "Come over. I got somethin ta show ya".

Tim started dragging the trash cans back up the driveway.

"Maybe after I finish my deliveries," Tim said. "I told my mother I'd get them done before I leave."

Stanley dropped the cigarette on the street and crushed it out.

"Who cares?" Stanley called. "Tell her you'll do them later".

Then as if on cue it started to drizzle, and the first rumbles of thunder sounded in the distance.

Stanley grinned at Tim. "Well, there ya go. You're off the hook. Might as well hang out here till it stops rainin'."

***

Tim Ryan had only been in Stanley Bolton's house a few times and those visits were short as if Stanley didn't want to be in the house too long. Maybe he was ashamed of its shabby appearance or the smell of burnt coffee and cigarettes that filled the living area. Now, Stanley seemed more at ease with him being there.

"Follow me," Stan said as he opened the door that led to the basement.

Tim heard the clanking of pots and pans coming from the kitchen then the voice of Mrs. Bolton.

"Stanley? What are you up to?" she called.

"Nothin," Stanley said.

"Stanley?" she said again with a distinct sternness.

"Just tradin' some baseball cards with Tim Ryan."

"In the basement?"

"It's cooler down there!" Stan shot back.

"Don't touch your father's tools."

What's going on? I didn't bring any cards. Tim thought as he started down the dark stairs. True, collecting baseball cards was one of the hobbies Stan had shared with him but, Tim had a strong feeling this had nothing to do with that. Just then he heard the basement door close. The click of a switch brought the lights below to life.

"Yeah, Stan. What are you up to?" Tim said. The concerns he sometimes had about Stan's reputation made him wonder if this friendship was worth it. And here he was being all mysterious about something plus lying to his mother on top of it.

"Shsssh! I'll show ya. Just get down there."

The basement smelled musty. Two lone light bulbs hanging from the rafters cast a yellowish hue over the white cinder block walls. It felt damp and definitely cooler than the upstairs room. A wooden workbench cluttered with tools occupied a far-left corner. A card table with two chairs sat in the center of the room with a large publication — about the size and thickness of an Encyclopedia volume — resting in the middle.

Tim took a step forward, looking intently at the item laying there. The publication cover was jet black with a swirling gold border. The title — the letters raised and written in Old English type — also blazed in a shiny gold.

"What's this?" Tim said, as he shot Stan a confused look.

"It's somethin I ordered that might keep this summer from bein' borin'," Stan said.

"I'm not bored!"

Tim glanced at the book again. "Why are you showing me this?"

"Because you're the only one I know who's really into this stuff".

Tim read the title once more.

Lovecraft's

Spells and Conjuring's

"You know this stuff isn't real," Tim said. "Besides, I'm not into junk like Ouija boards and curses".

Stanley tapped the book with his finger. "This has nothin ta do with curses. And…how do ya know it ain't real? Suppose it is. I've read stuff that said the Lovecraft stories about the Old Ones are true. Not made up. How cool would that be?"

"Sounds like you've got a plan for using this," Tim said.

Stanley sat at the table and opened the publication to a page he had dog eared earlier.

Thunder boomed outside and heavy rain battered the small, single basement window located at the top of a back wall. The lights flickered and they gave each other a wide-eyed look.

"Accordin' ta this," Stanley said as he returned his attention to the page in front of him. "A magical being named Malhela — one of those Lovecraft calls the Old Ones — can predict things. It can also get things for the person who conjured it."

Tim sat down across from Stanley.

"So? You really think that conjuring up this being is going to tell you the future and get things for you? Get what things?"

"Yeah, if what this book says is true. *And…* who cares what it gets? Maybe baseball cards, cigarettes, money. Who knows?

"This is dumb," Tim said.

"Hold on! Just read this," Stanley said. He slid the open book over to Tim.

The paper upon which the description of Malhela was written appeared to be faded tanned parchment. It felt gritty to the touch as if sprinkled with sand. *How old is this thing?* Tim wondered. *The cover looks new, but these pages feel like they were buried in a sand box or something.*

Despite his common sense telling him this was baloney, Tim had seen enough movies and read enough books concerning this subject that his curiosity was getting the better of him.

He read the description.

<u>Malhela</u>: *Considered a prophet; seer of future events. Also known to be a harvester or gatherer of* **what** *is not fully known. Chameleon by nature.*

Malhela is mischievous, clever, unpredictable, impatient, spiteful and at times vicious. Can be fiercely loyal and protective of the one who calls.

Thought to be immortal.

Malhela requires payment for services rendered. The one who calls may not be aware of the compensation taken.

Nota Bene: A counter incantation is required to return Malhela to the realm of Cytizuz if her services cannot be fulfilled. This publication does not contain such prose.

<u>**Invocation**</u>

Exaudi me, o Sublimis! Egredere, Malhela et fac iussa mea. Exi, Malhela et da vota mea.

In hoc consentio ad emendam electionis tuae, quae in acceptis tuis servitis reddetur.

Laudon nomen tuum! Malhela! Malhela! Malhela!

Tim looked up. "This looks like Latin."

Stanley gave a quick smile that Tim didn't like.

"And…now ya know why you're here."

"What? I don't know Latin. I think you're cracked…Stanley."

Stanley straightened in his chair and glared across the table. "Come on, Ryan. Ya told me ya were learnin Latin last term in that Catholic school ya go to. So, don't be a Fink. Just try it. And…hurry up before my mother gets suspicious."

Tim stared at the page.

This is nuts. Tim thought. *What am I doing? I don't know enough Latin to translate this junk. Maybe I can pick out a few words, translate them and get him off my back with some mumbo jumbo?*

Stanley planted an elbow on the table and rested his chin in the palm of his hand. "I'm *waitin'.*"

"Why don't you do this by yourself, since you're so keen on finding out what happens? You know how to read." Tim said.

"I can't read this stuff. I could say somethin' wrong and screw up the conjurin'. Don't tell me you're chicken? *You are a Fink!*"

"Shut up! And…don't call me a Fink."

Being careful not to mess up his hair, Tim scratched the back of his head as if thinking of what to say. As he brought his hand back to the page his finger left a small fragrant stain from the Brylcreem he used. He didn't notice. He started his so-called translation. "Remember. This may be all wrong, but I think it's like a prayer to this Malhela being. Asking it to appear and grant something. I'm not sure …wishes or desires? I don't know. There's something about a payment but I can't make out the rest. The last part seems like a chant praising the name Malhela over and over. That's all I got." Tim slid the book across the table.

"Okay that sounds good enough ta me. So, go ahead…read it out loud."

Now, Tim started to feel a bit nervous. Movies like Night of the Demon and Burn, Witch, Burn crept into his mind. Not far behind were Lovecraft's Tales of Cthulu that had totally creeped him out when he had read them. Maybe this is a bad idea.

"No. This is your idea. You read and I'll help you," Tim said as he moved his chair back from the table.

"No dice. We'll read it out loud together. Deal?"

Tim gave a reluctant nod of agreement.

"Okay, let's … Wait! We need somethin first."

Stanley jumped up and went to the large white cabinet that stood under the basement window, opened the door, and pulled out a big, blood red candle.

Tim just shook his head. "You've got to be kidding."

"This is the way it's done in every movie I've ever seem about conjurin."

Stan placed the candle next to the open document and lit it with his lighter. He pulled his chair around the table, sat next to Tim, and smiled. "Ready?"

Together they slowly read the *Invocation*. Pronouncing the Latin words as best they could. When they finished both sat back in their chairs. Unconsciously holding their breath, arms folded in nervous anticipation. They gave each other a questioning look. Nothing happened.

The candle flickered once but that could have been anything. Nothing changed. The basement remained the same; cool, damp, and empty. All was quiet except for the continuing patter of the rain on the window.

"Looks like you wasted your money, Stan."

Stanley just shrugged. "Who cares?"

Just then they heard a sound that made them freeze where they sat.

The basement door flew open followed by rapid footfalls.

"What're you guys doing down here?" said Stanley's younger brother Jonathan. Who now stood at the foot of the stairs with an issue of Mad Magazine under his arm.

Stanley jumped up, knocking over his chair. "Get outa here ya little creep," he yelled.

"Mom! Stanley's playing with candles down here," Jonathan shouted as he headed back up the stairs.

A word slipped from Stanley's lips that Tim had never heard him say before. "Shit."

Stanley quickly blew out the candle and waved his hand over it to disperse the residual smoke. "We better go up before she comes down here snoopin," he said.

As they started up the stairs Stanley abruptly stopped. "Wait here," he said to Tim and went back down. He hurried to the table, picked up the candle and put it back where he found it, then grabbed the book of spells and stashed it under the stairs in the dark, dusty space beneath the bottom step. Satisfied with this hiding place Stanley rejoined Tim on the stairs.

***

As darkness fell on Cabel Street, a glowing cloud appeared above the roof top of the Bolton residence. It swirled in a slow clockwise motion, gradually increasing in size as it took on a vertical ovoid shape. Florescent colors churned within the cloud changing from white to pink to gray and finally to a pale blue. Silently the center of the ovoid irised open and the cloud began to sparkle and vibrate as it evaporated into a hazy mist revealing a shadowy figure, shoulders hunched, as it crouched behind the roof top chimney. Cautiously it raised its head and breathed in the night air.

CHAPTER 2

After the conjuring: Day one - Morning

Malhela felt the warmth of the morning sun on her wings and gingerly unfolded them from around her body. Instinctively she became one with the surroundings. Her appearance was now that of the mottled red stone structure next to her. She would not be seen.

With arms raised and back stretched, she slowly scanned the area below. Once again, called from the Dark Realm into the world of the mortals. But when? What era was this? The air was clean and free of soot. The sky, a brilliant blue.

The few mortals seen since arriving looked different. Shaven, fully clothed, and as far as she could tell, weaponless.

Weaponless? Unusual. Was this a *time* of docile beings? Did they not hunt for their food? Or was this some form of trickery intended as a trap?

Past encounters with mortal men always resulted in some form of combat. Though she couldn't die, pain could be experienced. Past wounds had taken too long to heal. It would be wise to remain suspicious as well as alert.

Obviously, this was not the place of the ancient mariners she had visited before. This was a new world, a new time for her to explore and perhaps play in. This would be exciting.

The quiet sounds of this world's early morning stimulated Malhela's sharp hearing. Bird song was everywhere. Insects buzzed. A small dog barked somewhere in the distance and in the dwelling below the noise of annoying mortals waking.

She flexed her wings and once again sniffed the air. Where was the conjurer? She knew well the scent of mortal males and had identified two of their kind last night, though they were juveniles. One of these — perhaps the conjurer — had an unusual scent that pleased her. Male musk with an intermingling of citrus. She caught a hint of it in the air now and grinned. He can't be far. Then before a direction could be determined a strong odor overcame it.

A strange moving object, like a four wheeled carriage with no horse, rattled down the thoroughfare below, spewing the stink from its rear. The odor— thick with the smell of some oily substance — caused her nose to twitch in disgust. She turned her head, hissed then spat at the object.

Annoyed and agitated she cast her keen sense of smell outward, a mile in all directions, trying to regain the scent. No success. It had dissipated.

Angered, Malhela lept into the air. Soared low over the moving object and splattered it with feces. As she swooped into an upward turn, she looked back and uttered a curse of damnation at the moving nuisance. It sputtered to a stop at the end of the thoroughfare.

Returning to the uncomfortable rooftop she hovered over the protruding stone structure pondering this irritating location. According to the Law of the Realm, a being passing through the veil via conjuring would be permanently linked to the point of arrival on the other side making it mandatory to return to this location after every undertaking until released from the spell. In other words, this could be Malhela's roost for a long time.

A poor start to this adventure.

Suddenly a voice in her head shattered the reverie. Not a spoken word, more like a thought. It came from one of the juveniles she had detected when she arrived. Apparently, he lived in the dwelling beneath her. Could he be the conjurer? The voice was similar but somehow incomplete. She could always identify the one who did the summoning. A certain feeling, like urgency, responsibility or duty would stream from the conjurer and envelope her. But oddly, not this time.

Curious now Malhela scrambled headfirst down the side of the dwelling to a window and peered inside. There, in what must be a sleep chamber stood one of the males from last night. He paced around the room like some trapped animal, muttering something unintelligible. His scent, strong, musky, mixed with the smell of burning vegetation assaulted her senses. As she watched, his voice once again sounded in her head. His language vaguely familiar. Likened to that of a Celtic tribe she had once harassed. The word he repeatedly pronounced as "money", echoed in her head.

It didn't feel like a summoning for service. Nothing felt right since she arrived. Could this conjuring be a mistake?

That would be an interesting turn of events. Trapped in this time and place forever until someone released her. No mission or purpose. No commands or demands to fulfill. It would be a life of unfamiliar freedom.

It may not be so bad, but something still felt incomplete. The other male — the one who's scent was delightful — could be the answer. But where was he?

All at once the reason for the strangeness became clear. The two males had corrupted her *Invocation* — an invocation created strictly for the voice of one individual — by speaking the sacred words together. This was blasphemy, a mockery.

Ignorant mortals! What would happen now? This would be a totally unknown experience that might never end. It could be fun, or it could be maddening.

Suddenly, the slamming of a door brought her attention back to the window. The male had left the room.

Aggravation, frustration, and a dose of anger began to well up inside her. She pushed off the wall and flew to her rooftop perch before she lost her temper and did something rash.

Then a more basic instinct made itself known. Hunger.

A youngling, especially a newborn would sufficiently satisfy that. A sniff of the air brought disappointment. There was no newborn cultivation nursery here as existed in the realm. At least not within the reach of her senses. A search would be imperative if she found herself trapped here.

Meanwhile, there was that small dog.

CHAPTER 3

After the conjuring: Day one - Morning

Tim Ryan hurried about his room getting ready to go deliver his newspapers. He had been delivering a daily newspaper, *Newsday,* for over a year. His route had successfully grown to sixty-four customers — the largest in this section of Hillsville — guaranteeing a weekly payment in tips between twenty-five and thirty dollars. Not a bad take for a 14-year-old. Saving this money, plus the meager allowance from his parents, gave him a sort of freedom to buy whatever he wanted without asking permission or having to beg his mother or father for additional money. So, this was a responsibility he eagerly accepted and took seriously.

He knew today's paper was usually a small one with no inserts. Delivery wouldn't take long. He could be done by two thirty and have the rest of the afternoon to himself.

The weatherman promised more record temperatures for today, so Tim put on a pair of khaki shorts— he hated the way he looked in them — and a pale blue T-shirt. He always tried to look presentable to his customers— though he rarely saw them until collection day. It helped with the tips and there were a few cute girls on his route who might take notice.

Tim's transistor radio tuned to WMCA played *Sleepwalk* by Santo and Johnny, an oldie but goodie from 1959 as he applied a "little dab'll do ya" of Brylcreem to his hair. He looked in the mirror and raked the comb through it fashioning it in the style now worn by his idol Ed "Kookie" Burns who played the cool, car hop on the TV series *77 Sunset Strip.* Satisfied with his look, he sat on the bed and laced up his not so white sneakers, turned off the radio and headed downstairs.

"Be back after I finish the route." He said to his mother who was busy squeezing fresh lemons into a glass pitcher for lemonade.

"Okay" she said. "Don't slam the screen do…" Too late.

He mounted his old beat-up Columbia bike with the oversized basket on the front and sped out the driveway heading for the Newsday office in town.

***

Three blocks done, two to go. Tim thought as he surveyed the number of papers still left in his basket. He would definitely have enough time to play a little baseball when he got home. The hot weather never bothered him. He'd see who was around.

As he moved on to the next house he suddenly stiffened and slammed down on the Columbia's brakes. "Oh, crap," he said out loud to himself. *Not this jerk again?*

Blocking the sidewalk in front of Tim stood an older boy dressed in black. He wore a buttoned-down short sleeve shirt with the collar turned up and chino slacks. Jet black hair styled in the "flat top" look.

"Well, well. It's the 90-pound weakling again. And look at those chicken legs! Oh man. How do you stand up on those things?" He let loose with a mocking laugh.

Tim didn't know the kid. He had run into him last week. He was big, intimidating and had given him an ultimatum if he found him on this block again.

"So…Pantywaist, I told you last time you would have to pay if I saw you around here again. Hand it over." He stuck out his beefy right hand.

Before he could stop himself, Tim said, "Why should I?"

"Because there's a toll for using this block, dummy. Hand it over."

"I don't have any money," Tim lied. He actually had three dollars in his shorts pocket.

The kid in black took a step forward and Tim pushed off on his bike hoping to slip around him. No luck. Suddenly, he felt himself being jerked off his bike. Fiery pain shot through his left elbow as he hit the cement. His bike fell, scattering newspapers all over the sidewalk. In that instant Tim thought *I wish I could do something to this punk! Make him leave me alone.*

He gingerly examined his elbow. It was scraped and bleeding. As he sat up, he thought he heard crying and turned to see the kid in black lying in the street. Blood streaming from the side of his face. Tim immediately thought the kid had been somehow hit by a car. A quick scan of the area revealed no cars, trucks, or buses anywhere. *What happened to him?*

Sniffling, the kid in black got to his feet. "You're done for *faggot*." He shouted and hobbled away.

Tim pulled a Kleenex from his pocket, dabbed his elbow till it stopped bleeding then collected his papers from the sidewalk. He placed them as neatly as possible back in the basket and prepared to finish his deliveries. Just then he thought he heard a giggle. A girl giggling.

Oh great. One of the girls on this block saw that whole thing.

Embarrassed, he quickly looked around to see who it was but saw no one. He stood listening. *Maybe it was a radio or someone's TV?*

With a shrug he headed to the next customer's house accompanied by an odd feeling that he was being watched.

CHAPTER 4

After the conjuring: Day one - Morning

Returning from her morning feast Malhela caught the smokey scent of the male who lived in the dwelling beneath her. She — still angered by the corruption of the *Invocation* they had committed — struggled with a means to punish them. She *could* just kill them but how would she get back to the Realm? They may have the counter spell. She watched as he came down the thoroughfare and entered the dwelling.

Wanting to know more about this mortal, she fluttered down, landing in front of the dwelling and gazed through a large window.

The male sat in a dilapidated chair — that appeared to be swollen — listening to a talking box. The area around him, cluttered and dirty, reeked of the burnt vegetation odor. The sunlight streaming in through the glass lit up his face. She saw him clearly now for the first time. He had the look of a primate. Could his ancestors have been what the Old Ones called a Cro-Magnon? A white stick protruded from his lips sending plumes of smoke swirling around his head. This was the source of the burning vegetation smell. She had seen mortals in the past doing something similar with oddly shaped smoking devices clenched between their teeth, but the fragrance given off was not offensive, sometimes pleasant.

Amongst the clutter, in a far corner of the room behind where the male sat, something caught her eye. Malhela's head jerked back as if she'd been slapped. A dead bird lay in the bottom of a rusty cage. A bad omen where she came from. Yes, even her kind were superstitious.

She hissed and spat at the hateful being sitting there in front of her. Unfortunately, the sputum hit the glass. She bared her teeth when she saw him stand up. With a low grumble she took to the air.

As Malhela landed on her roof top perch, preparing to inflict a nasty consequence on the primate below, the wonderful citrus scent of the other male wafted over her. She closed her eyes and took it in. Any stronger and it could be intoxicating.

She turned her head slowly, following the scent and spotted him across the thoroughfare, riding a two wheeled conveyance at a speed similar to a small horse, heading away from a dwelling that must be his.

Forgetting about the primate, Malhela jumped from the roof — immediately blending with the blue, white sky — and began following.

Soaring, high above, she continued the monotonous pursuit, watching him go from one dwelling to another delivering what appeared to be scrolls. Was this male a town crier in this world? Or messenger?

Suddenly a larger male dressed all in black blocked the pathway of her rider. Words were being spoken and she saw her male of interest stiffen. The male in black moved quickly and threw the other to the ground. All at once Malhela heard her fallen rider in her head. *I wish I could do something to this punk! Make him leave me alone.* The scent of strong citrus drifted around her and then the familiar tingling sensation accompanied by the feeling of utter responsibility and duty, struck her. She could understand the words he was sending to her; proof that some of the spell's magic was working. Yes, he definitely had taken part in the conjuring, but his vibe was stronger than that of the primate. Without further thought she reacted. Hitting the larger male with full force, slicing his face with three of her dagger like fingers, sending him into the nearby roadway.

Flapping her wings vigorously Malhela reared back, hovering over the male in black, intending to strike again when she saw her rider get to his feet, pick up the scrolls scattered in the pathway, place them in a large basket and move on to make the next delivery. Just then she saw the male in black get up, mutter something and stagger away like a drunk. An uncontrollable giggle burst from her, and she quickly slapped a hand over her mouth. Hopefully her rider didn't hear it.

Malhela's mood quickly shifted when she realized she had responded to a request from a conjurer, and nothing had changed. Further proof that the invocation was faulty.

Finally, her rider returned to his dwelling. Malhela — bored and hungry — circled overhead watching as he rode up a narrow path that ran between the dwellings. He stashed his conveyance in a large structure that stood directly behind the dwelling. It had two oversized doors in the front. Could this be a barn or stable?

An idea occurred to her as she examined the structure from all sides. She grinned her impish grin and glided unseen through one of the open doors. No more bothersome rooftops.

Fluttering to a landing on what appeared to be an empty loft Malhela thought this would do just fine. Suddenly, the voice of the primate interrupted her musings. He had entered the area via the same pathway taken by her rider and knocked on the back entrance door to the dwelling. It swung open and the tangy fragrance drifted out mingling immediately with that of the primate's. The same comingled scents were present at the time of the summoning. Her suspicions were confirmed. The two mortals had spoken the conjuring *Invocation* together thus corrupting it and most likely trapping her here forever.

Hunching forward Malhela hissed and shook her clenched fists at them.

***

"Hey Ryan, feel like goin ta the field an smackin' the ball around a bit?"

"Hold on. Let me grab my stuff." Tim finished adjusting a Band-Aid on his elbow as he turned away from Stanley.

***

Tim Ryan and Stanley Bolton pumping hard on the pedals of their bikes, raced into the Hillsville High school athletic field toward the baseball diamond.

The athletic field— which also included tennis courts, a football field as well as a running track and strategically placed bleachers— had been encircled with an eight-foot high chain link fence, in an effort to keep the grounds from being ruined by troublemakers. Outside the fence a sidewalk, edged with towering Maple trees, ran the full length of the field along Division Avenue.

Directly off Division Avenue to the left, between 4th and 5th street a playground had been constructed on a two-and-a-half-acre plot of land. Authorized by the town fathers — at the behest of the area's many young mothers with children — it proudly offered: swing sets, monkey bars, seesaws, a Spin - it - Yourself merry go round, a wading pool with fountain and an all-time favorite, the Hedge Maze, as well as numerous shaded benches for tired mothers. Over the years it had become a place of enjoyment for both parents and children. This warm July afternoon would see that change.

CHAPTER 5

After the conjuring: Day one – Mid-afternoon

"No fair!" Tim Ryan yelled from right field. "You're too close. Get back to home plate, you cheater."

He and Stanley Bolton were playing their own version of Home Run Derby. The score was tied 2 to 2 and Tim knew Stan would try to take advantage somehow.

To score you had to hit the ball over the head of the man in right field. A ground ball was an out and so was anything caught.

Stanley stood between home plate and the pitcher's mound. An easy shot over Tim's head from here. Turning, he took two steps towards the plate then suddenly spun around and hit the baseball as hard as he could.

The baseball rocketed over Tim's head and…over the fence. Tim jumped and crashed into the fence trying to catch it. The ball landed in the middle of Division Avenue and took a wicked bounce into the playground across the street.

"Nice going, *Stanley!*"

Stanley dropped the bat when he saw where the bouncing ball was headed.

"Dammit," he muttered.

***

Mary Wheatley and her five-year-old son Johnny braved the playground's afternoon heat by spending time at the wading pool. Johnny splashed about while she sat on a nearby bench enjoying the cooling mist drifting over from the fountain. She glanced around and counted six other children in the pool with her son. Not too crowded. She liked that. Bobby Vinton sang "Roses are Red" from someone's nearby transistor radio and Mary hummed along as she pulled the latest issue of *Ladies Home Journal* from her oversized purse. She would spend a couple of hours here relaxing while Johnny wore himself out in the water.

Meanwhile, Johnny wanted to be with the boys and girls at the other side of the pool. So, after initially trying — without success — to wade his way over to them he decided to get out and walk around. As he started in their direction, he stopped when he heard a little girl laughing and the jingling of bells. The sounds were coming from the Hedge Maze. He had been through this park attraction with his father, so he knew all about it.

Two large animal topiaries carved into the hedge— a bear and a gorilla — guarded the entrance. The hedge walls were approximately eight feet in height and about three feet thick. The dense leaves smelled like pepper mixed with berries. The trails were narrow hard packed dirt. On hot days like this the air inside the maze felt heavy and wet.

The twisting and turning passageways were always in shadow. Bright sunlight never seemed to break through or shine above the dense vegetation. Some corners deep within the maze were completely dark even in the middle of the day. Good places to hide. And most important of all the features; only one way out.

Those entering the maze for the first time spent at least forty-five minutes trying to escape.

The jingling continued. *The ice cream man?* Johnny wondered, *What's the Good Humor man doing in there?*

The little girl was still laughing. Johnny had to see what was going on.

Mary Wheatley, engrossed in a fashion article about the First Lady, Jaqueline Kennedy, had forgotten about her son when something hit her bench with a loud thump. Startled she jumped up knocking her purse to the ground, spilling its contents. As she stooped to gather her things, she saw a baseball roll away from the bench. She looked up and saw two boys standing behind the fence on the other side of the street. "You hoodlums! Somebody could've been hurt. I have a mind to call the police." With that she quickly turned to look for her son.

While this was taking place Johnny had scampered into the Maze in search of the Good Humor man and the little girl.

***

Circling high above like a bird of prey, Malhela had followed the two males to this area. Quickly losing interest in the game they were playing she focused her attention on the smell of younglings dashing about in a small pond with a sprouting fountain in the center. That delicious scent made her realize just how hungry she was.

Flying lower she wondered how to separate the group of young-lings; spread them out so she could capture one. Then an opportunity presented itself as one of the younglings stepped out of the pond.

Spying an area with high, thick foliage Malhela concocted a plan using a trick she had used before. She sniffed the air and looked around to make sure she would not be interrupted then swooped between the two large animal shapes into the shadows.

Crouching in a dark, far corner from the entrance she blended perfectly with the surrounding foliage and began her giggling routine which included her vocal imitation of bells.

***

Inside the maze Johnny came to a T and stopped to listen. The jingling came from the right. "Hello?" he called. Now the giggling started again prompting Johnny to go right. "Hey little girl…where are you?"

He moved forward toward the sounds. Some overgrown hedge branches reached out scratching his arms and legs. Now he was feel-ing itchy as well as hot and sweaty. *Maybe I should go back,* he thought. Then the sound of the bells grew louder, tempting him. "Is the Good Humor man in there with you?" A giggle answered him, and he stepped around a bend in the hedge into a deep gloom. He stopped when a strong putrid odor wafted over him. Johnny wrinkled his nose. *Yuck! It smells like garbage in here.* The giggle was right in front of him along with the sound of someone clapping happily. As he stepped towards it two creepy looking yellow eyes suddenly materialized in front of him. Johnny quickly turned to run. "Momm…"

Suddenly the shadows pulled him in. He felt no pain.

***

"Johnny!" Mary Wheatley shouted. "Where are you?" She quickly scanned the playground. He was nowhere in sight. She ran to the children still playing in the pool. "Did you see my son? Blonde hair, wearing a yellow bathing suit."

"He went in there," said a little girl as she squeezed water from her hair. She pointed to the maze.

"Oh, for Heaven's sake," Mary said and hurried in that direction.

***

"Go get the ball Stan,"

"Why? It's your ball."

"You hit it!"

"So what?"

"Okay…I'll go, and I'll apologize to that lady, so she doesn't think *I'm* a moron. But you can go scratch the next time you want me to play Home Run Derby with you."

"Don't be such a baby. I'll go with ya."

The two boys entered the playground and found the woman sitting on the bench almost in tears. Two other mothers were standing around her, keeping a close watch on their own children as they talked to her.

Tim excused himself then said, "We're really sorry ma'am. We didn't mean…"

The woman interrupted. "Did you see my son?"

Tim and Stanley looked at each other. "Uh? What?"

One of the mothers, a tall thin woman wearing a wide straw hat said, "She can't find her son. Have you seen him?"

"No," Tim said. "We just got here. But we can help you look for him."

Tim and Stan scanned the park.

"What's he look like?" Stan said.

The woman gave her son's name and description.

Tim looked around again.

"The children said he went into the maze, but I looked and couldn't find him."

"We'll go back in. Maybe you just missed him," Tim said.

Mary Wheatley, now flat out crying, muttered a thank you.

The mother in the straw hat said there was a phone booth on the corner, and she would go call the police.

Tim and Stanley headed for the maze.

***

"Hey, Johnny Wheatley! Tim called. "You in here? Your mom's looking for you."

Tim Ryan and Stanley Bolton moved single file along the trails winding through the maze, repeatedly calling Johnny's name. Stan wiped sweat from his face with the back of his hand. "Man, it's crazy hot in here. The kid probly passed out or somethin."

As they moved deeper into the labyrinth Tim stopped. "What's that smell?"

Stanley took a whiff. "Limburger cheese."

"You've had Limburger cheese?"

"No," Stanley said.

"Then how do you know what it smells like?"

"I heard it smells real bad."

"You're nuts. Come on, let's split up. I'll meet you outside. You *do* know how to get out of here ...Right?"

Stanley shot him a dirty look and stomped off calling Johnny's name.

After meeting outside the maze exit Tim and Stanley looked for Mrs. Wheatley. They saw her still sitting on the bench now talking to a policeman. Stanley stopped and grabbed Tim's arm.

"What?" Tim said.

Stan tilted his head and pointed with his chin towards Mrs. Wheatley and the cop. Their baseball sat on the bench next to the woman's purse.

Great! Tim thought. He gave Stanley a quick look and said, "Let's go. Just be cool."

"Excuse us Mrs. Wheatley. We just finished looking in the maze. We checked everywhere. Johnny's not in there. He must have come back out. Sorry." Tim said.

"And you are?" the patrolman asked.

"Tim Ryan"

The officer turned to Stanley.

"Uh...Stanley Bolton"

After a few more questions they were allowed to leave. As Tim turned to go Mrs. Wheatley held up the baseball and handed it to him.

"I think this belongs to you," she said. "And thank you both for trying to help." With that she broke down sobbing.

CHAPTER 6

After the conjuring: Day one – Evening

Tim Ryan noticed his father's car in the driveway and knew he was late for dinner. *Probably should buy a watch one of these days.* He lifted the garage door up and stored his bike just inside. As he did, a sudden gust of wind blew by him into the garage. He looked at the driveway behind him then at his backyard. *Where'd that come from?* With a shrug he pulled the door closed.

Sheepishly, Tim opened the back door and entered the kitchen. His family, already seated at the dinner table, turned to look as he entered.

"Nice of you to show up," his father said giving him a stern look. "Go wash your hands."

Tim's mother didn't say a word but looked relieved. His eight-year-old sister Emily just smirked at him.

Returning to the table Tim said, "Sorry, lost track of time." He pulled out his chair and sat down looking only at his dinner which was probably cold. Saying nothing.

Finally, his mother said, "What kept you?"

Swallowing a forkful of mashed potatoes Tim recounted what happened at the field and the playground. How he and Stanley Bolton helped look for a missing little boy.

"Did they find him?" Emily asked.

"I don't know. Another police car pulled up as we were leaving."

"Terrible. I hope they found him," said Tim's mother.

Emily wiped her mouth with a napkin and said matter of factly, "I like that playground. Especially that Hedge Maze game."

"That's where the kid's mother said he disappeared."

With that his father's eyebrows raised. "Oh? I think we'll stay away from *that* for a while Em."

"Oh, *Dad*…Why?"

"He doesn't want you disappearing. That's why. But it's not a bad idea," Tim said with a chuckle.

Emily made a face and stuck her tongue out at him. It had pieces of corn on it.

"That's enough you two," his mother said.

"Under the circumstances, I'll give you the benefit of the doubt for being late this time," Tim's father said. "But there will be consequences if it happens again. Understand?"

"Yes sir," Tim said.

With after dinner chores completed, Tim headed to his room to see if he had enough money saved to buy a watch. He opened his small bank safe and removed the dollar bills clipped together. He counted out forty-three dollars. *Whelan's has cheap watches. I'll stop by there tomorrow.*

He tried to practice his guitar but found his mind drifting back to the missing kid, Johnny Wheatley, and the uneasiness he felt when searching the maze. He couldn't explain it. Perhaps it was the awful smell they encountered. *Maybe something died in there...that's what the smell was.* Though his room was quite warm Tim shivered at the thought.

***

Sated, Malhela settled into the nest she had assembled from various items found lying around the loft. Boxes made of stiff paper, old pieces of cloth, a remnant from today's meal, a bag of dirt, a small bundle of straw and an oversized pillow. This was so much better than the uncomfortable rooftop.

Feeling relaxed and a bit drowsy she tuned her hearing to the sounds around her. From inside the house came music, played on some unusual lute. Conversations drifted up to her from the dwelling. What was this language? She knew it but couldn't remember the meaning of the words being spoken. She had to understand these mortals if she ever wanted to go home.

Closing her eyes Malhela drifted back in time searching the languages she had experienced in the past. The language of the old Celts sounded similar to that of this world's mortals, but it wasn't right. She moved on.

Suddenly, a memory broke through the fog of her history. A memory of a time when she and the Old Ones had decimated the mortals with disease and pestilence. A time when Cytizuz had planned to invade, conquer, and subjugate their world. The mortals had called it the *Black Death*. It had been a troublesome time for her as well. A careless mistake had allowed her to be captured by an old crone— who rendered her completely helpless by stabbing her in the back and leaving the knife in place. The crone was one of very few people who knew how to incapacitate a harpy.

She held her in an escape proof cage for many months treating her like a pet. The crone spoke to her daily in a language known as Old English. Malhela learned quickly and it served her well.

Bringing herself back to the present, Malhela realized the language she now heard was a form of that Old English. With a little effort, communicating with these mortals would be possible.

Now she had a goal of sorts. But first she had something else to consider. The last time she had been away from the realm too long her abilities had weakened. That was the time of the old crone. She would need to be more alert. Already her *blending* required more concentration than usual and only a day had passed.

Finding the spell to get her home would be the priority and learning the language of these mortals would be the key.

She wrapped her wings around her, curled up on the pillow and listened closely to the words drifting from the dwelling across the way. Repeating them as she remembered their meaning.

CHAPTER 7

After the conjuring: Day Two- Early afternoon

Once again Tim Ryan neared the end of his paper route. *I sure hope that jerk isn't around.*

As he turned the corner onto the block where he ran into the troublemaker yesterday, he felt his anxiety quickly disappear. There, parked in front of his first customer's house was a Nassau County police car. *Ha! No bully today.*

Tim put down the kick stand on his Columbia, walked up the front steps of the house and carefully placed today's paper inside the front storm door. Returning to his bike he saw a large, muscular police officer step out of the car and approach him.

"What's your name, son?" the officer asked.

"Tim Ryan. Is this about the little boy that went missing?"

Abruptly, the other car door opened and out stepped the troublemaker. He wasn't dressed in black. Today he wore a white, buttoned-down sport shirt with navy blue Chinos and black loafers. There were three small bandages on the right side of his face. With arms folded he just stood by the car glaring at Tim.

Tim's jaw dropped. *What the…?* Immediately, Tim felt nervous. He looked at the Police officer, then the bully, and back to the police officer. He didn't know what to say…or do, for that matter.

The officer stepped up on the sidewalk in front of Tim.

"My son here says you cut him yesterday. That true?"

Son!? Now he was scared.

The nametag over the officer's badge read Sgt. D. Sanfield.

Tim dragged his eyes away from the name. "No Sergeant. That's not true."

"Do you have a knife, Tim?"

"No sir. My dad won't let me have one."

"Please take everything out of your pockets, son."

Tim did as instructed and presented three one-dollar bills, a rubber band, two beat up baseball cards and a square of Bazooka bubble gum to the Sergeant. Who gave the items a cursory glance and returned his gaze to Tim.

The officer pointed to the three cuts on his son's face. "How do you explain that Mr. Ryan?"

"I …I can't. He knocked me down and when I looked over, he was in the street crying."

"Was not!" the troublemaker yelled.

"I thought he got hit by a car or something," Tim said.

The troublemaker unfolded his arms and pointed at Tim. "You shoved me into the street somehow. I *could have* been hit by a car."

Sergeant Sanfield shot his son a look. "I don't want any more trouble between you two. Understand? If it happens again, you'll both spend a night behind bars."

Tim nodded.

The troublemaker continued to glare, and Tim imagined steam coming from his ears.

"Danny, get in the car. Tim you be on your way. Remember no more trouble."

No more trouble? I'm not the problem, Officer.

The troublemaker turned to get back in the car and unexpectedly shouted "Owww!"

Tim and the Sergeant both looked.

"Something just bit my ear!" He said.

Seconds later the Sergeant's uniform hat flipped off his head, landing in the street. He calmly bent down and picked it up while carefully scanning the surroundings.

"Freak gust of wind," he said.

"My ear," his son whined.

"Is it bleeding?"

"No."

"Probably a bee sting or yellow jacket. Get in the car."

Once Tim moved further on, Sergeant Sanfield turned to his son. "Now…What really happened? You expect me to believe *that* skinny kid got the better of you?

His son, maintaining a defiant look, said nothing.

"How many times have I talked to you about trying to strong arm the kids in the neighborhood for money."

"I didn't!" Danny said.

"Don't lie to me," his father said grabbing his son by the shirt collar and pulling him closer to him. "This has to stop!"

***

Malhela, of course keeping a close eye on the young male with the wonderful scent, watched the entire scene unfold from atop the four wheeled, orange and blue conveyance. She liked the colors, and it had a convenient rack to perch on.

After spending the night re-learning the language of these mortals, she translated the words more quickly. Listening to the current conversation revealed the name of her citrus scented male. Tim Ryan. A breakthrough. Now she could make plans.

Right now, she felt mischievous plus she didn't like the tone of the words being spoken to her Tim Ryan. So, she nipped the ear of the male she had wounded yesterday and knocked the cap from the head of the large adult male. Fun!

Malhela trailed Tim Ryan back to the vicinity of his dwelling as well as her roost. She intended to observe him more closely. Maybe even try speaking to him? Find out exactly why he had summoned her and if he had the counter spell. From across the road, a familiar voice rang out interrupting her thoughts. The primate.

"Hey Ryan! Stick ball game on Elm afta suppa. We can play till the streetlights come on. Can ya make it?"

Malhela heard Tim say something in response, but she wasn't paying attention to him. She was focused on the primate. She didn't like him, and he needed to be taught a lesson.

He stood in front of his dwelling with one of those paper sticks hanging from his mouth. He held a small, shiny silver object in his hand which gave off sparks when he repeatedly flicked a tiny wheel at its top. It dawned on her that he was trying to set the stick on fire with this device. Malhela chuckled. Maybe he would like some help? She squinted, focusing her sight on the silver object and quickly waved her hands as if swatting away an insect. A long flame shot from the device, burning the primate's two fingers and the tip of his nose. He let out a loud scream, dropping the device. She grinned. A small taste of what lay ahead for this mortal. He would regret his part in summoning her.

***

Tim told Stanley he would meet him after dinner and ride over to Elm Street with him for the game then started walking his bike up his driveway. He had no sooner turned his back on Stanley when he heard him screaming, "Ow, ow, ow". He quickly turned and saw his friend jumping up and down holding his right hand.

"What happened?" Tim called as he hurried towards Stanley. He saw Stanley's cigarette lighter on the sidewalk then looking up noticed a nasty looking red blotch on the tip of Stanley's nose. The two fingers on his right hand were also red but had what looked like little blisters from the fingernails to the first knuckle.

"You better go run cold water on them," Tim said as Stanley turned and ran to his house without saying a word.

As Tim watched Stanley enter his front door, he picked up the lighter and instantly dropped it. "Ouch! That thing is hot," he said to himself. *Cripes! Can a lighter overheat or malfunction somehow?* He was contemplating if he should just leave it there or go get some work gloves from the garage to pick it up when he was distracted by a sound he had heard before but thought he had imagined. A giggle. A girl giggling. With a surprised look on his face, he eyed the empty street for the source, scrutinizing the nearby houses hoping to catch a glimpse of the mystery girl. *This is just plain crazy. It sounds like the same girl from the other day on the route. Am I being followed? Who could it possibly be?*

Tim scanned the block one more time but found no one.

CHAPTER 8

After the conjuring: Day two – Early Evening

With Eastern Daylight Savings Time fully in place, darkness fell around nine o'clock, allowing more time for outdoor activities. It was ideal for a stick ball game with neighborhood kids.

Tim rode alone to the game on Elm Street; Stanley couldn't play due to his burned fingers. Turning the corner, he spotted the guys he knew from this block and …Paulette standing on the corner with Janey — who seemed to always be with her. He suddenly felt happy that Stanley wasn't here to act like a moron in front of the girls. Paulette, a tall, thin young lady with light brown hair, a dazzling smile and great legs, had been on Tim's radar since the first time he saw her. He wanted to ask her to go to the movies with him but would inevitably chicken out at the last minute. Maybe tonight he would find the courage.

As the game got under way Tim took the outfield position down the street which happened to be near the corner where the girls stood. He said hello, then quickly turned and snagged a fly ball that came his way. Paulette applauded. "Didn't know you liked stick ball." He said with a smile.

"A little," Paulette said coquettishly.

Feeling encouraged Tim thought, *Gotta ask her tonight. Don't wimp out.*

From out of nowhere came a loud whistle that startled him. He missed catching an easy line drive allowing the other team to score.

"Hey Tim! Wake up!" Shouted one of his teammates.

"Sorry!" Tim said.

Then Tim heard someone call Paulette's name. When he looked out of the corner of his eye to see who it was his blood turned to ice water.

You've gotta be kidding me! Why is he here?

He couldn't believe his eyes. The troublemaker was strutting up the sidewalk on Terrace Street — which ran perpendicular to Elm — calling Paulette's name. Once again dressed all in black.

Tim caught a bouncing ground ball and threw it back. Trotting back to his position, he noticed the bully take Paulette by the hand and start to lead her away.

Not thinking Tim blurted out, "Paulette!" For some reason he suddenly remembered the kid's name was Danny Sanfield. What good would that do?

When the bully looked over his shoulder to see who called Paulette's name, Tim saw the three bandages still on his face.

Without a word, Danny Sanfield dropped Paulette's hand, ran into the street and punched Tim right in the mouth, splitting his lip and knocking him down.

Shouts erupted from the other boys as they ran with their sticks toward Tim and the bully.

"Get outta here Sanfield! Stay on your own side of town. We don't need your crap!" Yelled Billy Van — who was just as big as this Danny Sanfield kid — swinging his stick ball bat.

Wiping the blood from his mouth and trying not to humiliate himself in front of everyone by crying, an unbidden thought flashed in Tim's head. *I wish that punk was dead!*

Before Tim could get up Sanfield said, "Your *toll* is now paid... *Asswipe.*" He then walked back down Terrace Street dragging Paulette behind him, leaving Janey standing there looking bewildered.

***

Malhela glided with wings spread wide over the roof tops, keeping a possessive eye on her Tim Ryan. She circled over his head and spied an ideal perch. A street lamp. From this vantage point she studied the other males running, after hitting a round, pink object they called a rubber ball. Others catching and throwing it. Was this their idea of fun? Boring.

A warm breeze lifted a pleasing lilac scent up to her. It was mixed with the essence of something she knew well. Malhela quickly spotted the source. Two, healthy, pubescent females. *Birthgivers.* Producers of newborn younglings which were a delicacy.

Craning her neck to examine them more closely and inhaling deeply, she discovered they were not with child. Disappointed, she would watch for others.

Without warning a ruckus broke out in the street below her. The male dressed all in black called Danny Sanfield — according to Tim's thoughts — had returned and was once again attacking Tim Ryan.

Malhela reeled as Tim Ryan's thought screamed in her head. Not a command per se but a powerful wish filled with anguish. She was not a granter of wishes but maybe responding to this one would release her.

***

"Come on Paulette. Hurley's is still open. I'll buy you a sundae or whatever you want," Danny Sanfield said.

"I have to be home when the streetlights come on," Paulette said.

"Don't worry. We'll be back in time. I know a short cut."

That short cut was through a dark wooded area which began at Cherry Street and extended to Park Avenue where it opened out onto the sidewalk, not too far from Hurley's Ice Cream Parlor.

A make out session with Paulette and maybe copping a feel was Danny's real plan. This could be before or after the ice cream. It didn't matter.

Danny pulled Paulette towards the woods. "Let's go…Hurry."

"What happened to your face?" She reached out a hand toward the bandages.

Danny instantly grabbed it. "Nothing," he said.

Though Paulette really wanted to go with Danny to Hurley's, she was having second thoughts. "Is that why you hit that boy Tim?"

"It doesn't matter," he snapped. "Let's go!"

She hadn't known him that long and this was a side of his bad boy attitude that troubled her.

"I'd better not. I didn't ask permission or anything. Some other time?" With that Paulette pulled her hand away, turned and started walking back toward home.

Just then a blast of air whipped by, lifting her dress, and messing her hair. It was like a truck or bus had sped by. But the street was empty. Paulette straightened her dress and continued on.

"Maybe there *won't* be some other time," he shouted.

Paulette just waved and kept walking.

Danny Sanfield — thoroughly pissed off — didn't want to go home. His father had the night off and Danny couldn't handle another lecture about being the son of a police officer. So, he decided to cut through the woods into town and kill some time at the Whelan's Drug Store browsing magazines.

The wooded area had a trampled path. Danny knew it well, even in the darkness that now seemed to creep through the trees around him. He moped along with his hands in his pockets, swearing in a low voice at the tangled vegetation around him. The path took a bend into the thickest part of the woods and Danny unconsciously followed it. It was then that he heard something. He stopped and listened. At first all he heard were the ever-present crickets and peepers. About to move on, he heard what sounded like a whisper. He turned around clenching his fists. "Come on out," he called. "I'm in no mood for games."

"*Danny?*" A girl's voice whispered.

His eyes went wide, and he grinned. "Changed your mind?" *Maybe this night won't be a total loss after all.*

"*Danny?*" The whisper came again. This time more seductive.

"What's with the games Paulette? Is this you trying to be funny?"

Suddenly the thick bushes to his right moved as if someone or something were hiding there.

"That pretty dress of yours is going to be torn to shreds hiding in there." Danny liked the thought of a torn dress. "Come on Paulette. Stop teasing."

He was answered by an animal-like snort that startled him. "You're not funny, Paulette."

Then the dense shrubs on his left shook. "You're pissing me off now."

He peered into the increasing gloom. "Paulette?"

Another snort.

Then an idea popped into Danny's head. "If that's that candy ass Tim Ryan trying to get back at me, you're in for more than a split lip."

Now the response was a devilish giggle accompanied by a disgusting putrid smell that seemed to be creeping around him. He coughed and waved his hand in front of his face trying to minimize the stench before it entered his nose. "Only a coward uses a stink bomb Ryan. I'm going ring your neck when I catch you," He shouted.

Danny Sanfield turned toward the sound ready to teach this Tim Ryan a lasting lesson when he saw the eyes; yellow like that of a leopard or panther staring at him from the thicket. He heard a deep guttural sound almost like purring. For the first time in a long time, he felt scared. *What the hell is that?"*

Danny took a quick step back when he noticed something that looked like a large bat's wing sticking up from behind the eyes. He turned to run but his legs felt like lead. His mind raced. *What is this thing?* In seconds it was on his back. He tried to punch it but with no effect. Danny staggered backward attempting to bang this thing against a tree. In a blur it twirled off him and instantly faced him. The fangs and flicking forked tongue brought a scream to his throat. In a panic he swung his fists at it and bellowed in pain as his right hand disappeared in a spray of blood. Clutching his arm Danny stumbled and fell. His head was spinning. *So much blood. Is that mine?*

Before he could move it was on him again. And then came an exquisite pain. Like that of a hundred burning razor blades shredding his back. He cried out.

As he desperately tried to free himself from the thing's hold, he felt it grab his head and pull back. He fought with every ounce of strength he had left until a quick slash across his throat sent him spiraling into eternal darkness.

CHAPTER 9

After the conjuring: Day Three – Mid
Morning – Nassau County Police Department,
8th Precinct, Bethpage, New York

Lieutenant James Trabinski sat in his office at his cluttered Steel Case desk lighting a cigarette — his fifth of the morning — thinking about the Missing Persons' report he had just read. He didn't like it. The case didn't fall under his jurisdiction, but a five-year-old child disappearing from a playground in a place like Hillsville was disturbing. Things like that just didn't happen there. Hopefully, they will find the kid today safe and sound. But fifteen years' experience told him to keep an eye on this one. He pushed the file to the front corner of his desktop and placed a Statue of Liberty paper weight on it.

James Trabinski had worked his way from Patrolman to Lead Detective in those fifteen years and it wasn't easy. His devotion to the job, refusal to let a case go unsolved, had brought him a solitary life. Divorced three years now he could still hear his ex-wife saying he was obsessed, calling him a control freak, power hungry. None of it was true. You could ask anyone on the force who knew him. Jim Trabinski was a good man who just wanted to do a good job. He was dedicated.

The morning sun promised another scorcher of a day with temperatures in the high eighties. The clicking buzzing sound of the cicadas seemed to be everywhere. Already Trabinski's office started to feel uncomfortable, and he stepped away from his desk to turn on the new window air conditioning unit. He looked over his shoulder when he heard the outside door to the precinct open.

"Thought you had the morning off, Dave?" he said to the officer approaching him. The scheduling procedure stipulated that if an officer had a night off, he would also be entitled to being off the following morning.

"Got a minute Lieutenant?"

Trabinski moved back to his desk and crushed out the cigarette in an already full ashtray. "Sure. What can I do for you?" He pulled out his beat-up chair to sit down but remained standing when he heard the officer say, "Danny didn't come home last night. I think he may have run away."

Sergeant David Sanfield was a hard cop, but Trabinski could see in his face he was deeply concerned about his son. "What makes you think that?"

"He had a little scuffle with a neighborhood paperboy, so I needed to get the full story. I took him with me in the cruiser to confront the other boy and it turned out it was Danny's fault. He got mad and I had to pull rank. I dropped him at home around 3 pm and that was the last I've seen of him."

"Did he take clothes or anything?"

"It doesn't look like it."

"Okay, hold on," Trabinski said. With that he moved a stack of papers that hid his intercom unit and punched in Dispatch.

"Nancy?"

"Yes, Lieutenant?"

"Can you do me a favor? Send a BOLO to the units for Dave Sansfield's son Danny. Dave said he didn't come home last night. Didn't take anything with him so he's probably just skulking around town. Everybody should know Danny's description. And Nance? Do a *forthwith* on this.

"Sure thing. Consider it done. All units to be on the lookout for Danny Sanfield. Make it a priority," Nancy said.

"Thanks...you're the best."

"You say that to all the girls," Nancy replied and clicked off.

"Go home Dave. He may show up after he's cooled down. We'll call you if we find him."

Sergeant Sanfield looked as if he was going to say something but decided not to. He just nodded and turned to leave.

Trabinski watched the man as he walked away knowing full well this was not the first time Sanfield had had problems with his son. It seemed to be a never-ending struggle between the two of them. He hoped they would rectify their differences before it was too late.

As he lit another Camel cigarette, he saw patrolman Decker side-step Sanfield and hurry towards him.

"Lieutenant? You still have the 10-65 file on the five-year-old?"

Trabinski pointed to the Statue of Liberty paperweight on his desk. "Why?"

"Better grab it, sir. Unit 12 found something in that hedge maze at the Division Avenue playground. Sounds like it's a crime scene now."

**

Two patrol cars with lights flashing were already at the scene when James Trabinski arrived. Unit 12 — the K-9 squad — had been dispatched to search for the missing child two days ago and had found nothing. But something about that day's investigation of a hedged in area bothered Sergeant Todd Anderson. His lead dog Leo — a veteran German Shepherd — had concentrated for quite a while on a particular fetid area of that maze, eventually losing interest. Initially he thought Leo had sniffed out a skunk or something, but today on a hunch he brought Leo back for a second try. The hunch paid off.

Sergeant Anderson stood next to his car holding Leo's leash. "Fill me in Sergeant," Trabinski said leaning over to pat Leo's head.

Anderson recounted the events leading up to the discovery of a bright yellow piece of cloth.

"The mother said her son was wearing a yellow bathing suit. If this turns out to be a match, the case falls in your lap," Anderson said. "I'm sorry we didn't find it sooner. It was bright yellow for Christ's sake."

As Trabinski walked toward the taped off maze the Forensics van pulled to the curb. The examiner — wearing a white lab coat — caught up with him and they both entered the potential crime scene.

The morning sun had been baking the hedges while they in turn soaked up the humidity. Gnats flitted among the hedges.

"This is supposed to be fun? It's stifling in here," Trabinski said. Then sneezed. "And it stinks!"

"It's like a greenhouse," the examiner said.

Locating the marked area of discovery, the examiner, with Trabinski looking over his shoulder, slipped on a pair of gloves and gingerly removed a small piece of bright yellow fabric wedged deep between tight branches. He pulled a lighted magnifying glass from his case and scrutinized the torn edge of the cloth.

"That looks like blood, Lieutenant."

Trabinski studied the section of thick hedge for a sign the kid might have pushed or squirmed his way through the branches tearing the garment and cutting himself in the progress. But the closer he looked the less likely it seemed.

"More blood over here, Lieutenant." The examiner pulled apart the branches where the cloth had been and pointed to a reddish, brown stain on the ground at the base of the foliage.

"Terrific!" He said sarcastically. "Send me the full report as soon as you can. We'll need the mother to identify that piece of cloth."

Wiping the sweat from his brow with a handkerchief Lieutenant James Trabinski strode to his black, unmarked 1962 Ford Galaxie and grabbed the radio.

"This is a code 2. Repeat a code 2. Possible homicide at Division Avenue between 4th and 5th. Notify town officials… This park is shut down till further notice. Forensics on the scene. Unit One out."

***

The weather finally broke around one thirty that afternoon thanks to a quick thunderstorm and steady rain. Not ideal conditions for delivering newspapers. It took Tim Ryan twice as long to finish his route.

He always felt like a dork wearing the yellow, hooded rain slicker that his mother had bought for him, but there was no getting around using it today. His puffy lip, reminding him of last night's humiliation, didn't help his mood any. He had explained that injury to his parents as being hit accidentally by a stickball bat. Today's only bright spot was his route manager telling him he had won two tickets to the stock car races at the Freeport Speedway for tomorrow night. There were always contests going on to entice the carriers to get new customers. The carrier who signed up the most new subscriptions during the allotted period of time won. Tim had racked up five.

He had turned onto Plainview Road heading for home thinking about who he could ask to the races when he noticed a white 1958 Chevy Impala pull up alongside him. Driving slowly. Tim continued peddling. Without warning the car gave a blast of its horn. Startled, he almost lost control of his bike. Straightening up quickly, he peddled faster but the car followed. Another honk of the car horn. *What the heck is this now?*

The car pulled over to the curb and the driver's door opened. Tim was about to blast off but applied his brakes and came to a halt when he saw the man getting out of the car was the bully's father. Only not in his police uniform.

The rain had slowed to a drizzle, so Tim pulled the annoying hood from his head. He stared at the man who seemed at a loss for words or something. "You want a paper?" Tim said, pulling a dry copy from his sack.

The man almost smiled. "No thanks, son. I was wondering if you saw Danny?"

Tim put the paper back. "No sir…Not today," he said quickly.

Danny's father didn't say anything more and the silence between them started to feel awkward.

"I gotta go," Tim said.

The man had been just staring at Tim as if he was memorizing his features then tilted his head and pointed with his chin at Tim's face. "He do that to you?"

"Huh?"

"Your lip. Did my son do *that* to you?"

Cripes! Why is this happening to me? He didn't know whether to lie or tell the truth. Finally, he decided on the truth — the man *was* a cop — and told him everything that happened last night.

"What was the girl's name again?" Danny's father pulled a small pad and pencil from his shirt pocket. He began to write.

"Paulette Berdino. I'm not sure how she spells her last name."

"Address?"

"Elm Street…Second house on the left."

"And… Danny left with her after he hit you?"

"Yes, sir."

"Thanks for the help." He tucked the pad and pencil in his shirt pocket and got back in his car.

Tim watched the car pull away from the curb onto Plainview Road. *Somebody's in trouble.*

***

Sergeant David Sanfield located the second house on the left side of Elm Street and parked his car a few doors down. He knew that questioning the girl without clearance could get him in trouble. But who could really blame him? He was a concerned father. His son was missing, and he was just following up on a lead. Better to ask for mercy than to ask for permission. Besides, if his son had spent the night with this Paulette, he may still be here.

He walked up to the house — gave it a quick once over — slipped his badge out of his pants pocket and rang the bell. After a second ring the door was answered by an attractive woman in her early forties. "Yes?" A look of concern appeared on her face when she saw the badge the man was holding.

"Mrs. Berdino? Sergeant Sanfield, Nassau County Police. I was wondering if I could speak to your daughter for a moment. Paulette, is it?"

"Is there a problem?"

"No Ma'am. Is she home?"

The woman had a look of uncertainty on her face. "I think…"

"What is it mom?" A pretty teenage girl came to the doorway behind the woman.

"This police officer would like to ask you some questions, honey."

"Oh? What about?"

"You're not in any trouble, young lady." His tone friendly. "Are you Paulette?"

"Yes."

"Please step outside Paulette, if you wouldn't mind." The front stoop was wide, and he stepped aside for her to open the storm door and join him. Her mother watched with arms folded and a frown on her face.

"Paulette? Were you with Danny Sanfield last night?"

Her brown eyes widened. "For a little while."

"For a little while? When was that?"

Paulette shrugged. "Don't know the time. Wasn't that dark yet. We went for a walk. Danny wanted to go to Hurley's for ice cream, but I thought it would be too late when we got back so we didn't go. I have to be in the house when the streetlights come on." She glanced at her mother.

Sergeant Sanfield nodded. "Okay…Then what?"

"I came home."

"Mrs. Berdino?" He looked at the woman to watch her expression. "Yes, she was in the house a little after the lights came on. What's this all about?"

Ignoring the question Sanfield leaned back against the stoop railing. "Paulette? Did you see Danny today at all?"

"No. It's been raining so I wasn't out."

"Okay. Thank you, Paulette. Mrs.Berdino, Danny is my son. He didn't come home last night. I'm trying to find him. If you see him or hear from him, please call me." With that he handed Paulette a business card with a phone number on it and started down the steps.

"*Oh,*" Mother and daughter said at the same time.

Sergeant Sanfield stopped at the sidewalk and turned around. "Paulette? Did Danny say where he was going after he walked you home?"

Now, Paulette looked puzzled. "He didn't walk me home. He may have gone to Hurley's by himself…I don't know. He was still standing by the short cut when I left."

"Short cut?" Sanfield asked.

"By the woods on Cherry Street. Danny said there was a path that cut through to Park Avenue near Hurley's." This comment earned Paulette a harsh look from her mother.

"I know where it is," he said. "Thanks again."

As Sergeant Sanfield strode to his car, the rain returned.

CHAPTER 10

After the conjuring: Day Three – Late afternoon

After spending another tedious afternoon following Tim Ryan as he delivered his scrolls, Malhela drifted to the loft section of the barn structure and crawled into her nest. The rain and gloom outside reminded her of the Realm's drab season when the sun shone very little. She longed to be home with her sisters and wondered if they would come looking for her if she was gone too long.

The movements of the Sun and Moon told Malhela it had only been three days since she had been summoned, but not knowing the reason became more and more irritating. She needed to take a chance on communicating with this Tim Ryan or maybe even the primate— whom she learned was called Stanley. Perhaps, he was the better choice for communicating? After all, it was the roof of his dwelling that she found herself on after the conjuring. He may have the *Words* necessary to undo this spell.

Another visit to this Stanley's refuge would be necessary. Maybe a face to face visit this time? She would think more about this, but right now she was too tired and needed to rest. This enervation was worrisome. Feeling fatigued should not be happening. Last night's bloody fulfillment of Tim Ryan's pseudo command had drained her despite the fact she had eaten a portion of the victim. The meat of male mortals, though palatable, was not her favorite. Why was she so exhausted? Again, her thoughts returned to the incident long ago with the old crone and how weak she had become at that time. But that was the result of too many days away from the Realm. This was different though, and she was becoming more and more certain it was because of the tainted conjuring. Or perhaps it was the lack of proper nourishment causing this.

The reality that sources of tasty, satisfying as well as nutritious food were more difficult to find in this world — these mortals locked up *everything* — added to her frustration. Her diet would soon consist of cats, dogs, and vermin. Dreadful.

Malhela made herself comfortable in her little habitat, licking herself clean and preening her thick head quills. Listening, always listening to the chatter coming from the dwelling across the yard. The sound of her empty stomach growling would interrupt from time to time. At that moment she realized something she had overlooked. A female youngling lived with Tim Ryan. A meal was close by.

She glanced over her shoulder at the back wall window. The latch she had jimmied last night was still open. She could leave anytime she liked, but this lassitude overcame the hunger forcing her to sleep.

When she awoke night had fallen. A hazy moon shown high in the sky as she slipped out the back window into another humid evening. Her intent was to satiate her hunger with the female youngling, but something caught her attention. A faint sound travelled on a warm breeze to her keen ears. Malhela straightened and tilting her head to the side focused on the fading tone. There it was again, and not too far away either. She grinned. It was the wail of a newborn youngling. This would be her reward for surviving a day of aggravation.

Malhela spread her wings and darted skyward through the gauzy clouds that lingered in the sky after the day's storms. She homed in on the screaming delicacy. The crying led her to the top room of a well-lit dwelling in a settlement several furlongs from her nest.

Malhela grinned impishly when she saw the glass framework of the large window, where the crying came from, opened outward. She could step easily into the room.

Clinging to the glass framework she peered into the softly lit chamber. The birthgiver was there holding the newborn, soothing it. The crying had changed to cooing as the birthgiver rocked the delectable pink morsel in its arms. Malhela watched and waited.

It was taking too long, and she tired of clinging to the framework. She could quickly rush in, snatch the youngling from the birthgiver effortlessly — as she had done many times before — and be gone with her meal. This, however, might require killing the birthgiver, which was something her kind rarely did, if ever. It went against the code of the Realm.

Fluttering from the framework to the eaves just above the opening, she dug her talons into the gritty roofing, and hung upside down, bat like, to wait a while longer. It would be worth it in the end.

The sounds of the night filled the humid air. The buzz, clicks and peeps of insects surrounded her as she waited, her patience almost exhausted. Then a soft swishing sound came from within, snapping her to attention. She swung down to the glass framework and watched as the birthgiver gently laid the sleeping newborn into a cradle and quietly stepped toward the chamber door. Seeing her chance Malhela swung around to enter the opening and banged into some type of net blocking it. The birthgiver, almost out of the room, quickly turned and stared at the window. Malhela instantly blended with her surroundings. The birthgiver came to the aperture and examined the mesh. It was bowed inward from the impact, and she looked out as if searching for the cause. With the shake of her head, the birthgiver made certain the netting was secure, gave another look out the window, checked the youngling once again and left the room.

Silently, Malhela sliced the netting with one of her dagger like fingernails and slipped into the room keeping an eye on the doorway. The sweet powdery scent of the newborn filled the room. Without hesitation she lifted the youngling from the cradle. It whimpered and she quickly smothered it. With her prize in hand, she sprang from the chamber into the dark sky.

***

Tim Ryan spent most of the rainy afternoon calling friends from school to see who could go with him to the stock car races. After receiving "Gee I'd like to, but I can't…" from everyone, he decided as a last resort to call Stanley, who immediately said yes without even asking permission. It would be fun anyway, even if Stanley acted like a halfwit.

Hanging up the phone on the nightstand in his parents' room, Tim went upstairs to his. He looked out the window at the rain-soaked street.

No stickball tonight he thought, as he glanced at the small white clock on his desk. He had about an hour before his father came home from work. Plenty of time to do some practicing on his guitar — a candy apple red National electric guitar he had won in a contest sponsored by his music teacher. He needed to work more on the guitar lead for his favorite Ventures' tune *Walk Don't Run.*

He crossed the room, lifted his guitar from the case and started to plug it into the amp when his sister Emily burst into the room.

"I got dibs on the TV tonight," she announced.

Tim strummed an E chord and adjusted the volume. "Big deal. It's all reruns."

"Not the *Flintstones!*" she said in her best annoying voice. "And mom's probably gonna watch the Donna Reed show. So, you're outta luck."

"Fine." He didn't mind watching that program if he decided to watch any TV at all that night. Shelley Fabre was really cute and Paul Peterson cool. "Now get out of my room before I brain you."

That evening Tim couldn't sleep. For some reason he kept replaying the meeting with the bully's father. He now felt like a creep for giving him Paulette's name and address. This whole bully thing had a bad feel, and he didn't know what to do about it. He hadn't told anyone, especially his parents. Maybe that was the problem?

***

Malhela, now energized from her nourishing repast, decided to drop in on the primate — Stanley — and get some answers. She took flight, still clutching the pink cloth that had covered the newborn, swooping over the dwellings clustered below then shooting upward through the wandering clouds. In no time she circled the primate's dwelling. A dim light shown from Stanley's open bed chamber window. She descended and hovered there examining the mesh that blocked it. It was no different from the one she had just dismantled a few hours ago but this one had a small latch that upon jiggling allowed her to slide it open. She eased herself into the room without a sound and crouched, taking stock of the surroundings. Malhela had to pay attention to everything in this place, since this belonged to the mortal who openly displayed the dead bird. One never knew what a bad omen would bring.

The cramped room, lit by a small lamp sitting on the floor near a closed door, was muggy and had that burnt vegetation smell she had experienced before. On a small table in a dark corner a device with spinning petals, unfamiliar to Malhela, struggled to move the warm, smelly air around. The pages of documents scattered around the room fluttered as the device swiveled toward them. A piece of clothing blew from a pile and moved slowly across the floor.

Malhela noticed two sleep pallets on either side of her. One was empty, the other held the sleeping, Stanley. How convenient. She straightened and moved deftly to the foot of the pallet and perched herself on a chair that had been pushed against it. She stared down at his half naked, scrawny body and snickered. She was going to enjoy this.

She leaned forward gently running a hand down his leg as she whispered, "*Stanley?*"

CHAPTER 11

After the conjuring: Day four – 1:00 am.
Woodbury, Long Island

Lieutenant Cassandra "Casey" Talbot scrutinized the cut window screen in the upstairs room from where the reported infant had been taken. Normally, she would not have responded to a 10-65 call. A missing person didn't fall into the violent crime or homicide category that was her purview. However, the unit making the call had tagged a code 135—a possible kidnapping — to the 10-65. It sounded like something she should check out. So, here she was at the scene in the wee hours of the morning.

Casey Talbot grew up in Queens, New York. She had lived in a three-bedroom apartment on Lefferts Boulevard with her parents and three older brothers. The brothers were responsible for her learning to defend herself both verbally and physically. She graduated from Richmond Hill High school with high grades in 1950. She could have gone to college but there was no money for that. Her brothers had gobbled it up on their education. Being the youngest and a girl it was deemed not necessary. The Korean War had just broken out causing the local Army recruiters to step up their efforts. Casey saw a woman dressed in a uniform talking to students, days before graduation and inquired. Two weeks after graduation she signed up, defying the wishes of her parents.

Basic training for women in the army did not meet Casey's expectations. Because of her size, she found herself being directed toward programs for nursing— geared to assignments with MASH units— or communications as a radio or telegraph operator. Casey Talbot wanted to be a soldier and she lobbied for that every chance she got. It was during this time that she learned her personality and looks could get her places. She had charmed a staff sergeant into getting her transferred to the new training facility at Fort McClellan in Alabama. She completed basic training in 1951 as a Private First Class/Specialist with a "Sharpshooter" title as well as a first-degree black belt in Judo. The Drill Sergeant at Fort McClellan nick named her "Mighty Mite". She found herself assigned to duty in Seoul, South Korea as a base MP — Military Police. When time allowed, she learned Jui Jitsu from the south Korean soldiers while advancing her Judo skills to a second-degree black belt. In 1954 Corporal Cassandra Talbot received an Honorable Discharge and returned home.

After a brief respite, Casey answered a query for police officers in Mineola and was immediately hired, thanks to her military credentials.

Her petite, athletic figure plus movie star good looks — people told her she looked like Debbie Reynolds — landed her an undercover assignment. Pimps, rapists, porn brokers and small-time gambling bosses never knew what hit them. The termination of a child slavery ring and the capture of its dirt bag leader — which almost cost her life — made her famous within the department. Shortly after the conviction and sentencing of the ringleader — which seemed to take forever — Casey Talbot received accommodations leading to the title of Detective and a transfer to the 2nd Precinct, Violent Crimes Division in Woodbury.

Leaning closer to the window she examined the damaged screen that had been cut then forced inward as to allow entrance. *Make a note. Forced entry. Intruder carried a knife or box cutter to slice open the screen.*

Further scrutiny revealed three parallel scratch marks on the outside edge of the open window frame. They appeared to be fresh. The streaks in the metal frame were bright gouges. A stark contrast to the rest of the dull frame. *What could make marks like this?*

She turned to the officer behind her and pointed at the frame. "Has this been touched since you arrived?"

"No, Ma'am."

Casey winced. She hated being called Ma'am. "*Lieutenant* will do fine. Thank you. I want this window taped off."

The patrolman pulled a roll of crime scene tape from a duffle bag at his feet. "Yes, Ma…Lieutenant."

Images of the child slavery ring and missing children crept from a dark corner of her memory. Could this sick criminal operation be back? She knew the MO of the gang she had busted. *This is something new,* she thought.

"Okay, people. Listen up. I'm officially declaring this a crime scene."

The four officers snapped to attention. One, her partner Detective Carver, stepped forward. "Shall I wake up Forensics, Lieutenant?"

"Code 2. Thanks. Oh, and tell them to round up a doctor and bring him along." With that said Casey left the room to see what she could do for the stricken parents.

**

"Not *now*," Stanley said. He turned on to his side and pulled the pillow over his head.

Malhela straightened, a bit puzzled. With more command in her voice she said, *"Stanley!"*

"Go away," Stanley groaned.

Stunned by this remark she didn't know how to react. Was he giving her a command? Was she being released from the spell? No! The compelling sense of responsibility, the tingle of the call to duty that was part and parcel to a conjuring was not present. This was the incoherent mumbling of a sleeping mortal.

Frustrated and annoyed Malhela reached out and smacked Stanley hard on his rump.

"Ow! What the …?" Stanley threw his pillow aside, sat up and froze. Immediately wide awake he slid backward on his mattress away from the thing staring at him from the foot of the bed. *I'm dreamin...I have ta be dreamin.* He closed his eyes, gave his head a quick shake and looked again. The creature was still there. A winged shadow back lit by dim light.

Trying to control the fear that was welling up inside him, he kept saying, "Can't be real...can't be real."

"Oh, I'm real, Stanley," Malhela said softly as she floated from the chair to the side of Stanley's bed.

The creature had moved into the pale light and Stanley could see it a little more clearly. His eyes went wide, and he began to tremble.

The being, about five feet tall, had the body of a full grown, naked woman with leathery bat like wings on its back. Its slender, yet muscular arms ended with hands furnished with dagger like fingernails. The legs were shapely and sinewy. Instead of feet, hawklike talons tapped the wooden floor when it moved. Elfish ears extended from either side of the otherwise bald head except for — what Stanley thought were feathers — a thick cluster of white quills stemming from the top of its forehead. In the gloom, Stanley thought the skin color was like that of a person with a good summer tan.

An involuntary gasp escaped his lips when his eyes finally focused on the thing's partially lit face. His throat went dry, and he couldn't breathe.

Malhela leaned over Stanley and smiled. "*Stanley? Why am I here?*"

"Huh?" Stanley said, but it came out sounding like a moan. He couldn't tear his eyes from that face.

"*Why…am…I…here?*" Malhela asked again. She took Stanley's hand — the one with the burned fingers — in hers.

Stanley closed his eyes tight. *Oh shit! What if it's a Gorgon. I'll be turned to stone!*

"*I am not a Gorgon, Stanley. Now answer me,*" Malhela could hear his thoughts as if he were speaking aloud.

Stanley tried to pull his hand away. "Wha…What?"

Malhela, losing patience, snarled and twisted Stanley's hand. "*Why have you summoned me!?*"

Before he could answer she heard a sound outside the chamber door. She sniffed. Another male a bit older was approaching. This was not the time for a confrontation. The bad omen came to mind. Foiled and angry Malhela released Stanley's hand and slapped him hard across the face. She took a quick glance at the door then turned back to Stanley, hissed and spit on his head. In a blur she was out the window and gone.

Stanley's older brother Artie skulked into the room they shared and eyed his brother cowering on his bed. "What's your problem?" he said.

Letting out a breath that he didn't realize he was holding Stanley said, "Did ya see it? See her?"

"Her?" Artie laughed and looked around the room.

"I swear Artie. There was a girl…no… a woman, here. She had wings like a bat and…"

"Uh huh…sure. Where'd she go? Out the window?"

"Yes!" Stanley got out of bed and went to the window and looked out. He picked up a cloth that was lying beneath it and wiped the spit from his hair. Then dropped it back on the floor. He hadn't noticed it was pink in color.

"You're loco. Have you been hitting dad's Christian Brothers again?"

"Shut up, Artie!"

"Go back to bed, coo coo bird and… be quiet." Artie turned and started to undress. "Man…what's that smell?"

Stanley rolled over to face the wall. "*You!*"

CHAPTER 12

Day Four – mid morning, 2ⁿᵈ Precinct:
Woodbury, Long Island

After spending the early morning hours with Forensics combing the grounds as well as the home of William and Laura Purcell — parents of the missing infant — and finding nothing but scratch marks on the upstairs casement window frame plus identical ones directly above on the roof shingles, Lieutenant Casey Talbot returned to the precinct and issued an APB on the infant, Lilly Purcell, though she knew it was a waste of time and energy.

As she worked on the All-Points Bulletin, she noticed one that had been issued by the 8th Precinct concerning the disappearance of one John Wheatley. A five-year-old thought to have been abducted from the Division Avenue playground. *Why the hell didn't I pay attention to this when it came in?*

She got up from her desk and went to her office door. "Warren? Do we have any updates on the APB from the 8th regarding the missing five-year-old?"

Officer Warren Peters, busy filing a report on a domestic violence case, looked up. "Not that I know of Lieutenant. Want me to call them?"

"No, I'll do it myself. Thanks." She stifled a yawn. "Any coffee left in that pot?"

"I'll make some," Warren said getting up from his desk.

***

8th Precinct: Bethpage, Long Island

Sergeant David Sanfield had spent yesterday afternoon and the entire evening cruising Hillsville and its outskirts searching for his son. He questioned people at Hurley's Ice Cream Parlor as well as the other places he thought his son would hang out. No one had seen him. Now, he sat in his patrol car outside the precinct wondering what to do next.

Sanfield had lost his wife six years ago to Ovarian cancer. Danny was nine and blamed him for his mother's death. Whatever he did to relieve his son's grief had failed and the older Danny got the angrier he became. He told himself he was a good father, that he had to be tough on his son so he would survive this insane world. Maybe he'd been fooling himself? Even sending Danny to live with his aunt for a few weeks, hoping that a little female TLC would help, ended in disaster. Maybe he had pushed too hard, and Danny finally had had enough and took off.

He shook these thoughts from his head. He would let his fellow officers do their thing. Danny would turn up. Meanwhile he'd check in and find out the latest.

"Line three, Lieutenant. Second precinct. A Lieutenant Talbot asking for you."

Lieutenant James Trabinski quickly put his hand over the mouthpiece of the phone he was talking into. "Tell him I'll be right with him."

"Her…it's a her, Lieutenant."

Trabinski's eyebrows went up. "Tell her to hold on." He returned to the call. "Sorry, say again, sir."

"This is Doctor Corbin. I'm the pharmacist at Whelans Drugs. I have two teenage boys here who claim they found a body in the woods near Cherry Street. They're pretty shook up. They said they couldn't find a policeman to tell so they came here. I thought it best to call you immediately."

"Thank you doctor. Keep the boys there. We're on our way." He hit the dispatch button.

"We have a 10-54, Cherry Street, Hillsville. Scramble closest unit. Send a unit to Whelans' Drug Store on Park Avenue to pick up two teenagers. Trabinski, out."

"10-4 Lieutenant."

He took a deep breath, exhaled slowly and punched line three. "Lieutenant? I'll have to call you back. Got a 10-54 to run to." He was about to hang up when he heard her say, "Where?"

He wasn't expecting that response. "Uh…wooded area on Cherry Street in Hillsville. Not your jurisdiction. Why?"

"I'll meet you there," she said and hung up.

Trabinski looked at the phone, placed it back in its cradle then scanned the room to see who was available. Detective Pete Taylor had just come in and was about to pour himself a cup of java. "Detective?

Put a lid on that. You're with me," he said, jamming a pack of Camels in his shirt pocket and heading for the door. On his way out he bumped into Sergeant David Sanfield. "Sorry Dave…Danny come home last night?"

"No…No he didn't," Sanfield said.

Trabinski pushed through the door into the morning heat. "We'll keep looking," he said over his shoulder.

With the siren screaming, the black Galaxie roared out of the parking lot heading for Plainview Road. James Trabinski at the wheel. "Call it in Pete," he said turning to his partner.

Detective Taylor grabbed the mic from its dashboard clip and spoke quickly. "Dispatch? Unit one en route to Cherry Street scene. Copy?"

"10-4. Unit one en route. Over."

It only took Trabinski and Taylor ten minutes to get to Cherry Street but two of his units were already on the scene. *Nice response time gentlemen,* Trabinski thought as he pulled to the curb. He noticed two scared-looking teenagers sitting in the back seat of one of the cruisers. He lit a cigarette, stepped from his vehicle, and went to the boys. Pete Taylor right behind clutching his coffee cup. Officer Jake Stevens stood next to the blue and orange cruiser keeping an eye on its occupants.

"Morning Jake," Trabinski said. "You get their story?"

"Right here Lieutenant," Stevens said pulling a small notepad from his pocket. "At first, they weren't making much sense. Both talking at the same time…You know? Once I got them quieted down, they recounted their gruesome find. A body torn to pieces. It sounded a bit like an exaggeration to me until Hancock told me what they found back there." Stevens jerked a thumb in the direction of the woods. "Looks like they weren't. I was told to keep these two here and away from the scene."

Trabinski looked around and didn't see Stevens' partner anywhere but noticed a black 1960 Plymouth Fury parked nearby. "Where is Hancock?" He said.

Stevens stuffed his notepad back in his shirt pocket. "Went back to help, sir."

"Went back to help?" Trabinski said, offering Stevens a puzzled look.

"Yes, sir."

"Why?"

"He didn't say sir."

What's going on here? I'd better make this quick.

Trabinski blew smoke up into the air and bent down to the open car window. "You boys okay?"

They both said "yeah" at the same time but kept their heads down.

"I'm Lieutenant Trabinski. Can you tell me your names?"

"I'm Teddy," said the boy with red hair and glasses.

"Who's your partner here?" Trabinski pointed to the chubby-faced boy next to Teddy.

"My name's Larry," chubby face said. "Are we in trouble?"

"No, son…you're not in trouble. Just tell me why you were in the woods this morning."

Teddy took off his glasses, wiped them on his shirt and slid them back on his pointy nose. "Just collecting bottles…for the deposit money…You know?"

"Sometimes we find a lot back in there. Some good ones with a nickel deposit," chimed in Larry.

"Any luck today?" Trabinski asked.

"Nah," they both said. "We were doing one last search when we found…," Larry said.

It looked as if the boy couldn't bring himself to say anymore.

"That's fine boys," Trabinski said. "Thank you. Officer Stevens will take you home and explain everything to your parents."

Teddy and Larry nodded.

He turned to Stevens. "Okay Jake take these two home and get them a soda or something on the way. Check back in with me after you talk to the parents."

As Trabinski started toward the wooded area he saw the forensics van pull up. He spun around and yelled at Stevens who was about to back his cruiser into the street. "Jake! Who called Forensics? The area hasn't been designated."

"Hancock, sir. The Lieutenant told him to call in a code 2 for them."

"The Lieutenant!?"

"Lieutenant Talbot, sir."

"What the *Hell…*?" Trabinski stormed off into the woods. Detective Taylor trying to keep up.

It had been quite a while since Lieutenant James Trabinski had been in these woods. As a young police officer, he had helped nab a ring of reefer peddlers who had been operating from here. It was much more overgrown now. After yesterday's rain, the foliage was thick and lush. The earthy smell of mold and decaying wood hung in the humid air. The trail that snaked its way through the thicket was well travelled. The woods were strangely silent. Only the hushed voices from further up the path disturbed it.

Trabinski approached the voices. Four people stood gathered in the deep scrub about ten feet from the trail. Three uniformed officers plus a woman dressed in navy blue slacks and a white sleeveless blouse with a navy-blue jacket slung over her shoulder. Officers Malloy and Tracy from unit10 stood next to the woman — who was obviously Lieutenant Talbot — Hancock stood behind them with his head down.

"Lieutenant Talbot…I *presume*?" Trabinksi said stepping up to the group.

"Yes…Hello Lieutenant," the woman said and stuck out her hand.

James Trabinksi momentarily stunned by her good looks shook her hand. A firm hand shake. He introduced Taylor. Before he could say another word Lieutenant Talbot said, "Sorry to step on your toes Lieutenant. I officially declared the scene when Hancock here thought he knew the victim. If he's right, it's bad news. I told him to call forensics. They should be here any minute."

"They just pulled up." With that said they heard someone tramping along the trail. Two men dressed in white lab coats quickly approached.

"No rest for the weary…Ay Lieutenant?" The examiner said to Talbot.

"It's going to be one of those days," she said and pointed toward the body.

Trabinski put his hand on the examiner's shoulder. "Mind if I take a look first?"

The examiner stuck out his hand and gestured. "After you Lieutenant. Thought you had already examined the body."

Trabinski shot a quick glance at Hancock whose face was white as Talbot's blouse and pushed through the brush. The others followed, Hancock did not.

CHAPTER 13

Day Four – mid morning

Through the curtainless window the rays of the morning sun, filled with drifting dust motes, entered Stanley Bolton's room. Long shadows attached themselves to the legs of the lone bedroom chair as well as shoes and other scattered objects on the floor. Stanley sat on the edge of his bed, still in his underwear staring at the pink blanket hanging from the window where he had placed it last night. He had jammed the screen against it to keep it in place. It was one of the reasons he did not sleep well. The fishy garbage smell had come, he discovered, from the blanket. The putrid odor seemed to fill the area by his bed forcing him to get up and drape the coverlet out the window.

As Stanley sat thinking about last night's apparition, he realized he had been assaulted by this stench once before. *That's what we smelled in the maze when we were lookin for that kid. That thing musta been in there. And…what's with the pink blanket? Was it left here on purpose? Why? There ain't no girls in this house.*

He pulled his eyes from the blanket and scanned the room. His brother's bed was empty and unmade as usual. Stanley didn't know

83

where Artie went every day. He would leave early and come home late. Stanley didn't care.

His gaze landed on the chair pushed up against the foot of his bed where the creature had sat. *That thing was real. The smack in the face ... and the spit was real. Wait a minute. Did it speak to me? Cripes! I think it said something to me. I can't remember what it said.*

Then like a brilliant light being turned on in a dark room, Stanley knew. *Oh, shit! It worked! The conjuring worked!*

He jumped up from his bed and started rummaging through the clutter. *The book? Where's that book?*

After searching his room for an hour, Stanley could not find the Lovecraft book they had used for the incantation. *Where did we leave that damn thing?*

He racked his brain as he got dressed. *The basement! It's still in the basement. I hid it under the stairs. Duh! How could I forget that?*

Stanley finished dressing, placed the blanket in a paper bag he had found in his closet and dropped it out the window. He pushed the window screen back in place and headed for the basement.

What Stanley saw at the bottom of the dimly lit basement stairs made him stumble on the steps. Four neat bundles of newspapers and magazines, tied with heavy twine sat on the concrete floor at the foot of the stairs. This was his father's doing. *When did this happen?*

Stanley stepped over the bundles and hurried to the hiding place beneath the stairs feeling relieved that he remembered where he had put it. He moved the boxes aside that he had placed there and peered under the step, in anticipation of retrieving the book and putting it to good use. But he couldn't see it in the dark recess. *Must have pushed it further back than I thought.* He got down on his hands and knees, lowering his head for a better look. With his left hand he reached into the darkness and felt around for the book. Dust and spider webs stuck to his hand. "Shit!" He said quickly jerking his hand from beneath the step as a big spider came racing out of the shadows. In an instant he was on his feet stomping the hell out of the creepy thing. *I hate those damn things!*

Once again, he was down on his knees peering under the step but this time lighting the recess with the flame from his cigarette lighter. The space was empty. The book was gone.

He frantically moved the boxes and other junk around hoping it would still be there somewhere. It wasn't. "What the hell happened to it?" He muttered to himself.

Stanley stood and went over to the neatly tied bundles scanning each of them for the black cover of the thick book. It would be easy to spot if it was included here. No luck.

Thirty minutes of scrounging through every cabinet, drawer and shelf proved a waste of time. It could mean only one thing. Someone took it. *Probably father when he was cleanin' up and tyin' the papers. That's not so bad. He reads junk like that all the time. He probably stashed it in his night table drawer. I'll check that as soon as the coast is clear.* Then he shuddered at the thought of his mother finding it. She was always down here moving stuff around. *That would be bad.*

As he started up the basement stairs his thoughts turned to Tim Ryan. *I gotta tell him about this. Show him the blanket…make him smell it. Tell him what the creature looked like. He won't believe it. This is nuts!*

***

Malhela, after snacking on the yappy little dog that had lived in the yard behind her dwelling, sat sulking in her nest. She twirled the dog's collar around her finger as she replayed last night's visit to Stanley in her head. It had not gone as she had hoped. The more she thought about it the more certain she became that this conjuring was either a prank or a careless mistake. She had been summoned then apparently forgotten. But Stanley's dumbfounded primate reaction to her revealing herself last night may still lead to an answer. She had startled him and that was a blunder on her part. However, he didn't seem terrified as he looked into her eyes. Yes, his thoughts were hectic and confused. Yet, she could read his amazement as well as something else. Infatuation. *This* could be useful. Many male mortals through the ages had lusted after her and regretted it once she had no need for them.

She would watch for another opportunity to get Stanley alone. Right now, she didn't feel like doing anything. Even the wonderful, citrus scent telling her that Tim Ryan was approaching had no effect.

One of the two large doors at the front of her dwelling opened and Tim Ryan strode in. She watched him with listless eyes as he grabbed — what he called a bike — and left. Malhela knew she should follow him but had no desire.

Perhaps the dog she had eaten earlier had caused this malaise.

***

"*Shit!*" Lieutenant James Trabinski quickly rose from his crouching position next to the fly covered body. He ran a hand over his face as if trying to wipe the image from his eyes. His mind raced. *Focus…Focus Trabinski,* he told himself.

"I'm sorry Lieutenant. I was hoping Hancock was mistaken," Casey Talbot said. "Shall I tell Phil to proceed?"

Trabinski raised his head and looked at the stolid young woman standing next to him. "Phil?"

"Phil Tipton…our Forensics Examiner." Casey turned and pointed to the tall thin man in the white lab coat conversing with Malloy and Tracy.

"Right. I've worked with Phil before. I'll talk to him. Thanks anyway."

Casey stepped aside. "Sure."

Trabinski called the examiner over. "Phil…I want you to go by the book here. I know you're thorough, but this requires more than that. The victim is the son of one of my officers and we need to know what happened here as quickly as possible. No delays. Understand?"

"I'll make sure there's a code 2 on this investigation as soon as we're finished here. The official reports will be hand delivered to you and I'll personally call you with our findings before that." Phil waved his assistant over and stepped toward the body, as he pulled surgical gloves from his coat pocket.

Detective Pete Taylor — who had been shifting from one foot to the other with his hand over his mouth — finally spoke. "You think this is a gang kill, Jim?"

"Pretty brutal if it is." Trabinski gave a quick glance at the body and turned back to his detective. "Pete, go call the coroner. Code 2 on that too. And…find out where Sergeant Sanfield is this morning."

"Roger that." Taylor was about to leave when the examiner's voice grabbed everyone's attention.

"Lieutenant?"

Trabinski and Talbot both turned at the same time.

"Something a little odd here. May not mean anything, but the victim has no shoes." The examiner pointed to the shoeless feet clad with blood splattered white socks. "Could have come off in the struggle. We're going to need them."

Trabinski instructed Malloy and Tracey to spread out and search the area on the opposite side of the path while he took this section.

"I'll come with you," Casey said.

They searched in silence for quite some time, Trabinski deep in thought, dreading the task he had ahead of him. *Dave Sanfield will be devastated.*

The sound of someone pushing through bushes and sticks brought him back to the present, making him remember he was not alone out here.

"So …why are you here Lieutenant? Second Precinct slow today? He watched her as she worked her way through the thicket with a look of determination on her face.

"Just the opposite. I picked up a case this morning that seems to coincide with one of yours." She quickly broke off a branch that almost hit her in the face.

"Go on," he said.

"You have a missing child case on your books right now?"

Trabinski stopped walking when he came to a hedge of overgrown, thorned berry bushes and turned toward Talbot.

"We're wasting our time out here. Let's head back."

Casey swatted at a fly. They seemed to be everywhere. "You didn't answer my question."

"It's now a homicide investigation," he said.

"You recovered the missing child's body?"

"Not yet. A blood-stained piece of cloth was found at the scene where the boy disappeared. The mother identified the fragment as part of her son's bathing suit."

A pained expression clouded Casey's pretty face. "I'm sorry to hear that. My gut is telling me that an old nightmare of mine could be back."

"Old nightmare?"

"I helped break up a child slavery ring a few years ago. I got a bad feeling it's happening again."

"I take it your case this morning involves a missing child." Trabinski slowed his pace.

"An infant, taken from an upstairs room. Forced entry through the room's window. Whoever did this has upped their game. We found no clues on the grounds. Forensics thinks they may have used a grappling hook based on the marks found on the windowsill."

"A grappling hook? Seems a bit extreme don't you think?"

Trabinski could see the others just ahead and two men in navy blue windbreakers struggling up the path with a gurney. "Coroner's here," he said and quickly moved forward.

Phil Tipton, the lead Forensics examiner took Trabinski and Talbot aside as the Coroner's Department prepared the body for transport. "Jim...Casey? Thought you might be interested in my preliminary findings." His usual placid expression now replaced by one of grimness.

Trabinski's attention was on the medics who had just placed a black tarp over the remains of Danny Sanfield.

"Lieutenant?"

"Yes, yes…by all means."

"The killer had to be powerful. If the jugular laceration were any deeper, it would have resulted in decapitation. Plus, the right hand was severed from the wrist with great force. The ragged edges imply something other than a knife was used." Phil removed his surgical gloves and placed them in a plastic bag he had pulled from his pocket. "I can't explain the multiple lacerations on his back. The shirt has been completely shredded as if it went through a machine. We'll dig deeper…find out more when we get back to the lab. Your boys couldn't find the shoes. I take it you didn't either."

Trabinski gave a quick shake of the head and Casey said, "Nope."

The examiner mopped his face and the back of his neck with a blue striped handkerchief. "Be glad when this heat wave is over. You officially IDing the victim, Jim?"

Trabinski nodded and took the clip board from Phil's assistant and signed the top document. "Proceed with the autopsy, Phil. No delays. Round the clock if you have to. I want to be able to give Dave Sanfield a detailed account of what happened to his son. Whoever did this will pay dearly."

"Right," Phil said. "I'll be in touch." He shook Trabinski's hand, nodded at Casey and left.

During this exchange Casey had been watching Officer Hancock who was slouched against a tree directly across from the taped off crime scene. She gave Trabinski a light tap on the shoulder. "He's taking this pretty hard." She pointed to Hancock.

Trabinski had forgotten all about his officer and his connection to the Sanfield family. "Christ…I'd better talk to him."

Hancock looked up as Trabinski and Talbot approached. Malloy and Tracey were standing to his left, concern on their faces. Detective Taylor to his right was saying something in a low voice.

"Tough day gentlemen. Let's stay focused and find out who did this," Trabinski said. "Malloy…you and Tracey grab some tape and close off both entrances to this area. Pete…Call dispatch and have them assign a unit to the Cherry Street and Park Avenue entryways. Hourly patrols. My authorization if the captain should ask."

The three men hurried off to their tasks. Trabinski came up to Hancock and put a hand on his shoulder. "You okay Ed?"

Hancock took a deep breath and let it out slowly. "I can't believe it Jim. I feel like I let him down. I knew him since he was a little kid. Helen and I tried to help out when his mother died. He didn't have it easy with Dave working all those odd hours. You know how it is. We tried to keep him out of trouble, steer him in the right direction. I never imagined he'd end up like this.

"Last week he was around to the house telling Helen about this girl he was crazy over and when I heard he had run away I was certain it involved this girl." Hancock shook his head. His face was flushed. "I can't believe it. He's dead Jim!"

"Blaming yourself isn't going to help find his killer. Come on, Taylor and I will take you back to the precinct."

Hancock pushed away from the tree. Trabinski gave him a pat on the back and they both headed down the path toward the street. Abruptly, Trabinski stopped and turned to look at Lieutenant Talbot still standing by the tree. *How can a ray of sunshine like that be involved in such darkness?*

Before he could say anything, Talbot urged him to go with a wave of her hand. She nodded. "We'll talk."

CHAPTER 14

Day Four – Late afternoon

Tim told Stanley Bolton to be at his house at 4 o'clock. They had to be at the newspaper office before 5 to get on the bus that would take them to the stock car races at the Freeport Raceway. Tim's mom had offered to take them to the office. But Stan, keyed up about his late-night discovery, had to talk to Tim. He couldn't wait so he decided to show up a half hour early. He sauntered up Tim's driveway, his left hand behind his back clutching the bag with the pink blanket. *What am I gonna say if his mother wants to know what's in the bag? Shoulda thought of that before ya brought it dummy. I know…I'll just say it's garbage I found in the street, and it needs to be tossed. That should work. It does smell.*

As he stepped around the corner of Tim's house, he saw the left garage door open. He quickly scooted over, stashed the bag inside, near Tim's bike and moseyed over to the back door and knocked.

Instantly, the door opened. Emily, Tim's sister, stood there with a frown on her face. "What are you doing here? You're too early."

"Where's Tim? I need ta tell him somethin."

"He's getting ready. I think he's in the bathroom. Hey, what happened to your nose?" Emily squinted as if examining it more closely.

"*Just* get him, squirt," Stanley said.

"*Don't call me squirt!*" Emily said and closed the door in Stanley's face.

Stan threw his hands up in frustration and stepped off the stoop unaware that a pair of yellow eyes were watching him from a dark corner inside the garage.

"Stanley? Come in, come in. Have some lemonade. That was very rude of Emily." Tim's mother said.

Startled, Stanley immediately turned to face her. "Uh…Hi, Mrs. Ryan. Sorry I'm early. I wanted ta talk ta Tim about somethin."

"Have a seat," she said pouring him a glass of pink liquid. You can talk on the way to the news stand.

"Thank you, Mrs. Ryan." Stanley said as he took the glass. *Dammit!*

Emily sat at the end of the kitchen table giving Stanley her best mean face.

The ride to the Newsday office was a quiet one. Stanley hardly spoke — which was totally unlike him — and Tim kept looking at him wondering what was going on. Stanley seemed out of it.

Keeping his voice low Tim said, "You look beat. You stay up all night or something?"

"Huh? Oh yeah somethin like that. I'll tell ya on the bus." Stanley put his finger on his lips signaling to be quiet and pointed to Tim's mom and sister in the front seat.

Tim gave Stanley a puzzled look but didn't say anything else.

They arrived in plenty of time for the bus, said goodbye to Tim's mother — assuring her that Tim's Route Manger, Mr. Leber would bring them home — and proceeded to check in with the bus driver.

There were six other boys on the bus already, laughing and poking each other when they got on. Tim noticed an instant change in Stan as they moved to their seats. The noise had quieted down when a big kid with orange hair, sporting a flat top with slicked back sides turned and looked at Stan.

"Hey, Bolton? What are you doing here?" orange hair said.

"Well, if it ain't Butch Corrigan. *You delivering papers?* Unbelievable!"

"What's unbelievable is you being allowed out." Butch laughed. "After that cat in the mailbox bit we figured you'd be grounded for the summer."

"You still owe me five dollars, pal," Stanley replied.

"Ha! I don't think so. You cheated and the dice were loaded." Butch smiled and folded his arms across his chest.

Tim kept looking back and forth at the two of them fearing this would escalate into a brawl.

Stanley made a puff sound with his mouth and shook his head. "The dice were yours blockhead…Remember?"

Butch was about to say something when Mr. Leber came on board followed by four other boys. Instead, he thrust a hand into his pants pocket, pulled out a five-dollar bill and threw it at Stanley - who deftly snatched it from the air before it hit the floor.

Stanley saw the question on Tim's face and quickly said, "Knuckleheads from school".

"All right you thugs…settle down." Mr. Leber always called his delivery boys "thugs". No one really knew why, but he would laugh after he said it. He took attendance, laid down the rules of the trip, instructed them the bus would leave at 10pm sharp to bring them back home and that stragglers would pay the consequences. With that said he took his seat behind the driver. The old yellow school bus's engine cranked a few times, and finally started. The next stop Freeport Raceway.

The Raceway opened its gates for stock car racing in 1937. The half mile dirt oval track featured main, high stakes events on Friday and Saturday nights. Thursday nights and Sunday afternoons offered specialty shows like demolition derbies and midget racers on the inner quarter mile oval. It seated two thousand people on a good night. The smell of hot dogs, hamburgers, French fries, popcorn, and peanuts as well as cotton candy intermingling with that of gasoline and motor oil added to the charm.

Stanley took the window seat, looked around to see if anyone was listening and spoke to Tim, keeping his voice down. "You're gonna mess your drawers when ya hear this. I think it worked. Somethin actually came through."

"What worked?" Tim said.

"The conjuring. Remember the conjuring? I think it worked." Stan shifted in his seat. "Keep your voice down."

"The conjuring? It *worked* and… *something* came through?" Tim squinted his eyes giving Stan a look of suspicion.

"Exactly!" Stan said, scanning the seats around them again for eavesdroppers.

"What came through and from where?"

Stan rubbed the tip of his sore nose. "I *don't know* from where, but there was a creature in my room last night. And remember that odor we smelled in the maze when we were lookin' for that missin' kid? That's what this thing smelled like."

Tim's eyebrows went up on that one. "Were you dreaming?"

"Can ya smell somethin' in a dream? I wasn't dreamin' because the thing slapped me on the butt and woke me up."

"You can have a dream within a dream you know," Tim said.

"This *was not* a dream." Stan, in a hushed voice, went on to describe the creature.

"Oh brother," Tim said. "You expect me to believe a naked woman with bat wings and yellow eyes was in your room last night? And… you think she spoke to you. That definitely sounds like a dream to me. You've got to stop looking at those girlie magazines in the barber shop." Now it was Tim scanning the area for listeners.

At the front of the bus, Butch was treating his cronies to some new verses of Barnacle Bill the Sailor. "Who's that knocking at my door? Said the fair young maiden. It's only me, home from the sea, said Barnacle Bill the Sailor.

Shall we go to the dance, shall we go to the dance? Said the fair young maiden.

To hell with the dance now down with yer pants, said Barnacle Bill the Sailor…"

Mr. Leber pretended not to hear.

"What about the smell?" Stan countered. "I can prove that. She was carryin a blanket and dropped it when she flew out the window. The smell is all over it. I put it in a bag and stashed it in your garage to show you."

"You *what*? Suppose my parents find it?"

"Who cares? They won't know what it is or where it came from."

Tim unwrapped a piece of Bazooka bubble gum and popped it in his mouth. He didn't offer any to Stanley. "So far, I'm not hearing anything that'll make me *mess my drawers* as you say. Did you *mess* yours when you saw how terrifying it was?"

"That's the thing…she wasn't terrifyin' or scary. She was …well… her face was kinda …beautiful."

"*Beautiful?*" Tim said, trying to control his sarcasm.

"Yeah. Tim ya gotta believe me. Imagine Tuesday Weld's face only with the eyes of let's say a leopard." Stan's voice took on an almost dreamy tone as he spoke about her face.

"You are bonkers." Tim popped a bubble and shook his head.

Stanley, feeling a bit annoyed, pushed on.

"I wish I knew what happened to that book. We could sure use it," he said.

"What do you mean? You left it on the table in your basement when we left. What do we need it for?"

Stanley reached into his shirt pocket and pulled out a pack of cigarettes, slipped one into his mouth and lit it. He took a deep drag then exhaled slowly out the open window.

"No smoking in here, son," Mr. Leber called from the front of the bus.

Tim shot Stanley a stern look that said you better not ruin this trip.

"Uh…sorry." Stanley said to Mr. Leber and tossed the cigarette out the window. He held his hand out to Tim. "Give me a piece of gum will ya."

"Why is this book suddenly so important?" Tim asked, handing him a square of Bazooka.

"It may have stuff in it on how ta control this thing." He said noisily chewing the gum as he spoke. "Remember I told ya ta wait on the stairs? Well, I went back and stashed the book behind the bottom step…underneath it until I could come back for it."

"Okay?"

"It was *gone* when I looked for it this morning. It looked like my father had been down there cleaning up. It's possible he found it and kept it for himself ta read. He reads stuff like that sometimes. So, it could be with his other books. But if my mother found it, she would throw it out."

He looked out the window, thinking. Then quickly turned back to face Tim. "Hey…do ya remember the name? Ya know? The name of the being we were tryin' to call up?"

Unexpectedly, Mr. Leber announced they had arrived at the track, repeated the rules, what to do in an emergency, where to find him or the driver. He opened the bus door and ushered them out with a jovial "Have Fun!"

***

Meanwhile, still out of sorts Malhela snatched the bag left by Stanley, examined the contents, and tossed it into her nest with the rest of her souvenirs.

As night approached, she once again found thoughts of the Realm haunting her. She focused on her current situation and the reason for it.

A disturbing notion came to mind, bringing with it a sickening feeling of hopelessness. Was she being punished? What had she done to warrant punishment? Did the Lord of the Realm think — as he had done when she had failed to return from His *Black Death* invasion all those ages ago — that she was incompetent, reckless, or just plain careless? Jeopardizing the secrecy of the Realm once again?

She remembered being severely reprimanded when she finally returned to the Realm after escaping the clutches of the witch crone and being given a warning. But the ever-shifting dunes of time had sufficiently buried it in her mind.

It didn't matter what the warning had been. Malhela couldn't shake the feeling of exile.

CHAPTER 15

Day Four – Evening

Lieutenant James Trabinski sat in a dimly lit corner of the Broadway Café nursing his second Cutty Sark on the rocks. It was a quiet night at the Café, and he liked it that way, especially after the day he just had. Soft music— piano jazz—drifted through the restaurant helping to calm his nerves.

Breaking the bad news to Sergeant Dave Sanfield about his son had been difficult. The man — a seasoned cop — knew something was up by the expressions on people's faces in the precinct when he came off duty. He had looked around, not saying a word, scanning the faces of people he knew well. When no one made eye contact he squared his shoulders and seeing Trabinski at his desk with his head down walked toward his office.

He remained standing although he had been offered a chair. There was no reaction to the news of his son's death, other than a slight twitch of his left eye. He acted as if it were just another case briefing. Without being asked, he divulged the information he had regarding the kids who had seen his son last.

Sanfield didn't want to know the examiner's details just the measures being taken to find the killer.

Phil Tipton had been good to his word, cutting through red tape and getting the autopsy results to Trabinski in record time.

Sergeant Sanfield stood as if at attention conversing in a monotone voice. When he finally had nothing else to say he sat down, the color draining from his face. Leaning back in the chair he folded his hands in his lap and stared up at the clock on the office wall. His left eye started twitching rapidly. He was going into shock.

Everyone in the department scrambled to help. A quickly dispatched ambulance had rushed him to Central General for observation. He would be temporarily relieved of duty and granted a leave of absence for bereavement.

Trabinski finally looked at the menu the waitress had left on the corner of the table. He wasn't hungry but knew he had better eat something. The fish and chips looked appealing. He gave his order to the waitress and as she scurried off, the Café front door opened. A lone figure stepped into the shadows of the restaurant's foyer.

He raised his glass to his lips and took a sip while watching the new customer over the top of his glass. Normally, he wouldn't pay much attention to the clientele who dined here but this one walked with poise, maybe even authority. His curiosity turned to surprised recognition when the figure stepped into the dining room light. His eyes lingered admiringly on the person who stood a few tables from his. He saw the figure's head turn to the left then to the right, eyes exploring the tables as if searching for someone. Trabinski took another sip and lowered his glass watching as a waitress chatted with the new customer. *Hmmm…date night? With a significant other? This should be interesting.* No sooner had these thoughts entered his head when the waitress turned and pointed in his direction. *Oh, man…Don't know if I'm ready for this.* He sat back in his chair and folded his arms across his chest as the person strode purposely toward him.

"You have a knack for showing up unexpectedly, Lieutenant Talbot."

"You'd be surprised at how much you can learn by showing up unannounced." She gave him a quick smile. "May I join you? That is if you're not expecting someone."

Trabinski found himself feeling a bit uncomfortable. He was totally out of shape when it came to socializing with the fairer sex, especially those with Talbot's looks. She wore dark casual slacks and a distracting light blue, tight knit boatneck top. Her red hair was cut in a short Pageboy style with her bangs brushed to the side.

He realized he was staring and that she was waiting for an answer. "Sure…Why not?" He started to get up to pull the chair out for her, but she immediately seated herself across from him. She casually scanned the restaurant's Italian décor: small statues on corner shelves, potted plants as well as paintings—fresco imitations—tastefully hung on the walls.

"Nice place," she said.

"I like it. Name your poison, Lieutenant."

"Manhattan sounds good to me. And…no need to be formal, you can call me Casey when we're not on duty."

Trabinski ordered her drink and another Cutty for himself. The waitress slid a menu in front of Casey.

"How'd you know I'd be here?" He picked up his pack of cigarettes, offered one to her — which she declined — lit it with his lighter and blew smoke into the slow-moving ceiling fan.

"I'm a detective…remember?"

"Right…dumb question." Trabinski drained his glass and pushed it to the edge of the table as the waitress delivered Casey's cocktail as well as his third.

The waitress pulled a small pad from her apron pocket and slipped a pencil from behind her ear. "Would you like to order?" she asked Casey.

Casey handed back the menu. "Nothing for me thanks. I've already eaten."

As the waitress took the menu, she did a double take. "Say…has anyone ever told you that you look just like…?"

"Yes. A number of times. Don't have her money though." Casey interrupted.

"Wow…Debbie Reynolds and Dana Andrews sitting at *my* table." The waitress laughed. "Don't you think he looks like Dana Andrews?"

Before Casey could answer, a busboy delivered Trabinski's meal, and he and the waitress hurried away.

"She's very impressionable," Trabinski said. "So…what can I do for you?"

Casey reached across the table and stole one of his chips and took a small bite.

"Before I fill your head with my theories…How did it go this afternoon with your Sergeant? It had to be tough."

Trabinski munched on a piece of fried cod, washed it down with a bit of scotch then told her how it went with Sergeant Sanfield. He found her easy to talk to or was it the drinks doing their job. When he got to the part involving the coroner's report, she took a taste of her Manhattan that had just been sitting there untouched.

"They have no idea what caused all those lacerations on his back?"

Trabinski wiped his mouth with his napkin. "Just guesses. Whatever the weapon; it was razor sharp with a ragged edge. And to further cloud the issue, Forensics claims there were no traces of metal on any of the wounds."

"That rules out switch blades and box cutters." Casey took another sip.

"So, it would seem. We're now looking into handmade weapons: stone arrow heads, bamboo and even ivory."

"Was the victim a gang member? I wouldn't put it past the Druids or the Pagans to make their own weapons."

"Danny had been in trouble before but nothing gang related. We're looking at his priors too. Tomorrow, we start questioning all the neighborhood kids who saw him last."

Casey drank the rest of her cocktail and leaned back in her chair. "Does it seem odd to you that we have two missing children and a teenage murder victim all within a week?"

Trabinski lit another Camel cigarette — the other had burned itself out in the ashtray. "You mentioned that child slavery ring this morning. What makes you think it could be them? That was quite a few years ago…right? This is 1963 plus they were all convicted…right? Are any up for parole?"

"I'm looking into the parole aspects now. I don't know if it's a reoc-currence, but my gut is telling me these cases are somehow related."

The waitress sauntered over and asked her if she would care for another drink. Casey ordered a coffee and Trabinski did the same.

"Do you have any leads whatsoever on your missing child case?" Casey leaned forward and placed her elbows on the table clasping her hands together in front of her.

"None so far," Trabinski said.

"Exactly the same situation for me. No leads. The only evidence… if you could call it that are the three scrape marks we found on the roof and windowsill. Forensics is scratching their head on that one too."

Trabinski crushed his cigarette in the ashtray and lit another one.

"Those things are going to kill you, Lieutenant," Casey said matter of factly.

"Jim. No formalities off duty…Remember?"

Casey gave a pert little nod of her head. She flashed a smile at him. Two coffees arrived.

"Any suspects yet for you? Anyone who has a grudge against the family? Someone looking for ransom money? That kind of thing?" Trabinski felt like he was a babbling schoolboy. Trying to talk to a pretty girl for the first time. He reached for his coffee.

"We're checking family relationships, the father's business deal-ings, and relationships with the neighbors. We'll see what comes up tomorrow, but first impressions are usually correct. This young couple? They're innocents just starting out with their first child. I'd be very surprised if a ransom note showed up."

The waitress asked if they wanted anything else. Trabinski looked at his watch. It was getting late. "Just the check please."

"Your boys searching that wooded area again tomorrow?" Casey asked as she reached for her purse.

"That's the plan."

"Good luck. I hope they find something."

Casey started to take money from her purse when the check arrived, but Trabinski grabbed it and insisted on paying. "Thanks Jim. I'll get the next one." A sheepish smile this time.

Trabinski walked her to her car, the uncomfortable feeling accompanying him. Ever the gentleman, he went to open the door for her but again she pre-empted his gallantry and opened it herself. They shook hands — another awkward moment — and said good night.

Before she pulled away, she rolled down her car window and stuck her head out.

"Keep in touch and think about my connection theory."

Lieutenant James Trabinski waved as she drove off. He lit another cigarette and wondered if Lieutenant Casey Talbot was dating anyone.

***

Tim Ryan and Stanley Bolton arrived home around 11 pm from the stock car races. They moved quickly and silently up the dark driveway to Tim's garage planning on retrieving the bag with the pink blanket. They came to an abrupt halt at the corner of the house. They both grumbled their disappointment when they saw the garage door closed and locked.

"Tomorrow," Tim whispered.

"Right…tomorrow. Try ta remember the name will ya?"

The smiling face of John Glenn, the first American astronaut to orbit the earth greeted Tim as he entered his room. The picture was one of several astronaut and rocket photos decorating his walls along with a map of the solar system and color pictures of planetary landscapes he had purchased when he went to the Hayden Planetarium in New York City. Many a night he spent staring at those images wondering about the mysteries of outer space before he would fall asleep. But tonight, as he got ready for bed, his mind would not let go of the picture Stanley had painted for him on the bus. He seemed convinced that the conjuring had actually worked bringing some fantastic creature from an unknown world.

Tim plugged in the small fan situated on his desk and turned it on — the room was already muggy even though his bedroom window had been open all day — then he brought his night stand light to life, extinguished the bright ceiling one and crawled into bed. *Why did Stanley keep rambling on about the creature's name all the way home? Why does he expect me to remember it if he can't? All I remember was a bunch of Latin phrases and stuff. And stuff?*

He fluffed up his pillow, but it immediately deflated when his head hit it. Sitting up he put his hands behind his head, leaned against the headboard and closed his eyes. *Was the name part of that Latin mumbo jumbo?*

He tried to picture in his mind the page they had read from only four days ago. *Yes. It was part of the incantation. We had to say it a*

few times. What the heck was it? Maya? No but something like that.
Ma something.

Tim kept repeating that part of the name over and over. *Was it*
Marlena? No…I think it was Malhela. We had to say it three times. That's
it…Malhela.

***

In the dark corner loft of the Ryan's garage an uneasy Malhela
instantly raised her head as the sound of her name entered her mind.

CHAPTER 16

Day Five – Mid morning

The morning air, cooler than it had been in days, carried the refreshing fragrances of roses, honeysuckle, and gardenias as well as the sweet scent of alfalfa from a newly mown lawn, to Malhela perched on the peak of her dwelling's roof top enjoying the potpourri. Although only five days had passed, she felt a twinge of melancholy as this bouquet reminded her of the faery gardens of the realm. Lush, colorful, fragrant oases scattered throughout the land cultivated by the magical faeries for all to enjoy.

As usual she blended with her surroundings, now taking on the appearance of the rust-colored roof shingles.

Having shaken last night's dreadful feeling — that she had somehow offended the Lord of the Realm and been banished as a result — she casually surveyed the grounds around her. Her relief had come late in the evening with the call of her name from Tim Ryan. She felt more certain that her being here was the work of the two mortals she had come to know. They had summoned her for a reason and one of them was going to tell her why. She had no more patience for this game.

Unexpectedly, she saw Tim Ryan exit the back door of his dwelling and approach her own. Looking down she watched as he lifted the large door and went inside. After a few minutes he reappeared pushing his bike. He looked over his shoulder and stared into the opening for a moment as if he were searching for something then mounted his two wheeled conveyance and rode away.

Malhela took to the air. Today she would, once again, follow this conjurer.

**

Tim Ryan had two reasons for starting his day early; looking for the bag that Stanley said he had stashed in the garage and finishing his route early so he would have time to prepare for tomorrow's bike hike his friend Mike Grainger had invited him to join. Lucky for him his paper did not have weekend issues.

He lifted the heavy garage door — the reason it was often left open — entered the bay, checked his bike and searched for the bag that supposedly held a smelly blanket carried by the creature. No bag, but the smell of something like ammonia caught his attention. *Could be that stuff Dad uses to clean car parts. Nothing otherworldly about that. And...where's the bag? I'm going to clobber Stanley if he's pulling my leg about this.*

Tim grabbed his bike, gave one last look into the garage and rode down the driveway toward Stanley's house. The plan was to tell him there was no bag and that he remembered the name of the being stated in the book of spells. However, no one answered the door when he knocked — the doorbell didn't work — so that idea would have to wait. He sped off to the Newsday office.

After securing his load of papers into the canvas sack given to him by Newsday and placing it neatly into the front basket on his Columbia, Tim started down Kraemer Street to his first customers. The sidewalk was empty except for a speeding tricycle driven by a little kid coming at him. Tim moved aside and laughed as the boy raced by. The kid was wearing one of those Beanie and Cecil hats with the tiny propeller on top.

Where's his mother? Nobody's watching him? Tim pushed his bike back onto the sidewalk and watched the kid zip into the next driveway, disappearing between the houses. Tim shook his head, smiled, and started his deliveries. His mind was on tomorrow's 5-mile bike hike to Manetto Hill with his longtime friend Mike Grainger. Tim always thought he looked like Buddy Holly. Sadly, Mike had no musical abilities whatsoever, but his other interests coincided nicely with Tim's. They built model cars together, played baseball, and tennis as well as devoured all things science fiction and horror.

Tim knew why Mike had come up with this bike trek idea. He had a brand-new Schwinn Speedster he wanted to put through its paces. Tim was a little envious. Mike always had cool things.

His thoughts were interrupted when he thought he heard his name being called. He abruptly stopped in his tracks and looked around expecting to see the bully—Danny Sanfield. He saw no one. An anxious chill crept over him. *I don't like this. Feels like an ambush. What the heck does that punk want from me? He said my **toll** was paid when he split my lip.*

Mustering up his courage Tim called out, "I heard you Sanfield. So now you're gonna heckle me on my route? Don't you have anything better to do?" He listened and waited to see if he would appear. Nothing. "Your father said 'no more trouble'…remember. So, knock it off." Still no response.

Tim rubbed his neck then proceeded up the steps of his first customer and placed the paper inside their storm door. As he returned to his bike, he heard a voice, crystal clear with the soft sweetness of a shy young girl. "Tim Ryan?"

"What the …? Who's there?" Now he scanned the nearby houses with a different curiosity.

"I need your help," the charming voice said.

"Sure. What kind of help?" Tim said to the emptiness around him. His imagination creating an instant picture of the cute girl with the blonde hair who lived at the end of Kraemer Street. She wasn't a customer —though he had tried several times to sell a subscription to her parents— so he didn't know her name. "Don't be bashful. Come out where I can see you and we'll talk," Tim said trying to sound confident.

He stood listening for a few minutes. He looked up and down the block once again hoping she would appear. When no one showed themselves or said anything more, Tim wondered if the hot sun was getting to him. He picked another paper from his sack and strode to the next customer's house. As he headed up the cement pathway to make the delivery, he saw a woman in a print dress wearing a white apron standing on the sidewalk in front of the house where the little kid had zipped into the driveway. She scanned the street in both directions then called, "Georgie!"

Figuring she was looking for the kid on the bike, Tim shouted, "He just went up your driveway!"

The woman waved. "Thank you!"

Tim waved back, watching her hurry up the driveway. Suddenly, a scream shattered the quiet neighborhood. Momentarily startled, Tim recovered quickly and ran toward the sound.

The woman stood in the driveway with her hands over her mouth as if trying to prevent another scream from escaping. The tricycle the kid had been riding lay flipped on its side, rear wheel spinning. His Beanie and Cecil hat lay on the pavement next to a scuffed Buster Brown shoe. The little kid — Georgie — was nowhere in sight.

"Maybe he's behind the garage?" Tim heard himself say. He motioned towards the one car structure at the end of the driveway. The door closed.

The woman seemed to notice him for the first time. "What?"

"Maybe he went behind the garage," Tim repeated and started heading that way.

The woman followed. "Georgie?"

The open yard behind the garage gave no sign of Georgie ever being there.

Without a word the woman ran to the house and vanished inside, leaving Tim alone and confused in her backyard.

***

Malhela, following her usual routine of watching Tim Ryan from a high vantage point, soared beneath gauzy clouds. She had decided to confront him this time; find out what role he played in this debacle.

The ill performed conjuring increased her irritation with each passing day; she needed to act now.

Seeing an opportunity, she descended closer to Tim Ryan and called his name. Thinking she had his attention, she decided to try a different approach, telling him she needed his help. His unexpected response surprised her; caught her off guard without a reply of her own. *Don't be bashful? What does that mean?*

Before she could think of what to say Malhela became distracted; a look of delight appeared on her face. There, moving quickly up the path toward Tim Ryan, came a healthy-looking youngling. Her senses went to full alert; closely tracking the child between two buildings. She suddenly realized she had not yet fed and swooped down on her prey.

Without a sound her talons sunk into the boy's shoulders, lifting him from the thing he was riding. She quickly silenced the youngling and took to the sky.

This was a daring capture even though she remained camouflaged — which was becoming more of an effort every time she applied it — anyone, even Tim Ryan, could have seen the child rising into the air.

She flew high into the sun hoping to distort the view of her cargo from below, but this youngling weighed more than she expected, causing her to rethink her flight plan. She needed a closer destination.

A familiar wooded area loomed ahead. That would be ideal. She began her approach. Her dead prey seemed to be getting heavier. Just then the sight below stunned her. She quickly pulled up.

"Diable cio!" She swore in her native tongue. *Damn it all!*

The woods below were infested with men and dogs moving back and forth through the trees and shrubs. There would be no quiet feasting here.

Agitated and a bit frightened, Malhela took a bite from the youngling's meaty thigh, dropped him, and flew off holding a small shoe. She could hear the dogs' frenzied barking as she glided away.

***

"Holy Christ!" Sergeant Todd Anderson of the K9 division pulled a barking Leo — his lead patrol dog — back from the grizzly scene they had just discovered.

"Easy boy…easy now." He gently patted the German Shepherd's back and activated the newly issued Walkie Talkie. "This is K9…unit 12," Anderson said into the mouthpiece. "Do you read?"

"Malloy here. Go ahead 12."

"Got something here, Malloy. Northwest section of the woods on the Park Avenue side. It's a little kid. Looks like he fell from a tree and broke his neck."

"On my way."

"Better radio Trabinski first. He wants to know about anything we find out here."

"Roger that…Malloy out."

Lieutenant James Trabinski and Detective Peter Taylor had just finished interviewing the teenagers whose names had been given to them by Sergeant Sanfield when the call came in. The teenagers' stories all coincided and Trabinski's uncanny ability to tell if someone was lying reassured him these kids were not involved in the demise of Danny Sanfield. However, one name had come up in all their statements. A person who it appeared had a motive for going after Sanfield; a person whose name Trabinski remembered from his first conversation with Danny's father the day he disappeared. Tim Ryan. He would call on this Tim Ryan first chance he got. But now he had to make another disturbing sojourn to the woods on Cherry Street.

The siren pierced the morning stillness as Trabinski's Ford Galaxie screeched onto Cherry Street, bounced over the curb, and stopped on the sidewalk. The Forensics van arrived at the same time. The doors flew open and Phil Tipton, the examiner jumped out while his assistant exited the passenger side and opened the rear doors.

"We have to stop meeting like this, Lieutenant," the examiner said as he came up to Trabinski.

"You can say that again. I'm not superstitious but I'm beginning to think these woods are cursed."

Trabinski, Taylor, Phil Tipton along with his assistant ducked under the crime scene tape already in place due to the Sanfield incident and hurried up the well trampled path to the new discovery. They found Malloy and Sergeant Anderson with his dog standing deep within the copse almost fifty yards from the path. Neither said a word as the others approached. The dog turned his head and chuffed at them.

Trabinski stood over the twisted body of a young boy, maybe five years old dressed in a white short sleeved shirt with navy blue horizontal stripes and light gray shorts. The boy's head lay at an odd angle to his body.

Detective Taylor stood next to Trabinski looking up into the trees. "There's no way he fell from up there. He couldn't climb that high."

Trabinski gave a quick look up then scrutinized the thick brush crowding the trees. "Phil? Tell me this was an accident."

The expression on the Examiner's face held the answer but all he said was, "Look. See anything familiar?" He took the bag his assistant held, removed a 35mm camera and took some quick shots.

Trabinski and Taylor took a step closer to the corpse for a better look.

"Shit," Trabinski said.

"Not again," Taylor groaned.

"No shoes. What the hell?" Trabinski gave the Examiner —who now knelt next the body—a concerned look.

"Something else familiar here." Phil pointed to the boy's right thigh. "This wound... a bite mark if you will, at first glance seems similar to the one we found on the Sanfield boy."

"An animal?" Trabinski said.

The Examiner took a few closeup shots of the wound. "Perhaps. We're still studying the Sanfield wound. The difference here is this boy has been dead for maybe only thirty minutes. The body's still warm. And...the dogs would have prevented any scavengers from taking a chunk of flesh like that. I'm *guessing* right now, but I'd say this wound happened before his death. The cause of which is most assuredly a cervical fracture.

"In addition to the bite mark there are these puncture wounds on each of the victim's shoulders. No idea what could have caused those...A hook or something? A closer look in the lab hopefully will shed more light on it."

At the word "hook" Trabinski immediately remembered Casey Talbot's remark about a grappling hook possibly being used in her kidnap case. *She thought there may be a connection. Now this.*

Someone thrashing their way through the brush interrupted his thoughts. Tracy, Malloy's partner. "Lieutenant! We may have a possible ID on the victim," he said.

Trabinski quickly turned his way. "How?"

"A call just came in from a woman over on Kraemer Street."

"Almost around the corner," Detective Taylor offered.

Tracy took off his hat and wiped his forehead with his shirt sleeve. "Claims her son Georgie disappeared from her driveway. She said he was riding his tricycle and all of a sudden, he was gone. His name is Georgie Westmyer. Five years old. Wearing a white shirt with navy blue horizontal stripes and gray shorts."

"Dammit!" Trabinski said.

"She said they searched the street and her yard but only found his hat and one shoe."

Trabinski looked into Tracy's eyes. "They?"

"Local newspaper boy helped her search for him. Name's Tim Ryan."

Trabinski was searching his pockets for a cigarette but quickly stopped.

"What did you say his *name* was?"

"Tim Ryan."

CHAPTER 17

Day Five – Afternoon

Stanley Bolton painted the concrete parking space markers that divided the parking lot rows behind Hillsville Municipal Building; thoroughly pissed off at those who slapped him with this community service crap and a bit at himself for being so stupid. He probably would have received just a slap on the hand for the cat in the mailbox stunt if it wasn't for the damn cat exploding into the mailman's face — as he unlocked the bottom mailbox door — badly scratching him as well as scattering mail all over the sidewalk. This, he was told, could be considered a Federal Offense if the Post Office pressed charges.

He was also mad at himself for opening his big mouth and bragging about it; trying to impress the knuckleheads at school. Plus, the heat rising from the sunbaked parking lot macadam didn't help his mood any.

The Juvenile Court sentenced Stanley to four hours of community service— a service, day, and time of their choosing— twice a week for one month. Failure on his part to comply would result in a misdemeanor charge, a fine and possibly a night in jail. None of which appealed to him.

Today's assignment allowed him to ride his beat up, rusted old Raleigh bike to the site. His first appearance required him to be dropped off at the appointed place by his mother, who had to sign some kind of document when he arrived. Today he just had to verbally report in.

As he slapped white paint onto the dividers his thoughts returned to his night visitor and the missing Lovecraft book of incantations. He smiled at the thought of her body's firm curves and the way she stood naked and unashamed in front of him. *If she's real? Really, real from the incantation? I could command her ta be my girlfriend or better yet...lover. Man...that would be somethin.* He quickly directed his thoughts to finding the book when he felt himself becoming aroused.

Stanley had started referring to his visitor as "her" rather than "it" or "the creature" after he had seen her face; and became enthralled with her beauty.

He had not yet been able to search his father's nightstand—where he usually kept novels he planned to read— for the book. *What would happen if I just asked him? Maybe...but not today.*

His father tended to ignore Stanley on the days he had community service. When he looked at his second son — if he looked at him at all on those days — his eyes held disappointment. Sometimes, Stanley thought his father looked at him as if he didn't know who he was. *He probably doesn't. Who cares?*

Moving on to the next concrete marker he wondered about alternatives. *Maybe I can get another copy? Does the library have stuff like that? That might be worth a look. Crap! I don't have a library card. Oh...but I'm sure Ryan does. I'll go and see what they have, then get a hold of him if I find it.*

"Better step up the pace, Mr. Bolton. You've got an hour left and they all need to be painted. Unless you plan on coming back tomorrow."

The sound of the man's voice made Stanley jump; paint splattered his pants. He looked down at the white specks on his dungarees. "Dammit," he mumbled then quickly looked up at the large balding man who stood on the back steps of the Municipal Building, lighting a cigarette.

He was wearing a white short sleeved shirt that stretched over his pot belly—buttons straining— no tie, grey slacks, and polished black shoes This was Stanley's assignment supervisor. He was always around somewhere, watching. The man never seemed to sweat.

In his head Stanley said, "Drop dead!" Out loud he replied, "I'll get them done. No problem."

***

Back at the precinct Lieutenant James Trabinski paced his office, a ribbon of cigarette smoke trailed behind him like smoke billowing from a fast-moving locomotive, thinking about the events of the past few days. *Two kids missing, one dead and a teenage boy murdered. Is there a connection? Lieutenant Talbot seems to think so. How does this Ryan kid fit in with all this?*

Leaving his office, he walked over to the coffee pot and poured himself a cup, remembering something the examiner had said at the scene this morning. *The shoulder wounds looked like hooks could have been used. Grappling hooks?*

"Hey Pete? Can you get Lieutenant Talbot, second precinct on the horn for me? I'll be right back." He thanked detective Taylor and entered the file room.

He returned a few moments later with the John Wheatley file — the child abducted from the playground — dropped it on his cluttered desk and flipped the folder open scanning each page. There were only a few since no further details regarding the boy's disappearance had come to light. *What are we missing here? How could someone grab a kid in that hedge thing and get out without being seen…or heard? They would have to go over the top. How? A ladder or…a hook?*

He stuck his head out his office door. "Any luck getting a hold of Talbot?" He asked his detective.

"They said she's scheduled at the firing range in Hempstead for the rest of the afternoon.

"Okay…thanks" He read the last page of the Wheatley documents — it contained the witness statements — tapped his finger on the last name listed and scowled. *Tim Ryan…again.*

He finished his coffee and left the building.

The afternoon traffic slowed to a crawl thanks to the new construction underway on the Broadway expansion. Normally, a twenty-minute ride, it now took Trabinski double that to get to the Hempstead Firing Range.

The grappling hook theory Casey had mentioned now became a nagging *What if?* He wanted to do some brainstorming with her especially in light of this new Georgie Westmyer case. He looked at his watch. *Hope I haven't missed her.*

Trabinski entered the gray painted cinder block office, showed his badge plus ID to the desk sergeant, signed in as an observer, received a clear cellophane bag containing ear plugs and pushed through the heavy padded door into the range.

The walls of the main hallway were painted black as well as those of the shooter's cubicle connected to each lane. The only light came from the lanes themselves and the red Exit sign. The range consisted of ten lanes, each thirty yards in length, eight feet wide with automatic target retrieval pulleys. Each cubicle had a gun shelf and rack with extra paper targets.

Inserting the earplugs Lieutenant Trabinksi slowly walked the hallway peering into each cubicle he passed. Nine units were occupied but none by her. No shots were being fired from unit Ten, so he didn't bother looking. *Well, this was a waste of time.* But as he turned to leave, unit Ten erupted in rapid gunfire. He quickly stopped then took two steps toward the lane. There she stood — an M-1 Carbine pressed to her shoulder — firing in succession at a large paper target. He leaned back against the wall behind her, folded his arms and watched as the target—a silhouetted bust of a man against a white background— came toward her when she ceased firing. From where he stood it looked to him as if she had missed the target completely, but to his surprise as it got closer, he saw that every shot was a dead center head shot. She laid the rifle on the shelf, removed the used target, inserted another, and sent it back to the thirty-yard lane limit then picked up a 9mm Luger from the gun shelf. *There's a lot more to this little lady than just good looks,* he thought as she took a shooter's stance, feet apart, two hands holding the raised pistol.

The stance had pulled her slacks tight across her firm, curvaceous posterior distracting him. He forced his eyes back to the range target when she started firing. The target shivered a little but other than that it hardly moved. Again, the approaching target revealed all shots dead center. Trabinski couldn't control himself. He clapped his hands and whistled. He had never seen anyone shoot like that.

Casey put the Luger on the shelf and slowly turned to see what was going on behind her. A look of surprise, then a quick smile when she saw him.

Trabinski removed his ear plugs, and she did the same. "You're a regular Annie Oakley, Lieutenant. I'm impressed."

"I have my moments," she laughed. "What brings you here? I don't see a weapon."

"Your theory about the recent crimes being related. We had another situation this morning. I'd like to talk more about this theory. I think the sooner, the better."

"Another child has disappeared?"

"No…we found this one in the woods where we found the Sanfield boy. Unfortunately, dead."

He saw a flash of anger in her gray eyes.

"Let me pack up here. There's a diner across the street. We can talk there."

They sat in a booth at the far end of the diner. A small, chrome plated jukebox fastened to the booth wall played "Sincerely" by the Moonglows. Mugs of coffee were served. Trabinski laid a pack of

Camels on the table along with his lighter. Casey dropped two sugar cubes into her coffee.

"Tell me what happened this morning." She said getting right down to business. "And…what made you change your mind about these cases being connected."

Trabinski took a sip of coffee, grimaced and reached for his cigarettes.

"I still had a team of men, including our dogs, searching the woods for anything that might be related to the Sanfield case. The missing shoes…anything. One of the dogs started going crazy, dragging his trainer deeper into the brush. Just before the dog found the body of this little boy, the Trainer thought he heard a thud like something heavy hitting the ground. His immediate thought, he said, was that the kid fell out of a tree. An impossibility. A kid that size could never climb the tall trees in that section."

"What was the cause of death?" Casey asked.

Trabinski took a drag on his cigarette, then exhaled smoke from the corner of his mouth into the aisle. "Broken neck…confirmed by Forensics."

Casey shook her head. "Terrible. So…now we have *three* small children in less than a week. Other than that, what's making you think this one is connected to the others?"

"Forensics found puncture wounds on the victim's shoulders."

"Puncture wounds?"

"The examiner thought the wounds might have been made by a hook. Your grappling hook theory immediately came to mind."

Casey sat back in the seat and crossed her arms. "I get the picture."

"But something is off with this one. Phil Tipton, who happened to be the examiner *again*, said the boy had been dead for less than thirty minutes. The body is still warm. Then there's the shoes."

"The shoes?"

"Just like the Sanfield case, the body had no shoes. *But*...here's the kicker. One of the boy's shoes was found on the driveway where he lived."

"You mean this child may have been taken from his home in broad daylight?"

"Sure looks like it. The question is how. Does this MO match that Child Slavery thing you told me about?"

"No...this is different. I can't imagine a hook of any kind being used. For what reason? The abductees would have been considered damaged goods and rejected by the buyers back then. These current events don't make sense."

Just then a silent shadow loomed over them. They both quickly looked up.

"Would you like anything else?" The waitress said as she topped off Casey's coffee. Trabinski had barely touched his.

Casey ordered a fresh fruit cup; Trabinski a slice of cherry pie and a Coke.

"There seems to be a common thread though, with my cases." Trabinski brought his attention back to Casey.

"Can you tell me or is it protected information?"

Fruit cup, pie and a Coke arrived. Trabinski took a taste of the beverage.

"No...not protected. It may turn out to be a coincidence."

"I don't believe in coincidence," Casey said. "What's the thread?"

"There's this teenager whose name keeps turning up. He was involved in a scuffle with The Sanfield boy; helped search for the missing child at the playground and today supposedly helped the mother of *this* child search the neighborhood for him."

"Hmmm…You question him?"

"Not yet. I've got detective Taylor looking for an address. Did that slavery ring use kids to lure others into their trap?"

"No, but now you've got me rethinking the child slavery scenario. None of the original gang are out on parole, so that kills that idea. But the feeling that *all* these crimes are somehow connected is still nagging me."

Trabinski swallowed a piece of pie. "I'm open to any ideas."

Lieutenant Casey Talbot quietly nibbled on her fruit cup, deep in thought. Trabinski patiently waited for her response while he finished off his pie. He found himself struggling to keep from staring at her. He still marveled at the fact this gorgeous creature was a police officer.

"I just thought of something," she suddenly said snapping him out of his daydream. "You'll think this crazy, but I've had success with this before."

"Success is good. What's the idea?"

"Have you ever heard of Madame Florentine?"

"Not ringing any bells."

"She helped us…*me* finally wrap up the slavery ring years ago. She's psychic…uses crime scene objects to get readings…that kind of thing."

"A psychic? You're right, sounds crazy, but just a little. Has the department used her services prior to your case?"

"I only know of one murder case she helped with in Brooklyn. That's when I heard of her. I don't know if she does this kind of thing anymore. After her husband died, she moved to East Hampton. Last I heard she opened an Occult Book store. Might be worth a try…especially since we have nothing to go on here. What do you think?"

"I guess we might as well, especially since the forensics boys still haven't come up with anything useful."

"Let's do it. I'll make a phone call as soon as I get back…find out if she's willing."

"East Hampton?" Trabinski sounded doubtful.

"Right. A two-hour trip from the precinct…that's without traffic. Problem?"

The distance was not a problem; the length of time sitting next to her could be.

"I'll drive," he said.

"Maybe…," Casey said.

The waitress delivered the check and Casey quickly grabbed it.

CHAPTER 18

Day Six- Early Morning

Malhela's strategies for confronting Tim Ryan continued to be deterred by unexpected circumstances. This morning's attempt was thwarted when two unknown males— on those *bikes* — joined Tim on the main thoroughfare and sped away.

Four emotions struck her in quick succession: disappointment, frustration, aggravation, and anger, all contributing to her body's tenseness, which resulted in her exuding more musk than usual. Her nest in the loft reeked of the pungent fishy odor. She could do nothing to prevent this bodily function. Nor did she care.

Malhela fiddled with her collection of souvenirs; shifting them around in her nest when she heard someone coming. The scent told her it was the female youngling — Tim Ryan's sibling. She was in no mood for this interruption and readied herself to pounce.

***

Eight-year-old Emily Ryan — *eight and half,* she would tell everyone — eager to help her mother make jam this morning offered to retrieve the needed Mason jars from the garage. The large door was already up thanks to Tim leaving earlier.

As she moved toward the cabinet containing the jars an awful smell surrounded her. She wrinkled her nose and started to cough. Her eyes began to water so she headed for the open door but stopped when she heard something in the garage attic. Something moving around. Her curiosity — stronger than the odor — drove her to the foot of the attic stairs. She looked up into the shadows. Emily wasn't afraid so she took a step up for a better look but held the apron she wore up to cover her mouth and nose to lessen the smell. She was about to switch on the attic light when from out of the darkness came an intense hissing sound at the top of the stairs. Emily screamed, "Snake! Snake!" She raced out of the garage.

"Daddy! There's a snake in the garage attic. Get it outta there… *Please!*" Emily shrieked as she burst through the back door.

Her father, sitting at the kitchen table having a second cup of coffee and reading a Popular Mechanics magazine was startled by Emily's outburst. "What? A snake?" He got up from his chair.

"In the *attic!* It *hissed* at me …and it *smells really bad!*"

Emily's mother immediately came over and put an arm around her. "Stay here while your father takes a look."

Carl Ryan knew that poisonous snakes were extremely rare on Long Island. But something hissing in his garage attic, frightening his daughter, had to be dealt with, even if it was only a startled Milk Snake. He entered the garage, grabbed a long-handled pitchfork, and moved cautiously to the attic steps. He had taken only a few steps when the sickening smell hit him like a slap in the face. *God... What in the world?* Shuffling backward he went to the rear window and opened it wide; surprised it wasn't latched. The flow of fresh air immediately started to diminish the stench. He flipped on the switch for the attic light and slowly climbed the wooden stairs, pitchfork at the ready. At the top he found no snake but did see evidence that some type of animal was residing there. *Probably a raccoon...they will hiss if threatened,* he thought as he scanned the various objects strewn about in what looked like a nest. *But this odor doesn't smell like any I've ever run across.* As he checked the rest of the attic area for the animal itself, his eye caught sight of something that chilled his blood. He hurried down the stairs and into the house. The screen door slamming behind him. He grabbed the wall phone and started dialing.

"What are you doing?" His wife asked.

"Calling the police."

Officers Stevens and Hancock stood with Carl Ryan in the hot garage attic — sweat dripping onto their notepads — jotting down the objects scattered before them: a bloodstained pair of black Flagg Brothers loafers, a leather collar from a small dog, what appeared to be a pink baby's blanket hanging out of a ripped paper bag, several small bones, part of a yellow pair of shorts, a child's Buster Brown shoe and the human skull of a child.

Officer Hancock looked up at Carl Ryan. "Did you or anyone in your family touch anything here?"

"I was the only one up here. Nothing was touched. This is how I found it."

"Okay, Mr. Ryan…Thank you. That'll be all." Officer Stevens tucked the small pad in his back pocket. "We have to call this in," he said and headed down the stairs.

Hancock gestured for Carl Ryan to follow Stevens. "Oh and Mr. Ryan? Your garage is now off limits to everyone except Nassau County Police. Understand?"

Carl Ryan nodded.

As they stepped out into the now late morning sunlight Carl Ryan stopped Hancock. "Officer? What's going on here? I saw a look of recognition on your face up there. Is my family in danger?"

Hancock adjusted his sweat stained officer's hat on his head. "Just stay away from the garage sir. Others will be here shortly to ask you some questions. We'll be out front if you need us."

***

Malhela, about to take the youngling's life, hesitated when it screamed. She then lunged for her but the little *hundino* darted away, escaping into her dwelling. Fearing discovery now, abandoning the nest became her only choice. She sprang from her loft and flew out the front opening, climbing high blending into the blue above. Everything was going wrong. Delirious with rage she flew southeast killing anything that got near her; a shredded Robin plummeted to the ground, a headless Starling fell on a roof, even a lone squirrel minding his business atop a telephone pole became mincemeat.

Malhela blundered on having no idea where she was headed. Then, as she passed through a wisp of clouds, a strange looking mountain came into view. Perhaps a place to rest and think.

***

Lieutenant James Trabinski and Detective Peter Taylor arrived at 14 Cabel Street within minutes of receiving the call. He pulled his Galaxie to the curb in front of Hancock and Stevens' NCPD cruiser.

They hurried from their vehicle to the reporting officers, who were standing on the sidewalk scrutinizing their pads, comparing notes. "What have you got for me gentlemen?" Trabinski leaned forward to look at the information Hancock had written down in his pad.

"Better to see for yourself Lieutenant," Stevens said.

Hancock agreed. "Right...It could be the evidence we've been searching for all in a nice little collection."

"Where is it?" Taylor asked.

Hancock and Stevens led the way to the two-car garage located behind the house. "Everything is stashed up in an attic space." Hancock motioned toward the wooden steps. "Should be able to breath up there now."

"What?" Trabinski looked at Hancock then at Stevens. "What do you mean able to breath?"

"There was this horrible smell up there earlier...Made you want to gag." Stevens said, waving his hand in front of his face as if fanning the smell away.

"Right. Okay...Let's take a look." Trabinski followed Hancock up into the attic.

The late morning sun had been baking the garage roof for hours making the interior temperature of the attic feel like a sauna.

"Christ it's hot up here," Trabinski said as he examined the pieces of evidence. He mentally tied each object to a case at hand: John Wheatley, yellow bathing suit; Danny Sanfield, Flagg Brothers loafers; Georgie Westmyer, Buster Brown shoe.

The pink blanket and child's skull had to be Casey Talbot's missing infant.

Where does the dog collar and small bones fit in? Why gather it all in one place? He pulled a white handkerchief from a pocket and mopped his face and neck. "Okay…I've seen enough. Let's seal it up and get forensics out here."

Trabinski moved toward the steps but suddenly stopped as if he had just remembered something. He turned to his men. "What does that remind you of?" He pointed to the gathering of objects. Hancock took a hard look but just shook his head. Taylor squinted at the collection for a moment. "Reminds me of some sort of nest."

"Exactly!" Trabinski said.

"You think some animal did this?"

"I…don't know. But let's not rule it out," Trabinski replied.

As they came down the stairs they saw Stevens — who had remained below — talking to a man outside the garage. Stevens introduced him.

"Lieutenant? This is Mr. Ryan. He and his family live here. He's concerned that his family may be in danger."

Trabinski shook his hand and stared into his eyes. "Do you have a son named Tim?" He saw surprise on the man's face.

"Yes…yes, I do. Why?"

"I'd like to talk to him. Is he home?" Again, Trabinski watched his eyes.

"No. He's on a bike hike with some friends. I told him to be home around six o'clock.

Honest man. Trabinski read the truth in the man's eyes.

"I'll be back then. Please make sure he doesn't leave till I get here."

Detective Taylor joined the conversation. "Mr. Ryan, this is now a crime scene. Our Forensics crew will be here shortly. Please give them full cooperation."

As Trabinski took a step to leave the father grabbed his arm. "What does my son have to do with all this?"

Trabinski stopped and slowly looked at the man's hand holding his arm, then gave him such a threatening look that he quickly let go. "Just make sure he's here when I return."

CHAPTER 19

Day six – Late afternoon

Tim Ryan's new watch—he had purchased with route money to insure he wouldn't be late again— read six thirty as he turned off Plainview Road onto Cabel Street. He let his bike coast around the bend toward his house — his legs were tired from a day of vigorous pedaling — and skidded to a stop when he saw the scene at his home. *Oh no! Something's happened.* A few neighbors stood on their lawns faking disinterest.

A blue and orange Nassau County patrol car as well as a white van that resembled an ambulance were parked in front of his house. Two black cars; a Ford Galaxie and a Plymouth Fury, sat bumper to bumper in his driveway.

A jolt of fear set Tim back in motion. He jockeyed quickly past the cars in the driveway, jumped from his bike and hurried through the back door into the kitchen. Muffled voices coming from the living room drew him in, but immediately stopped when he entered the room.

Relief washed over Tim when he saw his parents and sister sitting on the big couch. They looked fine, just concerned. "What's going on?" He said eyeing the others in the room; two uniformed policemen, a tall thin man in a white lab coat, a stocky man wearing a white shirt with tie loosened and sleeves rolled up plus a very pretty woman in a gray skirt and pale blue top, that he assumed was a policewoman. Another man with slicked back blonde hair, wearing a tan sport jacket stood by the front door looking at a note pad.

"Come on in son," His father said. "These people would like to ask you some questions. Just tell the truth and everything will be fine."

"Sure…What about?"

Tim's mother raised a finger to pause the questioning. "Emily? Please go play in your room while we talk to your brother." She gave her daughter a gentle push.

"Is Timmy in trouble?"

The pretty woman leaned forward and smiled at Emily. "We just want to talk to your brother sweetie to make sure he's *not* in any trouble. Understand?"

Emily nodded and strutted to her room.

The stocky man in the white shirt stood up from the easy chair he had been sitting in — a favorite of Tim's father — and introduced himself. "I'm lieutenant Trabinski, Tim. I need to ask you some questions regarding a case we're working on." He motioned around the room at the others. "But first I want you to look at a bunch of items we found in your garage attic…see if you know anything about them."

Tim looked over at his parents. His mother just nodded — concern still in her eyes — but said nothing. His father — stony faced- gestured with his hand to go ahead.

"Okay," Tim said.

"Follow me son." Trabinksi moved to the back door. The others, except Tim's mom followed.

Tim couldn't remember the last time he was in the garage attic, but it didn't look weird like it did now. Yellow and black Police tape seemed to be everywhere; little paper cones with numbers marked odd items gathered on the wooden floor planks. The stocky man — Lieutenant Trabinski — directed Tim to a specific spot near the objects and stood next to him but positioned so he could see his face. The pretty woman — Tim had learned was Lieutenant Talbot from the 2nd Precinct in Woodbury— moved behind Lieutenant Trabinski. The limited attic space could not comfortably hold four people, so Tim's father stood on the top step looking on. The others remained below.

"Tim?" Trabinski said. "I want you to take a close look at the items on the floor in front of you and tell me if you recognize anything…or know anything about any of them."

Tim gave a slight shrug. "Never seen any of this. Looks like pieces of garbage to me." This came out a little snippier than he wanted. He gave a quick look towards his father to see his expression. It wasn't good. "Is that a human skull?" Tim asked, noticing it for the first time.

The adrenaline that had burst through Tim's body when he had arrived home and found police cars in front of his house had drained, opening the gate for the bike hike fatigue to set in. He felt tired, hungry, and confused.

"Nothing at all Tim? What about those loafers over there?" Lieutenant Trabinski pointed to the scuffed, bloodstained shoes that may have belonged to the late Danny Sanfield.

Tim leaned forward for a better look. "I have a pair like that. Bought them at the Flagg Brothers' store at the Plaza." He straightened and glanced at Lieutenant Trabinski. "What is all this? Why is it up here?"

Trabinski watched Tim's eyes. "That's what we're trying to find out, Tim. When was the last time you saw Danny Sanfield?"

"*Who?* Is this going to take long? I'm starving."

Trabinski was starting to feel annoyed with this kid. "Danny Sanfield, the boy who punched you in the mouth the other day. When was the last time you *saw him?*"

"Oh him?" Tim said with a smirk on his face. "I never saw him again after that night. After he knocked me down, he headed up Terrace Street dragging Paulette behind him. The guy's a real jerk. He tried to get money from me on my paper route a couple of times. Then he shows up and clobbers me for no reason. I can't believe his father is a cop."

Immediately thinking he had overstepped some law enforcement boundary he said, "Uh…sorry."

Trabinski read Tim's face as well as his body language. There was no trace of deception, but he prodded a little more. "Did you happen to notice if he was wearing a pair of shoes like those over there?"

Tim glanced down again at the filthy loafers. "Maybe. I'm not really sure. I wasn't looking at his feet."

Trabinski, feeling this was going nowhere was about to let Tim go when Lieutenant Talbot chimed in. "Tim? These items are all evidence related to recent crimes in the area. Serious crimes. What concerns us is the information we've received regarding your whereabouts at the time of three of the four crimes."

"*Huh?*" Tim offered a surprised yet innocent look to the pretty Lieutenant.

"Tim," Trabinski said. Your name appears in reports pertaining to three recent crimes in Hillsville. A little boy disappearing from the Division Avenue playground, a little boy disappearing from Kraemer Street, which happens to be part of your paper route, and the murder of Danny Sanfield. The boy who hit you." Trabinski never took his eyes off Tim's face as he told him these facts.

Tim all at once felt a chill. "That kid is *dead?*" He shot a quick look between the two police officers. "Wait…you…you think I *killed* him?"

"We're not thinking anything just yet," Lieutenant Trabinski said. We're only collecting information. However, doesn't it seem strange to you that all this crime scene evidence winds up here where you live?"

At this point Tim's father broke in. "Don't say anything else, son. I'll call my lawyer before this goes any further. Let's go."

"But I didn't do anything." Tim said scanning the faces looking at him.

Ignoring the father Lieutenant Talbot took a step towards the gathered evidence. "One more thing. Your name does not appear on the reports for the case I'm working on, but a piece of evidence related to that case is here." She pointed to a ripped paper bag with a pink baby's blanket hanging out of it.

Casey had been told by the missing child's parents that the infant had been cuddled that night in a pink cotton blanket. It was nowhere in the baby's room when it was searched.

"I'd like to know how it got here and why? Any ideas, Tim?"

Tim stared at the blanket for a long moment. *Cripes! That must be the blanket Stanley was talking about. What the hell is happening here?*

"I never saw it till now. No idea where it came from." Tim said quickly then joined his father on the stairs.

Lieutenant Trabinksi gestured to Casey to stay with him till the father and son were gone then in a soft voice said, "The boy was telling the truth right up to that last bit about the blanket then he waffled. He definitely knows something about it. And…he tensed up just before he spoke as if he was afraid to say anything. What do you want to do? This belongs to your can of worms."

Casey took another look at the evidence and rubbed the side of her nose with her finger. "So…he's not really a person of interest on your three cases but suddenly he becomes one on mine. You think he knows how the blanket got here?"

"That's my read." Trabinski said. "And…was that skull with the blanket?"

"Then that means I need to have another talk with Mr. Tim Ryan…alone."

"Right. Maybe if possible, catch him while he's delivering his papers before the lawyer gets to him. I'll give you his route details."

They both moved toward the stairs. "By the way," Casey said. "Madame Florentine said she'd listen to our story. Didn't say she'd help. Still want to go?"

***

Stanley Bolton's search for the Lovecraft book at the library turned up nothing useful. So, after sleeping late, he spent the time he had today while the house was empty — parents and little brother shopping; brother Artie MIA as usual — thoroughly scouring the place for his copy. It was nowhere to be found. Even his father's night table drawer proved a disappointment. He finally came to the maddening conclusion that his mother had found it and thrown it away. *The only thing left to do is to hit the magazine rack at Whelans. See if some other pulp issue has the same ad I ordered from. Rip out the page and reorder the damn thing. That'll work.*

He was so preoccupied with his search he failed to notice the commotion going on across the street at Tim Ryan's house. "What the …?" He said looking out through the blinds of his front window.

Stanley watched as two policemen left Tim's house and drove off in their patrol car. Then he noticed the white vehicle that looked like an ambulance parked there. Lights flashing. *Somebody got hurt or somethin. Better find out what's goin on.* But before he could turn away, he noticed two men dressed like doctors carrying clear plastic boxes walking single file down Tim's driveway passed two black cars parked there. From where he stood Stanley could see there were a few items in each, but not exactly what they were. When each container was placed in the white vehicle the two men hurried back up the driveway. Curious about the contents of these boxes Stanley headed for the front door and stepped out into the waning sunlight. He stood on the sidewalk and lit a cigarette discreetly watching his friend's house. Shortly the two men in white reappeared carrying two more boxes. Stanley surreptitiously eyed the boxes they carried. He could make out what looked like shoes and something else in the box carried by the first man. Unfortunately, this man blocked the view of the second as they approached the vehicle preventing Stanley from seeing the contents of his container. When he finally stepped aside Stanley caught a glimpse of something sticking up from the second man's box and almost fainted. *Shit! Shit! Shit! The blanket!*

CHAPTER 20

Day six – Early evening

The place Malhela found herself circling above had a familiar gloom to it. Even though the sun still had a few hours left before setting, it cast shadows across the ground of the strange, tall stacks of flattened materials standing in the dirt expanse. They resembled tilted temple pillars with jagged edges. Some stacks— further back from these pillars— had grown to the size of small mountains. Pieces of the flattened materials glistened in the dwindling sunlight like scattered jewels. A dirt road snaked its way around these odd compilations decorating most with a fine coating of its dust. An aged wooden barricade surrounded the entire expanse reminding Malhela of an ancient fortress — except for the large, heavy mesh gate with strong chains holding it closed that looked out of place.

As she hovered in the air scrutinizing the area below, she saw twisted hulks that resembled the four wheeled, horseless conveyances that congested the thoroughfares of this world. She did not understand these unusual foul-smelling carriages or how they worked. Perhaps they were magical or even alive somehow? Could this place be their grave-yard? There were various sizes and shapes of these derelicts scattered throughout this plot of land. She could see no mortals anywhere. This was a good thing.

Rapid movement on the road below caught her eye. From this height it appeared like a black ant scurrying in circles. She focused her vision on the moving object and breathed deep, picking up its scent. It looked and smelled like a hound of the realm. How could it be?

The Cashundoj de la Regno roamed freely through the realm in packs. Often, wreaking havoc in the villages, which would result in her kind being called to deal with them. Had one somehow come through with her?

Descending for a better look she spied a large black and brown hound with a long snout and pointed ears that did indeed resemble a hound of the realm. But the barking of this beast was different. Nothing like the guttural hiccup of a realm canine. She would take care of it shortly. But first she needed to investigate the mountain of debris she noticed that rose higher than the others. At its peak the compacted materials had been placed or had fallen in such a way they formed a triangular cave like opening.

She darted toward the dark cavity, landed on a flat surface that jutted out from its mouth, folded her wings, and slipped inside.

The last remnants of daylight seeped through the cavern's porous, angled walls painting gray, ragged images on what might be considered the cavern's floor. The interior had more space than her previous nest and allowed her to freely move about. This would be perfect. It just needed a bit of decorating to make it comfortable. The only drawback being it had only one way in or out. She would have to come up with something to remedy that situation. Now for the barking hound.

In a flash she landed on the snarling hound's back, digging her talons into its sides while grabbing its snout with both hands. She may be small in stature, but her strength was extraordinary. Pulling the hound's head up, she breathed into its nostrils and spat in its eyes. This method always brought the hounds of the realm under control. Apparently, it worked on this beast as well. Within moments it had quieted down and become docile in her presence. It now belonged to her. Guardian of her nest.

Rocco's Auto Wrecker and Junk Emporium covered two acres of land just off New South Road in Bethpage. It had been a scrap metal depot during World War Two and had prospered in later years when automobiles became increasingly popular, and people demolished them on a regular basis.

Rocco Espesito, a barrel-chested man of average height in his late fifties with thinning slicked back salt and pepper hair and a neatly trimmed mustache took over the business when his father died in 1955, keeping it profitable ever since. He took pride in his little enterprise and would walk the yard every evening after closing, taking inventory of existing treasures as well as new arrivals. He had taken to carrying his father's Remington Model 870 shot gun after a bunch of Hot Rodders jumped his back fence a few years ago in an attempt to grab some free parts for their souped-up machines. Heeding the advice given by the responding police officers on that particular evening Rocco brought in a night watchman. Caesar: a four-year-old, hundred pound, black and tan Dobermann Pinscher, who learned his job quickly, obeying Rocco's every command with treat-fueled enthusiasm.

However, this evening Caesar did not come when called. This was totally unlike him. Even on the occasions when he'd cornered a rat or a raccoon he would come running when he heard his name. Rocco had heard him barking but now all was quiet.

Rocco went back inside the shabby little store front situated near the entrance gate— where he stored valuable items such as rebuilt carburetors, water pumps and the like — and grabbed a box of beef flavored Milk Bone biscuits from a shelf and went back outside. Shaking the box, he called again. "Caesar! Come on boy…time for our rounds." After waiting a few minutes, he called again, but when Caesar still did not show up Rocco tucked the box under his arm, readied his shot gun and took off in search of his dog.

About twenty yards from the main gate a ten-foot stack of crushed autos and trucks stood on either side of the dirt access road. As Rocco passed between them, he came upon a mountainous collection of derelicts — including a bus that had been hit by a train — all in various stages of disintegration. It had grown to a height of almost thirty feet but would soon be reduced if the deal he was working on with a manufacturing company worked out.

To his surprise he found Caesar sitting at attention at the base of this pyramid of junk. "Caesar? What are you doing? You didn't hear me calling you?" Holding up the box of treats he shook it again to get a response. Caesar remained in a calm position with his tongue hanging out but ignoring the bribe.

"What is wrong with you? Are you sick, boy?" Rocco said in a gentle voice as he approached the Dobermann.

Without warning the dog started growling, lips curled, showing dangerous teeth. Vicious barking followed as it took an attack stance.

Startled, Rocco dropped the box of treats as he stepped backward from the angry dog. "Caesar! Stop…lay down!" But this seemed to agitate it more.

The grayish pallor of dusk had begun to blanket the grounds giving the piles of junk an ominous appearance that seemed all the more foreboding with the transformation of his faithful watchdog into a vicious drooling beast.

Rocco made one last attempt to quiet his dog when the yard lights came on. He instinctively looked up — Caesar's barking now turned into yelps— and gasped. There, high up circling behind the glare of the lamps he saw a giant bat.

"No wonder you're upset." He said to Caesar as he raised his Remington, ready to shoot if it came any closer. "Never saw one that big…"

Rocco Espesito staggered at the sight of the thing as it entered the halo of the yard lamp in front of him. The creature flew up, its wings extended, landed atop the light stanchion, and assumed a crouching position. "Madre di Dio!" He cried. "What …is it?" His amazement at seeing a naked woman with bat wings quickly disappeared when she leaned forward, hissed angrily, and spat at him. Rattled, Rocco fired blindly. He heard Caesar barking again. The creature was coming right at him. He fired again. Something struck him —Caesar — knocking him to the ground. His shot gun went flying. He struggled to get up, but she was on him before he could stand. A sickening odor enveloped him making it hard to breathe. His heart was pounding, and he cried out, "God help me!"

Suddenly he felt the thing's hands on the side of his head give a twist. He heard a snap, instantly followed by a flash of searing pain. The last thing Rocco Espesito saw as inky darkness swallowed him was the beautiful face of a woman with leopard's eyes.

Caesar looked up at his new master as if seeking permission. He sniffed the proffered hand then trotted toward the fallen box of spilled treats.

CHAPTER 21

Day Seven – afternoon

Tim Ryan sat brooding in his upstairs bedroom after being given the third degree by his parents when they returned from church. They told him several times that they trusted him so just tell the truth about his involvement with the items found in the garage attic. His mother urged him to go to confession if he felt he couldn't tell them. She was especially concerned about the human skull her husband told her about. Tim of course insisted he knew nothing about those objects, though consciously avoiding Stanley's damn pink blanket. He would have to go through more questioning tomorrow at the office of his father's attorney.

His father put restrictions on what he called "privileges" until this mess was cleared up. Tim wasn't sure what privileges his father had in mind but felt certain it didn't concern his paper route. Losing that would be the ultimate punishment. However, he was equally certain that going to movies, parties and dances would be out of the question. This was turning out to be the worst summer ever.

Staring out the window — it was raining — Tim wondered why he hadn't seen or heard from Stanley Bolton in the past two days. Yesterday was understandable with all the cops and commotion. But what about the day before? He had to talk to him, especially about the blanket that was now part of a police investigation.

Tim got up and began to pace back and forth. *This is all his fault anyway…he should take the blame. Why am I covering for him? His raving about how he got the blanket could be baloney he made up.*

As he passed his desk a third time, he glanced at this month's edition of Famous Monsters of Filmland pushed to the side on top of his desk and remembered something. He stopped, picked up the magazine and started flipping through the pages; Stanley's description of the being he encountered stuck in his head.

This issue had pictures from the new Ray Harryhausen film *Jason and the Argonauts*—it was on Tim's list of movies to see this summer— and he soon found the page he was looking for. The black and white picture was small, so he held the magazine up closer to see it better. The creature in the picture matched Stanley's description except for two characteristics: this one had horns and was ugly. Tim read the caption, "*The Harpy attacks!*"

He slowly closed the issue, placing it back on his desk. Now his doubts about Stanley's visitor deepened. *That knucklehead probably just saw the movie at the Hillsville Cinema and imagined the whole thing. He probably saw Tuesday Weld on a Dobie Gillis summer rerun before he fell asleep that night and fit her into his dream. Though he said it wasn't a dream… he can still be full of it sometimes. But where does the blanket fit in?*

Tim crossed his room to the bookcase that held the encyclopedia his grandmother had given him—*The Book of Knowledge*—selected the "H" volume and looked up Harpy.

As he read about the nature of this mythological creature, he realized he had read this information before in Stanley's basement a week ago. *Thief, wanderer, prophet, vicious, a chameleon, spiteful and mischievous, gatherer, immortal, magical.*

He rubbed the back of his neck. *This was in that Lovecraft book. Now I know why Stanley wanted the name. His whole nutty idea was to conjure something up that would get things for him or predict things that would get him money. A kind of slave. And...I have that name.*

Tim reread the encyclopedia's paragraph on the Harpy and had a startling revelation. The word "gatherer" flashed in his head like a warning sign. "Holy crap!" He said to the page in front of him then listened for a moment fearing someone downstairs might have heard him.

Replacing the book on the shelf, Tim sat on the edge of his bed holding his head. *Gatherer? If Stanley's creature is a harpy and actually gathers things, that sure would explain how all that stuff got in our garage attic. But why our attic?*

*Oh no...those Flagg Brothers loafers were part of the crime scene evidence stashed there. That lieutenant asked me if I recognized them, then questioned me about the Sanfield kid. Those shoes must have belonged to him. So, if this harpy **is** real and it's responsible for all that stuff being in the garage attic then maybe it killed that Danny kid and took his shoes.* He stood up and started pacing again. *It gathered things from its victims. This is bad...really bad.*

***

153

Across the street, Stanley Bolton, wearing a crown of cigarette smoke, paraded around his cluttered room waving a lit Marlboro and mumbling to himself.

"I sure hope he kept his trap shut...Did he rat me out? Shit...Did he give them the blanket?"

He took a drag on the cigarette then slowly exhaled. "Nah...The cops would've been here already if he squealed." Stanley stopped mid stride. *Cops? What the hell were the fuzz doing there anyway? Who were those guys in white and why'd they take the blanket and what was that other junk they were carryin? Somethin's up. We need ta talk. Maybe I'll just bop over there?* He walked to his bedroom window and looked out. It was pouring. "Shit! I hate rain." *Maybe I can get him on the phone.*

Crushing out the cigarette in an already overflowing ash tray, Stanley headed downstairs to the living room anticipating trouble, but to his relief found the phone available and no one in the room to bug him or listen in.

The smell of liver and onions cooking told him his mother was busy in the kitchen preparing dinner. His father's vacant chair at this time of day plus the absence of his little brother meant they were probably in the basement tinkering. That was a good thing.

He approached the phone. "Gonna make a call," he said furtively.

"Don't be long," his mother called from the kitchen.

Stanley dialed Tim's number. It wrang several times and he was about to hang up when a small voice said, "Ryan's Residence." *Emily... dammit.* He asked to speak to Tim.

"Who's this?" Emily said.

Taking a chance on being friendly he said, "Hi Emily. It's Stanley. Can I please talk ta your brother?"

"No," Emily replied. "He's not allowed to talk on the phone…*ever.*"

Surprised by that response Stanley stammered, "What?… What happened? Does it have ta do with the cops yesterday?"

"I'm not sure. After they found that awful smelling stuff in our garage attic no one would tell me anything."

Stanley prodded a little. "What stuff?"

"I don't know, but Tim had to go up there with them for some reason. Well…you can't talk to him anyway so goodbye." Stanley heard the click as she hung up. *Little brat. I don't like the feel of this.*

***

Tim came down from his room intending to grab a snack from the kitchen when he heard his mother ask Emily who was on the phone. He stepped up to the refrigerator, opened it and began rummaging around when his sister said the caller was Stanley. He turned quickly. "Why didn't you tell me?" he said, giving her an angry look.

"You're not allowed to have phone calls…remember?" She said.

Tim glanced at his mother. She was always more lenient than his father, but she just gave a quick nod and shrugged. Before he said anything a clever idea popped into his head. "Did he say why he called?"

Emily, on a step stool next to her mother helping to cut carrots for dinner shot a sarcastic "Nope" over her shoulder.

Tim applied his idea. "Oh no…I know why he called. I forgot to give him the baseball cards I owe him. I promised to give them to him yesterday when I got back from the bike hike." He didn't like to lie,

155

especially to his mother but he had to talk to Stanley now. "I'll just get the cards and run over there now and give them to him and come right back."

His mother turned, giving him a suspicious eye. *Crap! She didn't buy it.* Then said, "Dinner in half an hour. *Do not* be late."

"I won't," Tim said tapping his watch. "Thanks mom." He raced up to his room, gathered some bogus cards, threw on the hated rain slicker and flew down the stairs and out the front door before his father intervened.

Splashing through puddles, he crossed the street and knocked heavily on the front door of the Bolton's residence. The door opened at once with Stanley holding the handle. A momentary look of surprise crossed both their faces.

"We need to talk." They said at the same time. Stanley stepped aside but Tim hesitated before entering and glanced over his shoulder at his house expecting to see his father at the door. "I've got a half an hour …that's it."

"C'mon," Stanley said hurrying to the stairs leading up to his room.

The room looked worse than the last time Tim had seen it. A tornado could not have done a better job of messing up this place. And beside the ubiquitous clutter, the entire place smelled like a giant ashtray. The rain dripping from his slicker actually left clean spots on the wood floor. There was no place to sit except on Stanley's brother's unmade bed— the single chair near Stanley's bed was occupied by what looked like dirty clothes—so he leaned against a closet door.

"I think we're in big trouble," Tim said.

Stanley sat on the edge of his disheveled bed. "What the hell happened? Why were the fuzz at your place?"

Tim folded his arms. "You know that pink blanket you stashed in my garage?"

"Yeah…I saw this guy in a white coat coming down your driveway carryin' a box. The blanket was stickin' out. I flipped out when I saw it. Why'd they take it?"

"Turns out it's evidence in a police investigation…my father found it with a bunch of other junk up in our garage attic and …ready for this? *They* are all part of other police investigations. There was even a skull that looked like a kid's."

Stanley looked surprised. "*No shit…a skull?* How'd this stuff get up there?"

"I don't know but I have an off the wall idea." Tim checked his watch for the time and went on to tell Stanley about his discovery in the Famous Monsters of Filmland magazine and how it almost fit the description of what he saw as well as the information from the encyclopedia. He paused for a moment thinking then said, "You haven't seen that Jason and the Argonauts movie…Have you?"

Stanley, mentally worrying about the blanket, was half listening to his friend. "Huh? Movie? I haven't been ta any movies."

Satisfied that Stanley was telling the truth, Tim continued.

"Okay, if what you saw is real and you weren't hallucinating or something it's probably this thing called a harpy."

A look of confusion appeared on Stanley's face. "*Harpy?*"

"Right, but here's what freaked me out. I was wondering the same thing. How did these items get into my garage attic? When I read the traits of these creatures described in the encyclopedia, I remembered they were in that Lovecraft book. The two that jumped off the page at me were "Thief" and "Gatherer". *Gatherer!* It made sense. *Your* harpy gathered up those things and for some reason put them in my garage. But the cops think I had something to do with putting them up there."

"What? Why?" Stanley said, reaching for a gnarled pack of Marlboros.

Tim quickly explained the circumstances incriminating him.

"That's totally nuts." Stanley lit the cigarette, took a quick drag, and exhaled. "Wait…I was with you when we looked for that kid in the maze. That cop took my name, too. How come they're not talkin' ta me?"

Tim checked the time again. "Probably just haven't gotten to you yet."

"*Shit!* They'll see my name on the damn community service roster. I'll be public enemy number one."

"On the what?" Tim said.

"Never mind."

Tim saw he didn't have much time left so he got to the heart of the matter. "Stanley? If we really did conjure up a harpy, it may have killed those kids and that jerk I had the run in with. We could be considered…What do they call it? *Accessories!* We could go to jail. And…no one would believe us if we told the truth. There's only one thing we can do. Did you find the book?"

Stanley shook his head. "Not yet. I'm tryin' ta find another pulp that might have the ad plus the order blank for it.

"It wasn't with my father's books. I'll look once more but I got a feelin' my mother found it and tossed it."

"Crap! That's not good." Tim said. "I gotta go. Here…take these. My excuse to get over here." He handed Stanley the decoy baseball cards and turned to go. "Let me know if you have any luck finding the book or another copy."

As Stanley stood to see his friend and possible accomplice out Tim suddenly stopped and turned back. "Cripes! I almost forgot. I remembered the name."

Stanley's eyes went wide. "You did?"

"Malhela… It's Malhela."

Shortly after Tim Ryan had left, the Bolton family actually sat down together for dinner—a rare occurrence. Stanley was surprised to see his older brother Artie seated at the table. *He must have just come in.* Equally surprising was his spiffy appearance. He now had a crew cut, was clean shaven plus wore a dark T-shirt that wasn't wrinkled. *Must have a date or somethin'.* Stanley took a seat next to him.

After his mother doled out portions of mashed potatoes, corn plus slices of liver with bacon and onions on each of their plates she sat, gave his father a quick glance then turned to Artie.

"I'm happy to see you here for dinner Arthur. Is it a special occasion? You look nice," she said. Her tone bordering on sarcasm.

Artie put down his fork, took a sip of milk and with a tone matching his mother's said, "You might say it's a special occasion…for me especially. I'm moving out. So…this is a kind of last supper."

His father choked and his mother said, "moving *out*? To where?"

"I joined the Peace Corps," Artie said.

"That volunteer organization President Kennedy set up back in sixty-one?" His father asked.

Stanley couldn't resist a jab at his older brother. "Never took you for a do gooder."

"What will you do? I thought you needed some type of skill?" His mother asked.

Artie explained that he had been in their training program for months learning carpentry and such. "I have a skill," he said.

"We didn't give you permission to join this," his father chided.

Stanley leaned back in his chair as if getting out of the line of fire. *Uh oh…here we go.*

"Don't need your permission to join. I'm eighteen and a high school graduate. It was either this or the army. I picked this. Tomorrow morning I'm taking the nine fifteen train into the city to join up with my assigned group. We fly to Africa the next day …a place called Guinea."

Stanley stared at his mother's face. It looked as if it had turned to white stone. Her mouth hardly moved when she asked, "For how long?"

Arthur shrugged. "Don't know."

Little brother Jonathan, ignoring the liver on his plate, didn't say anything, just kept looking back and forth at everyone's faces. Then mustering up enough courage said, "Can I have your transistor radio?"

Not another word was said during the rest of the meal. When everyone was finished Arthur left the table and went upstairs to pack. Stanley followed, trying not to reveal his joy at soon having the room all to himself.

Once they entered the room Artie turned to Stanley. "You know? You should think about joining this group once you graduate...*if* you graduate that is. There's this thing going on in a place called Viet Nam and I heard the army's going to draft guys to go fight there. Unless you want to get caught up in that mess the Peace Corps would be the way to go."

"I'll be fine," Stanley said. "I've got my own plans."

CHAPTER 22

Day Eight – Late morning

Lieutenant James Trabinski had just returned to the precinct after attending the funeral service for Danny Sanfield. The morning rain, leftover from yesterday's storm, added to his somber mood as he sat at his desk signing a document authorizing an extended bereavement leave for Sergeant David Sanfield. He was concerned the man might not recover from this tragedy.

As he took a gulp of coffee he groaned — it was cold and flat. *Perfect...* Without thinking he opened a side desk drawer and pulled out a new pack of Camels, quickly tore off the cellophane wrapper, tapped one out and lit it. He leaned back in his chair closed his eyes, took a deep drag on the cigarette, and exhaled slowly. *Better...*

A knock on his open office door startled him. A tall young man wearing a tan rain slicker that matched his pants stood there holding a thick light brown envelope.

"Lieutenant Trabinski? Wells Fargo courier service. I was instructed to deliver this directly to you." The man held out the package. "Please sign here." He held out a clipboard with an attached receipt. Trabinski leaned forward, signed the acceptance sheet, and took the envelope.

"Thanks," he said offering a dollar tip to the courier.

"That won't be necessary. Have a good day, sir." The man made a crisp military turn and left the station.

The top left-hand corner of the envelope read: Nassau County Medical Examiners Department.

Trabinski unsealed it and carefully slipped out the enclosed documents. An unofficial, handwritten note had been clipped to the first batch of papers. He took a drag on his cigarette and began to read:

Hello Jim,

Our forensics team worked feverishly to get these two reports finished. With the autopsies completed we released the bodies the next day for burial.

As you know there are a lot of medical and technical terms throughout the reports, so I thought it best for the sake of expediency to give you the Readers Digest version.

The autopsies of the two boys; Sanfield and Westmyer have revealed a certain protein embedded in their wounds. Alpha-Keratin. This is the substance that makes up human fingernails as well as animal claws plus the talons of various birds of prey. The reports go into detail regarding the amounts of protein for each wound etc. The Sanfield boy had a great deal, especially at the throat laceration.

I usually don't do this, I let you detective types put it all together, but I'll stick my neck out here. I believe the shoulder wounds on the Westmyer boy could have been caused by the talons of a large bird of prey. Your guess is as good as mine as to what type. Call me if you need anything else.

Hope this helps.

Good luck,

Phil

Trabinski leaned to his left, planting an elbow on the arm of his chair, placed two fingers over his mouth and reread the Lead Examiner's note. *A large bird of prey? Could something like that kill a full-grown man?*

"Lieutenant?" For the second time today, he had been jarred out of his thoughts. He pushed the intercom button. "Go ahead."

"Second Precinct, line one…Lieutenant Talbot."

He punched the glowing line one button on his phone. "Trabinski," he said, force of habit.

"I just received Phil Tipton's report," she said without preamble. "They found something interesting on those alleged grappling hook scratch marks I was telling you about. Doesn't make any sense but my instincts still tell me there's some connection. Their research turned up traces of …"

"Let me guess," he interrupted. "Alpha-Keratin?"

"Ha! I suspect you just received a report yourself."

"Right. Phil said the wounds on my victims were covered with it."

"What could it mean?"

"Beats me, but he had a theory."

"Let's hear it."

"Over coffee?" Trabinski needed something to lift his spirits and seeing her would sure help.

"Plainview Diner…twenty minutes."

As Trabinski pulled into the misty diner parking lot his radio announced a Code 10-91V, New South Road, Bethpage. *A vicious animal call. Probably a rabid raccoon.* Figuring this was an Animal Control situation he ignored it and entered the diner. Not surprised at seeing Casey already there, seated in a back booth gazing out the window, he moseyed up to her. "Come here often?" He joked.

"Wow. Haven't heard that one in a while." She laughed. "I went ahead and ordered you a coffee and a slice of apple pie."

"Aah…you read my mind. Thanks." He slid into the booth seat across from her. Despite the rain and muggy temperatures, she looked amazing, not a hair out of place, makeup perfect.

As Trabinski sat Casey's intuition picked up on his weak attempt at being in a good mood. "Tough morning, Jim?" Her tone concerned and sincere. "You look a little rough around the edges."

Lighting a cigarette Trabinski told her about the morning funeral service for the Sanfield boy and signing the bereavement papers for Sergeant Sanfield's leave of absence.

"Oh," Casey said. Her gray eyes filled with sympathy. "It's never easy."

Two coffees and a slice of pie arrived. Casey took a quick sip of hers. "So? I'm anxious to hear Phil's theory."

Trabinski rested his cigarette on the edge of the nearby ashtray then stirred two sugar cubes into his coffee. "Well, you know what this Alpha-Keratin is…Right?"

"Basically…Fingernails." She picked up the fork from her place setting and helped herself to a chunk of his pie.

"Right, plus animal claws and talons." He said.

"Okay?"

"Unofficially, Phil thinks the wounds inflicted on the young boy could have been caused by the talons of a large bird of prey." He took a taste of the pie himself.

"What kind of bird could pick up and carry off a child that size and weight?"

"Around here? I have no idea. In South America they have those Condors with ten-foot wingspans…"

"They have them in California too." Casey interjected.

"I have my guys checking the Bronx Zoo and one in New Jersey to see if they're missing any birds of prey. The other question I have is… What kind of *bird* is capable of killing a strong, healthy fifteen-year-old?"

Casey drained her cup and waved at the waitress for a refill. "I read somewhere that a trained Falcon could kill a full-grown man. And…?" She rubbed the side of her nose. Trabinski noticed this was something she did when an idea was brewing. "Falcons are strong enough to carry off an infant," she concluded.

"That could explain the Keratin on *your* scratch marks. But a Falcon could never lift the Westmyer boy."

Her second coffee was delivered. "Right. But how about this? What if there were two birds?"

Trabinski sat back and chuckled. "*Two* birds? *Working* together? How could that possibly work? Unless…"

Casey leaned forward. "Right! Two birds…one trainer."

Trabinski retrieved his cigarette from the ashtray and took a drag. "Not bad, Miss Talbot. That's a strong possibility. What's the motive? And could a Falcon cut through the window screen you mentioned?"

"Those are very good questions. None of this fits the child slavery MO either. The slavery kids were never killed or seriously harmed.

Something else is going on here, Jim, and I'll buy you a steak dinner at Tavern on the Green if these cases are not connected."

Trabinski smiled. "I'll hold you to that, but we're still in the dark here. No solid leads whatsoever. No motive."

She took a sip of her coffee and said, "What about the Ryan boy?"

"Aside from the fact he lied about that blanket, my gut tells me he's clean. And you might as well forget about trying to get anything more out of him, now that his father's lawyer is involved. The boy will keep his mouth shut."

Casey nodded.

"So…where do we go from here?" Trabinski said.

"East Hampton."

Two police cruisers, sirens screaming, lights flashing went by in a blur on the road outside causing Trabinski and Talbot to instantly look out the diner window next to them.

"Must be an accident." Casey offered. But Trabinski didn't think so. Unbidden, the code 10-91V immediately came to mind. "I'd better check this out."

Like trained soldiers they both stood at the same time. Trabinski slapped a ten spot on the table, Talbot grabbed her shoulder bag, and they hurried out the door to his car.

The radio came to life when he flipped the switch. "All units in vicinity of New South Road, Bethpage Code 10-54. Rocco's Auto Wrecking…" The message repeated. Trabinski started the engine. "Gotta go," he said to Casey.

Without a word she trotted around to the passenger side, opened the door, and jumped in. "Let's go," she said.

The rain was finally tapering off.

The scene that greeted Trabinski and Talbot as they pulled up to Rocco's Auto Wrecking and Junk Emporium was typical.

Flashing blue and red lights atop three patrol cars cast their colors across a high stockade fence as well as the beat-up Ford Pickup truck, parked off to the side of the parking lot facing the fence. Six uniformed officers stood in front of a heavy chain link gate — that matched the fence in height — talking to a couple of civilians. Two of the officers had guns drawn. The one detail that deviated from the typical was a large rain-soaked Dobermann Pincher, frothing at the mouth, growling, barking, and jumping at the gate.

Trabinski and Talbot made a quick exit from his vehicle and approached the group avoiding the many puddles scattered about the wet dirt parking lot. "Thought this was a 10-54 Sergeant?" Trabinski said pointing at the gun in the officer's hand.

"Still is Lieutenant. We just can't confirm. The gate's locked on the inside and every time we approach, that damn dog hits it. Sal and Marco over there are Rocco's nephews. They work here. They were supposed to pick up some parts in their truck." The sergeant pointed to the beat-up pickup truck. "They made the original vicious animal call. They have bolt cutters but are afraid of the dog. We were just about to put it down when you arrived."

"Where's the body?" Trabinski asked.

The Sergeant pointed with his free hand. "Back there, Lieutenant. On the road between those two stacks of crushed cars. It may be the owner. Can't tell from here. His nephews called out to him but no response."

"Hold off a minute before you put it down," Casey said. "The dog may just be protecting his master. Especially, since it can see he's hurt. Anyone know the dog's name?"

The nephew, Sal, hurried over. "His name is Caesar. He knows us but he sure doesn't act like it. We've never seen him like this before."

Casey came up to the gate. "I wouldn't get too close," the sergeant warned.

She squatted and spoke to the dog in a soft voice. "Caesar? Come here good boy. You're okay. Where's Rocco? Show us where Rocco is Caesar."

For a long moment the dog seemed to have calmed down and everyone looked at Casey in amazement. But as she stood the dog went berserk, throwing itself at the gate repeatedly, foaming at the mouth, teeth bared, wet fur sending a spray of droplets through the chain link. It was then that Casey saw something caught on the dog's back teeth hanging from the corner of its mouth; something shredded and bloody. It looked like a piece of clothing or meat.

Calmly, Casey opened her shoulder bag and in one fluid motion withdrew her Luger 9mm and shot the dog in the head. It fell backwards from the impact, twitched a few times, and expired.

Trabinski stepped next to her. "That was sudden…"

Casey checked her gun, placing it gently back in her bag she said, "The poor thing was mad. I think it may have been feeding on the body."

"Nice shot," the sergeant said.

"Use those bolt cutters," Trabinski ordered. "Let's get this gate open. Sergeant? Call an ambulance just in case this guy is still with us."

They all charged through the open gate. The nephews in the lead. Sal came up to what he thought was a bloody, overstuffed sack lying in the mud. "Oh, Christ!" he said when he realized what it was. He quickly turned and puked. Marco came no closer.

"Looks like you were right Lieutenant. Caesar had a feast…Not much left either. This poor soul didn't stand a chance." Trabinski said.

Casey walked a wide circle around the mutilated body—trying to keep from slipping in the soggy dirt—surveying the damage. "You think the dog killed him?"

"Maybe. Hard to tell just by looking. The guy may have had a heart attack and you know dogs, they're always hungry."

The sound of a wailing siren increased as the ambulance got closer.

"He won't have any use for that." Casey said.

Sal had recovered. He and Marco, both with faces white as chalk wandered trancelike back and forth, keeping their distance from the body, as if searching for something.

Casey caught up with them as they went around a pile of rusted fenders and hub caps. "What are you looking for? Maybe I can help."

The two men momentarily startled, stopped in their tracks, and looked over their shoulders. They both smiled sheepishly when they saw who it was. Her looks had that effect on most men.

Marco spoke first. "We're looking for uncle's Remington."

"He always took it with him when he made his rounds after closing." Sal added. His voice cracking.

"A Remington?" Casey said.

"A shot gun," Marco continued. "It belonged to his father. Kind of a prized possession."

Casey nodded. "A model 870 pump action?"

"Yes!" The nephews said.

"I know it," Casey said. "Powerful weapon. Good for close range only. Let's go tell the others…widen the search."

After an hour of searching for the missing shot gun and not finding it they all regrouped by their vehicles, making way for the forensics team—who had been notified by the ambulance crew— to analyze the remains of Rocco Espesito. Trabinski and Talbot leaned on his car watching the proceedings in silence. He noticed Casey rubbing the side of her nose.

"Something on your mind?" He said.

Casey stopped rubbing her nose and held her chin in her hand for a moment. "We've had four violent crimes plus a kidnapping in the span of a week's time. And at every crime scene something was missing. Right?

"Go on," Trabinski said.

Casey turned and looked up at him. "All those items found in the Ryan's garage were the items missing from related crime scenes".

"Right…So?"

"Now there's a Remington Model 870 pump action shot gun…a family heir loom to boot, missing."

Trabinski's face took on a pensive expression. "Coincidence?"

"I don't believe in them. Remember?" she said. "I think our perp is a collector…keeping souvenirs. We should do a record search for killers with similar MO's. See what turns up."

Trabinski nodded, "Makes sense. We could use a break."

***

From deep in the shadows of her new nest Malhela watched, through the dripping strings of rainwater coming from the edges of her nest entrance, the events unfold below her. She struggled to keep her anger at the loss of her guardian hound under control as she focused her sight on the red-haired elf like female responsible for its death. This birthgiver—if she was a birthgiver— differed from the others Malhela had come upon in this world of mortals. She sensed this one could be a threat. She had some form of magic that enabled her to fire deadly projectiles from her hand. Malhela would watch for this one and get her revenge when the time was right.

CHAPTER 23

Day Eight – Evening

Now having the room completely to himself —which felt strange for some reason—Stanley, succumbing to his mother's demand, had spent the day halfheartedly tidying up the place. With that completed his mind focused on what might happen if he called the name of the beautiful creature from another realm. He felt excited and a bit nervous. He'd not given any real thought as to what he would do if the conjuring worked. Originally it was all kind of a prank. And now this jive from Tim Ryan about her being dangerous complicated things even more.

There were two cigarettes left in the crumpled pack of Marlboros. He removed one, tucked it in the corner of his mouth and touched the flame from his lighter to it. He took a deep drag then slowly exhaled as he walked to the bedroom window and removed the screen. It would be dark soon. Should he wait? Or take a chance and call her name? He thought back to the first time he saw her and how scared he was. *I can't be scared if I do this. Can't show her I'm afraid. I'm supposed ta have the power since I summoned her. The power ta do what? Command her? I wish I had that damn book so I could read about her abilities again.*

Maybe she's like a genie that grants three wishes? No...Ryan said she was somethin' called a harpy.

Then as he watched the thin clouds drift across the face of the moon his thoughts wandered back to the way she looked that night. Excitement, like that of a first date, took hold urging him across the floor to the bedroom door where he instantly locked it. He had made up his mind. "Malhela? Come to me."

***

Malhela hunkered down in her nest peering out into the night. Her idea of a peaceful hideaway shattered by the continuous comings and goings of male mortals on the grounds below her. They had taken away the remains of her hound as well as the mortal she killed but still wandered about as if searching for something. She gave a sideways glance at the long cylindrical item she had taken from the dead man then returned to surveilling the annoying mortals.

The sun had risen and set eight times; a solution to her entrapment still eluded her. She could feel herself changing. Controlling her emotions as well as utilizing her magic — especially her camouflage — was becoming more exhausting with each passing day. She felt her anger bubbling up within her like lava waiting for a volcano to erupt. She was supposed to be clever, devious, and unpredictable, yet no helpful ideas came.

As she leaned forward watching the last of the mortals leave the yard and close the gate, she heard her name, then the command. The feeling of duty, of obligation was weak. She knew immediately who was responsible. *Stanley!*

With a hiss, she took flight. Now she would get answers.

***

Maybe she didn't hear me? Stanley thought. It felt like hours since he had called her. His excitement was beginning to wane. *Did I say it wrong? How's it spelled, anyway? I shoulda had Ryan write it down.* He moved to the open window and in a normal voice called her again, this time breaking it down into two words. "Mal-*Hela*...Come to me." He watched the sky for a few moments hoping to see her winging her way to him, but there was no sign of her.

Dammit! Is there somethin' else I'm supposed ta say besides her name? He was about to turn away from the window when he heard a flapping sound like someone slapping a carpet to clean dirt from it. The sound came closer causing his intended bravado to falter. He willed his hands to stop shaking. He willed himself to look in the sound's direction. And there she was. He took a step backward as she gracefully slipped through the open window into his room.

"What is it you want from me, Stanley?" She stood, hands on her hips, wings folded back, chin tilted up.

Stanley Bolton found it difficult to breathe. His thoughts became a chaotic mess. Feeling dizzy he clumsily backed into the chair near the foot of his bed and sat with a thump.

Though he had seen her briefly in the dark on that night, which felt like ages ago, seeing her now in the light was a whole different ball game.

"You are *so beautiful*." He breathed. His eyes filled with her nakedness, wandering from her full breasts to a flat toned abdomen to shapely muscular thighs then back to her amazing face. Her skin was a muted golden bronze. *Coppertone* popped into his head. Pointed elf-like ears plus white feather quills just above her forehead framed a beautiful face that still reminded him of the actress Tuesday Weld with the eyes of a leopard.

Malhela took two quick steps towards Stanley and grabbed him by the throat. "I have no more patience for whatever game you are playing…Stanley. You will tell me *now* why you have summoned me."

Stanley coughed. She released him. Instantly his jumbled thoughts were in her head. *Make love, go all the way, lover.* She felt the infatuation come off him like a wave of heat.

Stanley caught his breath. His arousal diminished but not extinguished. Regaining some composure he said, "You have ta do what I say…Right?"

Ignoring her piscine body odor, he leaned closer. "I read in a book that you could do things for me…maybe get things for me."

Malhela remembered the dead bird, the bad omen, on display in the room below. Thoughtfully she said, "Maybe?" She stepped away from him, flexing her wings. "Your incantation was flawed," she said. Her tone turning sinister. "You did not speak the words as an individual. Your voice was secondary to that of Tim Ryan. Alone, your commands are not compelling. I will grant you one insignificant request and then you will release me from the spell."

Stanley was a virgin, though he told his cronies otherwise, and getting laid was primary in his mind so he said, "Okay." He was surprised when she asked, "What is getting laid?" So, he explained as best he could.

Malhela shot him a puzzled look. "You want to *mate* with me?"

"*Yeah...*"He said, straightening in the chair, feeling hopeful.

"Impossible! It is not my time." *And you are repulsive,* she thought. But the idea of being released from this nightmare was strong, prompting another idea to materialize.

She lifted from the floor floating to Stanley. She straddled him, took his head in her hands — imagining him to be the more appealing Tim Ryan— and kissed him ferociously. She allowed him to fondle her as she inhaled through her nose and exhaled from her mouth into his while undulating her hips on his lap. She felt him quiver. Twice more she breathed into his mouth. When he arched his back, she pulled away.

Stanley fell back in his chair breathing heavily, eyes wide, mouth hanging open. Shooting stars, skyrockets and fireworks blazed through the clouds of euphoria in his head. He was vaguely aware of being wet.

Malhela sat on his brother's bed. "Now release me, Stanley," she said sweetly with a smile.

For a moment Stanley didn't know where he was nor cared. He had never felt this good...ever. He didn't want it to end. Finding his voice he said, "Can we do that again?"

"Say the words, Stanley!" Her eyes flashed a dangerous look at him.

"Don't I need Tim with me ta release you?"

Suddenly, Stanley felt weird. He couldn't feel his legs or his arms. "What's happenin?"

"*Say the words!*"She growled.

"I...I can't. I don't know them. They were in a book." His throat felt like a desert.

Malhela rose from the bed, circling behind him. "Where is this *book*?"

"I don't know. I lost it somewhere."

She hissed and dug her claws deep into his shoulders, but Stanley didn't feel a thing. "You lost it somewhere. Where is this somewhere?"

"If I knew I wouldn't be in this mess," he said.

"Does Tim Ryan know where it is?"

Stanley let loose with a barrage of dry coughs. "No…," he choked.

Unexpectedly, the knob on his locked bedroom door rattled. "Whata ya doin in there Stanley?" Little brother Jonathan called. *Why is he still up at this hour?*

Before Stanley could say a word, he heard himself say, "Go away." The words came out of Malhela's mouth.

"Why should I?" Jonathan whined.

"Leave me alone ya little creep or you'll regret it!" Malhela said in Stanley's voice.

As his brother went back down the stairs Stanley thought he heard him call his mother. For the first time in a long time, he wanted her.

Malhela walked to the window, her talons clicking on the wood floor, wondering what to do next, when a memory from her past brought a touch of hope. She turned to Stanley. "What was the title of this missing book?"

Stanley could hardly speak but managed to get out, "Water… need water."

"Was it the Necronomicon?" Malhela asked.

When Stanley just shook his head, she stifled a scream and uttered in her language, "Malbenu —i tiun forlasitan lokon kaj —iujn, kiuj lo—as ene!" Cursing this place and all who lived here. She gave Stanley a look that might have been pity then leapt from the window.

Stanley was surprised to see her return carrying a pail half filled with rainwater. She placed it on the floor in front of him about three feet from the chair and announced, "You are of no further use to me primate. May your quiet suffering be long." With that said, she went to the window and soared into the night, leaving Stanley Bolton alone and paralyzed.

CHAPTER 24

Day Nine – Morning

Another hot morning, not a cloud in the sky. The white sun was already baking everything its brilliance touched. Lieutenant James Trabinski wondered if he had made a mistake by recommending today for the East Hampton trip. His tan button down short sleeved camp shirt was already sticking to him.

Cruising up South Oyster Bay Road with all the windows rolled down in his Ford Galaxie, hoping to keep the interior reasonably cool, he ran the commercial radio dial searching for a station with decent music— the volume on his police radio turned low. He settled on one playing the song *On Broadway*. It had a 50's sound that he liked. The DJ announced the recording artist as The Drifters.

He had won the coin toss which decided who would drive today and told Lieutenant Talbot he would pick her up early. He would be at her Woodbury Gardens apartment in about ten minutes.

His thoughts then turned to the day ahead. *Hope this doesn't turn out to be a waste of time. It took some convincing to get Philbrick to agree to this. He likes his Captain's shield nice and shiny…no tarnish. Philbrick talk for "no screw ups". He certainly wasn't happy with me taking a piece of evidence.*

A beige heavy-duty envelope containing the yellow piece of cloth found at the playground scene rested on the backseat. *It will be interesting to see what this Madame Florentine comes up with when she sees this piece of cloth. It better be good.*

He turned onto Woodbury Road and shut the radio off as Johnny Cash sang about a ring of fire. *Yeah…feels like a ring of fire out there.*

As Trabinski approached the garden apartments he glanced at his watch. *Five minutes early.* The plan was to meet her out front. So, he made a quick right turn onto the entrance road and began checking for her building number. Through his windshield he saw a young woman who looked like a model from the cover of a fashion magazine standing on the sidewalk in front of a corner unit. He gave a soft whistle to himself as he pulled closer.

She wore tight yellow cropped slacks that Trabinski vaguely remembered being called *pedal* something, a white button-down sleeveless top, tied at the waist. It had a high collar with an open V neck. A yellow headband kept her red hair off her forehead. Dark sunglasses, a large colorful beach style bag and white tennis shoes completed the look. *Yacht club, anyone?* He thought.

"*Oh*…murder." He muttered to himself when he realized the vision of loveliness standing in front of him was Talbot. *Lieutenant? You can arrest me anytime you like.* He shook his head. *Keep it professional Trabinski. This is not a date.*

He pulled his car to the curb in front of her, stopped and quickly got out to open the door for her. "Good morning," he said with more enthusiasm than he intended.

She stepped to the car and opened the door herself. "Morning Lieutenant. Give a girl a lift?"

"By all means," he said, and they both slid into the vehicle. "Nice disguise Lieutenant."

"We going to be formal this whole trip?" She said good naturedly.

"You started it." He laughed.

"Had to pull some strings to get the evidence I wanted." She said as she placed her colorful beach bag on the floor between her feet.

"The blanket?" Trabinski asked as he pulled out onto the highway.

"Exactly." She pulled a transparent zippered pouch from her bag to show him then quickly put it away. It contained the pink infant's blanket found at the Ryan's garage. "I feel bad for the forensic boys who had to examine this the first time. It still smells *bad*. Thankfully, the pouch seems to be stifling it."

When she leaned forward Trabinski noticed a long thin scar on the back of her left shoulder that her blouse didn't completely conceal. *That looks nasty. Bet there's a story behind that.*

"There's coffee in the thermos and pastries in that white bag. Help yourself." He gestured to the items on the seat between them. "There's an extra cup in the glove compartment."

Trabinski maneuvered his Galaxie through traffic heading toward Sunrise Highway. "So, tell me about this Madame Florentine. What can I expect?"

Casey poured herself some coffee when they stopped at a traffic light. Then examined the contents of the pastry bag, eyeing a cheese Danish. "Any napkins?"

He gave her a sideways glance. "*Napkins?*"

"Never mind," she said reaching into her beach bag and pulling out a package of tissues. "Madame Florentine? I'm not sure what to expect myself. It *has* been a few years since we worked together. Remember she said she'd listen to us not necessarily help us."

"I do. But she did help you crack that child slavery case. How'd you get her to use her psychic abilities back then?"

Casey took a sip of coffee to wash down a bite of Danish. "I'm not really sure what changed her mind. I remember her being reluctant at first. It may have been because she couldn't have children of her own and felt sorry for anyone who had lost a child that convinced her to get involved. She was Dolores Florentine then and the whole psychic detective thing was new to her. She couldn't control it yet. The Madame Florentine bit came later. At one point she tried to convince me to give the case to somebody else with more experience. Concern for my safety being the reason. I guess you might say that little impromptu warning saved my life."

"That how you got that souvenir on your shoulder?"

Casey turned her head slowly towards him and with a slight smile said, "Sharp eyes, Trabinski."

"Yes, ma'am. Trained to be observant." He said, returning the smile.

Casey went on to tell him about the encounter with the gang leaders after Madame Florentine —by using a hair ribbon from a missing little girl— located their hidden operation headquarters at a Jamaica Bay boat yard.

They were caught "red handed" as they say with children bound and gagged stowed below decks on an old fishing boat. Though she had backup, the arrest got out of hand. The gang had decided to make a run for it. One had a gun and winged one of her team. It was while she wrestled the weapon from the gunman that she was stabbed in the shoulder with a seven-inch hunting knife by one of his partners. Had she not remembered the psychic's warning, she might not have used a certain Judo move on the gunman, which caused the man with the knife to nail her in the shoulder rather than the back. "That knife could have penetrated a lung, or my heart for that matter. Either way game over." She said.

Trabinski gave a low whistle. "You're a tough cookie lady. Most women in your position at that time…and some guys would have called it quits."

When she didn't say anything, he quickly said, "I'm glad you didn't."

"Really?" Casey said with a touch of surprise in her tone.

"Really," Trabinski said.

Realizing that this may have sounded like a come on he immediately changed the subject. "We got the information back from the Bronx Zoo and Central Park Zoo plus the Turtle Back Zoo in New Jersey. No birds of prey missing."

"I figured as much. I went ahead and checked with the New York Audubon Society, hoping they could give me names of trainers or owners of these types of birds. They were no help. But that doesn't rule out some nut job secretly training these birds to do his dirty work."

"Right…and that's why we're doing this little junket. Nail down this supposed nut job's motive."

They had been on the road for about an hour and a half. It was taking longer than anticipated thanks to the traffic lights on Sunrise Highway that seemed determined to turn red every time they approached. Trabinski was tempted to hit the siren and bully his way through these intersections, but he found himself enjoying the ride *and* the company so he resisted.

Trabinski's stomach made a gurgling sound. His breakfast of coffee and a Danish long since digested.

"Hungry?" Casey asked. "There's a Wetsons' up ahead on the right. Sixteen cents for a cheeseburger fits my budget. Shall we?"

After grabbing a bag of burgers and sodas Trabinski and Talbot were back on the highway carrying with them the wonderful aroma of French fries and burgers cooked with onions. The traffic lights were more cooperative on this leg allowing them to make up time.

Sunrise Highway became Montauk Highway bending southward near Bridgehampton, skirting the south shore of Long Island. From time-to-time glimpses of the ocean and the sun-drenched beaches could be seen through the passenger side window. The cry and cackle of seagulls echoed from the distant sky.

Being a city girl, Casey Talbot had never been this far east on the island and the beautiful beaches she was seeing made her think of the crowded, not so beautiful, Rockaway beaches she had frequented in her youth.

"It's beautiful out here," Casey said. "Wish I had beaches like these when I was kid.

"Yes, it is," Trabinski said. "They take pride in their beaches and parks out here."

Trabinski made a left turn, exiting Montauk Highway.

"It has been a long time since I've been out here," Trabinski said as they pulled into the Village of East Hampton. "But that thing is still there. Hasn't changed all that much." He pointed to a small windmill that stood at the junction of North Main Steet and Pantigo Road. The ornate wooden sign out front read "Old Hook Mill".

"Would you believe that's been here since 1806?"

The mill—originally named the Smock Mill—the last of the wind powered grist mills on Long Island was built in 1806 by Nathan Dominy the 5th, a well-known local craftsman. It was designed to grind 5000 bushels of grain into flour and feed. It included a corn cob crusher as well as an elevator to transport grain from the first floor to the third for processing.

In 1851 the mill was deemed obsolete thanks to a grist mill in South Hampton capable of grinding 25,000 bushels of grain. It fell into disrepair and was finally restored to working order for the Village of East Hampton in 1939 where it continued to operate until 1942.

Somewhere along the line the name was changed to the Old Hook Mill. No one seems to know why.

In 1959 it became an East Hampton historical site and museum.

Casey looked out the window admiring the quaint Dutch style mill. "When were you here last?"

Trabinski turned onto Main Street. Madame Florentine's store was up about a quarter mile on the right, according to the directions she had been given.

"Probably Forty-Seven…Just got out of the Coast Guard. I was stationed out at Montauk. Shore Patrol. The War was finally over so I bummed around here awhile till I figured out what I wanted to do with my life."

"A sailor, huh? I better not let my guard down," she said with a quick laugh. Then, "Oh, there it is," she said pointing to the bookstore.

Madame Florentine's Antediluvian Occult Books, Potions and other Sundries stood in the shadows between two towering Elm trees. The rustic, dark wood storefront had a large plate-glass window upon which the above words were painted in gold. A "Yes, We're Open" sign hung in the front door window. Three concrete steps led up to a wooden porch with a black wrought iron railing at its perimeter. From a ceramic bowl, placed on a small round table, the enticing scent of jasmine and incense wafted over two cushioned cane rocking chairs situated on either side, inviting visitors to enjoy the ambiance.

A tiny brass bell on the inside of the door jingled as Talbot and Trabinski entered. The dim interior, redolent with the musty smell of old books laced with a scent that might have been cinnamon created a welcoming atmosphere. Three claw foot stands with octagonal tops supported Tiffany table lamps. They were strategically placed in corners of the room. Soft violin music played from a hidden source. There were no customers.

The wooden planked floor with an oriental rug at its center creaked as they stepped forward. The deceptively large room looked to be a perfect square with three of its four walls holding floor to ceiling book-cases filled with books of the occult: The Complete Works of Hans Holtzer, Secrets of the Black Arts, Occultism and Common Sense, Tobin's Spirit Guide, Secrets of the Tarot, The Gods of Hell-Demon's List as well as hundreds of others. The back wall also contained a black wooden door with a large eyeball painted on it. A glass counter, waist high, filled with jars of various sizes and colors containing powders as well as liquids stood a few feet in front of the door. An ancient cash register rested on top of a red velvet runner which protected the glass. Trinkets along with various figurines shared the countertop. Amulets, wood chimes, planetary mobiles, wind chimes, as well as all manner of dream catchers dangled from the rafters.

Talbot sidled past a free-standing kiosk containing bags of spices, herbs, and dried mushrooms as Trabinski worked his way between two dark wood reading tables adorned with fat candles to look at more book titles. "Very homey," he said.

Before Talbot could comment a voice said, "Welcome Cassandra… It's been a while."

CHAPTER 25

Day Nine – Afternoon

A tall, thin, attractive woman with curly raven hair, accented by white strands that framed her face, stood by the open black door at the rear of the store. She wore long dangling silver earrings, a cream-colored gauze top with a red paisley design, scoop neck, as well as long slit baggy sleeves which gathered at her wrists. A flowing burgundy maxi skirt completed her ensemble. A silver chain with a circled pentagram hung from her slender neck. She had a heart shaped face, full lips, dark eyes, and a splash of freckles across the bridge of her straight nose. Her welcoming smile revealed perfect teeth.

Trabinksi was surprised by her youthful appearance. He had expected a much older woman. Someone more like Maria Ouspenskaya from the Wolfman movie perhaps.

"Hello Dolores," Casey said moving forward to shake her hand. "I love your store."

"Thank you…Come sit." Dolores gestured to the chairs at the nearest reading table.

Casey introduced her to Trabinksi then took a seat.

"Would you care for tea or lemonade?"

Casey accepted the tea, Trabinski lemonade.

The woman went back through the door from which she came and disappeared into a back room. Minutes later she reappeared carrying an ornate silver tray with a white pot of steaming tea, two matching cups and a tall frosty glass of lemonade.

"You look wonderful Dolores. Apparently, life in the Hamptons agrees with you." Casey said with a smile as the woman poured the tea.

"Life's been good. No complaints." Dolores took the chair across from Trabinski and sat gracefully.

"How's business?" Trabinski asked, picking up on the lack of customers in the store.

Dolores gave a proud smile. "Business is good. Especially in the evenings and on the weekends. Usually slow on days like this. Everyone is at the beach. I make up for any summer losses in October. You should see this place around Halloween. It's busier than Christmas time." Dolores laughed light heartedly but her expression quickly turned dour.

"I was excited when I heard your voice on the phone Cassandra…" Dolores said. "… And the thought of seeing you was indeed a happy one but now that you are here those feelings have become clouded. You bring with you something disturbing…unsettling."

Trabinski and Talbot gave each other a quick look then returned to Dolores.

The woman took a dainty sip of tea. "I agreed to listen to what you have to say but I'm feeling that whatever it is, Cassandra, it may be beyond any help I could provide."

Trabinski let Talbot do the talking. This was her contact.

"I'm not exactly sure what you mean but I totally understand if you have reservations about getting involved with police work again. We don't want to take up a lot of your time and we *won't*." Casey reached over and gently touched Dolores' arm. "Could you just take a quick look at the two items we brought. Tell us if anything comes to mind. Anything at all. Then we'll be on our way and let you get back to your business."

Dolores leaned back in her chair and folded her hands on her lap. "This has to do with missing children again…Am I correct?"

Casey had not mentioned the details of the case to her on the phone but was not surprised at her premonition. "You are."

Trabinski studied the woman as she sat quietly looking down at her hands. *She's struggling to make a decision here. Something is making her edgy.*

Dolores looked up then closed her eyes. She took a deep breath and exhaled ever so slowly. "Show me," she said.

Casey pulled the transparent zippered pouch containing the pink blanket from her beach bag. As she held it out to Dolores the woman suddenly jumped up, knocking over her chair, and splashing tea on the table. Her hands flew to her mouth, covering it and her eyes went wide with a look of horror.

Trabinski, seeing her stagger immediately stood and grabbed her before she fell. He eased her back onto her chair.

Casey was also on her feet. "Dolores? Are you alright? What did you see?"

For a moment Trabinski and Talbot thought the woman had gone into shock. She sat staring wide eyed into space. Then when Casey took her hand, she blinked, and a tear ran down her cheek. With a shaking hand she pointed to the blanket. "*Please,* put that away."

Casey quickly placed the pouch back in her bag, a look of deep concern on her face.

Trabinski crouched down next to Dolores and spoke in a calm voice. "We weren't expecting a reaction like that Dolores. Sorry. We had no idea how intense this might be for you."

Casey poured more tea into Dolores' cup and handed it to her. "Do you think you can tell us what happened? No rush if you're not up to it."

Dolores drained her cup and placed it on the table with a trembling hand. "I felt it when you first came in. Not strong, just a glimpse. But that *blanket* wreaked with a powerful evil. Inhuman."

"You mean an animal?" Trabinski asked, returning to his chair. "A bird of prey perhaps?"

"No…not an animal."

Casey pulled her chair closer to Dolores. "Dolores? When you helped me find those abducted children years ago you saw where they had been taken. If we show you the other item we brought with us could you do the same thing? It would help us find *these* children as well as who is taking them."

"Just a quick look?" Trabinski prodded. "We're hoping to find a motive for these kidnappings."

Dolores gave a slow nod as she mentally prepared herself.

Trabinski pulled the yellow piece of cloth from the padded envelope and placed it on the table.

Dolores instantly caught her breath and looked away. She waved her hand for Trabinski to remove the cloth. "These children cannot be found," she said.

"What do you mean? Can't be found." Trabinski said.

Casey asked, "Why?"

Once again tears trickled down Dolores' face. "They're dead. Murdered."

Trabinski made a hissing sound like steam escaping from an old-fashioned radiator and ran his hand through his hair. "Any notion about a motive?"

"I sense hunger." Dolores wiped her eyes with a napkin from the tray.

Trabinski gawked at her. "Did you just say hunger?"

Dolores shivered as if the store had suddenly grown chilly. "They were *eaten*."

"Wait a minute. You said it wasn't an animal." Trabinski snapped.

"Not an animal we know."

"Dolores? I'm not good at riddles. What kind of an animal is it? A pterodactyl or something like that?" Trabinski needed a cigarette. He urgently searched his pockets and realized he had left the pack in the car. He folded his arms. "We're dealing with someone…or something capable of lifting a five-year-old boy into the air, carrying him a half mile then dropping him. Our researchers found evidence suggesting a large bird of prey. Now you're saying the two kids represented here, one an infant in fact, were eaten but not by a bird of prey. Then eaten by what? A cannibal?"

Dolores looked up at Trabinski. Her face like that of a stern school-marm. "I'm sorry Lieutenant. I did tell you this may be beyond my capabilities. What I feel is evil, dangerous, and not natural. That is all I can tell you."

Trabinski stood up and began to pace. "Well, we appreciate you giving it a try Dolores, but unfortunately it gets us nowhere. How are we supposed to identify something evil, dangerous and...*not natural?*"

"Perhaps by starting here." Dolores waved her hand indicating the many shelves filled with books.

Trabinski groaned.

Casey moved around the table and stood next to Trabinski. "Can you try to see the killer, Dolores? Maybe give us a location?" She could see the woman looked tired. "Just once more. Then we're through. I promise."

Dolores sighed and gave a slight nod.

Trabinski once again removed the item from the envelope and cautiously pushed the yellow cloth closer to her on the table.

Only the sound of the soft violin music playing from a hidden speaker somewhere in the store disturbed the silence as Dolores with eyes closed concentrated on the killer of the two children. After several minutes in that state, she opened her dark eyes and in a voice that was almost a whisper said, "I see only shadows of its being. It surrounds itself with trash, and what seems to be scraps of oddly shaped metal. There are glimpses of objects that may be derelict cars or trucks. I can't see clearly. It could be a junkyard."

"Rocco's," Trabinski and Talbot said in unison.

Dolores covered her face with both hands. She sat that way for a few minutes then dropped her hands onto her lap as if she had no strength to hold them up any longer. She sent a questioning look to Casey.

"Thank you, Dolores. You've given us something to work on. Sorry, this has been so exhausting for you. We'll leave now ... Give you some peace and quiet." Casey said.

"No!" Dolores cried. "You must search the books before you leave. In my vision the killer's shadow contained an odd shape. Thinking about it now...it could have been a wing. Search the books for winged creatures of lore."

"And...How will that help?" Trabinski said looking over his shoulder at the myriad of tomes behind him.

"Wait," Casey said rubbing the side of her nose. "Dolores? Are you suggesting this killer may be supernatural?"

Dolores shrugged. "There are many tales of mythical beasts crossing from their world into ours, creating mayhem."

"Children's stories," Trabinski said.

"Every legend has a basis in truth," Dolores answered.

"Next we'll be looking for the Loch Ness Monster," Trabinski scoffed.

"Doesn't have wings," Casey corrected.

Dolores stood shakily and moved away from the table toward the bookshelves behind the glass counter. "Come with me." She approached the center section and pulled over a step stool, stood for a moment calming herself then stepped up selecting a thick volume titled Mythical Beasts: Fact or Fiction.

Trabinski, with a doubtful expression on his face and hands in his pockets stood next to Casey and watched as Dolores placed the book on the counter and began flipping through the pages.

After what seemed like an eternity to Trabinski they had a list of winged, magical creatures: Basilisk, Dragon, Gargoyles, Griffin, Harpy, Pegasus, Phoenix, and Firebird.

Trabinski gave a sideways glance at Casey — who was looking intently at the list — then back to Dolores. "Okay. Let's say one of these things is the culprit…How do we go about finding it?"

Dolores looked up from the list and fixed her dark eyes on Trabinski. "*It* will find *you* lieutenant."

CHAPTER 26

Day Nine – Morning
The Bolton Residence

The loud jangling ring of the house phone shattered the early summer morning quiet of the Bolton home. Anna Bolton, who had been sitting at the kitchen table drinking coffee and glancing through a new issue of McCalls magazine, jumped, almost spilling her coffee. "Blast it!" She said as she stood and reached for the phone. "Hello?"

"Mrs. Bolton?" A man's voice said. "This is Larry Jessup from the Juvenile Community Service Department. Your son Stanley was supposed to be here first thing this morning to fulfil today's service requirement."

"Yes…I know *that*, and he knows *that*. He's not there?"

"No Mrs. Bolton. He hasn't shown. Did he leave the house this morning?"

Having spent an evening dealing with feelings of anger, self-doubt and sadness brought on by her oldest son leaving to join the Peace Corps, she had not paid any attention to this morning's activities. She heard her husband leave for work and had assumed Stanley had left too. She wasn't even sure of the whereabouts of her youngest son at this moment. Feeling a bit ashamed she said, "I'm not sure. I thought I heard him leave. Hold on …I'll check his room."

In a few long minutes she was back. "Mr. Jessup? His bedroom door is closed and locked. I think he may have overslept. I'll wake him and get him down to you right away."

She could hear the man clearing his throat on the other end. "Alright Mrs. Bolton, you do that, but remember the court has no tolerance for those who try to skip their service responsibilities. I won't write him up this time since it appears to be an honest oversight. Please make sure your son understands the circumstances if he fails to fulfill the court order."

Anna Bolton wanted to scream but controlled the tone of her voice. "I will," she said politely.

"Thank you, Mrs. Bolton. We'll see Stanley shortly. Have a nice day." Click.

Being a large woman Anna lumbered up the stairs again to her son's room, breathing heavily, she pounded on the bedroom door and rattled the doorknob. "*Stanley Francis Bolton!* You get your lazy rear end out of that bed right now and unlock this door. You hear me!"

She waited. No sound came from within the room. "Stanley! You're late for your community service. They just called. Get up now. I'll drive you down there. Let's go!"

Still no response. "Stanley! Wake up! I know you can hear me. Open this door. You can't avoid this. It will only make matters worse."

Anna knew Stanley could be as obstinate as a mule plus he had a penchant for defiance. Her face started to flush with anger at this thought and her reaction was immediate. She threw her weight against the door, cracking the jam. Lifting her pudgy hands she pushed hard, the door opened with a bang.

She strode into the room prepared to deliver a stern tongue lashing when she saw her son sitting in a straight chair with his head down. "Stanley?" She stepped around the chair accidentally kicking a bucket of water placed on the floor in front of him. She caught her breath when she saw his face. It, as well as his arms were gray. He was still wearing the same black T-shirt and dungarees he had on at dinner last night. His eyes were closed, and his arms hung limp at his sides. "Sweet Jesus," she said softly. "Stanley, what have you done?"

At that moment Stanley opened his eyes and struggled to lift his head. His mother quickly took his hands. They felt cold as death. His lips were dry and cracked. He forced his mouth to open and tried to speak but only a ragged, choking sound emerged.

The Bolton's family physician, Doctor Martin Wells, one of the few doctors who still made house calls these days, arrived at the Bolton residence within minutes of receiving Anna Bolton's frantic call. Fortunately, his office was close by on Plainview Road and his schedule had not yet taken command of his day. He was ushered into the house and up the stairs to Stanley's room. Anna Bolton right behind him. Jonathan Bolton, with an open Readers Digest in his hand suddenly appeared from somewhere and was instructed to remain below.

A look of deep concern overtook the Doctor's normally jovial expression when he came into the room and approached the boy seated in a straight-backed wooden chair. He immediately placed his black leather bag on the floor, opened it and removed a stethoscope. He stepped forward, gently lowered the blanket that had been placed over the boy by his mother — because he was so cold — lifted the rank t-shirt and touched the stethoscope to his chest listening to his patient's heart. He felt both sides of the boy's neck examining the glands. As he did this, he noticed slits on the shoulders of the t-shirt as if cut by a razor blade. Two in the front and one directly behind those on both shoulders. Each slice in the t-shirt fabric stuck to the wound and appeared to be caked with dried blood. He wondered if these wounds were the result of some drug experiment the teenager was conducting on himself.

"Mrs. Bolton, we need to get your son to the hospital immediately. He's extremely dehydrated." Doctor Wells straightened then dropped his stethoscope back into his bag. "I don't like his gray skin pallor. That's usually an indication of organ failure, kidneys possibly or a reaction to the use of some stimulant. Could be an infection or allergic reaction to something he ate? We won't know till we get him admitted. We need to move quickly. Where's your phone?" With that said Doctor Wells hurried from the room and down the stairs to call an ambulance.

Jonathan Bolton was still standing at the foot of the stairs silently watching and listening. He stepped back and gave the doctor a curious look as he rushed by him. He wondered if he was about to lose another brother.

***

Meanwhile, as Stanley Bolton was being rushed to Central General Hospital, Tim Ryan waited nervously in the office of his father's attorney William Maddox.

He sat in a comfortable high back, brown leather chair next to his father, who occupied an identical chair, across from a large mahogany desk. Tim picked at his fingernails as the lawyer behind the desk finished a phone conversation.

"Sorry to keep you waiting Carl. I had to take that call." The lawyer said to Tim's father as he hung up the phone. He took a cream-colored folder from the top of a neat stack at the corner of the desk and opened it. He adjusted his round wire framed glasses on his aquiline nose, read a page in silence then looked up at Tim.

"Looks like you have a knack for being in the right place at the wrong time, Tim. This police report…" He tapped the sheet in front of him. "…has you at the scene of two serious crimes involving young children as well as being a person of interest involving the death of a police officer's teenage son. I'm thinking this is all coincidence coupled with conjecture on the part of the police. But… Before I proceed as your attorney, I need to ask you some questions myself and you *must* answer them truthfully. Understand?"

Tim looked over at his father then back at the attorney. "Sure…I guess."

The first round of questions concerned the missing child at the playground and the lost bicycle boy from Kraemer Street. Tim had no problem answering those and the attorney seemed satisfied. The second round involved the murder of the bully, Danny Sanfield. "I didn't even know anything happened to him till the cops told me," Tim said to the lawyer. He answered this group of questions truthfully and with sincerity. Again, the attorney seemed satisfied. Tim's nervousness was subsiding. *This isn't so bad.*

The attorney looked at his watch and stroked his bushy mustache —which Tim thought looked absolutely silly on the man's face — with his index finger then turned over the page he had been writing on. The flip of that page sent the strong scent of aftershave in Tim's direction. It smelled like a household cleaner his mother used. He stifled a cough as the attorney said, "Alright Tim, just a few more and we can wrap this up."

This series of questions concerned the items found in his garage attic. Tim confidently breezed through them until it came to the one about the pink baby's blanket. The question, basically the same as the others, simply asked him if he knew *how* it got there. He felt himself getting tense and was about to give his pat "I have no idea" answer when his conscience reminded him, he *must* tell the truth or risk the consequences. *What exactly are those consequences?* The fact that he was hesitating brought questioning looks from the lawyer as well as his father. "The *truth, Tim*," his father said in a quiet but stern tone.

Tim looked down at his hands then slowly brought them up and started cracking his knuckles. A quirky thing he did when extremely nervous or scared.

William Maddox exchanged glances with Tim's father. "Tim? If you have information about this piece of evidence, you must reveal it. This is a police matter not some game. I can help you if you are involved somehow but only if you tell me truthfully what you know.

Tim straightened in the chair, focused his eyes on the object at the front edge of the desk; a wooden gavel affixed to a mahogany stand with a gold engraved nameplate featuring the attorney's name, and said, "Stanley brought it over."

Tim's father turned in his chair facing his son. "Stanley Bolton?"

"Yes, sir," Tim replied.

The attorney wrote the name on a legal sized yellow lined note pad. "Go on Tim. Please explain."

Dammit! I can't say anything about the harpy that Stanley said carried the blanket. They'll never believe it. Maybe just leave that part out?

"Stanley said he found the blanket and that there was a story that went with it. He wanted to know what I thought about it. He said he put it in the garage for me to look at until he was able to talk to me, but I never saw it till the police showed it to me."

"Why didn't you say something then son?" his father asked.

"I don't know. I guess I didn't want to get him in trouble."

Writing again the attorney asked, "What was the story?"

"Don't know," Tim lied. "He never got around to telling me."

The attorney looked directly into Tim's eyes. "Anything else, Tim?"

Tim looked up at the office ceiling as if trying to remember something then said, "I don't think so."

"Where does this Stanley Bolton live?"

Tim's father answered immediately. "Just across the street from us." He gave the address.

More writing then William Maddox closed the folder and addressed Tim's father. "Carl? I'm confident I can keep the police off Tim's back, but I will have to divulge this information to the police immediately. And Tim, you're not required to talk to anyone about this except for your parents and me of course. Understand?"

Tim nodded.

After escorting Tim and his father from his office William Maddox opened the Ryan folder again, scanned it quickly, found what he was looking for then called his secretary via the intercom. "Valerie? Please put a call through to a Lieutenant Cassandra Talbot at the 2nd Precinct in Woodbury for me. Thanks."

CHAPTER 27

Day Nine- Late evening

A dense fog, like a warm wet blanket draped itself over Hillsville and the surrounding area. The young teenage couple sitting on a bus stop bench at the corner of Old Country Road and South Oyster Bay, didn't seem to mind. The lone streetlight shed its gauzy light down on the boy and girl as they made out, hands exploring each other and giggling. No doubt the bus they waited for would be late. They were in no hurry to get home. The girl, sixteen, sat sideways next to the boy with her left leg positioned over his lap. She sighed as he gently ran his hand up her thigh and under the hem of her shorts while kissing her neck. Suddenly, she pulled away. "Did you hear something?" She said returning to a proper sitting position with her knees together and feet flat on the pavement.

The boy chuckled. "Only you breathing."

They both sat listening, not saying a word. Only the choir of crickets and katydids disturbed the quiet.

"I'm not taking you to anymore of those horror movies," he said.

They had just come from a double feature: *The Terror* starring Boris Karloff and *The Blanchville Monster.*

They both laughed but the girl had a look of uncertainty on her face.

The boy put his arm around her, pulled her close and returned to kissing her neck while his hand casually slipped under her loose-fitting top.

"Tommy...*stop*. I'm too nervous now," she said gently pushing him away.

"C'mon Laurie. Lighten up," he pleaded. "There's nobody here."

The girl leaned forward and peered up the murky street. "What if the bus comes?"

Then a metallic ping caught both their attention. It sounded like someone had tapped a coin or a ring against a metal pipe. They both looked up at the steel stanchion holding the streetlight, but the lamp's glare prevented them from seeing anything. They both stood when the ping sounded again, only this time it was a quick ping, ping as if the source were moving. The girl turned to her left, the boy to the right. A gust of wind followed by a whooshing sound swept over them bringing Laurie and Tommy's evening to a bloody end.

***

Malhela, distraught over the information she had extracted from Stanley, especially the news that even Tim Ryan would be of no help, felt gutted and empty. The thought of returning home to the Realm seemed impossible now. She decided the rules and codes of the Realm no longer applied and she would do what needed to be done. It now came down to not being captured. Imprisonment for an immortal was a long, long time. She was truly lost. Betrayed by the tomfoolery of two adolescent mortals. Her body ached for vengeance, retribution. Any mortal would do.

On top of this, she desperately needed real sustenance to keep up her strength. She would no longer consume the flesh of the foul-tasting, bushy tailed rodents that inhabited the trees.

The dark of night had become her only friend. Her ability to blend in with her surroundings had diminished greatly, forcing her to abandon the daylight hours. Tonight, her prowling would be assisted by a thick fog that had crawled in from the south.

Driven by her malignant feelings as well as hunger, Malhela dove from her metallic nest into the mist.

As fate would have it, she soon came upon two adolescent mortals entwined on a wooden bench under a clouded streetlight. She silently glided to the thick metal arm that held the lamp and landed. Her talons clinked against the surface. She assumed a crouching position and watched the couple below.

One, was a young birthgiver, small in stature, but healthy in appearance, the other a strong looking male. Knowing this to be an indiscretion on her part, she decided to take the girl despite her birthgiver status. She had never tasted the meat of a female. She imagined it to be sweet. The male was of little value.

Malhela sized up the female. *She might be light enough to carry to the nest if handled correctly.* With that thought in mind Malhela leapt from her perch and swooped down on the unsuspecting couple. In a blur she broke the male's neck and slit the female's throat.

Before attempting to carry her prize to the nest she wanted to make sure it would be worth it, so she dragged the birthgiver away from the light, further into the dark fog and took a small bite from the thigh. An involuntary groan of delight escaped from her bloody lips. The taste was wonderful. Not as good as a newborn but many times better than that of a male. *Maybe the old realm code forbidding us to take sustenance from a birthgiver was a ruse? In the realm being honorable was not a law.* She took another mouthful, savoring the taste before swallowing.

This valuable parcel could keep her nourished and strong for many days to come if she could get it to the nest.

Malhela picked the girl up and discovered she had the strength to carry her. A power seemed to course unexpectedly through her body. Pleased but puzzled by this sudden energy she adjusted the body in her arms to a more comfortable position, took a running start and sprung with her bounty skyward.

No sooner had she taken flight when the yellow headlight beams from the long overdue bus cut through the haze, spotlighting a twisted shape on the street.

Once, inside her nest Malhela discarded the birthgiver's garments and took her fill.

Fully sated she sprawled out and wrapped her wings around her, welcoming the night mist as it entered the aerie caressing her outstretched body. Her frantic mind started to calm, allowing her to contemplate what the future may hold. Would her desperation get to a point where she would break down and summon the Lord of the Realm for help, knowing full well it would not be a joyous reunion? Or, would she carry on with this existence until the last of her magic disappeared, making her just another unwelcome creature of the night, disposing of mortals till finally subdued?

She propped herself up on one elbow and rested her head on the palm of her hand. There was something else crawling around in the back of her mind; an idea she couldn't quite catch. She closed her eyes and replayed past events in her mind, names and places. Instantaneously, the elusive idea came forward. It involved Tim Ryan. His ability to communicate with her was the stronger of the two conjurers. She had already responded to one of his commands by doing away with that brute that tormented him. She knew it had not fulfilled the spells requirement because she was still here. Had she overreacted? Maybe it wasn't an actual request? She recalled being slightly intoxicated by his scent. Maybe that was the reason for her compliance? Whatever it was, there existed the possibility that she could seduce him into making a serious command. One strong enough to release her from this ordeal. She liked this idea. It gave her a bit of hope.

Now she had to figure out a way to get to him.

***

Casey Talbot stood in her apartment looking out her bedroom window hoping Jim Trabinski got home safe in this awful fog. It had been a long tiring drive back from East Hampton and she had been tempted to ask him to stay. The day with him—aside from the disturbing visit with Dolores Florentine— had been enjoyable, the conversations were easy and honest, and the overall atmosphere had a positive feel. In short — though she didn't want to admit it — she felt comfortable being with him. But in the end, she thought it was better *not* to ask him. Things could get complicated real fast. "He'll be fine," she said to her reflection in the window glass.

She closed the bedroom blinds, undressed, showered, slipped into a cool nightgown, and picked out her clothes for tomorrow. With these tasks completed she walked over to her large oak, two drawer night-stand — a gift from her oldest brother — sitting caddy-cornered at the corner of the room opposite the window and checked the new Record-O-Phone answering machine that she had charmed her captain into procuring for her. It occupied the entire top of the nightstand. The indi-cator showed she had one new message. Turning the chrome selector knob to *play message* a male voice, tinny and a bit scratchy immedi-ately came on. "Hi Lieutenant, Les Fuller here at the precinct. We got a call from a lawyer named Maddox who's representing someone named Tim Ryan. Says to let you know right away that a kid named Stanley Bolton is connected to a piece of evidence you're concerned with. He said you can call if you have questions. The number is WE5-2468. So, I hope your new-fangled machine there delivers the message in good order. Over and out…Fuller."

Stanley Bolton? Who's this now? She glanced over at her bag sitting by the closet door that contained the blanket. *So, Jim was right. Tim Ryan was not being truthful about the blanket. This Stanley Bolton must be a friend and the Ryan kid didn't want to squeal on him.* She wrote down the lawyer's number then eased her feet into her comfortable slippers and shuffled into the kitchen to make chamomile tea. *This Ryan kid is like a bad penny. The feeling that he…and now this boy Bolton are connected to these crimes is stronger. The question still remains…How?*

The tea kettle whistled. She poured the boiling water over the tea bag waiting in a pink ceramic mug and sat at the table watching it steep. The fragrant steam drifted to her nose. She closed her eyes and inhaled the delightful flowery scent. *It's the little things…*

As she stirred a teaspoon of honey into the beverage her mind wandered back to Madame Florentine and two particular, puzzling things she had said. *What did she mean, "It will find you?" She didn't actually answer my question about a supernatural connection… just presented us with a list of mythical creatures. Where was she going with that? Was that her answer to the bird of prey theory? Sorry Dolores… I can't buy it.*

Casey took a sip of tea. *Perhaps it wasn't such a good idea to go see her? But then there was her vision of what could have been a junk yard and the shadowy shape that was hiding there. Did she really pick that up from the yellow piece of cloth or did she just read us? The situation at Rocco's was still fresh in our heads. Well, it won't hurt to pay another visit. Maybe we missed something?*

She felt the calming effects of the tea kicking in. *Maybe…?* She gently rubbed the side of her nose. *Maybe she meant it will find you at the junkyard? No, too easy.*

***

Lieutenant James Trabinksi gave a sigh of relief as he pulled into his fog shrouded driveway. It was a treacherous night to be on the highway. He could barely see the front of his house. As he reached behind him to collect the padded evidence envelope containing the yellow cloth, his police scan radio came to life. He had turned it back on after dropping Casey at her apartment. It announced a code 10-57, possible hit and run with a fatality at the corner of South Oyster Bay Road and Old Country. *I knew I should've left it turned off.*

Technically, he was off duty, but the location of the incident was close. *Better check this out. It will nag me all night if I don't... plus this could turn out to be a real snafu with this fog.*

He lit a cigarette, and slowly backed the Galaxie out of the driveway. He hit the siren when he turned onto Plainview Road and drove as fast as the fog permitted to the scene.

Hancock and Stevens, working the graveyard shift, were already at the scene. The flashing lights of their cruiser resembled haloed fairy lights in the clinging vapor. The ghostly shape of the idling bus loomed over a body lying in the road. Fog swirled in the headlight beams giving them the appearance of smoking heat rays, like those of the Martian war machines in *War of the Worlds,* directed at the broken human in their path.

The two officers, talking to the bus driver, were not surprised when they saw Trabinski pull up. "Hell of a night to be out Lieutenant," Hancock said.

"What? You don't like pea soup Ed?" Trabinski said stepping over to the body that Hancock had covered with a blanket from the patrol car. "What've we got?"

Hancock filled him in. "Bus driver found him laying right there. He thought the kid had been hit by a car. It's possible he had been hit on the sidewalk and dragged by the looks of the blood trail."

"But…," Jake Stevens interrupted. "The blood is only on the sidewalk and there's no blood in the street or on the body. So, I'm not sure that idea works."

Trabinski examined the swath of blood, following it into the smothering mist to where it abruptly ended. As he doubled back, he noticed a spray of blood across the bus stop bench. *Stay off the moors at night,* popped into his head. "This is no hit and run gentlemen. See this?" He pointed to the bloodied bench. "Know what it is?"

The two officers stepped up for a closer look. "Christ…another killing," Hancock said.

Stevens leaned in. "Somebody got their throat slit tonight and it sure wasn't the kid in the street."

Trabinski nodded. "And …I've got an awful feeling that *somebody* was a teenage girl."

Hancock stepped away from the bench. "What makes you say that lieutenant?"

Trabinski pointed at the rear leg of the wooden bench. "*That…*," he said.

There, on the ground leaning up against the rear leg was a purple jeweled handbag spattered with blood. The strap broken. "You call Forensics?"

"On their way, but it will take a while in this slop." Stevens said.

"Yep," Trabinski said. "Jake? Get back on the pipe and tell them this is dog worthy. Tell them it's a code 2. That girl was murdered then dragged away. We'll see if we can ID her and the boy when Forensics gets here."

"Right," Stevens said and headed to their cruiser.

Trabinski went over to the bus driver who was seated on the bus doorsteps holding his hat. "Sorry to hold you up like this. Once our forensics team gets here, we can let you go." He turned to go but stopped. "What's your name sir?"

"Bud Thompson," the driver answered.

"Bud? Were you traveling north on South Oyster Bay when you made this stop?"

"Yes, sir."

"This may seem like a ridiculous question…but did you see anything, anything at all as you approached the corner."

"No sir. I was crawling along, trying to keep my bus on the road. I was lucky I saw the boy when I did. I could've run him over."

Trabinski thanked the man and strode over to the covered body. Hancock standing by. "You do a preliminary on the body Ed? Probable cause?"

Hancock folded his arms. "Remember the cause of death for that five-year-old boy we found in the Cherry Street woods?"

Trabinski looked at his man. "I do. Broken neck."

Hancock pointed to the body. "Same thing."

Trabinski stuck a cigarette in his mouth, pulled his lighter from his pants pocket and lit it. He heard the fog muted wail of the forensics siren in the distance as it slowly approached from the north. But his mind had inadvertently taken him to Rocco's junkyard.

CHAPTER 28

Day Ten – Morning

Anna Bolton had just returned from dropping off her son Jonathan at a cousin's and was trying to make herself presentable before visiting Stanley in the hospital when she heard a knock at the front door. She was going to ignore it but when the wrapping came again, she went to the front window and peered out through the open blinds.

A very attractive young woman with dark red hair, wearing a tan suit and a light blue open neck blouse with a small collar, accessorized with a small Coach shoulder bag, stood on the front steps with her hands behind her back looking around. *What's she selling? Probably cosmetics by the look of her. I don't have time for this.*

"I don't need whatever it is you're selling," Anna said loudly through the closed door.

"Nassau County Police, ma'am. Please open the door.

Momentarily dumbfounded by the reply, Anna realized what this was about. Her blood pressure began to rise as she yanked open the front door. The red-haired woman held up her gold badge.

"If this is about Stanley missing Community Service," she snapped. "I already called and explained. You people need to do a better job of talking to each other."

"I'm Detective Talbot. I'm not here about community service ma'am. Is your son Stanley at home?"

"What's this about then?" Anna said with a lot less bluster.

The policewoman tucked her badge back into her skirt pocket. "I need to ask him some questions about his involvement in a case I'm working on. Is he here?"

"No. He's in the hospital. I'm going there now."

The detective looked surprised.

"I'm sorry to hear that. What happened?"

"We don't know. The doctors think it's some kind of infection," Anna said.

"I won't hold you up then. I can talk to him when he recovers. Thanks for your time." The detective turned to leave but stopped and looked over her shoulder. "If you don't mind my asking, what hospital is he in?"

When the Bolton woman gave Casey the name of the hospital, she thought *Central General Hospital? Not far. I think I'll make a stop there myself.*

She stood by her car watching the haggard looking Bolton woman drive away. *Not a happy woman...*

Casey pulled her car keys from her purse, stepped off the curb and was about to open the driver's side door when she noticed Tim Ryan across the street standing in his driveway holding his bike, watching her. He started to turn away when he realized she had seen him, so she hurried across the street to corral him.

"Tim? Wait...I need to talk to you."

"I don't have to talk to you," Tim said maneuvering his bike toward the back of his house.

Casey quickly stepped in front of him blocking his way. She quickly scanned the area to see if they were alone. She noticed the side kitchen window of the Ryan house was open. So, she took a step closer to the boy and in a hushed voice said, "I know, I know. We'll keep this conversation just between us. What do you say?" She flashed him her most beguiling smile and waited as his eyes surreptitiously checked her out. *They're all the same regardless of age.* When she saw him blush, she knew she had him.

"Tim? Is Stanley Bolton your friend?"

"Sort of...," he looked down as he spoke.

"Tim? Look at me. I spoke with your attorney today. He told me that Stanley Bolton gave you the blanket. So, it doesn't make me happy that you lied to me as well as Lieutenant Trabinski when we asked if you knew anything about it. But I understand. Nobody likes a squealer."

"Uh huh," Tim agreed.

"It's very important to me that I know where Stanley got that blanket. Did he tell you how he came to have it? Remember this is just between you and me."

Casey saw the reluctance in his eyes. "Did you know that Stanley's in the hospital?"

His wide-eyed look of surprise answered her question. "Tim? You and your friend can help me catch a killer. Tell me what you know."

"You won't believe me if I tell you." Tim shifted from one foot to the other.

Casey leaned forward and flashed the smile again. "Try me."

She listened closely as Tim quickly recounted the story about a stupid incantation from a book Stanley had purchased and the supposed appearance of this creature called a harpy in his room. Stanley claimed the creature left the blanket. He said the blanket smelled like the creature. The same awful smell that gagged them in the playground maze when they helped look for the missing boy.

Casey was familiar with the blanket's fetor.

"So, have you seen this, this…harpy?" Casey asked.

"No," Tim answered. "Only in pictures."

"Do you believe him? Sounds a bit farfetched to me." Casey said but her mind was stuck on the word *harpy.*

"I'm not sure. Stanley can be full of it sometimes."

"Thank you, Tim. You've been a big help." Casey put her finger to her lips then said. "We didn't have this talk." She patted Tim on the shoulder and was headed back to her car when he asked, "Do you believe it?"

She turned her head towards him. "I'm not sure."

Back in her car Casey's mind immediately transported her back to Madame Florentine's store and the list of names representing flying mystical beasts. The name Harpy was on that list. *It will find you. A shadowy winged shape. Bird of prey. And now the name harpy comes out of Tim Ryan's mouth. A supernatural killer? Maybe I need to read up on these Harpies? Figure out what we're dealing with. Why am I even considering this? I must be losing my mind. But first things, first...the hospital.*

Earlier, she had radioed into the 8th Precinct and left a message for Trabinski, filling him in on the conversation with Tim Ryan's attorney and advising him she was on her way to interview the Bolton boy at his home. Now, she wondered if she should call him again with this latest information. For some reason she needed to talk to him, hear his voice. Her gray eyes looked back at her from the rear-view mirror. *Snap out of it, Casey. Don't make a fool of yourself.*

She started the car and drove off towards the hospital.

Inside Central General Hospital Casey presented her credentials at the nurse's station and inquired about Stanley Bolton.

The nurse, an older woman with bleach blonde hair and a stern expression handed Casey a paper to sign. "He's still in Intensive Care, Lieutenant. You'll have to wait if you want to see him. One visitor at a time. His mother is in there now."

Casey nodded. "Understood." She noted the name J.Simmons R.N. engraved in white on a black plastic badge pinned to the woman's uniform.

The nurse took the document from Casey. "It's none of my business but you may be wasting your time."

"How's that?" Casey gave the woman her own stern look.

"The boy can't speak. Can't form words. He just makes croaking, rattling sounds. It's almost like he had a stroke." When the nurse saw Casey frowning at her she quickly added, "Forget I said that. I'm not supposed to give out that kind of information."

Casey ignored that last bit. "Alright, I'll speak to the attending physician then. Please have him paged. It's important. Thanks."

With a huff Nurse Simmons grudgingly obliged.

A few moments later Casey heard a man's voice come from behind her. "May I help you?"

Casey quickly turned. A handsome man in his late fifties with a full head of snow-white hair and a friendly face, dressed in a charcoal pin striped suit stood before her. A stethoscope dangling from his neck. "I'm Doctor Wells. What can I do for you?"

Casey introduced herself and shook his proffered hand. "I won't take much of your time Doctor. What can you tell me about Stanley Bolton's condition? He may have important information on a case I'm working on. I need to ask him a few questions."

The doctor removed the stethoscope from his neck and stuffed it in his jacket pocket. "At this point Lieutenant, I don't know when that will be possible. We're running several tests to determine exactly what is causing his condition. He appeared to be dangerously dehydrated when I examined him at his home. *That* is being remedied as we speak. However, this infection, if it turns out to be that, has severely damaged his vocal cords. I hate to say it, but he may never be able to speak again. Hopefully, he will regain strength in his arms and legs. When I first examined him, they were limp as if the bones had been removed."

Casey gently rubbed the side of her nose. "What kind of infection can do that?"

"To be honest…we don't know. We suspect that whatever it is, came from the lacerations on the boy's shoulders."

"Lacerations?"

The doctor looked at his watch. "There are three lacerations. Two in the front and one in the back directly behind those in the front. Both shoulders have these. They are deep crescent shape cuts with slightly ragged edges. We're trying to determine the cause. At first glance we thought, it might be from sharp fingernails but now we're not certain." He looked at his watch again. "I really must continue my rounds, Lieutenant. That's about all I can tell you. Please excuse me."

Fingernails? Casey held up her hand to prevent the doctor from leaving. "Doctor? Were those lacerations tested for Alpha Keratin?"

Doctor Wells removed his stethoscope from his jacket pocket and gave Casey a patronizing look. "Lieutenant? We're running every test possible to determine what this infection is. It takes time. Now, if you don't mind, I must be going. I have patients waiting."

"Thank you, Doctor." She handed him her business card. "Please call me if you think of anything else."

The doctor took the card, gave a quick nod, and hurried away.

Casey removed her suit jacket and slid into the front seat of her Plymouth Fury and rolled down her side window. *Lacerations and fingernails? Sounds familiar. Okay. What do we have?*

She turned the ignition key and the V8 roared to life. *The policeman's son…multiple lacerations, throat cut, evidence of keratin…Fingernails. The young boy found in the woods…lacerations…no, these were puncture wounds on his shoulders…evidence of keratin but not thought to be fingernails. This gave birth to the bird of prey theory. And now we have a paralyzed Stanley Bolton with shoulder lacerations, possibly caused by fingernails. I don't like where this is going. I can't believe where this is going. And… Tim Ryan's little tale is not helping.*

She pulled out of the hospital parking lot and headed to the Hillsville Public Library.

***

Detective Peter Taylor, early as usual, took Lieutenant Talbot's call. He had written the message down and placed it on Jim Trabinski's desk. He planned to have a little fun with his boss about spending an entire day with the sexy lieutenant from the 2nd Precinct but ditched the idea when Trabinski walked in looking exhausted and pissed off. The man, unshaven, wearing a tan short sleeved shirt — that looked like he had slept in it — no tie and casual looking khaki slacks went straight to the coffee pot and poured a cup.

"Rough night Jim?" Taylor asked.

"You hear about the hit and run last night?" Trabinski asked stirring sugar into his cup of steaming java.

Taylor swiveled his chair to face his boss. "I did. Figured it was Traffic's problem so paid little attention to it."

Trabinski sampled his coffee. "It's our problem now. It wasn't a hit and run. Two teenagers were murdered. A sixteen-year-old boy, identified by working papers in his pocket, Thomas Reinhardt and his girlfriend Laura Decker whose bloodied purse contained her high school ID. Her body is missing. The blood trail we found indicated she had been dragged from the scene. A bus stop bench was also sprayed with blood which could have only come from a severed jugular. The boy's body was found in the street. His neck broken. We had the dogs out

222

all night looking for her but found nothing. The girl's parents called the night desk when she didn't come home last night from a movie date with the Reinhardt boy. What the hell am I going to tell them?"

"Shit...Do you think we've got a serial killer on our hands?" Taylor asked.

Trabinski put his cup down on the counter, pulled a crumpled pack of Camels from his shirt pocket, extracted the lone cigarette, and lit it. "If we count Rocco Espesito, we now have three victims with broken necks. And of course, Danny Sanfield, whose throat was cut. I'd say you're not far off on that Pete."

He took a drag on the cigarette, picked up his coffee and started for his office.

"Message on your desk from Lieutenant Talbot. She called this morning. Involves that Ryan kid again." Taylor said.

"Okay...thanks." Before entering his office, he stopped as if he just remembered something. "Pete? Get a hold of Todd Anderson over at the K-9 squad, will you? See if he can meet us at Rocco's Auto Wreckers this afternoon. He was off last night so he should be available. Thanks."

Trabinski entered his office and picked up the note. Without bidding, the image of Casey Talbot in her movie star outfit yesterday appeared in his mind's eye. As tired as he was a smile still managed to force its way onto his face. He flopped into his chair and read:

Tip from Tim Ryan's lawyer. His client did know where the blanket came from. You were right about him lying. He fingered a kid named Stanley Bolton who supposedly had the blanket first.

Going to interview him now. Catch up with you later.

He placed the note by his phone, sat back in his chair and ran both hands through his unruly dark hair. *Who the hell is Stanley Bolton? And why is the Ryan kid covering for him?*

Pete Taylor knocked on Trabinski's door and stuck his head in. "Anderson's working graveyard tonight. Mid to eight. Still want him there?"

"Yes, tell him to do a sweep with Leo. I swear that dog is smarter than a human. See if he can scare anything out of the shadows. Meanwhile you and I will pay a visit this afternoon. Do a casual walk through."

"Something troubling you, Jim? We've been all over that place. What are we looking for?"

Trabinski drank the rest of his coffee. "I don't know…but somebody told me it will find us."

Detective Pete Taylor had known Jim Trabinski a long time. Riddles never had a place in his detective toolbox. He straightened from his leaning position on Trabinski's office door frame and crossed his arms. Squinting his eyes at his boss he asked, "*It?*"

CHAPTER 29

Day Ten – Afternoon

Lieutenant Casey Talbot, delayed on her way to the public library by construction traffic on Broadway, stopped at Schlosser's Deli to accommodate her rumbling stomach. She ordered a tuna salad sandwich on whole wheat, a cup of rice pudding and a cold bottle of Yoohoo from the deli refrigerated glass case. *Yoohoo was made to go with rice pudding.* As she paid for her lunch the tall athletic looking young man of about eighteen or nineteen, behind the counter flirted with her, trying to chat her up. With a bemused smile Casey thanked the boy and returned to her car. *Thirty years old and still got it…*

In a quiet, secluded corner at the rear of the Hillsville Public Library, Casey selected a large golden oak table with four matching chairs to do her research. She unwrapped her lunch, took a bite of sandwich and started perusing the six books the librarian had been kind enough to provide for her: The Mythology Book, Mythical Creatures and Magical Beasts, Mythological Creatures: A Pictorial Dictionary, Encyclopedia of Beasts and Monsters in Myth, Legend and Folklore,

Mythical and Fabulous Creatures: A Source Book and Research Guide, Compendium of Magical Beasts.

The librarian offered to bring more if these were not enough.

What exactly am I hoping to find here? She paged through the first book. *This is all the stuff of imagination. There are no facts.* After taking a gulp of Yoohoo she pulled the next volume from the stack and flipped it open. Finding a section dedicated to the creature known as Harpy, she studied the pictures and began to read. An involuntary smirk appeared on her face. *This is the stuff of a **male** imagination. Naked women with wings of all sizes and shapes. Brother...guess these guys had nothing better to do with their time. Oh, and look at this. They have even listed the personality traits of these things.* She pulled a pen and a small pad from her purse and began to note the traits. Harvester, Gatherer, Thief, Wanderer, A Seer, or Prophet. They have chameleon like abilities. They are known to be vicious, mischievous, spiteful, impatient as well as unpredictable. Some require payment for services rendered. All are immortal. All have magical powers.

Casey put down her pen and took another bite of her lunch. *Useless information. Flying immortal prostitutes with magical powers? Nonsense.* But she still underlined the words "gatherer and thief. Pushing that book aside she picked up the third publication in the stack. Before opening this one she sat back, finished her sandwich, took a sip of Yoohoo, and pulled the cardboard top off of the rice pudding container. Using the plastic spoon supplied by the Deli she scooped a small portion of the dessert and quickly took a taste. *You eat too fast,* her mind said. With the spoon still in her mouth she perused the book in front of her. *This is a waste of time. I think I'm done here.* She was about to close the book when a picture caught her eye. It was a black and white illustration depicting a trio of Harpies grabbing babies from the arms of screaming, crying mothers in some medieval setting. One creature was shown biting into the infant's chubby leg.

A sudden tingling crawled up her neck like a small electrical charge. The plastic spoon fell from her mouth. "No," she whispered. Casey immediately saw the pink blanket in her mind's eye. The upstairs room where the infant slept, the cut screen and the scratch marks on the windowsill all were there like a vivid color photograph. *You don't believe in coincidences…Remember? So, it must be true.* She gently rubbed the side of her nose. *It all fits, but no one will believe it. Hell, I don't believe it. They'll slap a Section eight on me for sure. I have to tell Jim. Dolores may have been right. Tim Ryan said they may have conjured up this thing. I wonder if Dolores has any insights on that subject?*

***

Lead Detective Lieutenant James Trabinski and his partner Detective Peter Taylor arrived at Rocco's Auto Wreckers and Junk Emporium around 3 pm. The junk yard had not reopened after Rocco's death due to legal difficulties regarding which nephew or cousin would take it over. Not a problem. Trabinski had a key to the newly installed Masterworks lock and chain.

The partly sunny afternoon painted shadows everywhere in the yard. Some stemming from the base of randomly stacked mountains of flattened metal appeared as mysterious threatening beasts. Others appeared as strange, black, featureless, one-dimensional buildings lying flat on the ground. The pungent fishy smell of old tires mixed with the cloying odor of motor oil, drifted through the premises. Only the sound of two men's footsteps crunching across the hard packed dirt disturbed the quiet of this automotive graveyard.

Trabinski and Taylor stood at the spot where Rocco's body had been found. "I feel like I'm in one of those Twilight Zone episodes," Trabinski said. "Ever watch that show?" He asked Taylor.

"I've seen a few. I can only watch it after my wife goes to bed. She said it gives her the creeps. Ever see the one where these monks have this howling guy in a cell held closed by a wooden staff and this sales-man or lost traveler, whatever he was, lets him out only to discover it was the devil he released?"

"Missed that one. Sounds like it could explain a lot of things. Feels like the Ole Boy is playing his nasty games with us this past week." Trabinski strode through a valley of debris, his head turning one way then another searching for anything that might have been missed before. The memory of Madame Florentine's so-called vision of what *could be* a junkyard compelled him to make this visit.

Pete Taylor kicked a rusted hub cap out of his path. "Tell me why we're here again."

Trabinski kept moving. "I don't know. Just a feeling."

"Does this have anything to do with that psychic you went to see yesterday. You haven't told me yet how that turned out."

Trabinski patted his shirt pocket then his trousers as he walked. "Damn…You got a smoke, Pete? Left mine in the car."

"Winstons," Pete answered as he reached in his sport jacket — he always wore a sports jacket regardless of the warm weather — for the pack.

"In a pinch." Trabinski reached over as Pete tapped one out. "The trip yesterday may have been a waste of time. I say that because the woman gave us nothing really concrete."

"Con artist," Pete said.

Trabinski strode over to a rusted derelict of a Ford panel truck; its rear doors hanging open. He looked in the front seat then did the same at the rear doors. "I don't know if you could call her that. She's not one of those who advertises her psychic abilities. There was nothing in her store to indicate that at all." He took a drag on the Winston and scowled in disgust.

"So? Was she the real deal?" Pete coaxed.

"Casey thinks she is."

Taylor shot him a puzzled look. "Casey?"

"Lieutenant Talbot," Trabinski said, a little embarrassed at his slip of the tongue.

"Oohh…" Taylor said with a smirk and a wink.

"Knock it off…wise guy."

"Yes sir, if you say so…" Taylor couldn't prevent the grin that popped onto his face. "So, this woman didn't seem authentic. Was that it?"

Trabinski looked up at a pyramid of hub caps in various sizes and wondered how they remained in place. "Well, her reaction to the evidence we presented her was authentic. It was a great act if it wasn't. At one point we thought she was going to pass out after having just announced that the two missing children we're searching for were dead. Eaten by something."

"Oh brother. Sounds like a nut job to me."

"I know what you mean, but along with that she claimed to have a vision of a place that sure sounded like a junkyard by her description." Trabinski took a last drag on the Winston then tossed it. "That little tidbit has been banging around in my head since I got back."

"Okay," Taylor said. "That explains why you feel you should be here. But what is this *it* that's supposed to find us?"

James Trabinski toyed with the idea of telling his partner about the bird of prey theory and the supernatural slant the psychic put on it but decided it might not be a good idea. *They'll have a padded cell waiting for me in Bellevue for sure if they think I'm running with that idea.*

"Could be a figure of speech. I don't know. *It* could be anything we might have missed, and it doesn't necessarily have to be here in this place. In the meantime, let's eyeball as much as we can now. If we don't have a sudden revelation, then Todd and Leo will do one final sweep tonight."

***

Tim Ryan delivered his newspapers in a daze. So dumbfounded by the news that Stanley had been hospitalized he didn't even notice when a twenty something blonde in a skimpy pink negligee opened her door and took the paper from him. He didn't want to think about why his friend was there. Even if it was something ordinary, like a broken arm or something, he was afraid. Afraid that the pictures his imagination was sending would turn out to be real. Afraid that the harpy had done something to Stanley and maybe he was next.

Maybe I should talk to that policewoman again about this? No…she'll think I'm cracked. This is not good. I've got to find out what happened to

Stanley before I do anything else. Maybe his dopey little brother Jonathan would tell me?

With a new purpose Tim sped up his deliveries.

***

In Central General Hospital the nutrients: vitamins, proteins, and minerals along with saline plus the antibiotics being administered intravenously to Stanley Bolton were doing their job. Sensation had returned to his right arm. He could now move it gingerly and was able to lift a spoonful of jello to his mouth. The gray pallor was receding from his face and his eyes had more sparkle. His left arm as well as his legs remained numb but Doctor Wells, pleased with Stanley's progress so far, authorized his transfer from intensive care to a single, personal care room. He told Stanley's mother to plan on him being in the hospital for at least a week. The prognosis of Stanley's voice ever returning remained poor.

CHAPTER 30

Day Ten – Evening

Casey Talbot had tracked Trabinski to Rocco's Auto Wreckers. It would be hours yet before sunset, but the gloom of evening had started to swallow up what was left of sunlight. She pulled into the dirt parking lot and stopped next to his dusty Ford Galaxie and got out of her car. Feeling that she wasn't dressed for traipsing through dirt and rubble she decided to wait.

Leaning against her car's front fender she scanned the outer perimeter of the premises. She marveled that the old faded, splintered wooden fence that surrounded the place was still standing, let alone capable of keeping out intruders. Her gaze took her to the front gate which stood open at an angle. She knew exactly why Trabinski was here. *Dolores' junkyard vision. I hope what I have to tell him makes sense.* She heard voices approaching and straightened. Without thinking she combed her thick hair with the fingertips of her right hand. She folded her arms across her chest watching as two men came through the gate and locked it. Trabinski and Taylor.

Casey frowned when she saw Trabinski. *He looks totally beat. This may not be a good time to present more of this crazy stuff.*

James Trabinski came to an abrupt halt when he saw Casey standing there. *Why am I not surprised?* He chuckled quietly to himself. *She is a sight for sore eyes though.*

Pete Taylor almost ran into him but smiled when he saw why his partner had suddenly stopped. He immediately wiped the smile from his face when he caught Trabinski looking at him.

Casey stepped forward and greeted them. "Lieutenant… Detective."

Both men returned the greeting in unison. "Lieutenant."

"I'll be in the car," Taylor said and quickly moved away.

Trabinski in that instant felt self-conscious about his appearance. He hoped he didn't smell too bad and almost cringed when Casey stepped closer to him.

"Didn't you sleep when you got home last night?" She asked.

Trabinski rubbed the small of his back. "I don't remember."

"You don't remember?" Casey asked with a touch of sarcasm. "You look terrible."

"Gee…Thanks," Trabinski replied. Then, turning serious, he told her about the murdered teenagers. "The kid had a broken neck. We couldn't find the girl's body, but we suspect her throat was cut based on the amount of blood we found. Sound familiar?"

Casey, with her hands on her hips turned away and Trabinski thought she was going to leave but she looked back at him with concerned eyes. "Jim? I have another idea about these crimes and if I'm right we've got a very serious situation on our hands. I have a great deal to tell you when you're up to it. Call me." Casey handed him a business card with her home phone number handwritten on it.

Trabinski looked at his watch. "We need to act now on any pertinent information that may help. We've made no progress whatsoever and I'm tired of going in circles." He ran a hand over the stubble on his face. "I'll go get cleaned up, then swing by for you at eight. We'll grab dinner at The Broadway Café and see if we can come up with a solid game plan. I want us to solve these crimes without the help of those on high…If you know what I mean?"

Casey nodded. She knew exactly what he meant. The last person they wanted involved in this was the Chief. Plus, if this case dragged on another week the FBI would be poking into the kidnappings. "Okay. See you at eight but I think you should go home and sleep."

"I'll be fine," Trabinski said.

As Casey slid into the front seat of her car a thought snuck into her head regarding tonight's get together. Something trivial but potentially troublesome. *I wonder how long it will take the rumor mill and gossip mongers to start talking about us working together on these cases?* She smiled to herself. *They should mind their own business if they know what's good for them.*

Lieutenant James Trabinski felt odd as he rang Casey Talbot's doorbell. The night was warm but comfortable. Crickets and katydids sang to the oncoming night and the heady fragrance from a potpourri of flowers artistically placed along the front of the apartment took him back to the night he had first taken his now ex-wife out on a date. The purpose of tonight's meeting started to feel less important. He even felt self-conscious about the clothes he chose to wear; a navy-blue camp shirt with white pin stripes untucked with tan trousers and Bass

Weejuns. *What are you in High School?* He mentally chided himself. *This is not a date!*

But then she opened the door and took his breath away.

She was wearing a cream-colored satin blouse — that seemed to cling in all the right places— with an open neck collar and a fitted light gray skirt that hugged the curve of her hips. Her red hair glistened in the hallway light. A tan leather shoulder bag and matching kitten heel pumps completed the stunning vision.

For the first time in a long time James Trabinski was tongue tied. All he managed to say was, "Ready?"

Casey sized him up. "*Well* … Don't you look nice. Feel better now?" She caught a whiff of Old Spice after shave. Seeing the "deer in the headlights" look on his face she smiled and quickly said, "Shall we go? I'm starving."

After a few awkward moments of silence in the car Trabinksi recovered from his stupor and complimented Casey on how lovely she looked. At a stop light on Woodbury Road, he had fully regained his composure and turned to her. "Can I ask you something personal? It's none of my business *really* but I'm curious."

A frown appeared on her gorgeous face. "I guess so…"

The light turned green and Trabinski nudged the gas pedal. "I know we haven't known each other that long so the topic probably wasn't appropriate before. You never mention a boyfriend or that you're dating someone. In the interest of knowing who I'm confiding in I thought it would be good to have such information. I mean a woman with your looks and brains must have someone."

Casey laughed. "What's your question?"

Trabinski cleared his throat. "Are you seeing anyone on a regular basis? Do you have a boyfriend?"

Casey thought about having some fun with him. *He's cute when he squirms.* But she felt a compulsion to open up to him. *Something feels right. Something good may be developing here. We'll see.*

"I don't," Casey said. "I'm a cop remember. Hard to keep guys interested when their girlfriend is out all hours of the night doing things she can't talk about. When I first started on the force, I was under cover. They called me a "decoy". I worked for the Vice Squad. You can well imagine how that would sit with a guy, especially if he was the jealous type. So, never found a guy who had the glue for that kind of relationship. Not the end of the world though. I'm pretty happy the way I am."

Trabinski acknowledged her predicament. "Yep, I get it. Been down a similar road myself. Only, I was married to a woman who decided that two years of marriage to a cop wasn't her cup of tea. She complained that I loved the job more than her. That I would give it up and do something else for a living if I really loved her. Meanwhile she was getting special deliveries from the mailman, if you know what I mean. So that was the end of that. Been single ever since."

The Broadway Café came into view. Trabinski made a U-turn and pulled up next to the curb in front of the restaurant. "Wait here," he said to Casey. He quickly exited his car, went around to the trunk, opened it, and pulled out a red canvas bag. With a shrewd glance up and down the street he placed the bag over the parking meter. It read "Out of Order." With that little problem solved, Trabinski opened the passenger door for Talbot and extended a hand to help her out.

"Why…thank you kind sir," Casey said coyly as she gracefully left the vehicle and stepped onto the sidewalk.

They entered the dimly lit café and were pleased to see that Trabinski's favorite table in the back corner of the dining room was available. The Café manager Ed Brigandi knew Trabinski and came right over as soon as he saw him enter. He shook his hand, smiled, and bowed to Casey then gestured towards the empty table.

Trabinski went to pull out the chair for Casey, but she beat him to it. With a smile she said, "I'm capable of pulling out my own chair. Not a diva you know." He nodded. "Right." Then took his seat across from her.

A short, chubby waiter who reminded Trabinski of Lou Costello offered to take their drink order. Casey hesitated, looked at the waiter then said, "I'll have what he's having."

Trabinski's eyebrows went up on that one. He gave a slight shake of the head in disbelief and ordered two Cutty Sarks on the rocks. After the waiter left, he couldn't hold back a chuckle. "Is there no end to your surprises, lady?"

Tugging at the hem of her skirt while shifting to a more comfortable position Casey replied, "Probably not…"

"Wouldn't take you for a Scotch drinker."

Casey grinned. "Oh, I can hold my own. I learned to drink when I was stationed in Korea. The horn dogs at the base were always trying to get me drunk on Soju. I was usually the last one standing."

"Soju?" Trabinski asked.

"Korea's version of Sake."

Lou Costello arrived with the drinks, presented menus, recited the specials then shuffled away.

Trabinski leaned back in his chair. "I guess we better get down to business before we forget why we're here."

"I agree." Casey opened her purse, removed a small note pad, and flipped it open. "What I'm about to tell you is just plain nuts, but you'll see a lot of it fits together." She took a long sip of scotch. "Just listen. Keep an open mind and don't say anything till I'm finished. Okay?"

Trabinski nodded. "Go ahead. I'm all ears."

Before she could continue the waiter inquired about their dinner choices. A little annoyed by the interruption Casey ordered Chicken Francaise with Jasmine rice. Trabinski selected Trout Almondine with Capellini and handed the menus back to the man.

Casey placed the pad on the table. "Okay. First, I went to see this Stanley Bolton boy based on the tip from Ryan's lawyer. That had all the markings of a dead end. He's in the hospital with some strange infection, unable to speak. There's more to that. I'll tell you in a minute.

As I was leaving the Bolton residence, I spied Tim Ryan across the street watching me."

Trabinski sat forward. His interest piqued.

"I cornered him and after a little persuasion he opened up about his friend and the blanket. When I asked him how Stanley came into possession of the blanket, he told me about an incantation from a book of spells and a nocturnal visitation Stanley had from a conjured creature known as a Harpy. Farfetched story, right? Tim thought so too.

"So now I head to the hospital thinking I might be able to speak to the Bolton kid there. No dice. The kid is paralyzed and can't speak at all. I go around this dead end and speak to his doctor. Who proceeds to tell me they suspect the infection attacking the boy came from bloody lacerations found on the boy's shoulders. The deep cuts were crescent shaped like ragged fingernails. We've heard this before...Right?"

The meals were served, and they both ordered another drink.

Casey went on to tell Trabinski about her library trip and her research into the Harpy nonsense. "After wading through book after book of ridiculous ramblings I was about to call it quits when I saw this page with a black and white illustration showing these winged creatures...Harpies stealing infants from the arms of horrified mothers. One of the beasts in the picture was taking a bite from an infant's leg. That's when it hit me. All the evidence we have points to this ...this flying monstrosity. What if those kids actually did conjure up something from another world. What *if* Dolores *was* right?"

With eyes squinted, brow furrowed Trabinski hung on every word. His right hand reached over and picked up the new pack of Camels as if it had a mind of its own. Still concentrating on Casey, he removed the cellophane wrapper, tore open the pack, slid out a fresh cigarette and lit it all in one fluid motion.

Casey took a fork full of the steaming rice, blew on it slightly and tasted it.

After a couple of contemplative drags on his smoke Trabinski said, "Then we add the two victims from last night. As much as I hate to say this, the blood trail from the girl ended so abruptly it was as if she either disappeared or was lifted into the air. And the kid's neck was broken which we've also seen before. But as you said this is completely nuts and that's exactly what our superiors are going to think. This is the 20th century not the dark ages. However, let's say it's all true. This thing…this Harpy is flying around secretly kidnapping young kids and killing others. How do we go about stopping it? By the way. What is this thing supposed to look like anyway?"

He crushed out his butt and took a taste of the Trout.

Casey fastidiously dabbed her lips with the cloth napkin provided by the waiter. "You'll love this. According to my *current* research they are historically visualized as beautiful, naked women with various wing descriptions. Some have bat-like wings, others are bird like."

"Unbelievable. I'm sure someone would have reported seeing something like *that*. And that's a good question. Why *hasn't* anybody seen this thing … besides that Bolton kid?"

"Supernatural…remember? Magical. They supposedly have the ability to camouflage themselves."

"*Wonderful*," he said sarcastically. So? Any ideas on how we stop a supernatural, magical, flying *naked* woman?" He knew an idea was coming because Casey was rubbing the side of her nose.

"I was thinking we should call Dolores and find out what she knows about conjurings. Find out if such a thing is even possible. Could a couple of teenage boys actually do this successfully? What do you think?"

"I don't know. Even if she's willing it could take too long. We really need to act now," he said, twirling capellini onto his fork.

Casey nodded.

"Okay then with bait," she said. "A decoy. I can pose as a teenage girl. Alone on the street or wherever we choose."

Trabinski almost choked on his Capellini. "No way in hell that's going to happen."

A smug look appeared on Casey's face. "I was a professional decoy for years. I can do this. Besides…You have a better idea?"

"Hold on a minute. What makes you think this…this harpy or whatever it is will come after you? Except for the girl last night and Danny Sanfield most of the victims were children."

Casey tasted her chicken Francaise and waggled her fork at him. "What about Rocco and the boy last night? For some reason this killer is selective."

"Selective? In what way?"

"The children are missing, except for the little boy you found in the woods and the teenage girl is missing. Right? The bodies of the males have been left at the scene. I hate to say this while we're having dinner but remember Dolores said the children had been eaten. I'm thinking this thing has a taste for children and females. So…" She leaned forward and pinned Trabinski with a charming look of defiance and continued. "Since we won't be putting any children in harm's way, I'll pretend to be a teenage girl whose car broke down and we'll see what comes to help her. It's the only way. Agreed?"

Trabinski chugged his Cutty Sark then held up his empty glass and rattled the remaining ice at the waiter for a refill. "I still don't like it," he said.

***

Midnight – Rocco's Auto Wreckers and Junk Emporium

Sergeant Todd Anderson, Unit 12 K-9 Squad accompanied by his new rookie partner Patrolman Eileen Cummings along with Leo—Anderson's decorated German Shepherd— arrived at the junkyard five minutes past midnight. A rolling ground fog covered the expanse. One lone yard light with a cone shaped metal shade connected by an S shaped rod to the roof of the ramshackle store, struggled to illuminate the area.

Anderson noticed the other yard lights were all off. Flashlights would be needed. He also took note of his partner's apparent nervousness. This was her dream job ever since she was a little girl. She absolutely loved dogs and Leo seemed to like her. Anderson knew this was her first real assignment and she didn't want to screw it up, even though this was a nothing follow up sweep which didn't amount to much. He had no concerns. She was a stocky well-built girl; thoroughly trained, able to handle herself in a situation and extremely knowledgeable about the squad.

They exited the Ford station wagon especially built to carry dogs in the rear. Anderson attached the leather restraint to his dog, handed Cummings a heavy-duty flashlight and headed to the gate. The low-lying mist swirled around their feet as they walked. Anderson opened the lock with the key Trabinski had left for him.

Cummings turned on her light and began to play the beam into the darkness. "Are all your night shift assignments like this?" There was a slight tremor in her voice.

To bolster her confidence Anderson said, "Here." He handed her Leo's leash. "Take Leo and check out the area around the store. Wait for me there. I need to let dispatch know we changed our itinerary and stopped here first."

The rookie took the leash. "With pleasure." She lovingly patted Leo on his head. Who in turn gave her a short *chuff* of approval and licked her hand.

Minutes later Anderson had joined Cummings at the rear of the building. Leo was sitting quietly at her feet with a look that might have meant, *Okay? What's next?*

"Do you have any idea what we're looking for?" Cummings asked.

"None. We already went over this place and came up empty, but the Lieutenant insisted we do another sweep. Something is bugging him about it. He was actually here this afternoon. So, let's get it over with."

Giving Leo a tug on his leash Cummings led him into the murk. Anderson right behind her.

As they proceeded through the dark gloom, guided by their flashlight beams they came to a massive black shape that could have been a towering volcano. Their lights danced over it and upward revealing a huge pile of flattened metal positioned in such a way as to create a mountainous appearance. At its peak there existed a triangular opening resembling a cave one might find on a natural escarpment.

Suddenly, Leo tensed, then with a surge of strength that ripped the leash from Cummings' hand bolted into the darkness.

"No! Leo stop!" Cummings cried and started to run.

Anderson thought he heard a yelp come from deep in the shadows and raced towards it. "Leo! Here boy!" Unable to see clearly, he tripped over something in his path and went tumbling headfirst in the dirt. With a curse he scrambled to his feet. "Leo! Come here boy!" Just then he realized he had lost sight of Cummings. No sign of her or her flashlight. "Cummings!" He shouted. No reply. The entire junkyard was quiet as a tomb. Swinging his light back and forth he retraced his steps, carefully avoiding the stray truck bumper that had tripped him up. "Cummings!" He called again. A moan caught his ear just as he saw movement and the faint glow of a flashlight submerged in swirling clouds of fog. As he approached the foot of the metallic mountain, he saw Patrolman Cummings struggling to stand. "Hold on…take it easy. I got you." Anderson eased her into a sitting position against a solid car door remnant. "You, okay?" His light revealed a bruise on her face just below her right eye.

"I'm alright. Just embarrassed."

"What happened?" Anderson asked. He flashed his light quickly past her eyes checking for a concussion.

"From out of nowhere something hit me."

Anderson straightened up. "Leo?"

"No. it wasn't a dog." She abruptly sat forward. "Where's Leo? He didn't come back?"

Anderson shook his head. "No…and this isn't like him at all."

Cummings got to her feet. "We've got to find him. He may be hurt."

Gingerly they both walked into the murkiness calling his name to no avail. After a few moments of waiting and listening Anderson asked Cummings, "What do you think it was that hit you?"

The rookie cast her light beam around her as if searching for it. "I have no idea Sergeant, but it stunk. And I can tell you I haven't smelled anything that disgusting since my days as a kid doing clean up at the Fulton Fish Market."

CHAPTER 31

Day Eleven – Morning

Before he came down to breakfast, Tim Ryan sat at his old wooden desk wracking his brain for an idea, a way to see Stanley in the hospital. He had no luck getting information from Stanley's brother Jonathan, so he still had no idea what had happened to his friend. He didn't even know the name of the hospital but surmised it was Central General because it was nearby. *I could ride my bike there if that's the place. But would they let me in without a parent? Dammit! How am I going to do this? I wonder if that policewoman would take me.*

The tantalizing aroma of bacon cooking came wafting up the stairs into his room accompanied by the sounds of pots and pans being jostled around and his sister's constant yammering. Then his mother's call alerting him breakfast was ready. *Maybe I'll think of something while I'm eating…if Emily ever shuts up.*

Seated at the head of the small oval kitchen table, Tim — deep in thought — dug into his scrambled eggs ignoring his sister seated next to him. His daydream was unexpectedly interrupted by his mother.

"Tim? Did you know that Stanley Bolton is in the hospital?"

He almost spit out his mouthful of eggs. He swallowed his food with a gulp and without thinking said, "No!" Faking a surprised look. "What happened? Who told you?" He took a quick sip of orange juice.

"I was talking to Mrs. Tillis this morning. She's a friend of Stanley's mother. Apparently, Stanley cut himself and the cut became seriously infected."

Trying not to appear overly interested Tim just said, "Oh."

His mother went on to say Stanley was in Central General and that he would probably be there for at least a week. Then she said something so surprising that Tim thought he misheard her. "What?"

"I said…Would you like to go see him?" She wiped her hands on her pink apron and gave him a smile.

"Uh…yeah sure. I can bring him some comics and stuff." *I can't believe it. Miracles do happen.*

"So, help me clean up when you're finished eating and I'll drive you over there for the noon visiting hours. That way you'll be back in time to deliver your papers."

Tim glanced at his sister then shot a questioning look at his mom.

"Emily will be spending the day with Joanie Purcell in her pool. We'll drop her off first." She chuckled at the relieved look on her son's face.

Emily made a goofy face at him and mouthed the words, "na … na…na, na, na, *na.*"

"Thanks mom. That'll be swell." Tim avoided using the word "swell". It sounded dorky; like something from that silly Leave it to Beaver show. He would have said "groovy" or "ginchy" but felt it was the more appropriate word for his mother's ears.

As Tim walked through the white sterile corridors of the hospital with his mother, he was reminded how much he disliked the smell of alcohol. It brought back the anxiety he felt when he was younger, waiting in line with his classmates to receive the Polio vaccine at the school nurse's office. This anxiety only added to the tenseness he already felt about seeing Stanley. He cracked his knuckles a few times till they wouldn't crack anymore. His palms felt sweaty though it was relatively cool in the hall. When the elevator doors finally opened for them to proceed to Stanley's floor, he took a deep breath. *Don't be such a baby. It's only Stanley.*

At the nurses' station Tim and his mother were informed by a pretty nurse with black hair that only two people at a time were permitted to visit the patient. "Someone is in with him now. I can give you a single pass. However, one of you will have to wait till the other comes out."

"That's fine," Tim's mother replied. She patted Tim on the back. "You go son. He's your friend."

"Room 211," the nurse said with a sympathetic smile.

Tim briefly wondered who was already in there with Stanley as he pushed open the heavy solid oak door. When he stepped into the room redolent with the scent of alcohol and something else, he couldn't identify, he saw Stanley's mother sitting there. He was surprised how old she looked. He didn't remember her hair being so gray. She was seated in a black straight chair with her back to the room's only window. The morning sunlight shining through the glass seemed to give Stanley's mother a halo of sorts. A white privacy curtain had been partially drawn so only the foot of the bed was visible to Tim. The room was as quiet as a library except for a slight beeping and the rustle of pages from Mrs. Bolton's magazine.

"Hi Mrs. Bolton," Tim said sheepishly. He was always intimidated by this woman.

She reacted as if she hadn't noticed his entry. "Oh, Tim…hello." She stood. "Are you here by yourself?"

Tim did a little nervous two step, shifting from one foot to the other then back again. "No ma'am. My mom's outside in the waiting room. I brought these for Stanley." He pulled two rolled up comic books from his back pocket. *The Adventures of Superman* and the new *Blackhawk* issue.

"Stanley will be happy to see you. I'll go keep your mother company."

When she left the room Tim hesitated to go around the curtain. His horror movie imagination was going into high gear. *What if he's all shriveled up or his face is all droopy like the scientist in that Tarantula movie?*

Just then a grunt from the other side of the curtain snapped him back to reality. He stepped gingerly to the other side of the curtain and there was Stanley holding up a large pad with scratchy writing on it.

I AINT DEFF DUMMY. HEARD YOUR VOICE.

Tim shook his head. *Same old Stanley.*

"I thought you might like these…" Tim placed the two comics on the stand next to his friend. He was glad to see that Stanley looked better than he had anticipated. He did have tubes running from what looked like a chrome coat rack on wheels to his left arm. One was attached to a plastic bag filled with a clear solution that dripped periodically into it. The other connected to a gray sleeve wrapped around Stanley's upper arm. It ran to a small white box with a square screen blinking numbers. Above the screen were the words Systolic/Diastolic. Other than the silly looking nightgown he was wearing — it had small geometric designs on it— he looked okay.

Stanley made a clucking sound as Tim sat in the chair vacated by Mrs. Bolton. Then scratched on the pad with a number two pencil using his right hand.

THANKS

Tim leaned forward putting his elbows on his knees. "Stanley? What the hell happened to you? I heard it was some kind of infection."

Stanley gingerly shook his head and wrote, **SHE HAPPENED** !

"You mean the Harpy did this to you?"

SHE'S DANGEROUS. PARALYZED ME WITH A KISS. TOOK AWAY MY VOICE. DOCTOR THINKS I WON'T TALK AGAIN. EVER!

GLAD I CAN AT LEAST USE ONE ARM.

Tim, thunderstruck by what he was reading, sat back in the uncomfortable chair. "You...You kissed it?"

KISSED HER. COULDN'T HELP IT

"You are truly nuts. So, she paralyzed you because you kissed it... uh her?"

SHE WANTS TO BE RELEASED. TOLD HER I DIDN'T KNOW HOW. SHE GOT MAD.

Before Tim could respond the pretty nurse with the black hair entered the room, momentarily diffusing the growing anxiety in the air.

Stanley quickly placed his writing pad face down on the bed stand with the comic books.

"Hello Stanley. I need to check your vitals before you have lunch," she said. Her voice was pleasant and assuring. "It won't take long."

She smiled at both boys then removed the clipboard fastened to the foot of the bed, read it quickly removed a thermometer from her uniform pocket and stuck it in Stanley's mouth. She checked his pulse then removed the thermometer and wrote down info with the pen attached to the clip board. She looked over at the Systolic/Diastolic machine and jotted down the numbers appearing there.

Tim was so distracted by this curvaceous woman in white he forgot what Stanley had written. *I sure wouldn't mind her taking care of me.* He was startled when he heard her say, "Excuse me. I need to get over there to check the IV drip." She pointed to the solution bag hanging from the stand at the right side of the bed where Tim was sitting.

"Oh, sorry," he said. He stood and as she squeezed past, he caught a whiff of a clean and enticing fragrance that in his mind made her even more appealing. *Ivory soap. She uses Ivory soap.*

After jotting down more information on the clipboard sheet the nurse stepped around to the other side of the bed and lifted the blanket exposing Stanley's feet. "Can you wiggle your toes for me Stanley?"

He tried but nothing happened.

"Can you feel this?" She leaned over and tickled the bottom of his feet.

He nodded and grinned.

"Good. That's a start." She replaced the blanket over Stanley's feet. "Now wiggle the fingers on your left hand for me."

When he did, she gave him an encouraging smile, finished writing on the clipboard, hung it back on the foot of the bed and said, "Doctor Wells will be in later this afternoon to examine your throat. In the meantime…Are you hungry?"

Stanley nodded.

"Good. I'll send someone in shortly with today's lunch selections. I'll check in on you later as well," she said then turned and left the room.

The boys watched her leave and Stanley made a pleasant groan. He grabbed his pad and pencil, grinned and scribbled:

I WANT HER FOR MY SPONGE BATH

Coming quickly back to reality Tim said, "We can't let ourselves get sidetracked like that. We've got problems. What are we gonna do? We don't even know where she is. And if she's the killer the cops are looking for, we could be in real danger. Look what she did to you." Tim started cracking his knuckles.

Stanley ignored his friend's rant and wrote:

SHE KNOWS YOUR NAME. ASKED ABOUT YOU

Tim felt as if all the air had been sucked out of the room. "What!? Cripes! Is she watching me?" Then it dawned on him. "Shit Stanley, *she* must have been in my garage attic. Should I go back and tell the police?"

TELL THEM WHAT? Stanley quickly scribbled.

Tim started pacing in front of the window. "I don't know, I don't know. What did you mean she wants to be released? Released from the spell?"

I THINK SO. SHE TOLD ME TO SAY THE WORDS AND RELEASE HER.

"What words? I don't have any *words*. And you never found the damn book. What am I supposed to say?"

Stanley awkwardly tore off the used pages of his pad and crumpled them up as best he could with his right hand. He handed them to Tim, gesturing toward the garbage can next to the bed.

Tim saw that Stanley looked tired. He took the pages, crumpled them up some more and tossed them in the receptacle. When he turned back to face his friend, he saw him scribbling again. He didn't like Stanley's answer to his question.

ASK HER

Just then the door opened, and Mrs. Bolton walked in. Tim could see his mother waiting in the doorway. Tim gave Stanley a frustrated look. "Okay, Stanley. Gotta go. Hurry up and get better. Enjoy the comics. See you around." With that Tim hurried from the room more anxious than when he first entered.

***

8ᵗʰ *Precinct*

"*Vanished?* What do you mean vanished?" Trabinski said to the disheveled looking officer standing in front of him.

"Yes, sir. That's the only way to describe what happened." Sergeant Todd Anderson's voice was that of a person who had spent the night yelling. "Leo just disappeared into the fog. Cummings and I must've circled that junkyard a hundred times looking and calling for him. Nothing. No barking or whining. Nothing. Unless he found a way to get through the fence, which I highly doubt, he vanished without a trace."

Trabinski pointed to the chair in front of his desk. "Have a seat before you fall down."

With a groan of relief Anderson sat. "We couldn't determine what or who knocked Cummings down. Too damn foggy. Left a good shiner on her face though."

"Had to be someone powerful to knock her down. She's a sturdy gal. Could it have been Leo? Something spooked him?" Trabinski asked. Still uncertain about Casey's harpy theory he continued with a more grounded line of questioning.

"Cummings is sure it wasn't a dog that clocked her. She said it smelled like rotten fish. Besides, Leo doesn't spook easily."

Trabinski closed his eyes and massaged his forehead with his fingertips. A headache coming on. "What are you going to do about Leo?" He asked in a tired voice.

Anderson stretched in the chair. "I have a team combing the area outside the junkyard for him. Meantime I'm going to recruit his sister Cleo as his replacement. She's older but still knows the game.

Trabinski suppressed a laugh. "Leo and *Cleo? Really?*"

"What's wrong with that?" Anderson asked with a pained look on his face.

"Nothing, nothing…sorry." The headache was building. Trabinski opened his desk drawer. He grabbed a bottle of Anacin, opened it, tapped out two pills, popped them in his mouth and washed them down with cold coffee.

"Lieutenant? If you don't mind me asking, sir. Why'd you send us out there last night?

Not knowing exactly how to answer that question truthfully, Trabinski told a little white lie. "We received an anonymous tip that the perp we're looking for may have been hiding there. Wasn't sure if it was legit so I sent you for one more look. Seems like you scared up *something.*"

"You think that's who ran into Cummings?"

"Possibly…but how did this person get past Leo?"

Anderson stifled a yawn. "Right. That's a good question. And why didn't we hear anything? Like someone running at least."

"I just authorized an around the clock surveillance of the place until further notice. You can probably call off your team. If your dog is out there somebody will spot him. Thanks for your help, Sergeant. Now go home and get some rest."

"Thank you, sir." Anderson stood and left the office.

Slowly rocking back and forth in his swivel desk chair Lieutenant James Trabinski lit a cigarette, the headache was subsiding, and he momentarily wondered about Anderson's dog. *Now we have a well-trained police dog disappear in that junkyard. And... we had a well-trained guard dog turn savage ... in that junkyard. Coincidence or do we actually have some kind of supernatural influence in effect there?*

With that thought in mind he became seriously concerned about the dubious plan he and Casey had concocted last evening.

CHAPTER 32

Day Eleven – Late evening

Malhela squatted before the remains of the birthgiver chastising herself for another error in judgement. Though it was a good idea at the time — perhaps driven by the wonderful flavor of her flesh — bringing the body to her nest had brought consequences she had not expected. Mainly, the enormous number of flies that had appeared in a short amount of time. She was used to these annoying pests. They would occasionally buzz around her when her musk was strong. But now, drawn to the smell of blood, they crawled and flitted over most of the body. She swept them away as best she could.

Besides this inconvenience the meat had lost its sweetness, turning sour almost overnight. She would remove some sections as rations and dispose of the rest. She could always find another birthgiver now that she had cast off the restrictions of the Realm.

The final nuisance came in the form of courageous, defiant crows who had entered her domain as if it were their own. One had the audacity to peck at her. A fatal move. The others were quickly dispatched by her new guardian; a big, tan and black hound whom she had subdued the night before as she had the other beast in past days. This one, however, was more intelligent, already understanding her commands as if trained specifically for her needs. It now lay in the shadows cleaning the last remnants of meat from the birthgiver's shin bone.

Adding to her self-doubt, the recent activity on the grounds below heightened her sense of being hunted. Looking around her nest she realized the front opening still posed a problem. It was the only way in or out. Perfect for trapping her inside. She had totally forgotten to rectify that situation when she first noticed it. After a few moments of deliberation, she cleverly rearranged the metal sheets at the rear of the cavern creating a worthwhile escape route. As she peered downward through the new aperture, she noticed the flattened metallic pieces at the back of her mountain of debris had randomly formed a zig zag stairway. Ideal for her new guardian to climb or descend, alleviating the necessity to fly the hound into the nest. She would make sure he remained here during the daylight hours to avoid encounters with snooping mortals.

Selecting what she felt were still choice pieces of meat from the carcass Malhela wrapped them in one of the birthgiver's garments and stashed them in a square tin container she had found in the rubble.

Holding up the container for her new hound to see, she said in a gentle voice, "Do not eat." She then pushed it into a deep corner of her nest.

As she bundled what was left of the birthgiver in the tattered garments that remained she abruptly stopped. She quickly stood. Her keen senses on full alert. She thought she heard a voice calling.

Carefully stepping to the entrance, she stared into the night, her head slightly tilted listening. After a moment she heard it again in her ears and in her head. A voice calling. All at once recognition shook her. Her breath caught in her throat. Then an impish smile crept onto her face. *Tim Ryan.*

***

After returning from the hospital with Stanley's scribbled words still fresh in his head Tim Ryan spent the rest of the afternoon a nervous wreck. So anxious and tense that his stomach had tied itself into a knot making him feel nauseous while he delivered his papers.

He couldn't eat dinner and retreated to his room with a glass of Alka-Seltzer his mother had handed him. *This won't help.* He thought as he entered his room and closed the door.

Moping to his desk he flipped on his transistor radio and plopped down in his chair as Jan and Dean came on singing about "*Two girls for every boy…* "in Surf City. He felt overwhelmed by the chain of events. His head hurt. Confused, worried *and* scared, Tim argued with himself. *What would happen if I did nothing? Maybe it will go away, or the cops will get it. I can just wait it out. This **rots** big time!*

Acting as a soundtrack for his thoughts the radio now delivered *Let Me In* by the Sensations.

You can't wait it out, moron. She knows your name…even asked about you. Well…that's what Stanley said anyway.

A quick knock on his bedroom door derailed his train of thought. His mother, fearing he had contracted something from Stanley entered and stuck a thermometer in his mouth to check for fever. "Normal," she said after waiting a few moments then removing it from his mouth.

"Drink that." She pointed to the full glass of water that contained the antacid. "Are you going to sleep?"

"I don't know," Tim replied. "Maybe."

"I'll close the door, "his mother said and left the room.

Tim took a gulp of the fizzing drink and suddenly belched. He didn't feel any better. He put his thought train back on the tracks. *She asked about me. Asked what? How the hell does she know my name?*

As his thoughts drifted the background music provided appropriate lyrics crooned by Roy Orbison, "Just running scared…So afraid…".

Yeah, that's about it alright. Running scared.

He got up, went to the bookcase, and removed the encyclopedia volume that contained the information he had read before regarding Harpies. Laying it on the top of his desk he flipped to the page already dogeared and turned off his radio so he could concentrate without distraction. *There may be something here I can use. Like special words to say or something that will chase her away.*

After reading and re-reading the article Tim slammed the book closed and held his head in his hands. *Nothing. Not a damn thing about special phrases or magical words to abolish the Harpy. Wait a minute…* He sat straight in his chair and gazed at the crucifix hanging on the wall next to his desk. *Could that keep her away? Pull yourself together knucklehead. She's not a vampire. But…she is a kind of demon. What about an exorcism? That might be the answer. Talk to Father Murphy. Yes! I like it! Yet…How would I go about it? I would have to convince Father Murphy to be here and then summon her to appear. I wonder if I could summon her to appear in church. Convincing Father Murphy may be easier said than done. He might think I'm possessed. That would really be the icing on this crazy cake. Crap! This is totally going nowhere.*

Tim let his eyes drift away from the crucifix to a small cubby in the top corner of his desk's shelving. A narrow, frosted glass bottle etched with a crimson cross at its center, topped with a black stopper sat there. It contained Holy Water collected from the church font by his mother. Every room in the house had a bottle. Tim remembered when his mom had placed it there. The day his room was finished, and he moved his stuff in. It gave him another idea. But it still required him to summon the harpy.

He crossed his arms over the volume on his desk, leaned forward and rested his chin on his hands, playing this new idea over in his head. The main concern, *what if it doesn't work?*

With a start he sat upright in his chair. He was surrounded by darkness. He turned his head slowly, momentarily uncertain of where he was, when his eyes focused on the dim glowing face of his clock strategically placed on his night table next to his bed. "Eleven thirty?" He whispered. "I fell asleep."

He stood and carefully stepped away from the chair quietly moving towards the night table where his reading lamp waited. Instinctively he reached out his right hand and pushed the switch at its base bringing light into the room.

A cool night breeze sifted through the screen and blinds of the open bedroom window. Tim had decided to go ahead with the summoning and debated whether or not to change his clothes before confronting the harpy. He was still wearing his newspaper delivery jeans and

T-shirt. He chose to keep them on just in case he had to make a mad dash to escape. He didn't want to be in his pajamas if that happened. Trying to prevent his bedroom door from squeaking Tim opened it ever so slowly and peered down the stairs. No lights and all was quiet. He listened a bit more to make sure his parents and Emily had gone to bed. Satisfied, he gently closed the door and locked it. *Probably not a good idea. You have no way out now.* He quickly unlocked it and moved to the window, raised the blinds, and quietly removed the screen. With that task completed he went to the wall, removed the crucifix, and placed it on his desk next to the encyclopedia volume. Now for the critical ingredient of his plan, the Holy Water. He removed the bottle from its cubby and sat it carefully next to the cross. *Guess I'm ready.*

In his stocking feet— he had removed his dirty sneakers when he arrived home after delivering his papers — Tim shuffled to the window. He cranked it open as far as it would go and gazed at a night sky, finally free of gloom. The stars were brilliant and the moon bright as a spotlight. No clouds to be seen.

The nervousness was back fueling his horror movie imagination once again. Scenes of moonlight madness played in his head. Most involved werewolves. Some, grave-robbing ghouls as frighteningly depicted in the film *Mr. Sardonicus.* Tim suddenly shivered. *I gotta be out of my mind. This is the real deal not some movie.* He moved back to his desk and stood so he could reach the Holy Water. *I'll douse her with it when I get the chance. She knows my name. She asked about me. I guess I have no choice.*

He took a deep breath and exhaled slowly to calm himself and cracked a few knuckles. *How do I summon her? Call out her name or just think really hard?*

Tim did both and waited. He glanced at his clock. Midnight. Other than a hypnotized moth that came through the open window orbiting his lamp, nothing happened. According to the clock only five minutes had passed but already his legs were getting tired from standing at rigid attention awaiting her arrival. He relaxed. *Great…just great. It didn't work. Now what?*

He turned his back to the window and started towards his bedroom door intending to go downstairs, brush his teeth and call it a night when the ambiance of his room changed.

Tim's ears knew every creek, groan, rattle, knock and squeak of his room but now it was as if cotton had been magically stuffed in them muffling everything. The pressure felt like being in a plane. They needed to be popped. He held his nose and swallowed, clearing them. It was then that he heard a whisper of movement behind him accompanied by the foul odor reminiscent of the one he and Stanley had survived in the playground maze. He stood stock still, fists clenched. Suddenly he heard a soft, sweet, melodious voice. It made the hair stand up on the back of his neck. *She's here!*

"Tim Ryan?" The female voice asked. "I am with you."

Tim mustered his courage and turned around. Pure astonishment would be the only words to describe the look on his face. He quickly realized his mouth was hanging open and shut it. His mind became a hurricane of thoughts. *Holy crap…she is beautiful. Stanley was right. Completely naked. Shit…what do I say? The smell. Where's the Holy Water?*

Doesn't look that dangerous. Breasts, bat wings. Tuesday Weld. No… more like Stella Stevens. Fumbling for something to say Tim stupidly said, "Malhela?"

Malhela offered a little girl giggle. "I am pleased you know my name."

As she approached Tim, she held her head in the air sniffing then paused to look him over. That delightful citrus fragrance was on him.

Tim went to step back but she grabbed him by the shoulders and pulled him close. She drew his head down to sniff his hair. Her firm breasts right in his face. They wreaked of her bodily stench and Tim turned his head trying not to gag.

Malhela ran her fingers through his hair then stopped and sniffed them. The wonderful oily ambrosial covering them drifted into her nose. She leaned her head back moaning with pleasure. "What is this substance, Tim Ryan?" She held out her fingers.

"Huh?" All Tim could see was a sun-tanned hand, long fingers with filthy dagger-like fingernails.

"In your hair," Malhela pointed to his head.

"Ah? Oh this…" Tim cautiously moved toward his dresser and picked up the tube of Brylcreem lying there. Glad to put even a little distance between them. *God…she smells. How could someone who looks so good smell so bad?* He opened the cap and handed it to her.

Malhela grabbed the tube from him as if it were something valuable; a dollop accidentally squeezed onto her hand in the process. She brought it to her nose and inhaled deeply. She moaned again and immediately started rubbing it all over her body. Her head swam, she giggled again.

Tim's fears were starting to fade. *What in the world is going on here? At least she smells a little better.* Still not fully comprehending that a naked woman was in his room he closed his eyes and gave his head a quick shake. When he opened them, he saw her swaying seductively. *What the...?*

"Malhela? Are you drunk?" This sounded like a dumb thing to ask but too late. He gawked as she stretched her arms toward the ceiling, flattening her abdomen, spreading her legs, and fluttering her dark wings. Tim's eyes wandered down her torso to the hairless cleft between her legs. Intrigued, his eyes lingered there — Tim was still a virgin when it came to the details of female anatomy — a pleasant tightness began to manifest itself in his groin but was soon eliminated by shame and its partner guilt. He forced himself to look away. *I am definitely going to Hell.*

"I have not drunk anything," Malhela replied. With a swift little wiggle, she gracefully lowered herself onto the floor and sat in the lotus position.

Tim sidled over to his desk and the Holy Water. *I may not need it. She acts as if she's zonked on Brylcreem. What'll I do if she passes out?* Seeing she still held the tube, he tried to take it from her but decided not to when she bared her teeth and hissed at him. The sight of two sharp fangs rekindled his fears. He glanced at the bottle with the crimson cross at its center on his desk. *Might still need that.*

"This goes on the tube to keep the cream from coming out all over the place." He handed her the cap to the Brylcreem.

She took it, sniffed it, and dropped it on the floor in front of her.

Tim sat on the edge of his desk watching her as she rubbed the Brylcreem on her chest like it was Vick's vapo rub. He caught sight of the clock on the night stand behind her. Twelve thirty. *This is taking too long. I have to get her out of here.*

"Malhela? Stanley told me you wanted to ask me something. What is it?"

She whipped her head around. Her leopard eyes glaring at him.

"The primate still lives? This Stanley must be more durable than I anticipated. I will do better next time." She said in a dreamy soft voice.

"Why do you want to hurt him?" Tim tried hard to sound brave.

Malhela was now applying the cream to her thighs. The entire room smelled of it; thankfully somewhat diminishing the rotten fish stench. "He is worthless to me. A deceitful betrayer worthy of elimination. To him, bringing me here was a thoughtless stunt. A game played at my expense. I trust that you will be different." Malhela's tone had lost its sweetness.

Tim stood up and began pacing quietly in front of his desk. *Don't piss her off.*

"I won't betray you." With nervousness building he said, "What do you want me to do?" He stopped his pacing. His eyes focused on her pretty face.

"The question is … What do *you* want *me* to do? What was your purpose in calling me from the realm Tim Ryan?" Malhela smiled sardonically.

"I…I had no purpose. I was just helping Stanley read the Latin phrases in this book he bought. I didn't think the incantation would work. How can I make it right? Can I help you in some way?"

Malhela immediately stood up causing Tim to flinch. "Ask me for something you deeply long for. Command me to perform an all-important task. Ask me about an event in the future. But you must do this with sincerity. Then, once I have provided you with my service, I will return from whence I came. Freed from this wretched world of yours."

Tim put his hands on the top of his head. He had an idea. *Could it be this simple?* He brought his hands down and crossed his arms. "I have something that I really need for you to do on my behalf. It's really important."

"When my wings enshroud me, say the words and it will be done."

Tim waited.

Malhela straightened, brought her feet together as her leathery wings wrapped around her from head to talon.

Tim cracked his knuckles. With as much emotion as he could muster, he said, "Malhela, I command you to...*return* to your realm." He stepped back as her entire visage began to shake. Her figure blurred. *She's going to disappear!*

When his reading lamp suddenly went out Tim thought it was over. Malhela was gone. But as he felt his way through the darkness searching for the wall with the overhead light switch, he heard a heavy sigh behind him. He knew he was near his desk and fumbled for the Holy Water, knocking it over. He froze when he heard Malhela's sultry voice.

"You have failed me, Tim Ryan. Now I am doomed to spend the rest of my days here. But...I will not spend them alone. As retribution for your deficiency, you will be my slave till you die."

"No!" Tim said louder than he intended. He made a quick blind move and crashed into his desk chair, knocking it over. Instantly she was on him, clutching him close, kissing him, her fetid breath filling his nostrils as her wings enfolded him. He couldn't breathe and his head was spinning. All at once he felt very sleepy and as he nodded off, he felt himself being lifted.

Tim's mother, asleep in the back bedroom, woke with a start at the sudden noise from her son's upstairs room. Tim's father groaned sleepily, "What is it?"

"I don't know. I think Tim may have fallen out of bed." Tim's mother swirled into her robe, flipped on the hall light, saw Emily standing in her doorway rubbing her eyes and without missing a beat ushered her back to bed. "Go back to sleep."

She hurried through the living room to the foot of the stairs leading to Tim's room and flipped on the secondary switch turning on the lights up in his room. She rushed up the stairs to the closed door and opened it. "Tim? Are you alright?"

Her eyes went wide, and her hand flew to her mouth as she took in the sight. An empty bed, unslept in, an opened, twisted tube of Brylcreem on the floor, the window wide open, the screen leaning against the dresser and an overturned desk chair. No sign of her son anywhere. Fighting hysteria, she fled to the top of the stairs calling out for her husband. "Carrllll!"

CHAPTER 33

Day Twelve – Morning

Lieutenant James Trabinski, Lead Detective for the 8th Precinct had just received the call he was hoping to avoid, Captain Walter Philbrick wanted to see him immediately. So, grabbing a cup of coffee he sauntered to the captain's office at the far end of the building. *Well, I guess the shit's going to hit the fan bright and early today.* Moving down the corridor he saw that Philbrick's door was uncharacteristically open.

Trabinski had no beef with the captain yet. He just didn't care for the man's pompous demeanor and so he prepared himself for what was coming.

"Good morning, Captain. Got your message. Something you wanted?"

Walter Michael Philbrick, an ex-marine decorated for services above and beyond during the Guadalcanal campaign stood behind a large, highly polished mahogany desk. A barrel-chested muscular man with a salt and pepper military flat top haircut, impeccably dressed, threw the newspaper he was holding on his desk, front page up.

"Have you seen this?" As usual there was condescension in his tone.

Trabinski picked it up and read the second headline circled in red.

COUNTY COPS STYMIED BY
PLAYGROUND DISAPPEARANCE

Philbrick took the paper back from Trabinski.

"The family of that missing child complained to the mayor. They obviously went to the press too. To aggravate things even more, the mother of the boy abducted from his driveway also wrote to the mayor sighting a lackadaisical response on our part. So, you know how this works Lieutenant. Your Honor, the mayor has now put a nasty bug in the chief's ear; the chief is all bent out of shape, my ass is in the wringer. And …yours is next. Why have we fumbled the ball on these cases?"

Trabinski took a gulp of his coffee. "The evidence collected ran cold. But we're confident we have a lead on the perp's whereabouts. It's under surveillance around the clock."

Philbrick eased into his plush leather chair. "You think this perp is responsible for both crimes?"

"Possibly more," Trabinski replied. "You may not have seen the report yet. Two teens were murdered the other night. Same MO as the boy we found in the woods as well as that of Danny Sanfield."

Philbrick drummed his fingers on his desk. "If you know where this lunatic is hiding, go in and grab him. What are you waiting for?"

The tone of disdain in Philbrick's voice told Trabinski to choose his words wisely.

"We're working in coordination with the second precinct. They have a strikingly similar case. I'm meeting with them at noon to solidify the plan. We should be able to wrap this whole thing up in a few days."

Uninvited, Trabinski stepped around a plush leather visitor's chair and sat. *Just like this guy to leave you standing.*

A look of disbelief covered Philbrick's face. "A few days? Unacceptable Lieutenant. We need to act now. The chief wants to see us this afternoon. Your meeting needs to be postponed. What is this plan you're discussing?"

Stalling for time while he thought of how to present the plan, he answered the question with one of his own. "Why does the chief want to see us? He's tangled with the mayor before and come away none the worse for wear."

"This time's different," Philbrick said smugly. "The mayor is up for re-election in November and he's threatening to call in the Staties if we can't get the job done. And quickly without any more press." He opened the desk drawer and pulled out a yellow lined pad, selected a pen from his Paper-Mate pen and pencil desk set and looked sternly at Trabinski. "I want to hear this plan before we go see the Chief. If it has holes in it or sounds like a wet dream to me it's *not* going to happen. We need something foolproof to give him. And just so you know what the stakes are here, he was mumbling something about making changes. What that means? I don't know. But you can fill in the blanks, I'm sure."

Trabinski exhaled a long breath sounding like a leaking tire. "We don't have all the details worked out. That was supposed to happen at today's meeting. Captain? You want immediate action? Then cover for me with the chief. I'll be wasting precious time sitting there listening to him vent. This killer is devious, cunning, and quick. Our plan, which so far, intends to use a decoy, will only succeed if we get the details right this afternoon and put them into play immediately."

Philbrick wrote something on his pad. "A decoy? As in a police-woman decoy?"

Trabinski hesitated. "That's the idea. Lieutenant Talbot from the second precinct has volunteered."

Philbrick started to object then paused as if remembering something. "Talbot? She's ex- military, isn't she?"

"That's correct," Trabinski answered. "She's done this type of work before."

"I'm not thrilled with the idea but at least she's more than capable of handling it." Philbrick stood up. "I'll deal with the chief; you get this plan in gear. And Lieutenant? By the numbers. By the numbers Lieutenant…no screw ups."

Trabinski stood as well. "Understood. I don't want any of those either. And thanks." He moved to the office door and said over his shoulder, "Oh, and give my regards to the chief."

Originally Trabinski wanted to meet with just Casey at the diner, thinking he might be able to talk her out of putting herself in harm's way as well as seizing the opportunity to ask her on a legitimate dinner date. Of course, she overruled him and diplomatically suggested the Ready room at her precinct. She would take the lead on this set up because her experience took precedence. Trabinski couldn't argue with that line of thinking. But above all else he worried about her safety. He found himself not caring if the plan worked or not, just as long as she wasn't harmed in any way.

As he came down the hall towards his office, he saw Detective Pete Taylor waving to him with a look of urgency on his face.

"What's going on?" Trabinski asked as he approached.

Taylor tilted his head and pulled on his ear. "You're going to love this. It's the Ryan kid."

"Again? What's he involved with now?"

"He's missing."

Trabinski shook his head. "Probably ran off."

Taylor picked up a small pad from his desk and glanced at it. "His parents don't think so. Hancock responded and took their statement. They heard a loud bang from his room around twelve thirty at night and immediately went to check on their son. His desk chair was on its side near the bedroom door, the window was wide open, and he was nowhere to be found. Hancock states there were no items in the room that could have facilitated a climb from the window, so unless the kid grew wings and flew there was no way he could have safely made a jump from that window to the ground thirty feet below. He noted the little sister's comment though he felt it was of little importance."

"Or? He staged the room that way for whatever reason and snuck out of the house via the front or back door," Trabinski commented then gestured for Taylor to continue. "Go on...What was her comment?"

Taylor flipped to another page on the pad, chuckling to himself. "She said the smelly thing that put all that stuff in the garage attic took him."

We never paid much attention to the sister. I don't remember asking her anything. She knows something and we missed it. Or...she's another psychic.

"Is Hancock still at the scene?"

"Yes, finishing paperwork. Dotting the I's and crossing the T's. You know how it is."

"Good. Tell him to inform the Ryans that I'll be there after I finish up at a meeting this afternoon. And tell them not to touch anything in their son's room."

"Right," Taylor said.

Trabinksi looked at his watch. "Hold the fort for me till I get back. And Pete? Philbrick's on the warpath so keep it tight around here."

Taylor nodded. "Ten-four."

There was no doubt in Trabinski's mind that Casey would take this plan seriously, working out details to perfection but was stunned when he strode into the 2nd Precinct's Ready room and saw her standing at the conference table with three men around her. Two were patrolmen and the other was a tall Troy Donahue look alike wearing a beige sports jacket with a paisley tie over a white shirt. He stood close to Casey looking over her shoulder. Trabinski felt a twinge of jealousy. *Not what I had in mind but it's her gig.*

As he approached the table Casey looked up, a hint of a smile came and went from her pretty face. "Right on time Lieutenant. Let's get started." She introduced him to her men. The tall good-looking guy turned out to be her partner Detective David Carver. Trabinski wondered why he hadn't seen this guy before.

Addressing Trabinski, Casey said, "We've been discussing the best location for this sting. You've got more riding on the success of this than we do so we'd like your thoughts on the logistics."

Trabinski gazed at the street map on the table in front of Casey, reached over and turned it around so he wasn't reading it upside down. He noted the streets that had been circled. "I don't think it makes much sense to pursue the playground and surrounding streets. *That* occurrence may have been a one off, or a test run so to speak. I'm sure Lieutenant Talbot has filled you in regarding the killings at the bus stop at the corner of Old Country Road and South Oyster Bay two nights ago. That may be a possible starting point. However, based on the series of events that have occurred at Rocco's Auto Wreckers it feels like the right place." He tapped the map indicating the junkyard's location. "My only concern is selecting the right area on the outskirts of the junkyard to safely insert our decoy. Once she's in place we need an immediate response point to assist her should she make contact."

There were mumbles of agreement from the men. Casey remained silent.

"What Lieutenant Talbot doesn't know is that we may only have one shot at this. The chief is now involved thanks to the mayor who is being pressured by his constituents to finish this. So…if we don't catch this killer in the next couple of days, he's calling in the Staties."

Casey raised an eyebrow in displeasure but made no comment.

Detective Carver slid the street map back in front of him. "What about this street?" Carver circled it with a pencil. "It runs alongside the junkyard and according to this, dead ends at wooded area."

"It's a possibility," Trabinski said. "There is a sidewalk along that street, and it does dead end at wooded area. There's an abandoned rail spur back there as well. We have to be careful though. This perp seems pretty smart and may become suspicious about a teenage girl driving alone down a dead-end street. Lieutenant? This is your call. What are you thinking?"

Casey pulled the map over and studied it for a moment. "What's over here?" She pointed to a blank space on the map just to the left of the Junkyard.

Trabinksi leaned forward noticing the determined look that he had seen on her face before. "Warehouse for some hardware company."

"Good. We may be able to use it." Casey straightened. She gave a quick assuring look to her men then sent a lingering thoughtful one to Trabinski.

"Okay. Here's what I want to do. Let's set up Rocco's as ground zero. Lieutenant? Since this location is under your precinct's jurisdiction, will you have your men do a little recon on that warehouse and if useable secure it? Might be a good idea to get on that as soon as we wrap up here."

Trabinski nodded.

"I want to think a bit more on this before I commit to my street position. It may simply come down to my car breaking down on the street in front of Rocco's. The warehouse recon will help. David? Once we have that info, please coordinate with Lieutenant Trabinski regarding manpower and equipment. One important thing we must keep in mind...and this is from data collected by the 8th precinct, this killer is quick, cunning, and powerful. Though it is our responsibility to apprehend this criminal and bring him in peacefully, I am authorizing deadly force if this caper goes south. Any concerns at this point?"

Silence all around.

Casey rolled up the street map. "Okay, good. I will notify you all tomorrow with my decision. Gentlemen? Let's make this happen. Thank you. That'll be all."

In her mind Casey wanted to be sure she was doing the right thing before she sent all these resources on a wild goose chase. Before selecting the final contact point Casey wanted another look at Rocco's and possibly some real proof this creature existed. She had an idea which precipitated the decision-making delay. She would sleep on it.

As they started to file out of the Ready room, Trabinski signaled Casey to wait. There was an awkward moment with Troy Donahue holding the door for her, but she waved him on.

Maintaining a professional air for appearance's sake Casey said, "Was there something else Lieutenant?"

Trabinski watched the door for a moment then looked her straight in the eyes. "The Ryan kid is missing."

"What? Did he run?"

"Maybe, but it doesn't sound like it. I'm heading over there as soon as I set up the warehouse recon. Ryan's little sister said something interesting to my officer about her brother being taken by the thing that placed those articles in the garage attic. I think she knows something."

"We never questioned her," Casey said.

"Right. Shall we go have a little chat with her?"

"I'll meet you there." She patted his shoulder, smiled ruefully, and left the room.

Once again Trabinski found himself dealing with distraught parents and it was wearing him thin. Lately, he doubted his ability to adhere to the motto "To serve and protect". Tim Ryan's mother continually dabbed her eyes with tissues, the father stoic but angry while the little sister sat rocking in a cushioned bent wood rocker watching silently.

After officially identifying themselves, which wasn't necessary for this family, Trabinksi and Talbot quickly examined Tim Ryan's upstairs room, noting the overturned bottle of holy water, the crucifix and the encyclopedia volume with the page earmarked for the article on Harpies.

Casey examined the desk chair lying on its side and noticed the crushed tube of hair cream beside it. Some of the white substance smeared on the floor.

"What do you make of this?" She pointed at the Brylcreem container.

"I have no idea. This whole thing is making me crazy." Trabinski replied.

Moving across the room they looked at each other, wordlessly acknowledging the same thought as they took in the view of the thirty-foot drop from the open bedroom window.

"Let's go talk to the sister," Trabinski said.

"Jim?" She said softly. "Let me do the talking."

"Sure."

"Hi Emily. Do you remember me? We didn't get a chance to talk the last time I was here. My name is Casey. Can I ask you some questions about last night?" Casey squatted next to the girl's chair to make eye contact.

"You're pretty," Emily said.

"Why, thank you. So are you." Casey feared the girl may be in shock, so she gently took one of the girl's hands in hers and softly stroked it.

"Emily? You told the policeman who was here earlier that your brother was taken by the smelly thing that put all that stuff in your garage attic. Why did you say that?"

Emily stopped her rocking and looked up toward her brother's room. "My bedroom window was open, and a noise outside woke me up. When I went to the window to see what it was the same gross smell from that day in the garage attic came seeping in. I almost gagged. Then I heard Tim talking to someone. My room is right below his, so I sometimes hear things."

"Could you hear what the person was saying to your brother?"

"No. But at first I thought it might be a girl."

Casey looked up at Trabinski then quickly returned to the little girl. "What made you think he was taken?"

"I heard him say, "No" in a loud voice then there was a crash."

Casey withdrew her hand and started rummaging through her purse. "Was there anything else, sweetie?"

Emily started rocking again. "No…nothing else. My mother came in and put me back to bed. I thought I heard someone's curtains flapping but I'm not sure."

Casey stood. "Thank you, Emily. You've been a big help. Don't you worry. We'll do our best to find your brother." With that she handed the girl a grape Tootsie Roll pop.

Emily brightened and looked at her parents. "Can I?"

Her mother said nothing, but her father nodded approval.

Trabinski and Casey once again exchanged that knowing look, advised the Ryans they would be kept up to date regarding the search, gave them the ok to straighten their son's room and quietly left the house.

Once back at their cars Trabinski said, "I can't believe how absurd this is. 1963 and we're chasing something out of the dark ages with strength enough to carry off a fourteen-year-old boy without a trace. How are we supposed to catch such a thing? Throw a net over it?"

"Perhaps." Casey slid into her Plymouth's driver seat.

"Why don't we go grab a bite to eat and talk more about this?"

Casey looked up at him with an expression he couldn't read. "I'd love to Jim, but I've got work to do." She closed the car door, gave him a quick wave, and drove off.

Trabinski lit up a smoke. "Yeah...me too."

CHAPTER 34

Day Twelve – Late afternoon

The July sun channeled into the shadows of Malhela's nest, bathing her in its light as she sprawled on a bed of leaves and pieces of stained cardboard, she had scrounged from the yard below. She studied the boy, Tim Ryan, across from her propped up against a wall of dark metallic plate. His eyes were wide open but glazed, his mouth stuffed with the sleeve of his shirt, which she had ripped off and his hands shackled by a strip of metal she had twisted around them. This last accomplishment surprised Malhela. Twisting the metal to fashion the manacle took little effort. Her strength had somehow returned. She had not considered this till now but carrying the boy last night was also effortless. This was a good thing. Perhaps her magical powers would strengthen as well. Somewhat confused by this she searched her mind for the possible source of the improvement and grinned at her sudden realization. *It can only be the nourishment obtained from the birthgiver's flesh. Another reason for the Realm forbidding us to indulge in feasting on these females. Their flesh makes one more powerful, increases one's strength. I will continue to pursue this possibility. If true and I am destined to remain here I could rule these mortals as a goddess.*

The boy began to squirm; the hypnotic trance she had put him in last night was wearing off. Her magic had not improved.

***

Theresa Valenti, cub reporter for the *Long Island Daily Press* under the tutelage of Ace news hound Ted Newman spent the morning with him talking to people, especially mothers at the Division Avenue playground. The park had reopened. Only the Maze attraction remained closed; most likely permanently. A patrolman on duty refused to comment on anything she inquired about.

Theresa, a short, skinny but not boney girl with coal black hair, brown eyes, a pug nose, and a small mouth with thin lips wanted her own *By Line*. She followed Newman's lead, taking every bit of advice to heart. Even though pounding the pavement, sometimes to no avail, tended to be dull as well as boring at times, the thrill of receiving a news tip and following it up couldn't be beat. Especially if it resulted in *Breaking News*, a big story. She experienced some of this feeling when Newman told her they were granted an interview with the mother of the boy who disappeared from his driveway a week ago. But this was Newman's story, and she was along for the ride and to learn. She needed her own. She needed a scoop.

After the interview she and Newman returned to the office where fate dealt her an opportunity. She overheard someone, she wasn't sure if he was a reporter, mention a tip regarding increased police activity at a place called Rocco's Auto Wreckers. She knew where that was located and dashed out the door not saying a word to anyone.

Daylight was starting to fade when Theresa drove her beige Volkswagen onto New South Road and parked within walking distance of the junkyard.

She waited and watched for a few minutes as police officers hurried about the out skirts of the yard. When a white van with the words **Nassau County Medical Examiner** on its side drove down a street next to the junk yard and out of view, she decided it was time to go ask some questions.

Theresa Valenti, feeling confident, bravely approached the first police officer she came upon.

"Excuse me officer. Valenti from the Daily Press," she said politely but firmly while presenting her press card. "This looks serious." She pointed to the van. "What's going on?" A pencil and pad immediately appeared in her hands.

The officer, a gorilla of a man, towered over her. He looked tired. "You shouldn't be here ma'am. No press allowed. Please return to your car."

"I was dropped off," She lied.

"Come with me." The officer said, leading her around the fence and into the dirt parking lot where his patrol car sat with lights flashing.

"You're arresting me? You *can't* arrest me!" She protested in a high squeaky voice.

The officer guided her to the vehicle. "I *will* if you don't do what I tell you." He opened the passenger side door. "Now sit here and be quiet till I come back. Then I'll drive you to where you need to be. Or is someone coming back to get you?"

"Come on officer." She looked at his name tag. T. Swift. *Swift?* "Please officer Swift, give a girl a break. I need a story for my editor. I'll get fired if I don't come back with something. Just give me a little tidbit. I can punch it up, sing your praises for the way the department is handling this situation. What do you say?"

"Just stay here," he said and closed the door.

Theresa watched him leave, waited a few minutes then exited the vehicle quietly closing the door behind her. She crept along the stockade fence, past the chained up-front gate to the corner she had just been escorted from and peered surreptitiously around the fence at the unfolding scene.

In the advancing gloom Theresa could only make out two police officers, other than Officer Swift as well as three men in white lab coats scurrying into a wooded area at the dark end of the street. With pad in hand, she jotted down some observations plus her own thoughts on what had happened. Unexpectedly, the two patrolman turned around heading in her direction. *Oh no!* She darted back the way she came heading toward of group of abandoned fifty-five-gallon oil drums gathered at the far end of the parking lot. She would not sit in that police car again, so she hunkered down behind the drums to wait for an opportunity.

By the time the Medical Examiner's van departed— followed by the two unknown police officers— darkness had crept in around her. Just as she wondered where Officer Swift was — his patrol car still sat in front of her — he appeared. She watched as he marched up to the car and looked inside. Not seeing her, he straightened, scanned the area then got in, started the engine, looked around once more and put the vehicle in gear backing slowly out of the lot. *He thinks I left. Good. Now let's go see if they left me any scraps to write about.* She waited till the taillights of the police car were out of sight then stood up and quickly moved along the fence. As she approached the chain link portion of the fence, she thought she heard a noise on the other side of the locked gate. Always the curious reporter, she turned to investigate and was instantly stunned by the figures standing there: a disheveled-looking teenage boy, his hands bound by what appeared to be a strip of metal and his dog.

"Can you help me?" the boy said in a monotone voice.

"Oh my God!" Theresa came closer to the gate. "Are you hurt? The police were just here. You should have called out to them."

The boy stared as if in a trance. The dog sat casually by his side; mouth open with its tongue hanging out. "Can you help me?" The boy said again.

Theresa, collecting her wits, began writing in her pad thinking she might salvage something from this trip after all. "What's your name?" When he didn't reply she said, "What's your dog's name?"

"Can you help me?" was all he said.

Theresa looked around and saw headlights on the side street where all the commotion was earlier. "You stay right here. I think there's a policeman around the corner. I'll go get him and we'll get you out of there." She said quickly scribbling the boy's description on her pad.

Theresa Valenti, cub reporter was on the verge of the biggest story ever. Unfortunately, she would never get to write it.

As she was about to go look for the police officer, she heard a fluttering sound behind her; the dog suddenly barked, startling her and when she turned to see what he was barking at felt a searing pain jolt her neck, a blinding white light instantly flashed in her eyes. A second later her last thought *What?* dissolved into pure black as she collapsed to the dusty ground.

***

Malhela, pursuing her theory regarding the flesh of birthgivers being a source of increased strength—no longer concerned with flies or crows—carried her new prey into her nest for sampling. She was proud of her Tim Ryan slave as well as her guardian hound for the part they played in her little trap. It also delighted her that her timing was perfect; waiting till the male mortals — whom she had learned were called police — left the premises. She would take care of the large, worrisome one that stayed behind after she fed on her new victim. If the theory became fact and she grew to be an all-powerful goddess this nest would become her fortress and all interlopers would be done away with.

***

Evening –

Lieutenant Casey Talbot paced around her dining room table as if she were doing laps in some imaginary marathon. Her thoughts playing then replaying ideas for the next step in the plan to catch or take down this criminal or creature whatever the case may be. Rubbing the side of her nose she stopped and gazed down at the yellow legal pad resting on the tabletop, reading the notes jotted there. *That warehouse will be useful. Jim confirmed it was in a transition phase and nearly empty. The owners were cooperative. That's good. There are second floor windows. Perfect for a man with a rifle. A straight line of fire if I decide on the street in front of Rocco's.* She looked at her watch. *Jim said the yard was under surveillance around the clock. That'll work. I'll do a quick recon myself then decide on the best location.*

With that she slipped into her tennis shoes, checked her 9mm Luger, placed it back in her shoulder holster rig, donned a lightweight cream-colored wind breaker and left her apartment.

As Casey approached Rocco's Auto Wreckers and Junk Emporium, she noticed a beige Volkswagen parked in the shadows at the curb. She pulled her Plymouth up next to it and shined her vehicle's spotlight into its interior. Empty. Force of habit made her jot down the license plate number. *Hmmm. I'll keep this spot in mind. It's close enough to Rocco's. Could be ideal.*

Moving slowly toward the junkyard she caught sight of a police cruiser parked on the side street they had discussed near the warehouse. She couldn't see the occupants inside the vehicle due to the absence of streetlights along that stretch of road. *I'll announce myself in a minute. Wouldn't look good if they shot me.*

She drove into the parking lot, parked in front of a bunch of rusted fifty-five-gallon oil drums, killed the engine, and sat listening to the night. It seemed oddly quiet. *Okay. Let's get to work.* She exited her car and scanned the area. *I think I'll cross this spot off the list. Might be too obvious...even for a harpy. Shit! Could we really catch or even subdue such a thing? Maybe we should equip everyone with nets.* Casey started to feel uncertain about the success of this decoy plan.

The humid night made her wind breaker stick to her, so she removed it and tossed it in the car. *I'd better check in with the boys. Let them know what I'm doing here. Odd they didn't see me…or hear me pull in. They're in big trouble if they're asleep.*

***

Malhela paused her mastication when her keen ears picked up the sound of one of those horseless conveyances entering the vicinity. Her guardian raised his head and offered a soft *woof.* She looked quickly at the boy and saw he remained in the trance she had re-applied then crept to the nest opening and peered into the dark. A slow menacing hiss signaled her displeasure at what she saw. Immediately, she turned and whispered in the boy's ear, then did the same with the hound. *This will be enjoyable.*

***

Casey started across the parking lot but abruptly stopped when she saw movement out of the corner of her eye. Two figures moved through the shadows, approaching her on the other side of the locked gate. She turned towards them, removing her Luger from its holster at the same time. Casey was stunned for a second as the two figures stepped into the spotlight circle provided by the only working yard lamp.

"Tim? Tim Ryan?" Casey stepped closer to the chain link gate and scanned the yard behind him. The boy resembled a modern-day street urchin; filthy clothes, a t-shirt with one sleeve torn off, dark circles beneath lifeless blue eyes, no shoes on his feet and unruly hair smattered with dust, leaves, and something else. Disturbingly, his hands were bound by a twisted piece of sheet metal.

Beside him stood a friendly looking German Shepherd. Its black eyes watching her closely.

"Can you help me?" Tim Ryan said in a low, weak sounding voice.

Without thinking Casey blurted, "Who did this to you?"

"Can you help me?" He replied, sounding like a recorded message.

"Yes, yes of course. Stay right there. I'll get help." *Expect the unexpected. I'll get the boys in the cruiser over here then call this in. God! What's that awful smell?* She took a step and froze when a sultry female voice said from behind her. "Are you an Elf?"

Casey twirled, pistol at the ready. *Hell's bells! Will you look at this. And it speaks English.*

Before her stood a butt naked, bronzed skin macabre beauty, with the menacing eyes of a leopard, partially extended leathery bat wings as well as white feather like quills protruding from the top of her forehead. Casey noted the claws on each hand. She was surprised to see that this creature was her height.

"Well…Aren't you a slutty little Tinker Bell? I guess clothing is optional where you come from?" Casey flipped off the safety on her Luger.

"Are you an *Elf?* Show me your ears!" To Malhela the Elfoj de la Regno —Elves of the Realm— were powerful, magical allies. She remembered *this one* had used a magical device that launched projectiles which killed her first hound. Most likely the same one that was pointed at her now.

She could certainly use an ally if the being in front of her was truly this world's answer to an elf. If not, she would kill it.

Casey, not sure where to go with this played along. "That's right I am an elf. What's it to you?"

"Then you shall be my comrade in arms. My ally." Malhela said.

"I don't think so. Thanks just the same." Casey adjusted her stance.

Malhela tilted her head, glaring at the elf woman. "You have no choice," she whispered in a threatening tone.

"Oh…I have plenty of choices." *One being…I'll shoot you in the leg, you murdering bitch and go for help. Or just kill you outright.*

In the blink of an eye Casey's pistol went flying. Knocked from her hand by a powerful blow from the harpy. She felt a sharp stinging sensation just below her left ear immediately followed by a burning slash across her chest. Blood trickled down into her cleavage. Half her blouse hung like a triangular flag from her shoulder.

Casey staggered back surprised by the speed of this creature. "So? You want to play dirty?"

Malhela placed her fisted clawed hands on her hips. "Play *dirty?*"

Assuming a Jiu Jitsu stance Casey instantly spun, launching a powerful kick to the harpy's throat. The creature stumbled back choking. Without hesitation Casey pummeled the harpy with punches and kicks; giving it no time to react. The mythological beast went down on one knee and Casey kicked it in the side of the head, drawing what appeared to be blood. With a horrific screech the harpy bolted away into the night sky.

Casey leaned forward, hands on her knees catching her breath. She looked askance at the gate and saw the boy still standing there as if at attention. The dog, however, was gone.

"Stay right there," she said to the boy. "I'll be right back."

Blood still trickled from her neck and chest, and she wiped it away with her fingers. *I need to call this in. Must tell Jim this damn thing is real.*

She straightened, picked up her pistol and instinctively went to put it in the holster but realized that half her blouse now hung over it like a drape. She quickly tried to repair the damage by tucking the shredded cloth in the top of her bra, but it wouldn't stay. *Damn it all. Wind breaker.* Covering herself as best she could, she moved to her car, discarded the holster and the tattered blouse, tucked the Luger in her waist band and quickly donned the wind breaker. All the while scanning the dark sky for the harpy's return.

Puzzled by the lack of response from the parked cruiser Casey hurried toward it. The driver's side window was open, and she could see the silhouette of a large man sitting there; his head leaning back against the seat.

What the hell? He is asleep! There'll be a serious reprimand in store for this goof off. But as she came closer, she grimaced at the sight of a ragged slit across the man's throat. Quickly gathering her wits, she peered in the window for his partner but found no sign of such person. She reached over and closed the man's eyes.

"Big mistake being here by yourself." *The bitch killed that poor slob.*

On her way back to make the call Casey found the area behind the locked gate empty. Tim Ryan was gone.

Suddenly, Casey Talbot did something she had learned to control over the years of military as well as police training. She lost her temper.

Grabbing the chain link gate with both hands she shook it violently, shouting into the darkness, "Your days are numbered, you God damned slut! The next time we meet … *YOU'RE DEAD!*"

***

Lieutenant James Trabinski, jarred from a sound sleep, wondered who the hell was pounding on his front door at this wretched hour. *This can't be good.*

Shuffling across the floor in his underwear he opened a night table drawer and pulled out a .38 Special. Checked the round then groggily went to the front of the house. Leaving the chain lock in place, he opened the door and peered through the narrow opening. He was instantly awake.

"Shit!" Placing his revolver on a side table he quickly unlocked the door and flung it open.

Casey stood there, hair a mess, flecked with dust, blood on her neck, and her half-unbuttoned wind breaker revealing a bloody gash on her chest.

"Hi," she said in a tired voice while at the same time offering him a half smile that made her look like a little girl who had just been caught doing something naughty.

Trabinksi gently took her by the shoulders and brought her into the house.

"What the hell happened?" He eyed the ragged laceration on her neck just below her left ear. It needed to be cleaned immediately. The one on her chest didn't look much better.

"Come with me," he said before she could answer his question.

He led her into the bedroom, carefully sat her on the edge of the bed and rushed into the adjoining bathroom. Within seconds he was back with bandages, a damp face cloth, Hydrogen Peroxide, and cotton swabs. He pointed to her wind breaker. "Take that off."

"I can take care of myself," she said but her tone wasn't convincing.

"Yeah… I can see that. Let's get you fixed up so these don't get infected. Come on."

The word "infected" immediately brought Stanley Bolton to her mind and his illness presumably caused by this harpy.

Casey quickly unbuttoned the rest of the wind breaker and Trabinski helped her shrug it off.

Had the circumstances been different Trabinski in the presence of this beautiful woman with her charms exposed to him, would have entertained thoughts of a romantic interlude, but instead he concentrated on mending her bloody wounds. His fear that her safety could be in jeopardy had just been confirmed.

With a gentle touch he tended to her injuries.

"Now…tell me what happened."

As he waited for her reply, he saw her hands begin to shake. Then she instantly grabbed both his hands, squeezing them. She fixed her eyes on his and said in a soft conspiratorial voice, "Jim? *It's real*. I fought it. The God damned harpy is real."

CHAPTER 35

Day Thirteen – 2 am.
Rocco's Auto Wreckers and Junk Emporium

Lieutenant Casey Talbot had radioed in a 10-13, Code 2: Urgent - Officer down while still at the junk yard. She had waited till the units and ambulance arrived before leaving to advise Trabinski. On the way to his residence, she took it upon herself to call in a Level Four task force which allowed the 2nd and 8th precincts to combine forces. She gave instructions to converge on the junk yard immediately and await further orders.

Now, after receiving first aid as well as a white T-shirt three times her size from Trabinski and bringing him up to speed on the situation; with emphasis on Tim Ryan being held hostage she was back at Rocco's with Trabinski by her side surrounded by a team of law enforcement professionals. They had decided to tell the men what they were about to face regardless of how absurd it sounded. Their lives would depend on it.

Six patrol cars crowded the dirt parking lot. Their flashing lights created a bizarre carnival atmosphere partially illuminating the groups of dark figures milling about.

Detective Peter Taylor broke away from the group he had been conversing with and hurried to Trabinski. "A real shit storm went down last night Lieutenant. We found the remains of that missing teenage girl in the wooded area behind the junk yard. Some newspaper reporter disappeared. They found her car parked up the street. Then Swift gets knocked off after he volunteered to take a solo watch when his partner called in sick. And now this. What's going on around here?" He swept his arm in a circular motion indicating the scene around him.

"It could get worse. Stay alert. We'll fill you in shortly." Trabinski looked over at Casey who had gone to her car, put on her windbreaker, opened the trunk, and started searching for something. He picked up his bullhorn.

"Alright people listen up. I've just been informed we have a hostage situation here. A teenage boy named Tim Ryan is being held by the piece of shit that most likely killed officer Swift and probably murdered Sergeant Sanfield's son as well as abducting and murdering three Hillsville children.

"This killer is unlike any you have ever encountered. Extremely dangerous. Though it is our sworn duty to apprehend such a criminal with as little violence as possible, deadly force may be the only option in this case. Watch each other's back, stay sharp. Our primary objective is to rescue the boy unharmed." Trabinski looked over his shoulder for Casey and saw her approaching with a rifle in her hands. A large flashlight was attached to the Carbine's barrel by black electrical tape.

Trabinski continued. "Lieutenant Talbot came face to face with the killer a few hours ago and attempted to make an arrest but failed due to the agility of this degenerate. She'll give you the details." He handed the bull horn to Casey.

Taking the bull horn, she cradled the rifle in her left arm wincing as it brushed against her chest wound.

"Gentlemen? What I'm about to tell you is no joke. I can guarantee you won't believe me. I scarcely believe it myself, but it is fact. What we face here this morning is not human...*and* it's not an animal. Those of you that are already smirking back there in the shadows better take this seriously. You won't be smiling when you're suddenly attacked from out of nowhere. So, pay attention. The killer we're after is from another world. Not from outer space but rather from another time. Once thought to be mythological the creature is known as a harpy."

A wave of murmurs rolled across the parking lot.

"This creature is intelligent, powerful, and quick. She flies. Yes...I said *she*. You men will find her very alluring, so if I were you, I would suppress any illicit thoughts that may pop into your heads at the sight of her. They'll get you killed.

"She is hold up somewhere in this junk yard and is probably watching and listening to us right now. It speaks and understands English. As for the boy, Tim Ryan, he appeared to be in a trance when I saw him last night. His hands were shackled by a twisted strip of sheet metal. Oh...and there was a dog with him."

"What kind of dog?" Sergeant Todd Anderson asked stepping forward.

He and Officer Cummings had arrived with two new K-9-unit recruits. Cleo, Leo's sister and Skipper, a solid black German Shepherd. Both waited quietly in the Unit's vehicle.

Casey lowered the bull horn. "A big, friendly looking German Shepherd."

"That's got to be Leo. He's, my dog. We've been looking for him."

"Hope he's *still* your dog when we go in there." Casey said remembering her encounter with Rocco's dog Caesar.

Casey put the bullhorn back to her mouth. "Okay...those of you who have vehicles equipped with riot guns or rifles get them now. Make sure you have extra rounds. Sidearms will have to suffice for the rest. Make sure your flashlights are in working order."

While she waited for the command to be completed, she glanced over at Trabinski as he strode back from his car carrying a Winchester Model 12, 12-gauge pump action shot gun.

With a raised voice — she didn't want to broadcast her plans to the harpy — Casey continued. "Alright. Let's get this show on the road. We number fourteen, including Lieutenant Trabinski and myself. I'll lead team A, Lieutenant Trabinski team B. Since this creature could be hiding anywhere in the yard, we'll use a flanking maneuver. Team B to the right, Team A to the left. We've got a lot of area to cover so use those torches to check out every nook and cranny you come upon." Casey held up her rifle with the heavy-duty flashlight taped to it and flipped on the beam. "She's going to see us coming, so watch each other's six. Call out if you find the boy. Once we're inside I'm going to try and lure it out of hiding so stay alert. This thing could be in the sky above you." She turned to Trabinski and gave him a look that silently asked if he was ready. He nodded. "Two by twos, search, and cover people. Sergeant Anderson? You and Cummings lead us in with your dogs. You front Lieutenant Talbots team. Cummings will be my lead. Let's move!"

Trabinski positioned his team, unlocked the gate, and swung it open. He nodded to Anderson to proceed but saw the sergeant struggling with his dog.

"Anderson? Move out."

"She refuses to go through the gate Lieutenant. Don't know what's gotten into her."

Trabinksi looked towards Cummings and saw her dog backing away from the gate. *Trained police dogs balking at an assignment is not a good sign.*

"Looks like we go in without the dogs," Trabinski said to Casey who was standing nearby. She gave a quick nod.

"Pull them back Sergeant. We'll go without them."

The two teams entered the darkness.

Fourteen beams of light bobbed and panned across the yard revealing twisted hulks of rusted automotive relics; all potential hiding places.

***

In the dark depth of her nest, Malhela furious with herself for letting the Elfin witch get the better of her gently patted the gash on her head with a soft wet leaf. *The next time we meet, you're dead, the witch said.* She snickered to herself. *We shall see who is **dead** the next time we meet.*

Malhela froze. Listening intently. She heard the banshee wail that always signaled the approach of the police, only this time there were many.

From her high vantage point, she saw flickering-colored lights in the distance, moving fast in her direction. Her eyes flared as she watched more than three horseless conveyances with blinding red and blue flashing lights enter the barren lot below her. Police mortals spilled from them in twos. *Could this be their idea of a siege? Oh, if only my sisters were here. What fun we would have.* She drifted back into the shadows eyeing her slave and guardian. A devious tactic began to take shape in her mind.

***

Lieutenant Casey Talbot positioned her team then strode to the center of the junk yard's front lot, rifle in her right hand, the stock tucked securely under her arm, the barrel with flashlight aimed forward. In her left hand was the bullhorn.

"Hey Tinker Bell! I'm back." Casey turned in a slow circle killing the shadows with her light. "How's your head?" Casey took a step deeper into the yard shining her light in all directions. "Remember I said I'd kill you the next time we met? Well, I changed my mind. I've decided to let you live if you give me the boy unharmed." She continued sweeping her weapon's light. "So…let's not play games. I know you understand me. Just bring me the boy and we'll leave."

The yard remained quiet. Nothing moved. Then Casey heard a finger snap twice on her right. She turned her head slowly and spotted Trabinski kneeling behind a rusted Studebaker carcass. He pointed two fingers at his eyes then at the top of a mountainous pile of junk. Casey quickly turned shining her light upward revealing a dark triangular opening. She thought she saw something move there. She whistled at her team as she pointed to the opening. "Be ready," she called. "Watch the sky!"

Then it started to rain.

Perfect…just perfect. Casey flipped her windbreaker's hood onto her head. With her light still trained on the triangular opening Casey was about to speak again when a vicious growl followed by someone screaming startled her. A single gunshot accompanied the screams. Then silence.

Casey's team stood back-to-back searching the area around them. Flashlight beams danced back and forth.

"Carver's down!" Someone shouted.

"Shit! Get him to the gate!" Casey turned and found Trabinski standing next to her. He motioned to his team to spread out. "Where the hell is it? Could the damn thing be invisible?"

"Wasn't invisible last night," she said assuming a rifleman's stance. Just then a thumping sound broke the silence. "Son of a bitch! Knock it off you little punk! God damn it!" Someone yelled. Then a flapping sound came from that direction followed by a painful shout that ended abruptly.

"Watch the sky!" Casey repeated.

Trabinski looked towards his men and was about to speak when someone cried out, "It got Myers!"

"This isn't working," Trabinski said to Casey. "I agree," she replied.

He grabbed the bullhorn. "All teams fall back and regroup at the gate."

Suddenly, more growling and screaming. The flapping sound seemed to be everywhere. The thumping sound came again. More yelling. Random shots were fired. Rain blurred flashlight beams bounced in all directions. A patrolman's severed head rolled in the ensuing mud.

Confusion had taken over. The scene was turning into an every man for himself situation.

As Casey turned, trying to catch a glimpse of the harpy, she saw Trabinski go down, blood streaming from his head. She spun, finger slightly pressing the trigger of her Carbine ready to shoot his assailant when the sight of Tim Ryan pounding Trabinski's head and shoulders with a broom handle brandished like a baseball bat made her pause. "Tim Ryan! Stop right there and put the bat on the ground. Do it *now*. Don't make me shoot you."

The boy hesitated; the bat raised ready to strike again.

Casey sidled closer to Trabinksi who was lying unconscious in the rain-soaked dirt thinking she could block the kid from delivering another blow and disarm him at the same time. That was a mistake.

With her attention focused on the Ryan boy Casey failed to notice the dark shape bounding through the steady rain towards her. It hit her full force knocking her to the ground. She managed to hang onto her rifle and jabbed its butt into the slavering maw of the German Shepherd on top of her. The hood of her windbreaker slipped off in the struggle and the rain quickly soaked her head and face. The dog jumped back barking ferociously. Froth and saliva flew from its mouth.

Before Casey had a chance to make a move Tim Ryan swung the bat downward —as if it were an axe and he was splitting a log— across her knees. Fiery pain shot through her legs, and she screamed out a litany of swear words that would make a sailor blush. When she saw Tim Ryan raising the broom handle for another strike she tried to move her rifle into position to block the impact but felt her arm quickly pinned to the ground. Instinctively she turned her head and saw a taloned foot holding it firmly. A quick look toward Tim Ryan showed him standing frozen in place with the panting dog standing by his side. Casey struggled to free her arm and as she looked up, she saw the harpy looming over her; dripping diaphanous bat wings fully extended, naked wet skin glistening with beaded droplets of rain, leopard eyes aglow as if lit from within, muscular arms folded across her breasts. With a grotesque fanged smile warping its beautiful face the harpy said, "It is no use, elf. You cannot win."

Malhela stared down at her nemesis, "Did you think your death threat would frighten me?"

She applied more pressure on the elf woman's arm. "So now it is you who will die on this night."

Casey's knees were throbbing and her grip on her rifle was starting to loosen. Through gritted teeth she said, "Don't be so sure of yourself *bitch*."

Malhela hissed as she reached down, grabbed the elf's wet hair, and pulled her head back exposing the throat. "You should not have refused me," she said raising her hand, daggered fingers stretching.

Casey fought with her free hand, punching and scratching to no avail. Just as she saw the harpy's arm raise to strike her two quick shots rang out.

One bullet whizzed past Malhela's face, the other went through her raised hand. With an unearthly screech of pain, she leapt into the air, winging toward the top of the mountain of junk.

Pushing herself into a sitting position, Casey massaged her arm and flexed her fingers, wiped the wet from her eyes, steadied her rifle, aimed, and fired in rapid succession.

In her wavering flashlight beam she saw the harpy wobble as it climbed higher. Casey fired again. Through the mist she thought she saw the harpy's wings go limp just before it plummeted behind the metallic pyramid. She held her shooter's position for a few moments, waiting to see if it reappeared. Finally, she lowered her weapon and looked over her shoulder at Trabinski lying unconscious in the muck. Nearby, Tim Ryan sat cross legged, his head in his hands, the dog beside him.

Suddenly, Casey found herself being lifted up by strong hands. "We got you Lieutenant. Just take it easy," a patrolman said.

As she was being helped to her feet, she saw others attending to Trabinski and the boy. The dog was being led away on a leash by Sergeant Todd Anderson.

"Did you find the body?" She asked. "Find it and make sure the damn thing is dead."

Two patrolmen nodded in unison and hurried away.

The whine of ambulance sirens seemed to be everywhere as Casey was helped over to Detective Taylor squatting at Trabinski's side. "Detective? How is he?" She struggled to keep her voice from shaking.

"He took some nasty whacks in the head but he's one of those thick-skulled Polacks. Pretty sure he'll be fine."

"I'm going to hold you to that."

At the sound of her voice Trabinski's eyes fluttered open, a questioning look formed on his muddy, blood-flecked face.

Casey nodded. "It's over. The boy is safe. The harpy is dead. I think we can close this case." She hoped she wasn't mistaken.

Trabinski managed to smile then started shaking as if he was freezing even though he had a blanket over him, which was no longer dry due to the continuing rain.

"Don't you quit on me Lieutenant." Casey said, returning the smile.

Through the dismal rain white coated men carrying stretchers hurried toward them.

Before allowing the medics to help her Lieutenant Casey Talbot gave one last look toward the towering mountain of junk where the harpy had gone down. She motioned to one of her men to come closer. "I want to be notified immediately when the body of that thing is found. Regardless of the time."

"I'll make sure it happens, lieutenant," the patrolman said and headed away.

Refusing to be placed on a stretcher Casey hobbled with the help of two medics to the waiting ambulance.

CHAPTER 36

Day Fourteen – Mid Morning
Central General Hospital

Slices of morning sun entered the hospital room through the open blinds, brightening the soothing pale blue walls, giving them the appearance of a cloudless sky. It added a needed cheerfulness as well as a relaxed atmosphere to this site of healing.

Lieutenant James Trabinski sat propped up in the hospital bed assigned to him, a white bandage wrapped around his head. A black eye and swollen bruised cheek bone made him look like a defeated prize fighter. "How's the Ryan kid?" He asked Detective Pete Taylor who was standing at the right side of the bed.

"Seems to be doing fine. They have him in a room down the hall for observation. He claims he can't remember a thing about what happened. His parents are with him now. The father is worried you two will press charges for assault and battery." Taylor replied.

Casey Talbot seated in a chair at the left side of the bed with her crutches leaning on its arm, right leg in a cast from knee to ankle stretched out in front of her said, "Probably not."

"Damn embarrassing to be brought down by a skinny teenager with a broom stick." Trabinski added. "I won't be pressing charges."

Detective Taylor faced Casey and gave her a sympathetic look. "Sorry for the loss of your partner Lieutenant. I didn't know the man, but Carver seemed like a good cop."

Casey looked down at her hands. "Thank you, detective. He will be missed."

"How many did we lose, Pete?" Trabinksi asked.

Taylor took a deep breath and quickly let it out. "Four, if you include Swift. We lost Myers and Howard and Detective Carver of course."

Trabinski shook his head and winced at the instant jab of pain.

Casey shifted in her seat trying for a more comfortable position. "By the way," she said. "Thanks for taking those shots when you did. She had me pinned. Not sure how that would have turned out if you hadn't shot her in the hand."

"No thanks needed," Taylor replied. "I shouldn't have hesitated, but I was gob smacked by the sight of it. Sexiest monster I've ever seen. That distraction plus rain in my eyes caused the shots to miss their mark. I was aiming at its head. Sorry Lieutenant."

Casey waved away that last apology. "Did they find the body?"

"Not yet."

Trabinski and Casey shared a worried look. "I didn't even see the damn thing. Could it have disappeared or vaporized when you killed it?" He asked.

"I have no idea," Casey said rubbing her bandaged left leg. "Let's just hope they find the body soon."

Detective Taylor looked at the clock on the wall. "Well, I better get back to the precinct. Paperwork will be piling up. Plus, I need to let the captain know that this thing is pretty much wrapped up.

" One more thing. They found the missing reporter …what was left of her that is, up in that mountain of junk as well as more bones, an old shotgun, and a tin box containing chunks of meat. It must have been the creature's nest or something.

"Okay I'd better go. Talk to you later. And don't go milking this Lieutenant…you look too comfortable in that bed."

"Get out of here!" Trabinski said good naturedly.

Taylor said his goodbyes and left the room. The door closing behind him.

Now alone Casey stared at Trabinski's face. She wrestled with the feelings welling up inside her. She had trained herself not to be emotional, but the training seemed to be failing here. She cleared her throat, breaking the awkward silence.

"You know? Yesterday, when I saw you go down, I instantly thought it can't end like this… I'm glad it didn't." Casey said with tenderness in her voice. She offered him an enticing smile.

Trabinski reached over and took her hand. "Me too."

A soft knock came at the door.

Casey started to get up. "That'll be my brother. He's going to take me home."

Trabinski still held her hand. "Just a minute," he said to the door. He needed one last look at her face before she left. Then without thinking he said, "There's a new restaurant in Huntington called the Blue

Grotto. Heard it was pretty good. How about we check it out when we're both healed up?"

Casey tilted her head coyly. "Are you asking me on a *date* Lieutenant?"

"You might say that." He gently released her hand and smiled as best he could.

As Casey left the main hospital entrance with her brother, she noticed a nurse pushing a wheelchair. A thin teenage boy sat in it leaning his head on one hand. A large woman walked alongside him. Casey immediately recognized her. Mrs. Bolton. The boy must be Stanley. *I should probably speak to him.*

The nurse waited with Stanley while his mother went for her car. Casey hobbled up to him. "Are you Stanley Bolton?"

Startled, the boy looked up at her.

"He can't answer you," the nurse said. "He lost his voice."

But Stanley nodded his response.

Casey adjusted her crutches for a more comfortable stance. "Stanley? I'm Lieutenant Talbot, Nassau County Police. Don't have my badge so you'll just have to take my word for it." She smiled as she studied his pale complexion and tired eyes, hoping that what she had to tell him would make him feel at least somewhat better.

"I spoke to Tim Ryan. He told me everything."

A troubled look appeared on the boy's face.

"Don't worry Stanley." Casey said in a reassuring tone. "We discovered that everything Tim told us was true."

A look of surprise replaced the troubled one on Stanley's face.

Casey turned to the nurse. "I need to speak with Stanley alone for a minute. Do you mind?"

The nurse moved back a few feet and stood next to Casey's brother.

Casey lowered her voice. "Stanley? We know about the harpy. I actually saw it and we killed it. It's all over."

Stanley abruptly straightened in the wheelchair and withdrew a pencil and pad from beneath the blanket covering his legs. He scribbled…

NOT OVER. CAN'T BE KILLED! IMMORTAL!

***

In what he called his club house, which in actuality was nothing more than a large attic crawl space, nine-year-old Jonathan Bolton sat cross legged among his toys.

This served as a secret hideaway for Jonathan who came here whenever possible to escape the pressures put upon him by his brothers and parents. It was surprising that no one had ever questioned his whereabouts when he spent time here.

The entrance to his inner sanctum was a four-foot square opening in the ceiling of an upstairs utility closet. He would use the step ladder stored there to climb up and push over the piece of plywood covering the opening. Before entering he would climb back down and close the closet door. So far, he had never been discovered. And today was no different. Now that Stanley was back home all the attention was on him.

The air temperature in the room varied with the conditions outside which inspired Jonathan's imagination. When it was cold, he would bundle up and pretend he participated in an Alaskan or North Pole adventure. When hot like today his imagination sometimes took him to darkest Africa on a Jungle Jim adventure or into the deserts with Chick Chandler and Tubo Smith, the Soldiers of Fortune.

Today, he and his Roman soldiers were on a quest to the temple of Fortuna in the hills of Rome in search of great treasures.

Most of Jonathan's possessions were stolen. He had learned quickly from his brother Stanley how to be a sneak thief. Stealing had become a successful habit. He felt very proud of himself for lifting his brother Arthur's transistor radio before he left for the Peace Corps. He would play it up here using the ear plug to avoid detection.

Another habit, if it could be called that, was reading. He read everything and anything he could get his hands on. And having read that the Romans spoke Latin he stole *The Beginners Book of Latin* from the library the last time his father had taken him there and studied it thoroughly.

So, to succeed on this quest and obtain the treasures, one had to read the Latin inscriptions from a book of spells which was in his possession, since he was the Alchemist of the group.

He ordered his men to surround the temple sitting high on a snow-covered mountain— a sheet covered stack of magazines— and to await his next command. They all stood poised with their swords raised for action.

Jonathan eased his way across the hard wood planked floor expertly preventing any creaking from the boards and withdrew two books from an old wooden soapbox standing on its side. One was the book stolen from the library. The other happened to be the one he had gleefully stolen from Stanley weeks ago.

The Alchemist returned to his troops, knelt before them, and reverently placed the books on the ground. He carefully opened the Latin textbook to the page he wanted then turned in a ceremonial manner to the publication with the black hard cover and its swirling gold border. Gazing at the raised gold Old English lettering the Alchemist read the title:

Lovecraft's
Spells and Conjuring's

***

Deep in the wooded area behind Rocco's Auto Wreckers and Junk Emporium languished an abandoned railroad spur overgrown with weeds and tall grass.

Originally intended for running freight to and from the warehouse on New South Road, it fell prey to rising construction costs and never reached completion. An open trench dug about four feet deep to accommodate electrical signal wires on the left side of the tracks now filled with thick brush and litter became Malhela's place of healing.

Angry and in pain from three gunshot wounds Malhela used the last of her adrenaline to crawl into the trench and cover herself completely with the detritus at her disposal. She didn't know how long it would take her to heal this time, but she would hold onto this hatred for as long as it took. She pulled her knees to her chest and wrapped her wings tightly around herself forming a healing cocoon.

Drifting into unconsciousness Malhela thought, *I was careless. This is the work of the omen. It doesn't matter now. What is done is done. But these mortals will know my wrath when I return.* With a sigh she let the darkness take her.

A CALL TO EVIL
PART TWO

CHAPTER 37

July 1964

The high noon sun cooked the black parking lot macadam as Stanley Bolton pushed six empty shopping carts to their collection station at the front of the Penn Fruit Market. He had been encouraged by a female classmate—who had come across him sitting alone at the top of the athletic field bleachers, smoking, looking forlorn— to stop moping around the school and do something to overcome his dark mood. She had empathy for him; knowing what it was like to be rejected. She even offered to help, which gave him a boost.

The school year had opened that September to the sad and disturbing news about the deaths of cheerleader Laurie Decker and popular school athlete Tommy Reinhardt. Rumors regarding how they died spread like wildfire through the school, but Stanley had a sick feeling that the harpy had killed them. He had no details to justify the feeling except for the one rumor that said Laurie had been missing for a few days before they found her body. If the harpy had murdered them, then he and Tim Ryan were responsible for their deaths by unleashing it.

Stanley carried this thought with him throughout the school year. It was the essence of his dark mood.

Stanley knew he had to get out of the house this summer. Things at home had become a real drag over the past year with his father having a mild heart attack and his brother Artie reported missing in the jungles of Guinea— the latter had turned his mother into a sulking zombie. Little brother Jonathan seemed to take things in stride. So, Stanley decided before school ended to work at this grocery store. Stanley didn't know that his family's misfortunes were the aftermath of Malhela's curse.

It was an easy part time job for a kid who couldn't speak. They paid him a dollar an hour to keep the parking lot clear of abandoned carriages. He had to wear a white polo shirt and a dorky red apron with the store's name on it while he worked. Not a big deal since the job had other benefits like employee discounts, free samples of cheese as well as other goodies free for the taking.

Stanley's inability to speak was a constant reminder of the drastic mistake he made last year. Luckily, he regained full use of his legs and left arm in early August. The memory of the harpy was always lurking somewhere in the shadows of his mind waiting to spoil his day. He often wondered what had happened to her. The policewoman had told him they killed it. But that was impossible. The book said she was immortal. He often had nightmares about her returning.

Stanley wanted to be rid of this smothering malaise, so he took his classmate up on her offer.

Janey Del Grasso, one time sidekick of Paulette Berdino was a chubby five-foot two young lady —whom Stanley thought was chubby in all the right places—had instilled a new confidence in him. She even helped to change his appearance by turning his single eyebrow into two separate ones—a painful process of shaving and plucking the unwanted pilosity—as well as restyling his hair. She said he looked like a young version of her favorite comedian Jerry Lewis. Stanley gladly accepted that comparison and hoped the "monkey boy" comparison would finally go away.

When she fixed her big brown puppy dog eyes on him and flashed her angelic dimpled smile, he felt he had a reason to put away his "Who cares?" attitude.

Some days he felt like an entirely different person; almost happy.

Seeing Stanley fumble to pull a pad and pencil from his pocket every time he wanted to say something, the store manager gave Stanley a small ringed steno pad fastened to a thick string lanyard to wear around his neck. Suggesting it would help him communicate more easily. At first, Stanley thought it made him look like an idiot but soon discovered it had advantages.

On a whim he wrote on the pad's cardboard cover with black magic marker: **WOULD YOU LIKE SOME HELP?**

Initially, he found that by showing this to elderly women or elderly couples with a cart full of grocery bags gained him a sympathetic response. Most times a twenty-five-cent tip would be his reward for placing the bags in their cars and removing the empty carriage. Soon he discovered it worked on young mothers with screaming kids. The tips magically increased to fifty cents on rainy days. He always remembered to flip the cover over to the words: **THANK YOU!** Stanley was surprised as well as pleased that this little side hustle had drawn no complaints. Many afternoons he would go home with two to three extra dollars in his pocket. More dough to spend on Janey.

After returning home from the hospital last July, Stanley had seen Tim Ryan a few times. He would stop by to see how his recovery was coming along; talk for a while about meaningless things then leave. He would never bring up the harpy in their conversations and would change the subject if Stanley did.

Tim always seemed preoccupied those few times Stanley saw him; like his real thoughts were somewhere far away and he didn't want those thoughts revealed. Even when Stanley scribbled his questions about what took place while he was in the hospital, Tim refused to talk about it. Stanley had a strong feeling that something pretty scary had happened during that time causing his friend to be so closed mouth.

With the coming of the new school year Tim's visits stopped and Stanley rarely saw him. He never found out about Tim's abduction by Malhela.

Now with another summer in the making the new and improved Stanley Bolton made plans to reconnect with his friend and convince him that a serious discussion was needed about the harpy's supposed immortality.

***

As the last remaining months of 1963 slid into a miasma of sadness and confusion due to the assassination of President John F. Kennedy, Lieutenant Cassandra Talbot—though inundated by Federal law enforcement bulletins concerning the matter—still could not dismiss the words Stanley Bolton had written regarding the harpy being immortal.

She remembered seeing the word *immortal* when she researched the creature that day in the library but gave it no credence since most of the description came across as medieval hog wash. The only way to prove this as nonsense was to find the body once and for all. Case closed. Trabinski didn't buy the immortality bit either when she told him.

When not working or spending time with the recuperating Jim Trabinski she would replay the battle with the creature on that rainy night in her mind; watching it fall through the mist as she fired her weapon at it. She reread all the reports on the fruitless search for the body. This prodded her to perform her own personal search for the harpy's remains once her knees were completely healed.

Finding proof of the creature's death bordered on obsession. She knew every nook and cranny that Rocco's Auto Wreckers and Junk Emporium had to offer. But came up with nothing more than sore feet. She even dragged Trabinski into the wooded area behind the junkyard one sunny, frigid day in early December —even though the ground was frozen and covered with ice crusted leaves — thinking between the two of them they might spot something, anything that might have been missed.

Trabinski, knowing full well the reason she was doing this, tried to gently reel her back to reality.

"Casey? Darling, there's nothing else we can do now. I know you don't want to hear it but there's no way we'll find anything in this tundra."

She had quietly acquiesced. But just like Stanley Bolton the nightmares of this evil beauty returning were all too real.

Now, one year later Lieutenant Cassandra "Casey" Talbot immersed in the heightened stress of the current law enforcement issues facing not only Long Island but the country as well, wondered if the harpy was truly gone. They never found the body. Perhaps it *had* disappeared—vanished into thin air— after being shot as Jim Trabinksi said. That would be a good thing, but she doubted it. There was no feeling of closure to the case though there had been no further incidents after that night.

The harpy's dark menacing image would sometimes drift into Casey's daydreams adding to the tension that surrounded her lately on a daily basis. Her only bright spot in all the gloom was Jim Trabinski and the time she spent with him. Though his days currently were as anxiety ridden as hers, he always had a way to make her smile or laugh plus he understood how she felt about not finding proof the harpy was dead. He would avoid the subject unless she needed to talk about it.

These days Casey found herself clinging to that bright spot.

***

Tim Ryan had received a clean bill of health from Doctor Wells— his family's doctor as well as Stanley's—and was released from Central General Hospital two days after the junkyard conflict with the harpy. He said he couldn't remember anything about that night or how he got there, however, at home alone in his room or by himself delivering papers he would experience mental snippets or mini flashbacks of certain random events. Some so disturbing he would find himself shaking as if he were freezing despite the summer heat.

In one snippet he was sitting in what seemed like a cave, hands bound, unable to speak watching in horror as the harpy ripped the flesh from the body of a dead young woman and ate it. The woman's dark lifeless eyes stared straight at him as if pleading with him for help.

A year later Tim would still see those eyes sometimes at night when he closed his own to sleep.

During the final days of the summer of '63 Tim kept to himself. Thinking; feeling guilty about his part in bringing this horror into their lives. He wanted to tell Stanley about the flashbacks but feared having what they called a nervous breakdown if he forced himself to remember. Better to try and bury them instead.

He found himself shying away from movies, magazines and TV shows that might trigger the memories. He even stayed home—claiming to feel nauseous—when his father took the family to see *Jason and the Argonauts* at the drive-in theater. He didn't think he could handle the fight scene in the movie involving the harpies.

After delivering his newspapers Tim would spend his time building model cars, fighter planes and rockets as well as playing his guitar.

He couldn't wait for that summer to end.

On the first day of school Tim felt out of place like he was in some kind of dream state. The High School building with its gray stone façade looked the same but he felt odd when he entered; like a ghost who didn't belong there. He walked in a daze down the same sterile beige hallways that welcomed him as a freshman; halfheartedly acknowledging the greetings from fellow classmates.

Perhaps the realization that he was now a sophomore with an entirely new curriculum to endure contributed to his uneasiness. Or subconsciously he feared having a flash back while sitting in class. How in the world would he explain that?

As the months passed, Tim discovered that music was his talisman against the mini flashbacks. He had been invited to play lead guitar in a band called *The Dynatones* and devoted as much time as possible to prove he was worthy of the invitation.

He would hum songs in his head and often start figuring out how to play them on his guitar when there were lapses in class participation. This method seemed to keep the flashbacks at bay.

The band played a number of the high school dances plus private parties as well as the newly formed Teen Club dances. The endeavor made him feel happy— regardless of feeling he didn't deserve to be. The music gave him comfort.

For Tim Ryan the summer of 1964 brought with it positive vibes.

With the advent of the British invasion, music was changing. It was an exciting time. Every song had a new and different sound. Tim would scramble to learn them as soon as they came out. The groups from England even looked different. Their hair styles and clothing were cool and unique. This inspired Tim's band to imitate the look. Tim traded his Ed "Kookie" Byrnes' hair style for that sported by the members of a new band from Liverpool called The Beatles. His parents hated it, but surprisingly little sister Emily didn't.

Adding to Tim's overall good mood was the possibility of *The Dynatones* performing at the New York World's Fair that opened at

Flushing Meadows in April. This was a big deal. Only the really good bands got to play there.

The bothersome mental snippets were rare, and Tim felt confident he could control them.

Tim thought this summer vacation was off to a good start. So far…

***

Lieutenant James Trabinski sat in his office reading an all points report on some nut job in Massachusetts called the *Boston Strangler* who was raping and murdering women in the Boston area. *The whole world's going to hell in a hand basket,* he thought. Every police department in New York was on alert as a precaution in case this sicko decided to expand his business.

He unwrapped a piece of Beeman's chewing gum and popped it into his mouth —he was trying to cut back on the cigarettes— as he read a report dated July 30th, 1963, giving the details of the strangler's MO.

That date took him back to Rocco's Auto Wreckers and Junk Emporium and the July night they fought the harpy. He hadn't thought much about it since that time. Things had quieted down. No more children disappearing, or teenagers being brutally murdered. Even though Casey had concerns about the creature being immortal, a year had passed without incident. It felt like the case was truly closed.

He thought back to when he had been released from the hospital, recuperating three days at home from his head injuries and finally returning to work. He had been summoned to Captain Philbrick's office to explain Detective Pete Taylor's sketchy report on the junkyard altercation. Still sporting the purple, brown remnants of a black eye Trabinski was greeted by the captain who commented on the eye's improvement—he had actually visited Trabinski in the hospital—then got down to business.

"Lieutenant? What is this nonsense? Do you expect me to believe this?" The captain said holding up Taylor's report and shaking it slightly.

"No, I don't sir. I don't believe it myself, but it's all true."

The captain placed the report on his desk and flipped through a couple of pages. "Was the body ever recovered?" He looked up at Trabinski with a skeptical expression on his face.

"It was never found. We think the creature vaporized when Lieutenant Talbot shot it. She's continuing to search for more information on this thing."

"I can't present this to the chief the way it reads now. I'm going to file it as SUI—Still Under Investigation—with an addendum stating the suspected killer has been incapacitated and see if that keeps the mayor and the State Police off our necks at least till after the election."

Trabinski nodded. "I understand. I'll have to use that line when I speak to the parents of the missing children. I'm sure they won't like it."

"Use it on the press too. They'll be sniffing around for information on the reporter they lost."

The captain opened the top drawer of his desk and slipped the report inside. "I want to be kept up to date on any further developments involving this creature. No matter how trivial. We can't have people thinking there's a monster roaming…*flying* around their neighborhoods."

Trabinski gathered up the loose bulletins as well as notifications regarding antiwar protesters into a neat stack and placed them in the OUT box on the right-hand corner of his desk. With the clutter removed he reached over and flipped the pages on his desk calendar to Saturday, July 4th. He grabbed a pen and jotted down: *Casey/take boat to Captree Island/Fireworks.* Then returned the calendar pages to the current date. So far, their schedules were in agreement for that get together. A rare occurrence these days.

***

Jonathan Bolton, quietly troubled by the bad luck that had befallen his family managed to breeze through his fourth-grade school year with high grades. This achievement actually brought a smile to his ailing father's face. However, it had no effect on his mother. Most days she would just sit and stare out the window no matter how he tried to cheer her up.

The holidays—usually his mother's time of year for promoting festivities—were like any other day. It was almost like her mind was lost in the jungles of Guinea with his brother Artie.

Christmas, however, wasn't a total loss. Stanley had managed to scrounge a small anemic tree from a Christmas tree lot downtown—the guy selling the trees felt sorry for him. He got the tree for a dollar. They carried it home and decorated it the best they could. Jonathan's big surprise came on Christmas day when a cousin who lived nearby stopped in with presents and food. The gift given to him was a 24-inch Huffy Cruiser bike. It was used but looked brand new. Now he could go places on his own.

As usual Jonathan constantly read.

After his oldest brother was reported missing Jonathan delved into anything he could find on the country of Guinea.

Located on the west coast of Africa it had once been controlled by the French who spread their traditions and beliefs throughout the country. Unhappy with the way the French were running things the natives rose up in rebellion finally ousting the French on October 2nd, 1958. Unfortunately, the new government of the people lapsed into a pseudo dictatorship aligning itself with the Soviet Union causing more unrest.

Jonathan learned that rebels seeking to overthrow this dictatorship were brutally defeated by the government around the time Artie went there with the Peace Corp. Many people including tourists and possibly Peace Corp volunteers were killed or imprisoned.

He would rather his brother be alive and, in some prison, than lost in jungles rampant with lions, poisonous snakes, pythons and malaria carrying mosquitos. There was at least hope in that way of thinking. But none of this information would be good for his mother to hear.

Determined to find a means to release her from the fugue she inhabited Jonathan turned to the book of spells he had stolen from Stanley. He would sit in his attic hideaway—bundled up like an Eskimo—during the winter months searching the pages and taking notes. It was tedious clandestine work, often times interrupted by his father calling. Occasionally, Stanley would rouse himself and go see what his father needed. This helped to reduce the number of times Jonathan had to scramble cat-like from his hideaway.

Finally, his diligence paid off in June of the new year when he came across a list of ingredients at the back of the book under the heading *Salutem et Bene Esse*—Health and Wellbeing.

He quickly wrote the ingredients down in the notebook he used for his Latin translations: *Licorice root, echinacea, peppermint, German chamomile, rosemary, ginger, cinnamon, and ground bird feather (preferably from a dead bird).*

The last ingredient made him think of his dead parakeet that was eventually laid to rest by his father in the back yard trash can. *I should have kept a feather,* he thought.

Jonathan had no idea what some of these ingredients were, but he would *read* and find out. He looked over the list and realized two things. Where in the book was the spell that required these? How was he going to get them?

He lay back on the blanket he had spread across the attic floor like a carpet, put his hands behind his head and stared at the ceiling rafters deep in thought.

A plan was brewing.

***

Stripes of mid-day sun penetrated the leafy canopy of the serene glade located behind the now defunct junkyard. The echo of chirping birds added to the peaceful ambiance. Insects buzzed and flitted through the tall grass and unruly weeds that partially concealed the continuous rust feeding on the remains of the abandoned railroad spur. Squirrels hustled about the trees dashing over piles of fallen winter branches that cluttered the landscape.

On one such pile a Starling sat pecking at ants as well as other hapless crawling insects. When the branches and twigs it was perched on began to shift the bird darted away squawking its annoyance.

The brush shivered and shook. Dead leaves and other accumulated debris began to fall away. From beneath the pile came a sound— a soft moan like that of someone waking then a quick squeal. Suddenly the pile exploded as two strong, shapely arms shot up from beneath it. Dagger like nails on stretched fingers pointed to the sky.

Malhela was back.

CHAPTER 38

July 1st, 1964 – Noon

"Where are you going Jonathan?" Anna Bolton asked in a tired voice. She always sounded a bit hoarse these days.

Jonathan Bolton, now ten years old, had a growth spurt over the winter months and now stood almost as tall as his mother. He paused with his hand on the doorknob of the kitchen back door dressed in gray shorts, a white checkered camp shirt—untucked— white socks and black beat up Keds. An equally beat up red baseball cap sat rakishly on his head; black curly hair stuck out from beneath the hat above his ears.

"To the library," he said holding up the book he held in his other hand—*Tom Swift Jr. In the Race to the Moon.*

This was a half-truth. His real plan was to visit a new store that had opened at the corner of Old Country Road and Broadway in downtown Hillsville. The name on the big plate glass window, printed in white letters read *Apothecary.* Underneath that heading were the words *Herbalist/Tobacconist.* Jonathan hoped this place could supply all the ingredients —except for the dead bird feather—he needed for the healing potion.

His *Huffy Cruiser* brought him a newfound freedom which he used to explore downtown. It was on one such expedition that he discovered this establishment. He didn't know exactly what they sold there but remembered the word "Herbalist. He intended to find out on this mission.

Anna Bolton took a sip of tea—she still maintained the ritual of hot Lipton's Tea at noon regardless of her mood. "It's too far for you to go alone. Wait till someone can take you."

"It'll be overdue if I don't take it today."

"Tell Stanley to go with you," his mother countered.

Jonathan turned the doorknob and opened the door. "He can't. He's getting ready to go to work. Besides I've gone there by myself before. I'll be okay."

"What?" his mother almost spilled her tea.

"I didn't want you to worry so I didn't tell you. I know how to go. It's safe. Straight up Old Country, cross Broadway at the light, go to New Bridge and make a left at the light. The library's right there. See…easy."

"Come right home after that. Don't go anywhere else. You hear?"

"Yes *mother.*"

Sticking to the sidewalks it took Jonathan fifteen minutes to get to the library where he quickly handed in the book and headed back to Broadway and his intended destination.

Once there he stopped, dismounted, and extended his bike's kickstand, placing the bike near the window so he could see it while inside the store.

He pulled the list of ingredients from his shorts pocket —along with a ten-dollar bill he had borrowed from his mother's purse— and read it over. He took a deep breath, let it out quickly and opened the door to the Apothecary. *Okay…Here goes nothing.*

The smell was the first thing to hit him when he entered the dimly lit store. He was no stranger to the scent of tobacco but the combination of that and other unidentifiable fragrances made his nose itch prompting an immediate sneeze.

"Bless *you*," a pleasant voice said.

Jonathan scanned the small interior. The walls held shelves filled with labeled bottles. Beneath the lowest shelves small baskets of what looked to him like weeds and grains were neatly placed on the hard wood floor. He stood there not sure of what he should do.

"May I help you, young man?" the pleasant voice asked.

As his eyes adjusted to the low light he turned and spotted a tall thin young woman standing behind a cash register that sat atop a long glass case. Behind her were racks of various cigarette brands and a sign stating you must be eighteen years old to make a purchase. Jonathan hoped that didn't apply to the items he needed.

She had long straight blonde hair, parted in the middle, adorned with a black paisley head band. She wore a short black dress with puffy sleeves and a plunging neckline. A narrow gold rectangular pendant with a matching chain hung from her slender neck bringing attention to her decolletage. Her skin was like that of a porcelain doll and her eyes a sparkling green. Dark eye shadow and ruby red lipstick added to her unique appearance.

She offered Jonathan a dazzling, welcoming smile.

Jonathan had never been in the presence of a beautiful woman before. Sure, he had been around pretty girls in school but none of them looked like this. He was suddenly feeling shy and unsure of himself. He fumbled with the list of ingredients almost dropping it.

"I…I uh…need these items," he said holding out the list.

The young woman stepped from behind the counter. "Let me see," she said still smiling.

As she reached for the list Jonathan noticed the color of her long fingernails matched her lipstick and the reason she was tall was the boot-like high heeled shoes she wore.

"I think I can help with these," she said nodding. "How much do you need?"

"Huh?"

Though Jonathan had found the page in the book of spells with the recipe for making the healing elixir he had forgotten to write down the amount needed for each ingredient.

"How much were you looking to purchase?" the woman repeated.

"I…ah? My mother just gave me the list. She didn't say how much. Ten dollars' worth I guess."

"Uh huh," the woman said eyeing Jonathan as if he were some kind of unusual specimen. She leaned towards him—the gold pendant swung out almost hitting his nose. Her breath smelled like peppermint. "Is your mother going to prepare a healing potion with these?" She ran a finger down the list.

Momentarily flabbergasted by the question Jonathan fumbled for the right way to answer it. "I uh…have no idea. Maybe. Is that what all this stuff is for? She hasn't been feeling well lately."

The woman straightened and with the wave of a hand said, "Follow me. I know how much she'll need."

Jonathan walked behind her. She led him to a corner wall lined with shelves filled with bottles of different sizes and shapes. She moved quietly across the floor as if she were gliding then stopped in front of a section of shelving and positioned a small step ladder in front of it.

For some odd reason he started to feel nervous about this. *I should just leave. Go home, write down the amounts I need and come back another time. And not by myself.* Just as those thoughts had finished percolating through his head the woman looked over her shoulder and asked, "What's your name young man?"

Jonathan didn't move any closer. *What does she want my name for?*
He folded his arms across his chest and tilted his head. "Why?"

"Oh, no special reason. I just like to know my customers' names. It's good for business," she said as she climbed up the step ladder to retrieve a jar with a black substance inside.

Her short dress revealed quite a bit of white shapely legs from Jonathan's point of view, and he felt his face getting hot. He quickly looked down at his feet.

"Come on. Tell me your name," she prodded sweetly. "My name is Phaedra."

She came off the step ladder and strode to the glass case placing the jar next to the cash register. "Okay. Don't tell me *then*. She laughed as she went to another shelf just below all the cigarettes and selected two more jars.

Jonathan looked up hoping he wasn't still blushing. "It's Jonathan."

The woman turned to face him as she placed the two jars next to the others. "Hello *Jonathan.* Welcome to my establishment. Now, come help me gather the rest of your ingredients."

She roamed through the store picking out the needed items handing them to Jonathan as she went along. The process temporarily delayed as she helped an older man who had come in to purchase pipe tobacco. Finally, all the ingredients were selected, and the amounts needed for the healing potion measured accordingly.

Jonathan watched closely as she cut and counted items. *She knows this potion all right. She's got the recipe memorized.*

When she finished, she placed each ingredient in a small dark brown paper bag which featured a white blank label. She wrote the name of the contents on the label.

"*Okay,* Jonathan. You're all set. That all comes to five dollars."

Surprised that he would have money left over he happily held out the ten-dollar bill to her but as she reached for it, she suddenly stopped. "I almost forgot," she said tapping a finger on the tip of her straight nose. "There's an ingredient your mother will need that wasn't on the list."

Jonathan knew the missing ingredient but innocently said, "Really?"

"I doubt the potion would work without it. Wait just a minute."

She retrieved a large jar from inside the glass case and placed it next to Jonathan's parcel—each separate small bag of ingredient had been neatly placed in a larger paper sack. The jar resembled the type the Deli used to store stick pretzels but contained something entirely different.

Feathers. She selected a white one and placed it with the other ingredients. "Make sure she grinds this to a fine powder."

Seeing this Jonathan couldn't help himself and blurted out, "Are you a witch?"

The woman drew her head back as if avoiding being hit, her pencil thin black eyebrows went up and she laughed. "A *witch?* No *not* really." She took the ten-dollar bill Jonathan had placed on the glass case top and punching up the sale on the cash register said, "By the way Jonathan. Where did your mother happen to find this list of ingredients for the healing potion?"

Once again caught off guard he faked a puzzled look, shrugged, and replied, "Beats me."

"Oh well. I was curious that's all."

The cash register drawer rang open, and she placed the ten in the proper slot and withdrew a five. Before she handed it to him, she leaned forward—the gold rectangular pendant once again swung outward—and locked her green eyes on him. "All I need is your address and our transaction here is completed. It's required by law for all Apothecaries."

Without giving it a thought Jonathan immediately gave it to her.

Phaedra Colefax, proprietor of *The Apothecary* knew the boy lied about not knowing the source of the list. She could read his eyes. Could he possibly have one of her editions? She could easily find out. She had his address.

An impish smile crossed her face as she watched him ride away.

The purchase of the ingredients had taken longer than Jonathan anticipated so he planned to say he was reading stuff at the library and lost track of time if questioned by his mother.

He coasted up the driveway, stopped by the kitchen window and peered in. His mother was nowhere in sight. *So far so good,* he thought as he wheeled his Huffy around to the back of the house and slowly lowered the kickstand. He stuck the bag of ingredients in the back waistband of his shorts and pulled his shirt over it. Another check of the kitchen through the back door window showed the coast was still clear. He nonchalantly opened the door and entered. The house was as quiet as the library, so he tiptoed through the kitchen to the living room and found his mother in her chair by the front window—her usual location for viewing whatever she was viewing through the open Venetian blinds these days—sound asleep, snoring softly.

*What a **break**!*

Without a sound Jonathan hurried up the stairs to his secret hideout entrance, climbed the step ladder, pushed aside the plywood hatch— that's what he liked to call it— and crawled up through the opening.

As usual for this time of year his hideaway was sweltering but it didn't bother him. Four thin rays of sunlight slanted down through the louvers of the roof vent providing a bit of air and enough light for him to see—turning on the light bulb dangling from the rafters only added to the heat.

He carefully placed the sack containing the ingredients on the blanket he used as a carpet and opened the book of spells to the dogeared page containing the recipe for the healing elixir. He carefully read the instructions.

Three necessary items: water, a mortar and pestle and a fire source were previously appropriated by Jonathan and ready to be used.

Much to his amazement he had found the mortar and pestle tucked in the back of a work bench drawer. The fire source would be provided by his father's Ronson cigarette lighter. It wouldn't be missed since his father cut back on smoking after his heart attack. The water was easy; one of his mother's Mason jars filled with tap water and tightly lidded.

Jonathan got to work cutting and slicing—using the sharp Penn knife that once belonged to his brother Artie—and grinding according to the directions. He diligently followed each step wondering if he should give *this* batch to his mother or pick a test subject. *Maybe I'll try it on Stanley first.*

As he pulled the feather from the sack and started cutting small segments to place in the mortar the young woman who helped him at the Apothecary came to mind. Her pretty face framed with flowing blonde hair floated in front of him.

He remembered her penetrating emerald, green eyes and melodic voice making him feel kind of drowsy. Then there was that rectangular gold pendant with the odd markings on it —he later found that it was called a cartouche—that kept glinting in his eyes now and then. *When I asked if she was a witch she said, "No, not really". What does **not really** mean?*

CHAPTER 39

The abandoned railroad spur.

Malhela gingerly crawled from the healing earth and stretched. She brushed leaves, dirt, small sticks, and other winter debris from her body as she fully extended her wings. Bright sunlight broke through the overhead leaves warming her. For a moment she savored the earthy fragrance wafting through the air around her.

Feeling apprehensive about being seen in the daylight, Malhela quickly scanned the area ready to flee. She breathed a sigh of relief when she found herself alone in the quiet glade. No mortals anywhere. Her wings slowly folded to a relaxed position.

She began shaking her arms and legs to limber them up, wondering how long it had taken for her to heal. How could she tell? Nothing looked familiar except the rail—now seriously rusted—that ran along the trench she had crawled into after she had been wounded. Everywhere she looked, tall grass, odd variations of weeds, vines, and thick foliage grew uncontrollably. The trees that created this wooded area were extremely tall and thick with leaves. *Vegetation has overtaken this grove,* Malhela thought. *Mortals have not been here for quite a while. Perhaps that means I have been buried here healing, for a long time. So, if that is true, I should be completely recovered.*

Malhela slowly raised the hand that had been pierced by a projectile. There was no sign of the injury. The wound had completely healed. She flexed it and made a fist. This was good.

Pleased, she examined the wounds on her chest and side. They too had healed but had not disappeared. Small, puckered nodules remained to remind her of her defeat. She hissed at the memory but controlled her anger. There would be time for that later. First, she needed to establish what—if any—abilities had returned to her and secondly to find a new nest.

So, concentrating on previous abilities she strode to the base of a large Maple tree and focused on blending. Her neck and shoulders began to ache as she held her arms at her sides. She stared with wide eyes at the greens and yellows of the glade. In an instant she felt the change; an imperceptible twitch, a brief tingle followed by a feeling of certainty. Her image now resembled the rutted brown bark of the Maple tree. She no longer had to limit her excursions to the dark of night.

This too was good.

Malhela smiled, remembering how she had escaped the old crone all those ages ago when her blending ability had returned.

The crone, after placing her in a large, screened cage, had removed the knife from her back and double locked the cage gate. Her captor must not have known that removing the knife would allow her healing process to begin. As time passed her ability to blend with her surroundings came back strong. So, one evening while the old crone was dining on bread and cheese and drinking red wine from the bottle, she blended with the cage. It now looked empty. Besotted with wine the old crone— surprised and confused — fumbled open the locks to examine the interior. Malhela darted past her to freedom. Days later a human disciple of Cytizuz said *the words* returning her to the realm.

Malhela, now fully camouflaged, strode to the edge of the woods and looked skyward. She needed to test her wings as well as find a new roost. With two swift steps she sprang into the air, wings flapping vigorously soaring high above the tree line. It felt wonderful to glide unseen among the cottony clouds drifting lazily in the pale blue sky. The world below looked like a sunlit expanse of miniature dwellings. She performed midair stunts— back flips, downward spirals, lazy eights, and full wing spread swoops— to exercise her wings. She laughed with delight.

A delight that was rudely interrupted by a thunderous roar above her. She dropped to just above the tree line, hovered, and looked up at something she had never seen before. *What kind of bird is this!?*

A large black metallic object with a pointed nose flew across the sky leaving a thin trail of what looked like white smoke behind. Its wings fully extended had strange looking egg-shaped things on each wingtip. A transparent bubble on top of its body near the nose looked like half a teardrop. The tail of this strange bird stuck straight up from a flat section. Before it raced out of sight, she noticed a white star on the side of its body.

Malhela watched until the object— a Grumman F9 Panther jet on its way to the Grumman, Calverton airfield— shrank to a black dot in the distant sky. *That was not a bird. Am I **now** in a time when mortals* *use magical vehicles to fly?* She drifted slowly upward, turning her head from side to side searching for another. *So...A new aggravation greets me. I should not be surprised. I must be more alert now that I know the skies are not safe. These mortals are like blatoj, they are everywhere.*

Cautiously she resumed her flight.

From this height Malhela searched the land below for anything suitable for a nest. She wondered if her old refuge was a possibility and drifted in a direction, she thought would take her there. But the ground below showed nothing familiar. The large expanse of terrain—except for a few piles of debris—appeared to be nothing but dirt.

As she circled, she saw there *was* something vaguely familiar about the grounds. The outskirts of the property had random sections of dilapidated stockade fences. There were large gaps between those still standing while some parts of the perimeter had no fences at all. At the northern end of the landscape stood the remains of a sagging wooden shack which leaned toward an open metal gate that hung at an angle from its hinges.

It immediately sparked a memory, taking Malhela back to the rainy night of her failed, humiliating encounter with the red-haired elf woman and her cohorts.

This land has been erased of all that was before. Was this their attempt to eradicate any trace of my presence here? Trying to forget me...Are they? I'll enjoy refreshing their memories.

She felt the hatred for the mortals of this world —suppressed during her time of healing— begin to rekindle itself.

Malhela felt certain she knew the area now so continued northward seeking a new nest as well as old acquaintances.

She had not travelled far when she noticed a large gray building on her right. Curious, she fluttered her wings to stop her forward motion and hung there, her taloned feet treading air as she surveyed the structure.

It too had the look of a place abandoned to time.

The structure had three levels, each with a row of windows. Most of which had been broken on the lower level. The faded gray exterior showed scattered blotches where the finish had flaked off. Wild, overgrown vegetation surrounded and climbed the building's foundation as if devouring it from the bottom up.

As she turned to continue her search elsewhere Malhela caught sight of an odd shaped shed at the far corner of the building's flat roof. She darted forward. *This looks promising.*

She landed in front of what looked like a large lean-to with ridged metal walls. It too was a faded pealing gray. A solid metal door hung open and screeched as if annoyed when she opened it further. The inside was dark, but her keen eyesight enabled her to easily investigate the room.

It was a long narrow space basically empty. The wall on the left had two bulbous objects fastened to it. Each with a wheel-like appendage on the front. Rusted pipes were connected to the objects and ran down the wall through the floor. In the corner sat a dusty, web covered wooden chair whose eight-legged occupant skittered away as the sunlight through the open door disturbed it. The only other inventory consisted of two metal buckets, a mop, broom, and a pile of old rags that had obviously been a home for some local rodent. The floor had a scattering of runaway leaves.

Malhela strode away from the enclosure to the low wall that edged the building's roof and gazed out at the surrounding area. The place was quiet, peaceful, and lacking mortals. *It will do for now.*

After collecting brush, twigs, and even large pieces of cardboard—which she found on the ground behind the building leaning against the wall—her nest was now comfortable. The only negative was the single entrance. One way in, one way out. It was doubtful she could remedy this predicament as she had with her previous nest. She was confident that she would hear or see interlopers long before they got to her.

Now, standing with her hands on her hips admiring her handy work, she wondered if any of her magic had returned. Would her mind over matter work? Would she be able to imitate voices and sounds again? Would she be able to pick up the thoughts of Stanley Bolton and Tim Ryan?

With that last thought foremost in her mind Malhela sprang into the warm afternoon sky heading toward the village where the two conjurers had lived. A bit off coarse due to her new point of departure she drifted eastward over a community she had not seen in the past. The dwellings looked the same as before, but these had bigger yards, and some had raised round ponds behind the dwelling.

The ponds caught her interest— three younglings romped and splashed in one —so she spiraled down to a rooftop and watched closely trying to figure out a plan of seduction. As she crouched there, thinking, she heard laughter coming from the walkway behind and below her. She turned her head and saw two nubile young birthgivers strutting toward another pond. Malhela was surprised to see they wore so little clothing. A devilish grin appeared on her face. *Very accommodating. Less work for me.* She leapt from the roof, soaring above the birthgivers as they entered the pond and watched them cavort in the water. She eyed the birthgiver with the short brown hair. *Mmm…meatier than the other. But how do I go about taking her?*

Momentary doubt caused her to gaze back toward the younglings. *Taking one of those would be easier … quicker. I may not have the strength yet to grapple with a birthgiver.* She did look thinner, and her breasts seemed smaller. She had to eat and soon, so she glided back and perched on the roof overlooking the pond with the younglings. *It will be risky but if I move fast and grab that little one who just left the water, I may avoid observation.*

As Malhela prepared to attack, an amazing thought hit her. An idea that —if it worked—would make daytime hunting worry free. *My **blending** ability is strong once again…as strong as if new and never used. Could I hold the youngling close and make it blend with me? It would look as if the youngling had simply disappeared. Risky yes…but worth a try.*

She scanned the yard for a guardian of the younglings and saw none but did find that a tall hedge at the perimeter separated the yard from an open field behind it. Perfect for hiding and enjoying her meal.

***

Malhela, soaring high in a north westerly direction, came upon a grouping of dwellings that looked very familiar. She casually rode the updrafts studying the structures below as she concentrated on connecting mentally with Stanley Bolton and Tim Ryan. Then her keen eyesight spied an object she definitely recognized; The old mottled rust colored chimney on the top of Stanley Bolton's dwelling, the first thing she had seen when she had originally entered this world.

She made a quick descent landing with a flutter on the roof's shingled peak. Once there she immediately recognized Tim Ryan's dwelling across the way. It all looked the same. Nothing had changed. *Maybe I haven't been asleep that long?*

Now taking on the appearance of the chimney Malhela experimented with the magic that enabled her to communicate through thought with the two conjurers. *Stanley? Can you hear me? It is I… Malhela. Stanley? I have returned. Hear me, Stanley Bolton! Remember!*

Nothing happened, so she attempted to reach Tim Ryan the same way but ended her call with *Open your mind to me, Tim Ryan!*

Still nothing. *That magic is gone. The connection lost. Contact must be physical from now on.*

Disappointed as well as fearful that all her magic had ebbed away over the time trapped here, she sighed and spread her wings to take flight. But approaching voices stopped her.

There walking up the pathway that skirted the road were a tall thin male, wheeling a bike and beside him a heavy set, large breasted birthgiver. She talked with animated gestures and giggled. He would stop walking and scribble on a pad, showing it to her.

Malhela relaxed her wings, leaned forward, and inhaled deeply. The scent of jasmine and lilacs accompanied by the slight coppery tang of a menstrual event came from the birthgiver. The male's scent she knew well. Though he didn't look the same there could be no mistake. *Stanley!*

The old hatred for this mortal who had foolishly and stupidly called her from her realm was instantly present. *So, he has recovered. I should have just **killed** him! I'll make certain there is no recovery next time. I may even have some fun with his juicy companion while I'm at it. Make him watch for a while before I eliminate him.*

She straightened her back and drifted upward to the top of the chimney. She crouched there glaring at the couple almost losing her grasp as a male on a bike came speeding around the bend in the road. Her leopard eyes went wide with surprise. *Tim Ryan?*

He too had changed. His hair was different, floppy with no delightful scent of citrus. He was a bit taller but still as thin as she had remembered. He skidded to stop next to Stanley and the birthgiver.

"Hi Janey, hey Stan. You two going to the Teen Club dance Friday night? My band's playing. You should come."

"We'll be there," Janey said flashing her renowned dimpled smile.

Stanley gave a thumbs up and nodded.

"We start at seven thirty. Gotta split. See you there." Tim said as he peddled into his driveway.

Malhela floated from the chimney to the roof peak. *Janey? Must be the birthgiver's name. I will remember it. I see that certain things have not changed that much. Perhaps the sun has only cycled three hundred sixty-five times? A year for these mortals. Not that long for an immortal. I will attempt to confirm this with Tim Ryan at whatever this teen club is, tomorrow night. Once again, I'll be following him. Just like old times. I could use his services again.*

As these thoughts ran through her head Malhela saw the birthgiver pull Stanley close to her and kiss him lovingly on the lips. He in turn reached over and gently ran his hand through her thick hair. A big smile decorated his face.

The hatred flared. *He cannot be happy! I will not allow it!* An angry hiss involuntarily escaped from her mouth.

Stanley abruptly pulled away from Janey.

"What?" Janey asked.

Stanley quickly scribbled; **DID YOU HEAR THAT?**

"Hear what? I didn't hear anything."

They stood quietly, listening intently.

The familiar sound that Stanley thought he just heard sent a chill down his back. He closed his eyes.

*Oh...**No!***

CHAPTER 40

Thursday July 2nd — Late morning

Lieutenant Casey Talbot had just left the beauty parlor and was feeling a bit uncomfortable with the outcome. She sat in her car looking in the rear-view mirror fussing with her new haircut. Pressed for time in the mornings, the relentless summer heat plus hectic schedules convinced her to try this new style. It was really short. The beautician said she looked "Cute as a button", adding it was an up-and-coming fashion trend called a "Pixie". No fuss no muss. Just wash, towel dry and go. Casey liked that idea. She wondered what Jim would think of this new look.

She fluffed her bangs. *Cute as a button? At my age? Hmmm…doubtful.* Then unbidden she heard the words "Show me *your* ears" in her head. A sudden rush of unwanted memories hit her: The harpy asking her if she was an elf, the harpy pinning her to the ground on that rainy night calling her an elf.

Casey sat back in her seat and pushed the thoughts away. She reached up and adjusted the mirror and examined her tiny almost round ears. *Nope. Definitely not an elf.*

She was supposed to have the day off but being a dedicated officer of the law, she felt she was never really off *duty*.

Her police radio had been on at a low volume broadcasting codes and incidents of little or no interest to her. She paid little attention to the constant flow of mumbo jumbo and police jargon which at times could be downright boring until a code 10-65—A missing person— caught her attention. She turned up the volume to get the details. It fell under her precinct's authority but wouldn't involve her yet. Still, an uncomfortable feeling crept over her. *This is the first missing person's report in a year. Don't jump to conclusions.*

Casey removed the mic from its hook and pressed call.

"This is unit one. Lieutenant Talbot."

A voice crackled through the speaker. "Go ahead lieutenant…"

"Give me the particulars on that 10-65 that just came in. Thanks"

Momentary static then the voice returned.

"Five-year-old disappeared from a back yard pool. Name is Eddie Franks. Uniforms at the scene."

"Let me have that address…"

Casey jotted down the address trying to quell the tension that abruptly overcame her. *Get the information. Don't get ahead of yourself. This could be nothing at all. Forget about that **immortal** nonsense till you have the facts.*

She told herself this was a good pep talk, but she didn't believe in coincidences. The words spoken by the fiendish creature popping into her head from out of nowhere could have been a premonition. A hint or a warning.

Casey pulled her Plymouth Fury to the curb in front of a stylish Cape Cod, not a typical Levitt house. The front had a stone veneer with a blend of tan, beige, and sand colors. Each stone varied in size and shape. White faux shutters adorned the windows and matching roof gables stood watch atop golden amber shingles.

An NCPD cruiser was parked in a newly paved driveway. She saw no one around.

Leaving her car, Casey started for the front door. A woman's voice said, "They're all in the back," and pointed towards the back of the house. Casey turned to see a young attractive woman— clutching a little blonde girl in a dripping bathing suit to her side—standing in a driveway adjacent to the Franks' residence. She pulled her badge from her shoulder bag and held it for the woman to see.

"I'm lieutenant Talbot, Nassau County Police. Do you know anything about what happened here?"

The woman looked down at the little girl for a second then back at Casey.

"No. My daughter was in the pool with the others. I was on my way over to bring her a towel when I heard Martha yelling that she couldn't find Eddie."

Casey bent down and smiled at the little girl. "Did you see where Eddie went, honey?"

The little girl—who may have been five or six years old—gave a quick look up at her mother then said, "No...He just dishappeared."

Casey straightened up. "Just disappeared?" She snapped her fingers. "Just like that he disappeared?"

"Uh huh," the little girl said.

"Thank you, sweetie."

Casey thanked the mother and asked for her name as well as her daughter's then proceeded to the back yard. She found two of her police officers—Haggerty and Reese. Haggerty talking to the distraught mother; Reese to another woman who stood off to the side with her arm around a little boy.

She quickly took in the surroundings. A small oval shaped swimming pool was situated about eight feet from the back of the house. Flat paving stones curved around the front of the pool giving sturdy support to the short ladder that allowed entrance from the yard. The other half of the ladder curved over the top of the pool's metal framework down into about three feet of water. Blow up toys—a yellow duck with an inner tube body, a flat segmented blue raft, a gray dolphin and a multicolored beachball—floated lazily in the clear water. Behind the pool a beautiful wide open grassy yard extended to a hedge row of medium height. A swing set sat at an angle near the hedge.

Casey studied the hedge row for a moment. A faint bell rang deep in the halls of her memory, but she couldn't determine what it meant.

She moved toward the others. They were gathered under an awning that extended from the house over a cement patio. Officer Haggerty interrupted his questioning—a look of surprise on his face—when he saw her approaching.

"May I join you?" she said.

"Of course, lieutenant."

Officer Reese—questioning the other mother—turned his head, trying not to look surprised, acknowledged her presence with a nod.

Introductions were made and Casey politely took over. Haggerty stepped aside and Reese paused *his* questioning.

"Mrs. Franks. I'm sorry to ask you to repeat yourself. I know this is very distressing, but I need you to tell me exactly what you saw."

The woman was seated in a fold up lawn chair, so Casey squatted in front of her and took her hand.

Sniffling the woman recounted the afternoon calamity. "He'd been in there quite a while, splashing around having fun with Toby…" she looked over to the little boy standing next to his mother. "…and Eleanor. He came out of the pool to get the beachball that had been sitting on the grass. I saw him pick it up and toss it in. Then …then he *wasn't* there."

"Were you sitting here the entire time?" Casey asked.

"No…I was inside watching through the screen door."

Casey stood up. Her thoughts reluctantly returning to last July and the disappearance of an infant girl from her upstairs bedroom.

"So, you were watching your son and he disappeared right before your eyes. Did you hear anything unusual?"

Mrs. Franks shook her head. "All I heard were the kids in the pool…and the beach towels flapping on the line next door." She pointed to a makeshift clothesline in her neighbor's yard next to their large pool.

Casey looked in that direction. *Not much wind for towels to be flapping.*

"Did you see anything odd…anything at all?"

"There was a shimmer." This came from Ingrid Hirsch, the woman talking to Reese.

Casey turned toward the trim, plain looking woman. "A shimmer?"

"Something like that. You know when you see heat rising from the street? It looked like that."

"And where were you when you saw this?"

"Standing right there." She pointed to a tray stand with a pitcher of lemonade and empty plastic glasses ready to be used. "I saw Eddie throw the ball into the pool and I turned to pour a glass of lemonade. When I turned back, I didn't see Eddie, just that shimmer effect. Then Martha started screaming."

Casey gave a questioning look to her men who instantly knew what she wanted; confirmation that this woman's statement jibed with what she had told them. They both nodded.

She glanced down at the little boy, still glued to his mother's side, and leaned forward placing her hands on her knees. "Hello Toby," she said in a calm voice. "Can you tell me if you *saw* anything? Did you see where Eddie went? Did he leave the yard?"

Casey read fear in his eyes. So, she stood and reached in her bag for an old standby that always worked. "Don't be scared," she said handing him an orange Tootsie Roll pop. "You can tell me Toby…Right mom?"

"Go ahead son."

Toby cautiously took the pop and unwrapped it and before sticking it in his mouth said, "It was a ghost. A ghost took him. Not a Casper ghost…a different kind."

"Now… *Toby.* Don't go making…"

Casey held up her hand to stop the mother from continuing.

"Toby? Your mom said she saw something shimmering. Did the ghost look like that?"

Toby took a few licks on the pop. "Sort of…I guess."

"Thank you, Toby. You've been a big help," Casey said with a smile.

"Okay," Toby replied. "Thanks for the pop."

"One more thing," Casey said, but hesitated. *This may come off as a dumb question.* "Did either of you *smell* anything? Like garbage or rotten fish?"

Mrs. Franks gave a quick shake of her head. Ingrid Hirsch with squinted eyes said, "*What?*"

"Never mind," Casey replied.

Lieutenant Detective Casey Talbot's head was spinning. *Not a ghost Toby…something much worse I'm afraid.*

She advised Mrs. Franks that an APB would be immediately issued for her son and that a patrol would search the neighborhood in the event her son had somehow left the yard and that she would keep her advised. Though she knew it would be no use.

Now, unfortunately, Casey had a bigger dilemma to contend with. *What do I say to these parents about protecting their children if this killing bitch has returned? Hell, how do we protect the community? I need to talk to Jim about this. I hope he can call tonight.*

Lieutenant James Trabinski being senior man in the precinct had been selected by Captain Philbrick to represent the 2nd and 8th precinct at a three-day law enforcement conference in Albany, New York. Casey was a little miffed at Phibrick for not selecting her too. But after venting to Jim about it she realized there was no way Philbrick—knowing they were dating—would send them together to something like this. He probably figured neither of them would get any work done.

She knew Jim would be home Friday afternoon and that she would have him all to herself on Saturday.

2nd Precinct— 8 pm

Casey sat in her office at her desk staring bleary eyed at another bulletin from the State regarding protocols in the event of Viet Nam war protests as well as racial incidents. So far nothing of this nature had occurred on Long Island and these bulletins were becoming redundant. *I wish they had more faith in our abilities. They keep sending these things as if we're a bunch of county chowder heads.*

She rubbed her eyes, stretched her arms over her head, groaned, then slowly brought them down to rest on the leather padded arms of her chair. She picked up her coffee cup and looked inside. Empty.

A quick glance out into the almost empty department—there were four, night shift officers preparing to head out on duty and two, night desk personnel shuffling papers—made her wonder if she should grab another coffee and trudge through some unread reports or call it a night. She rubbed the back of her neck. Her thoughts drifted back to the missing boy but were interrupted by the ring of her private line. She looked at her watch. 8:15. She grabbed the phone.

"Lieutenant Talbot…"

"Casey? *You're* at work? I thought you had the day off. I called your apartment first. When your answering machine came on I took a shot at calling the precinct and voila there you are…" Jim Trabinski said.

Casey smiled at the sound of his voice. "I thought I had the day off too but duty calls when you least expect it."

"I know what you mean. What happened?" Jim Trabinski asked.

With a sigh she leaned her head back against the leather headrest of her chair. "Well…I'm happy you called for two reasons. One, I miss you and two I need to tell you about today's mystery. But first … How is the conference?"

"I miss you *too* honey. So far, it's been pretty boring. It was a struggle to keep from nodding off this morning. Tomorrow there's a talk by a psychologist on a subject called Profiling. It may be interesting. We'll see. So, what's this mystery?"

Casey hesitated a moment unsure how to begin. "Jim? You know me. I don't usually jump to conclusions, and I don't believe in coincidences. Right?"

"Yes ma'am."

"Well, I responded to a code 10-65 this morning. When I heard it involved a missing child, I felt compelled to go. Jim? I'm worried, *really* worried.

"Tell me…" Trabinski said.

Casey recounted the details emphasizing the "shimmering" effect reported by a mother and her son. "The little boy who was watching from inside the pool said a ghost took the other boy. When I asked the two women if they heard anything, the missing boy's mother said she only heard her neighbor's beach towels flapping. Jim…there was no wind to flap any towels."

"Hmmm…I don't think I like where you're going with this," Trabinski said.

"I don't like where I'm going with this either. That annoying word *immortal* has been flashing in my head all day like a neon sign. I have a terrible feeling that damn mythological bitch is back and using her camouflage to its full advantage."

She heard him clear his throat then come back on. "Honey, you know we'll need more info. We can't go on a hunch. We have to be absolutely certain this time. Remember Philbrick wasn't real happy filing a "*Still Under Investigation*" for that last fiasco."

Casey ran her hand through her hair and was momentarily startled. She had completely forgotten how short it was. "I know, I know. I'm not happy with an SUI filing either. I just can't figure out how to proceed.

"Jim? Its been a long time since I've been afraid, and I have to tell you *I'm afraid.*"

"Don't worry. We'll figure something out."

"I sure hope so. By the way. When I scanned the backyard at the scene this morning, I saw a hedge row about five feet high at the back end of the property. It separates all the yards from an open field. For some reason it rang a bell, but I couldn't remember what it meant. Any ideas?"

There was a long moment of silence and Casey thought they had been disconnected.

"Jim? Are you still there?"

When Trabinski came back on there was concern in his voice. "Did you search the hedge?"

Surprised by his response Casey blurted, "What?"

"*Did you search the hedge?*"

"No. Didn't see a need," Casey replied sheepishly.

"Casey? I sure hope you're wrong about this. But I think you better search that hedge and the field behind. Get the dogs on it if necessary."

Casey leaned forward in her chair. "What does the hedge have to do with it?

"Nothing…if I'm wrong," Trabinski replied. "But, it confirms your hunch if I'm right."

CHAPTER 41

July 2nd — Malhela's Nest

After successfully capturing the male youngling at the pond Malhela decided to forego the hedge idea and immediately returned to her nest to dine. She was extremely pleased that her blending had enveloped her prey nicely and she had no difficulty carrying the load. Still, she craved the power offered by the flesh of a newborn or better yet a birthgiver. *I remember the sweet taste of the birthgiver and the surge of strength that coursed through my body that night. Younglings may fill an immediate need, but I **must** have the essence of the birthgiver to achieve my conquest of these mortals. My new blending abilities will be of great use.*

Later on, when Malhela left her nest—comfortably sated —her frame of mind still manifested a certain bravado, but the unexpected encounter with Stanley Bolton and Tim Ryan riled her. Everything came flooding back: The conjuring, the disorientation, the empty feeling of being lost forever in this wretched place, the anger, and the hate. It caused her to forget her original purpose for finding them and drove her back to the nest where she now sat brooding. The afternoon sun shone through the entrance onto her beautiful face.

Is this a futile idea? Conquer these mortals? The Lord of the Realm could not accomplish that…So how can I? They are many, I am one… alone. Alone!

Malhela covered her face with her hands and did something she didn't intend to do. She wept.

In a few moments she regained her composure. She wiped her eyes and breathed deeply. The summer air filled her lungs. *At least the air in this wretched place is acceptable.*

She brought her knees up to her chin and folded her arms around them, tightly contracted her wings and sat staring outward.

Birds darted through the surrounding trees while scores of insects flitted and buzzed about. Squirrels bounded up tree trunks and jumped carefree from one branch to another.

*They exist. Their only purpose is to get from one day to the next. So… **what** is my purpose? Just wander through endless, meaningless days?*

I am supposed to be clever and devious. Yet here I remain without a clever or devious thought in my head.

As Malhela continued to let these maudlin thoughts drift through her mind a face slowly manifested in her head—the red-haired elfish woman. At that instant an erratic twitch took control of her head and neck. She quickly stood and screeched in anger. ***Revenge** is my purpose! And I shall have it!*

She stepped out onto the flat roof of the building that supported her nest and paced the perimeter until the twitching stopped. An idea was taking shape, and it involved a certain past slave. Tim Ryan.

***

Jonathan Bolton sat in his small, nine by twelve-foot bedroom thinking about the hours he had spent last night in his attic hideaway with the pestle and mortar grinding up the ingredients for the healing potion. His right hand and wrist still felt sore from the continuous motion of the process.

His room—unlike that of his older brothers'—was neat and orderly. He made his bed as soon as he got up in the morning and would stuff his dirty clothes in a basket positioned at the foot of his single bed. An old, nicked, and scratched bookcase containing his most cherished possessions was snugged up against the wall next to a narrow closet door. The books were arranged in alphabetical order by title then according to height.

A thread bare oval carpet with faded black and red colors covered the center of the scuffed but clean hard wood floor.

He occupied the room's only chair, staring at the small bags of ingredients he had carefully placed on his worktable. He had planned on using Stanley as a test subject and then give it to his mother if it worked successfully, but now he had doubts. *What if I botch this up? I could turn Stanley into a Jekyll and Hyde or something.*

Jonathan leaned back in his chair and put his hands on top of his head. *I've read and read and still don't know exactly what the recipe measurements mean. A dash of this…a pinch of that? What the heck is a smidge?*

He brought his arms down and picked up the small bag of finely ground white feather—this took him the longest to crush and pulverize—and examined the contents. *What if I don't have enough to make two batches? Especially if I do the whole thing wrong.* He carefully folded the bag closed and repositioned it on the table with the others next to a larger sack. The name printed on that sack —Apothecary: Herbalist/ Tobacconist, 210 Broadway, Hillsville—offered a possible solution.

Jonathan jumped up, finished buttoning his hand me down camp shirt—another donation from his cousin—looked in his dresser mirror and attempted to brush his unruly curly hair. It was no use. His hair had a mind of its own. A thick crop of black that refused to accept a part of any style. He sighed.

It will have to do. Doesn't look too bad. For some reason —he probably couldn't explain— Jonathan wanted to look good for the person he planned on seeing.

He went back to his worktable and carefully placed each labelled small bag into the larger sack. The aroma of ground licorice root wafted around his head. *Hope mom doesn't question me about that.*

Now he wondered about carrying the sack back to the store. *This whole potion will be lost if the bag rips and everything spills out. That could happen even if I put it in one of the Huffy's side baskets. How am I going to do this?*

After thinking a few moments he snapped his fingers. *Got it!*

He opened his closet door, reached to the top shelf, and brought down a beat-up leather school bag—that he stopped using after Stanley said it was dorky—and placed it on the floor in front of the table. He released the clasp and opened it wide. *Perfect!*

As he securely placed the sack in the school bag another bothersome thought entered his head. *What if she needs the book?*

He glanced across his room to the mahogany nightstand positioned in front of the bedroom window. It had a lockable drawer which now contained a valuable—at least to Jonathan—piece of literature that he placed there secretly last night, the book of spells. He walked over and lifted his reading lamp from the top of the nightstand and removed the key hidden beneath. After carefully replacing the lamp, he inserted the key and unlocked the drawer. But he hesitated before opening it. *She probably has this. How else would she know the amounts to sell me for the potion? I shouldn't take it. Then she'll know I lied about the list being from my mother. Then what? She might even take it away. No…she wouldn't do that. Something about her makes me trust her.*

Jonathan opened the drawer and removed the book. He returned to the table and placed the book gently into the schoolbag next to the sack of ingredients. He gingerly closed the clasp, picked up the satchel and headed downstairs.

Now I have to get past mom with this. I may have a problem if she's still in the kitchen drinking her tea.

Quietly moving down the steps he stopped halfway to the bottom. His mother was in her usual spot, sitting in her wing back chair staring out the front living room window, her back toward him.

Slowly he proceeded to the bottom and stepped silently onto the floor thinking he could just slip by unnoticed.

"Jonathan?"

Crap! Nothing wrong with her ears. She always says she can hear the grass grow. Must be true.

"Yes, mom?"

"Would you be a sweetheart and open the blinds a little bit more for me?"

He placed the schoolbag on the floor next to the four-legged console table that occupied the space near the stairwell wall.

"Sure."

After adjusting the blinds to his mother's specifications, he turned and looked at her. It seemed to him that her hair was getting grayer every day and she had lost weight. He felt a tug of sadness as he took in her appearance. *This potion has to be done right. It has to work.*

"I'm gonna ride my bike for a while. I'll be careful...don't worry," Jonathan said and stepped away to grab his bag of valuables.

His mother—already in her travelling trance to wherever she went—just muttered a barely audible "Okay."

Scooting through the kitchen and out the back door Jonathan placed the schoolbag in one of the rear side baskets on his Huffy. It fit perfectly.

He released the kick stand, mounted his trusty steed, and took off for town.

Once again, Jonathan Bolton found himself standing in front of the Apothecary store. He felt excited but couldn't explain why. He was a great deal more confident than he was the last time. *Just be cool... like Stanley. Don't stammer and fumble for words. She's just a girl. Ask her nicely for help and see what happens.*

He lifted the schoolbag from the side basket and with as much bravado as a ten-year-old could muster he entered the store.

The tiny bell announced his presence when he opened the door. As before it took a few seconds for his eyes to adjust to the room's dim light. Suddenly, he felt stupid holding the schoolbag. He quickly put it on the floor next to his feet. He looked up—his vision improved—and saw her standing behind the counter attending to two men. She looked just as beautiful as she did the other day—maybe even more so. Today she wore the same style dress as before, but this was blood red in color. Her head band was a paisley design that matched the color of her dress. From where he stood, he could see the gold cartouche hanging around her slender neck and the sparkle of gold hoop earrings protruding from her silken blonde hair.

"Well…Hello Jonathan," she said in a welcoming tone. "I'll be right with you."

The two men turned to look at him. Both seemed annoyed at the intrusion. The man standing to her right at the corner of the counter may have been his father's age. He was a fat man with a completely bald head and a crooked nose. He was dressed in a black shirt and slacks but wore sandals on his feet. *What the…?*

The other man was tall and pale looking. He had black hair that covered his ears and a strange looking black mustache under a hooked nose. *Ming the Merciless,* Jonathan thought. He wore a red polo shirt and tan slacks, no socks and tennis shoes.

The bald man held a clear cellophane package of four cigars. Each had gold paper rings around them. The guy with the weird mustache was paying for a carton of Lucky Strikes cigarettes.

"Thank you for your support gentlemen. I trust you are both ready to begin.." Jonathan heard her say. Her tone was flat and business like, not the friendly melodic voice he heard moments ago. Both men silently nodded, took their purchases, and turned to go, eyeing him curiously as they passed him and left the store. *What's with those two?*

"*Jonathan…*Come in, come in. What brings you back so soon? Don't tell me the potion didn't work," she said as she stepped around the glass counter toward him.

Jonathan's initial plan to be cool and confident instantly disappeared now that she stood directly in front of him. He felt his heart speed up. The dress she wore— despite the color— was not exactly the same as he originally thought. It was much shorter; mid-thigh, showing a lot more of her shapely legs. He couldn't speak. His eyes moved repeatedly from her legs to her face.

At that moment the bag of ingredients and potion didn't matter to Jonathan. He only wanted to be with her. He wouldn't admit it, but he had a crush on this beautiful young woman. His first.

"Jonathan? Are you okay?" she said with a giggle as she leaned forward placing a hand on his shoulder. "Can I help you with something?"

"Uh…yeah. Hi Phaed…Phaedr…," Jonathan stammered.

"You can call me Phae," she said laughing. "That's what all my friends call me and we're friends. Right?"

Jonathan, regaining some composure, nodded.

She stepped back and put her hands on her hips. "*Now…*tell me why you're here."

He hadn't thought about how he was going to explain to her the reason for his return, but the words had their own plan and came tumbling from his mouth.

"Well…I feel stupid saying this, but I can't figure out the measurements for the ingredients. I thought you might be able to show me."

Her green eyes went wide with surprise. "I thought you said your mother would be making the potion?"

Jonathan scratched the back of his head. "No...I was going to make it for her so she would feel better. But I didn't understand the words describing the measurements for each ingredient and was afraid I'd mess it up. Sorry I lied to you."

Phaedra Colefax folded her arms across her chest and smiled at the boy. She was curious about him before but now he piqued her interest.

"Can you help? Do you know how to make the potion? I can pay you. I have everything right here." He pointed to the schoolbag at his feet.

"Jonathan? I know you lied. I could see it in your eyes." As she said this, she leaned toward him. The gold cartouche swung forward and flickered in his eyes.

"What? You did?"

"Oh yes. I'm quite good at detecting lies. But I'll forgive you this time." She stepped away from him and turned her back. "Before I help you, I would like to know where you found the recipe for the healing potion."

Jonathan gave a quick look at the schoolbag. "Uh? From a book."

Phaedra looked over her shoulder at him. "A book? What's the title of this book?"

"Do you need it to make the potion?" Jonathan replied avoiding the question.

"Maybe...maybe not," she said coyly. "It would help if I new the title *though*." She flashed him a smile and laughed.

Jonathan watched her strut to the glass counter and sit on a stool behind it. Again, she crossed her arms. "*Well?*" she said.

"Its…its title is…oh heck…*here.*" He bent down, undid the clasp on the schoolbag, removed the book and held it up to her. She reached across the counter. "May I?" she asked.

Jonathan immediately handed the book of spells to her.

"Oh, I *do* know this one," Phaedra said. Her tone was that of someone who had just found a long-lost item. "Where did you get this Jonathan?"

Jonathan put his hands in his pockets to keep them from shaking while he mentally debated telling her. But when he looked in her bright emerald green eyes staring at him, he felt compelled to answer.

"From my brother," he said.

"*Your* brother?"

"My older brother…Stanley."

Phaedra placed the book on the countertop. "And he gave this to you to make the potion for your mother? Why didn't he come with you?"

"Well…he doesn't know I have it."

"Oh, I see," she said with a laugh. Then turning serious she said, "Jonathan? I'm curious. Is your brother a disciple?"

"Huh?"

"A disciple?"

"I know what a disciple is. What do you mean is he one?"

Phaedra flipped through the pages of the book and stopped when she found what she was looking for. She looked up at Jonathan. "Is he a follower of Cytizuz? A member of the Church of the Ancient Realm?"

"I don't think so. Lately, he's a follower of Janey Del Grasso. Why?"

"Just curious…that's all," she replied with a fleeting smile. She tapped the book with her finger. "Here's the recipe. Let's go make some potion. Follow me."

Jonathan didn't need to be told twice. He trailed behind her as they entered a back room through a multicolored beaded curtain.

The room was long and narrow. Sunlight filtered in through a small dusty rectangular window located at the top of the right wall. It angled onto a square table covered with a —what appeared to be red velvet—cloth. A strange looking figurine sat at the center of the table with something burning in a tiny round bowl in front of it. A thin stream of wavering smoke rose from the bowl. It filled the room with an aroma similar to hot chocolate.

Alone in this room with the wonderful smell and her standing close to him at the table Jonathan felt amazing. His entire body felt pleasantly electrified and as he watched her start to prepare the potion the only thought on his mind was stealing a kiss from her.

"Jonathan?" she said sweetly, snapping him out of his daydream. "Please move the book to the corner of the table away from the ingredients."

As he moved the book, an important thought came to mind. "Phae? I don't want to be a pest, but would it be possible for you to make two potions? One as a back up in case I spill one or something."

"I guess so," she said with a chuckle.

The tinkle of the store's front doorbell interrupted their proceedings. "Wait here," she said. "I'll be right back."

Jonathan watched furtively through the curtain as two young men stood at the counter gaping at Phae as she checked their ID's and rang up their purchases. He felt a sudden pang of jealousy and was glad when they finally left.

Finally, the potions were ready, and Phaedra placed two small bottles of dark liquid into a doubled bag. "Now be careful with this," she said handing the bag to Jonathan.

As he carefully took the bag, he felt driven to ask her a follow-up question to the one he had asked her on his first visit. "Are you a *white* witch?"

She playfully tapped his nose with her finger. "I told you I am *not* a witch."

"You said *not really* when I asked you. So? Are you a sorceress then?"

"Hmmm…Why do you need to know, Jonathan?" She turned and picked up the book of spells from the table.

Jonathan gently placed the bag of potions in his schoolbag. "I don't know. I guess I'm glad you're not a witch. People used to do bad things to witches. And I wouldn't want anything bad to happen to you."

Phaedra handed him the book and with a tenderness in her voice said, "You are so *sweet,* and I like you too Jonathan." She leaned over and kissed him on the cheek. "I'll look forward to hearing about your success with the potion."

"Really?"

Blushing profusely Jonathan secured the book in the satchel and closed the clasp. He straightened up and gave her a wondering look.

"Really!" she said with a smile. "Now, you better get going. You have work to do."

Phaedra walked him to the door. "And…if you must know. In *some* places I am considered a High Priestess. Now, go." She gave him a gentle push out to the sidewalk. Then closing the door, she turned her back and leaned her head against it.

She rubbed the cartouche between her thumb and forefinger, smiling to herself. *I wonder what older brother Stanley wanted with the book? Has he dabbled? And if so …, what has he done? I may be able to use him. Recruit him. But first I need to know more.*

CHAPTER 42

July 2nd — The Bolton Residence, 6 pm.

Jonathan watched as Stanley and his father arrived home from work at the same time. Today, his father came home in his delivery truck. This was something he would do occasionally when he was working full time, but this was the first since he went back to work part time after the heart attack. He worked for Dugan's Bread Company delivering bread, rolls and sometimes donuts to different grocery stores in Queens and Jamaica. He was usually in a good mood —Jonathan had no idea why—when he was able to bring the truck home and today seemed no different. He carried a green box in his hands and Jonathan hoped it was donuts. He came up the walk, ignoring Stanley, entered the house, smiled at Jonathan, and went straight to the kitchen.

Stanley skidded to a stop in front of the house then hurriedly wheeled his bike to the side. As he came through the front door, he playfully punched Jonathan in the arm and headed up the stairs to his room. Jonathan watched him till he was out of sight. *He's in a good mood and so is dad. Hopefully it will stay that way after I slip Stanley the potion.*

Jonathan went to the kitchen —The aroma of franks and beans cooking filled the room—and poured a tall glass of iced tea. He ignored the box of Dugan's powdered donuts sitting on the counter and left. His father seated at the table was absorbed in the evening paper while his mother lethargically prepared salads.

He wasn't questioned.

Great! So far so good.

He went up the stairs as quickly as possible without spilling the drink and entered his room. Without hesitating he placed the glass on the worktable and poured the potion into the iced tea, stirring it with a spoon he had brought up earlier. *Okay. Time for the moment of truth.*

Jonathan picked up the glass and headed to his brother's room.

The door to Stanley's room was partially open and Jonathan could see his brother changing his clothes. "*Knock, knock,*" he said.

Stanley looked over and waved him to come in.

"I made this iced tea today. It's great…You gotta try it. Tell me what you think. Maybe I'll set up a stand and sell the stuff if you think it's good. Here." He handed the glass to Stanley. Seeing the suspicious look on his brother's face he immediately said, "This isn't a joke or trick or anything. It's the real deal. I swear."

I hope he doesn't tell me to drink it first.

Before taking the glass Stanley picked up his pad and pencil. He wrote: **YOU'RE DEAD IF THIS GIVES ME THE RUNS!**

"It won't. It's just iced tea. Mom's going to try it too."

Stanley took the glass and cautiously sipped the drink. His new individual eyebrows went up in surprise. He mouthed the words *Not bad* and took a gulp.

Jonathan grinned. "Good…Right?"

Stanley gave him a thumbs up then suddenly started choking and coughing. He dropped the glass, and his hands went to his throat. He gasped for air.

Jonathan stepped back toward the door. His dark eyes wide with fright. "No, no, no. I'm sorry…I'm sorry. No…this can't be happening! Stanley…I'm sorry. I only wanted to help."

Tears were streaming down his face as he turned to go for help. He froze in mid step when he heard, "*You* little creep! You poisoned m…"

Jonathan looked back, saw his brother with a goofy look on his face and started jumping up and down. "*Ha!* It worked. It worked. You can speak!"

"What the hell just happened?" Stanley said.

"How do you feel?" Jonathan asked, wiping his eyes as he re-entered the room.

"I can't believe it." Stanley ran a hand up and down his throat. "I feel fine. The ache in my throat is completely gone."

"I am *so happy* to hear that." Jonathan bent down, picked up the glass and started for the door. He had another patient to attend to.

Stanley grabbed him by the arm. "*Wait a minute.* What was in that iced tea?" His tone was one of curiosity not anger.

Jonathan gave a quick glance at the empty glass. "I… uh…it's."

"C'mon, spit it out you little twirp," Stanley said releasing Jonathan's arm.

Jonathan took a step away from his brother and struck a defiant pose. "It's a bunch of stuff from a recipe you wouldn't understand."

Stanley walked over and closed the bedroom door. "Try me. What stuff? What recipe?"

"It's a potion," Jonathan said. He started to worry about how this discussion would end.

"A potion? Well, it's a good one. Maybe you *should* set up a little stand and sell it. Where'd you get it?" Stanley leaned back against the door and folded his arms.

"I made it," Jonathan confessed.

At that point in the conversation, it dawned on Stanley that he was speaking clearly without effort after a year of painful silence. He stepped away from the door and looked Jonathan right in the eyes. "Little brother? I don't know what you're up to but whatever it is…thanks."

Jonathan smiled. "You're welcome. I gotta go help mom."

"Hold on. Not so fast. Where did you get the recipe to make this potion? It might make mom feel better."

If Stanley's thinking the same thing that I am about mom this could turn out better than I thought.

"I know," Jonathan said. "I'll show you, but you have to promise not to get mad or flip out."

Stanley squinted at his brother. "*Okay?* I promise but I reserve the right to clobber you if you deserve it," he said with a quick laugh.

"Okay…come with me." Jonathan opened the door and headed to his room.

Jonathan carefully removed the second bottle of healing potion from his schoolbag and placed it on the worktable. He looked over at Stanley who had taken a position in front of the closed bedroom door. "We have to give this to mom. Put it in her tea at dinner," Jonathan said.

"I don't know about that," Stanley said shaking his head. "We don't know if it will work on her."

"It'll work. Worked on you pretty quick."

As they talked, Stanley had a sneaking suspicion about Jonathan's source for the healing potion. Though it had been a year, the memory of the troublesome tome always lurked at the dark fringes of his mind.

"I need to know where you got it before we do anything," Stanley said.

Jonathan bent over and reached into the schoolbag. "Okay, okay. Just remember your promise." Slowly he lifted the book of spells from the satchel and held it up for Stanley to see.

Stanley sprang from the door and grabbed the book. "You little *shit*," he said in a voice just above a whisper.

Jonathan took a step back. "*Remember* your promise!"

"I should have known it was *you*," Stanley said, shaking his head and laughing.

Jonathan relaxed when he saw his brother's reaction. "I found the recipe for a healing potion in it and bought the ingredients." He reached over and flipped pages to the earmarked recipe.

Stanley glanced at the page, then at his brother. "This is all in Latin. How could you possibly read it?"

Lifting his chin Jonathan grinned. "Got a book from the library on how to read Latin and learned."

Stanley closed the book. "Very clever little brother. I wish I had thought of that." Then in a serious almost demanding tone he said, "What else have you used this for?"

Jonathan shrugged. "That was it…I think."

"What do you mean *you think?* Did you use it for anything else? Other spells? That kind of thing?"

"I don't remember using it for anything else. Why?"

Stanley shook the book at Jonathan. "You're very lucky. There's dangerous stuff in these pages. Stuff that could kill you. Don't ever take it again. You hear me?" With that he turned, opened the door, and took a step to leave.

Jonathan nodded. "Thanks for not being mad."

"After making me search and wonder for a year where this book could possibly be... I should wring your neck."

Just then they heard their father calling them to come eat.

"Won't they be surprised when they find out I can talk again," Stanley muttered.

Jonathan tapped Stanley on the back. "What about mom?"

"Mom? *Oh yeah...* grab the bottle.

CHAPTER 43

July 3rd — Mid-morning

Another hot, clear summer day greeted Malhela as she soared high above her nest in a sparsely clouded sky. She listened while scanning the expanse above her for the annoying mortals' flying machines. The visibility was unlimited, so it appeared that, for now, she had the sky to herself.

Her primary objective for this day was a re-connection with Tim Ryan. She knew where his dwelling was as well as the route he followed to deliver his scrolls. But she was uncertain that the route remained unchanged so decided to initiate her plan at his dwelling.

With wings fully extended she allowed the aerial currents to carry her on a relaxing undulating glide. It helped to clear her head of angry thoughts that may jeopardize her plan.

As she flapped her wings and banked toward the general direction of Tim Ryan's dwelling she remembered something important and changed direction.

In a few minutes she was hovering over the place where she had snatched the male youngling from the pond. Her interest, however, was on the larger pond adjacent to it and the healthy looking birthgiver swimming there. She could almost taste the sweet meat and feel the birthgiver's essence energize her.

Malhela fluttered—fully camouflaged—to the roof top overlooking the pond and watched. *I still lack the strength to carry this one. I will need an opportunity.* She glanced at the hedge row at the end of the yard. But as she began to formulate a plan the half-naked birthgiver climbed out of the pond, wrapped a large cloth around her body and entered the dwelling. Moments later Malhela's keen ears picked up sounds of movement coming from the open window just below her on the side of the building. She scurried down the side of the wall and peered in the window. Through gauzy curtains Malhela saw the birthgiver drying her hair with another cloth. *Taking this one will require more thought. She will be worth the wait.* With that Malhela took to the sky, heading in Tim Ryan's direction.

She arrived at the roof top of Tim Ryan's dwelling just in time to see him on his bike speeding from the pathway that ran alongside it onto the thoroughfare.

Malhela immediately gave chase.

***

Tim Ryan needed to finish his newspaper route early so he would have enough time to get back home and get ready for the Teen Club dance tonight. His band—The Dynatones— would be performing. They were scheduled to start playing at 7:30 which meant he had to be ready for Rick Vincentti to pick him up at 5:30 pm. It only took ten minutes to get to the Hillsville High School—the dances were held in the school basement—but setting up took time and he didn't want to be the reason for them starting late.

Rick Vincentti was nineteen and the only member of the band who could drive. He sang lead—because he could hit the high notes without going flat—and played rhythm guitar. He drove them to all the gigs in his father's beat up Plymouth station wagon. The car had a huge interior but filled up quickly with Bob Zarella's drums, Jack Murphy's big bass amp, Tim, and Rick's smaller amplifiers, three guitars and the PA system. Amazingly, there was still room for the four of them to ride comfortably to the jobs.

Tim knew that even though they had the packing down to a science he was the last to be picked up and loaded. So, he had to be dressed and ready to go when Rick got there.

When he skidded to a stop in front of the newspaper office Tim was relieved to see that his bundle of papers was there waiting for him. Sometimes the delivery truck was late, and he feared today would be one of those days.

He quickly loaded his papers into the canvas delivery sack and placed it securely in the front basket of his bike. *No dilly dallying. Keep customer chats short. Just deliver the papers and get home.* With those thoughts in mind, he raced toward Kraemer Street and his first block of customers.

Tim was making good time. He was already on his third block, and it was a short one. He looked at his watch and smiled. *Great. I'll have plenty of time to get ready.*

As he stopped his bike in front of the first customer on this street he saw a shimmer —his sister called them heat mirages—on the sidewalk directly ahead of him. *Well…that's odd. Don't usually see those things on the sidewalk.* He glanced at the street's surface but saw no shimmering heat rising anywhere. *Sidewalk must be hotter than the street. I'll just move right through it. Gotta finish.*

Before he took a step, he heard a soft sensual voice say, "*Tim Ryan?*"

He watched as the shimmer came closer. His feet suddenly felt glued to the concrete.

"I've missed you," the voice said.

The shimmer now flickered right in front of him, and the all too familiar smell of spoiled fish drifted over him.

"*Malhela,*" he whispered.

"Yes, Tim Ryan. It is I. Did you *miss* me?" the voice said sweetly.

Tim took a step back. He gripped the handlebars of his bike so tightly his hands started to hurt. His brain turned into a thoughtless block of ice. He spoke as if he had suddenly become a five-year-old. "*Go away! I don't want you here.*"

"Now, don't be like that," Malhela said gently as she took a step closer. "I need your help once more. That's all."

Before Tim could respond or move away Malhela grabbed his head with both hands pulled him close and kissed him. Her forked tongue slipped into his mouth caressing and tickling his. When Tim moaned softly, she pulled back and blew lightly into each of his ears. "*Now*, you will help me."

Tim's hands loosened on the handlebars and his bike fell over, spilling papers onto the sidewalk. He stood there stupefied. Suddenly a voice he hadn't heard in a long time jolted him back to reality.

"Hey Ryan? You goofing off or something? Looks like your posing for a picture."

Malhela issued a low hiss and took to the air.

Tim turned toward the voice. He felt like he had been asleep, and his vision was blurry as he saw two figures standing there. His eyes began to focus and at first, he recognized Janey Del Grasso. She gave a cute little wave, giggled, and then pointed to the person beside her.

"*Stanley?* You're *better?* You can talk again?"

Stanley and Janey were both standing on the sidewalk holding their bicycles.

"Sure seems like it," Stanley said with a laugh. "Want some help picking up your papers?"

"What?" Tim said and looked back at his overturned bike. The newspapers were scattered over the pavement. "Oh, crap. Yeah thanks."

As Stanley helped him gather the papers Tim asked, "What are you doing here? I thought you had work today. And more importantly... How'd you get better?"

"I have today off. Unfortunately, I have to work tomorrow till closing. Should be out in time to take Janey to the fireworks show." He placed three rolled up papers into the delivery sack, now back in the basket of Tim's bike. "I wanted to tell you the good news in person. The double good news."

Besides his change in appearance Tim noticed there was something else different about his friend. Then it hit him. He wasn't speaking like a punk. Tim wondered how that happened.

"*Double* good news?" Tim placed the last of the papers in the sack.

Keeping his voice low so Janey wouldn't hear Stanley said, "The other good news is …I have the *book*."

"*What? How?*"

Stanley leaned in a little closer to Tim. "Jonathan, the little thief, had it the whole time. I can't be mad at him though. He used it to cure me *and* my mother."

"Well, that's sort of triple good news. Now that you have it back what are you going to do with it?" Tim asked.

Just as Stanley started to reply he was interrupted by Janey's cheerful voice.

"Hey Tim? Why were you just standing there like a statue when we road up?"

Tim turned and looked at the cute, stout brunette who had been waiting patiently by her bike.

"Huh?"

Janey laughed. "You were just standing there staring straight ahead, like you were in a trance or something."

A frown crossed Tim's face. "I don't remember."

"Too much sun!" Stanley said with a chuckle. Then he said to Janey, "Or? His mind's on tonight's dance and what young lady he's going to try and charm with his music." They both laughed as Tim looked at his watch.

"Oh *crap!* It's four o'clock! I'll never finish in time to get home and be ready for the guys at five thirty."

"We can help," Janey offered. "Tell us what to do."

Malhela watched from above, delighted that she still had the ability to put Tim Ryan into a mind control trance. Perhaps she could use him to get her revenge on the frustrating Stanley Bolton. She would wait and see what opportunity presented itself in the hours that followed.

Tim raced his Columbia onto Cabel Street and saw Rick Vincentti's Plymouth station wagon already parked in front of his house with the tail gate open. He was surprised to see Jack Murphy loading his guitar and amplifier into the back. Rick was in the driver's seat with the window rolled down, smoking. Bob Zarella stood next to Jack watching to make sure his drums didn't get banged up.

"Hey Timmy." Jack always called him that when he was miffed at him for something. "Where you been? Watch broken?"

Tim pulled up next to them. "Sorry guys. Don't know what happened. I'll hurry and get ready." He started up his driveway and Jack stopped him.

"No need. We're doing the gig without you…gotta split," Jack said and closed the tail gate.

Tim's jaw dropped. "*What?* What do you mean?" He was so caught off guard he completely forgot that his gear was already loaded. Just then Murphy and Zarella broke out laughing.

"That'll teach you to be late. I talked to your father," Jack said still chuckling at the look on Tim's face. "He'll bring you to the gig as soon as you're ready. We'll go and set up. That way you can stroll in like some big rock star and just plug in and play." He punched Tim playfully in the arm.

Rick Vincentti stuck his head out the window and shouted, "Let's get on with the music…Shall we?"

***

Hillsville High School—Teen Club Dance—Evening

A pounding four-four beat came from the bass drum as Bob Zarella started off The Dynatones' opening song. Tim followed with a twangy, B string guitar riff and was immediately joined by Jack's bass and Rick's rhythm guitar chugging on an E chord. Then stepping to the microphones, they started singing in three-part harmony the 1959 hit by the Bell Notes, *I've Had It.*

The expansive High School basement had been decorated by the Teen Club committee— in charge of such things—to commemorate the Fourth of July holiday. Red, white, and blue paper ribbons were draped in the corners of the room enhanced by balloons—anchored to the floor by bricks wrapped in red foil— that matched the ribbon colors. Cardboard cut outs of various sized firecrackers as well as top hats with stars and stripes adorned the walls. Round tables were set up in a zig zag fashion throughout the room. Each table held bowls of pretzels, potato chips and popcorn. Ice filled coolers containing sodas lined the left wall between two doors.

The basement had a finished ceiling with banks of recessed lighting. A third of these had been turned off to create a mood conducive to dancing and other things.

The place was packed with teenagers, chaperoned by four adults who mingled among them and attempted to keep track of those who supposedly went outside to have a smoke. As usual the night started with boys on one side and girls on the other but soon the music brought them together.

Tim Ryan felt out of sorts. Uncharacteristically nervous about this gig. The jitters usually went away as soon as he started to play but for some reason, he couldn't shake these. He attributed this discomfort to being late for the pickup and having been driven here by his father. He decided to use an old trick he learned —when he first started playing with the band— that defeated stage fright nerves.

Just sing to the wall or the clock…or to a particular girl.

It was his turn to do the lead vocals on the next song and he stood in front of the microphone scanning those on the dance floor. He saw Stanley standing with Janey holding hands. *It would be stupid to sing to them.*

He was taking too long.

Rick Vincentti leaned towards him. "You forget the words or something? *What are you waiting for?*" He said in a low voice from the corner of his mouth.

"*Okay…okay,*" Tim whispered in reply. "Count it off…"

Tim found his target; a young lady about five foot seven, short —*what he called* bubble style— blonde hair, big blue eyes wearing a mini skirt with Go-go boots. He didn't know who she was, it didn't matter. He began to sing, "Come along and be my party doll…". His eyes met her's and she blushed. He felt much better.

As the night progressed Tim found himself singing the love songs that were his assigned selections in the band's performance to her; *Lonesome Town, And I Love Her* and *In the Still of the Night.* And she didn't seem to mind.

On the band's third and final break of the night she broke from her group of girlfriends and demurely walked toward him. "I love the way you sing," she said coquettishly.

Tim put down his guitar. "Thanks," he said. "I love the way you dance. *You're* really good."

She smiled. "Not really but thanks anyway."

"My name's Tim. What's yours?"

She stepped a little closer. "I know your name *Tim Ryan.* I'm Marcy.

"Pleased to meet you Marcy," he said half bowing to her as if she were royalty. "How'd you know my name?"

She laughed at his gesture then said, "I know Janey Del Grasso."

Tim looked at his watch. Designated break time was twenty minutes, so he didn't want to waste it. "I'm gonna grab a Coke and head outside. It's hot up there on that stage I gotta cool off. Want to come?"

"Sure," she said taking his hand.

Marcy Dubrowski had just turned sixteen. She would be a Junior at Hillsville High come September. She had broken up with her boyfriend a few months ago and was on the rebound.

She liked everything about Tim Ryan; his blue eyes, his almost blonde hair styled like one of the Beatles, his little boy smile, and the way he sang. She wondered if he was the *going steady* type.

Outside the high school building daylight savings time was allowing night to make an appearance and as the darkness approached, a camouflaged harpy peered through rectangular basement windows at the scene inside.

Malhela held her ears as she watched the young mortals jump, wiggle and gyrate. *What is this painful raucous? Is this some mating ritual between the males and birthgivers?*

Her interest was drawn to the large number of nubile birthgivers present before her. The possibilities were endless. As she pondered this, she spotted Tim Ryan —she had followed him from his dwelling—chatting with a healthy looking birthgiver. *Well, that one will do nicely.*

She turned her head toward an area where the young mortals seemed to be coming and going; a stairwell that went down to a door. Some males and birthgivers were mingling about smoking. A concrete pathway on the right of the stairwell ran along the side of the building snaking through bushes and shrubs of varying sizes and shapes. A high cluster of thick bushes situated where the walkway went around the end of the building looked ideal for grabbing unsuspecting prey.

Now…Let's see if the spell I put on him is still in place.

Malhela watched Tim Ryan walk with the birthgiver towards the door. She concentrated on sending him her command. *Tim Ryan? Bring her to me. Do you understand? Bring her to me…now.*

As Tim opened the door for Marcy, he suddenly lost all control of his actions. Words in his head told him what to do and he did what he was told. *Bring her to me.*

Reaching the top of the steps Tim said, "Come with me. I know a spot where we can be alone."

Marcy took his hand willingly and giggled as he pulled her along.

At the secluded edge of the building where the bushes were the highest and the light from the streetlamps did not intrude, Malhela blended with the overgrown shrubs, waiting as Tim and the birth-giver approached.

Tim brought Marcy into the dark at the corner of the building, put down his coke on the sidewalk and took hers carefully placing it next to his. He took both her hands in his. He took a small step back holding her at arm's length staring at her, not saying a word. Marcy offered a sheepish smile.

"*What* are you doing?" she asked. The blank look on his face gave her a creepy feeling. She was about to pull her hands away when she felt something like strong hands on both sides of her head. She looked down and saw his hands still holding hers. Before she could take another breath, her eyes went wide with shock and surprise as her head was twisted violently to the side sending a quick excruciating pain to the base of her skull, killing her instantly.

Tim still holding her hands, lowered her gently to the ground and released her. He then stood as if at attention with his hands by his sides.

Malhela moved fast and cat-like to her prey. She crouched next to the body and quickly dismissed Tim with a thought, *Go!* Then as she raised the birthgiver's leg to sample a piece of tender thigh before picking up the body, blending it to herself and carrying it away—hopefully to her nest—she heard a loud shout.

"Hey! What the hell's going on there?"

Caught off guard by this unexpected interruption, Malhela immediately thought *police* and fearing being shot again after a year's recovery, acted on impulse. Though completely invisible to the intruders she saw no chance in escaping with her prey at this point without being detected, so she spit and hissed in the direction of the approaching mortals and jetted skyward. She didn't see who had shouted until she was in the air. When she saw that her plan had been thwarted by older adolescent mortals and not police she seethed with bitterness.

The force of her leap caused Marcy's body to shift, splaying her booted legs on the walkway in front of the approaching group. Two boys and a girl all smoking had just come around the corner of the building. The girl dropped her cigarette and screamed.

Tim was slowly walking away like a robot.

The second boy yelled, "That's the kid from the *band.*"

The first boy said in a loud voice, *"Grab him!"*

The second boy was built like a football player. He put Tim in a headlock and dragged him down the stairs to the basement entrance. Tim didn't struggle or say a word.

They burst through the door onto the dance floor. The room immediately fell into a frightened silence.

One of the male chaperones, Mr. Toll, the high school Phys Ed teacher happened to be standing nearby when they came crashing in. He turned in surprise and hurried to them. He grabbed the second boy's arm. *"Let him go,"* he said with authority.

The hysterical girl cried, "He *killed that girl!*"

Mr. Toll squinted at the girl. "*What did you say?*"

The first boy—standing on the steps behind the second boy and Tim— said, "He killed some blonde girl at the back of the building. We saw him do it. Come on I'll show you."

The other three chaperones came rushing over. Mr. Toll took charge. He pointed to one of the women chaperones "Call the police." To the others he said, "Sit him at that table and keep an eye on him." He nodded to the second boy holding Tim giving him the okay to move him. Then he turned to the first boy. "*Show me.*"

There would be no more music tonight.

***

Malhela flew through the night in a blind rage. She had lost all sense of time as her temper tantrum prevailed. The half-moon hung high above her; she hissed, spit and punched at it. She snarled at the twinkling stars wishing they would disappear. She hated everything this night had to offer.

Finally exhausted from all her aerial thrashing and lack of nourishment Malhela drifted with wings spread wide on the currents. Her mind wandered. Suddenly she stopped mid-flight. She had forgotten. *All may not be lost.*

The dwellings with the ponds behind them came into view and she homed in on the one she had visited earlier in the day. This was the place where the healthy birthgiver lived.

Malhela flew to the window she remembered being the birthgiver's bed chamber. It was opened outward just like the other windows she had experienced. She peered into the dark room. Her leopard's eyes seeing everything clearly.

The birthgiver —dressed in a short gauzy sleeveless type of dress— lay fast asleep on a large bed. Her long legs were bent at the knees while her toned arms stretched over her pillowed head. Malhela sighed as she glanced at the window's opening. *She's too big.*

Then, so driven by hunger, she made a reckless decision, quietly slit the screen, spread it wide and slipped silently inside.

CHAPTER 44

July 4th—Early morning

Lieutenant James Trabinski had telephoned Casey before he left the Albany conference telling her he would be home later than originally anticipated, apologized sincerely, and told her he would pick her up in the morning at eight sharp for their day on the water. He'd been away less than a week but couldn't wait to see her.

At five minutes to eight o'clock he strode up to Casey's door. He was wearing a white linen shirt, open at the neck which hung loosely over his khaki shorts, a pair of brown boat shoes and his vintage off white Coast Guard Commander's cap positioned rakishly on his head making him look even more like the actor Dana Andrews from the 1943 film *Crash Dive*.

As their dating became more serious and he picked her up as often as their busy schedules allowed, he had initiated a simple code to let her know that he was at the door and not some salesman.

He stepped up to the entrance, wrang the bell once and did a 'shave and a haircut…two bits' knock on the door.

"*Come on in*, Jim," Casey called. "*It's open*"

He smiled at the sound of her voice, opened the door, and stepped inside. He was in a great mood and in a corny attempt at sounding like a cowboy just home from the range said, "Where are ya? You sweet *thaang.*"

"In the kitchen... *Tex,*" she laughed. "Packing up the sandwiches."

Jim came through the foyer, proceeded down the hall to the kitchen and entered the sun filled room. He stopped as if he had suddenly forgotten how to walk when he caught sight of her. Once again, this beautiful young woman had succeeded in taking his breath away. *What's this? A new hair style? She looks like a cute teen... Oh, man...I'll be accused of dating an underage girl. They can eat their hearts out.*

Casey stood at the edge of the kitchen table. She wore a white crocheted beach jacket, unfastened which revealed the top of a two piece, lime green gingham bathing suit. Tan Bermuda shorts and her favorite white tennis shoes without socks completed her outfit.

Seeing the look on his face, Casey immediately thought of her new hair style.

"You hate *it*...," she said with a pout as she touched her hair.

Jim finally blinked and managed a step closer to her. "Lieutenant? *I surrender.*" He held out his hands as if to be handcuffed. "*Take me...*I'm yours," he said grinning. "You can accompany me to my trial after I'm arrested for dating a teenage beauty queen."

Casey beamed. "No problem," she said throwing her arms around his neck and planting a lingering kiss on his lips.

Jim and Casey walked to his civilian car with their picnic supplies and coolers.

"I love *this* car," Casey said as Jim opened the trunk of his 1960 Chevrolet Impala Super Sport and stashed everything carefully inside.

The car was a white two door coupe with red trim on the side which was meant to resemble the jet stream emanating from a chrome futuristic jet at its front. Just behind the jet, written in script was the word **Impala** preceded by a crossed racing flag insignia topped by a chrome Impala figure. It had whitewall tires with chrome spinner hub caps. The red interior contained leather trimmed cloth bench seats an AM radio plus a small police radio—which Jim had installed after he bought the car. It would remain off on this day. After all this was his private vehicle and it wasn't mandatory to be turned on.

The power train for his pride and joy was a 348 cu.in. engine, four speed manual transmission on the floor and a Posi-traction rear end.

He bought it new for $2100 and only drove it on special occasions. Casey had been in it several times.

The drive to the Bay Shore Boat Basin was a quick thirty minutes. Jim and Casey's conversation was light and cheerful.

Casey told Jim the last time she was out to sea was on the Staten Island Ferry and she was really looking forward to this. They both had a chuckle over that.

Though Casey was in a chipper mood Trabinski got the impression that her thoughts were elsewhere. This was confirmed when—out of the corner of his eye—he saw her slowly rub the side of her nose. She always did this when something was brewing in her pretty little head. He decided to wait till they were on the boat before questioning her.

They drove into the Bay Shore Boat Basin parking lot and Jim parked in a faraway space from other cars to, hopefully, avoid dents and dings. They unpacked their gear and walked the dock as seagulls circled above, squawking, and chattering as if annoyed by their presence.

There were boats of varying sizes and shapes tied to the docks and Casey was amazed at the number.

"She's right up here," Jim said pointing to the fourth boat in the row, bobbing gently with the tide.

Casey followed his finger. "*That's yours?* I'm impressed," she said with an approving smile.

"Mine and Gary's," Trabinski said stepping closer to the boat he half owned with his old Coast Guard buddy. It was a 1958 twenty-five foot, Chris-Craft Cavalier Custom Cruiser, white with woodgrain hull. The boat featured sleeping quarters, a sink, dinette table, a two-burner alcohol stove, a bath, lavatory, a convertible canvas top, plush cushions positioned at the stern as well as a Zenith Marine band ship to shore radio.

Her name was *Lovely Leah*. It came with the boat and Gary felt it was bad luck to change it. Jim didn't argue—he had his own seafaring superstitions— so the name remained.

Trabinski helped Casey step onto the boat. "Who's Gary?" she asked.

"Gary Ojikha is an old Coast Guard buddy of mine. We shipped together during the war and became good friends. He's a full blood Shinnecock Indian, born and raised here on the island. He knows the ocean like the back of his hand. He runs a small fishing fleet for a living. We bought *Leah* together when I first made lieutenant. I rarely get to use her anymore, so Gary takes care of her. Today is a special occasion for me."

"She's a beauty," Casey said stepping gingerly onto the deck. "Do I need to know who Leah is?" she asked with a sly smile.

"We don't know who Leah is. The boat's registered under that name and we both felt it bad luck to change it."

"*Sure*," Casey said laughing. "I know you sailors. Girl in every port…that sort of thing."

Trabinski put the coolers on the dinette table. "What's that *supposed* to mean?"

Casey shuffled over to him and kissed him on the cheek. "Never mind."

Once out to sea it would be a thirty-minute sail to Captree Island.

Trabinski took advantage of the calm ocean and steered the boat casually with one hand while adjusting the throttle of the eight-cylinder engine to cruise at a comfortable 30 knots with the other. Casey stood next to him on the bridge quietly enjoying the breeze and the slight ocean spray though she seemed preoccupied.

"*So…*What's cookin' good lookin'? I've seen that expression on your face before and it usually means something's brewing in that pretty head of yours."

"*Really?*" Casey said tilting her head, offering a phony look of wonder.

Trabinski took his hand off the throttle and put his arm around her waist. "Really. Don't forget that I too am a detective, a *lead* detective if you will, and highly trained at being observant. So, let's hear it."

Casey put her arm round his waist and gave a gentle squeeze. "It's nothing. Let's enjoy the day."

"*Casey?* I'm captain of this vessel and I order you to divulge what's nagging you," he said, gently lifting her chin with his finger.

With an exaggerated salute Casey said, "Aye, aye captain if you insist."

"I do!" he replied.

She glanced up at the seagulls—who seemed to be keeping pace with the boat—then turned to Trabinski, took his hand, kissed it, and placed it firmly on the steering wheel as if what she had to say might cause him to lose control of the craft if he didn't use both hands. "I feel kind of guilty being here."

"I can understand that," he said. "I've had that feeling a few times myself but personally I feel we deserve to enjoy ourselves."

Casey nodded. "I know but I can't stop thinking about the little boy who disappeared from his back yard. It gives me a really bad feeling. I had them search that hedge at the back of the yard as you recommended. They searched the entire row behind the other yards as well and they came up with absolutely *nothing*.

"Then I think, what would the mother say if she knew I was out having a good ole time instead of trying to find her kid."

Trabinski turned the wheel. Captree Island was dead ahead. "I know exactly where you're going with this, and I still hope you're wrong."

Casey put her hand on his arm. "I'm sorry, Jim. I didn't want to put a damper on today, but you pulled rank."

"Yeah, yeah but let's consider this our own mandatory R and R. Our times alone together seem few and far between and this may sound selfish, but I don't care if it does. My time with you is very important. So…let's put work back in its ugly box and have some fun. That's Captree Island right there."

Casey took in the view and sighed. "Is that an order captain?"

"That's an *order.*"

Trabinski anchored the *Lovely Leah* in the shallows along a secluded shoreline of the island and turned to Casey. "Swim first? Eat later?"

Casey scanned the water around her. The sun was hot now that the boat had stopped its forward motion and she wondered about diving into a frigid Atlantic. The seagulls, circling above, laughed, and cackled at her as if mocking her indecision.

"Let's cool off!" She stepped off the bridge and strutted to the cushioned stern.

"Right behind you," Trabinski said.

Casey kicked off her tennis shoes, slipped out of her shorts, unfastened her crocheted beach jacket, and dropped it on the cushion fully revealing a lime green gingham patterned bikini.

Trabinski in the process of unbuttoning his shirt paused at the sight of her beautiful figure. *Oh, mercy. This little lady will be the death of me.*

A slow approving whistle escaped his lips.

Casey struck a quick pin up girl pose, fluffed her hair, and shot him a fetching smile then padded over and helped him undress.

When he could finally breathe, he said, "*Honey?* You look absolutely *stunning*. I am a *lucky man*."

"Yes… *you are.*" She laughed as she stepped onto the gunwale. "Last one in cleans the bilge," she called as she executed a perfect swan dive into the rippling water.

They swam for a while and Trabinski never took his eyes off her as she glided gracefully through the gentle swells. To him she was perfect in every way. Even the tiny mole next to her belly button was perfect. She was smart, witty, caring and undeniably beautiful.

As he watched her drift by, he smiled. There was no doubt in his mind about how he felt. He was head over heels in love with her.

"*What are you staring at?*" Casey asked as she scissor kicked toward him.

Trabinski swam a circle around her. "I'm not sure," he replied. "I think a gorgeous mermaid."

"*A mermaid? Where?*" Casey laughed and splashed water in his face.

They frolicked in the currents for another twenty minutes then Trabinski said, "I want you to see the island." They body surfed onto the beach and walked the dunes holding hands, letting the July sun dry them. The smell of fermenting sea grass drifted through the salty sea air as the breeze blew across the island causing the overgrown reeds to whisper a shushing tune. The cries of the gulls in the distance and the steady crash of the breakers had a relaxing hypnotic effect. Casey stopped walking, stepped in front of Jim, popped up on her tip toes and tenderly kissed his lips. "*Thank you,* Jim. I didn't realize how much I needed this."

"My pleasure," he said and returned the kiss. "You hungry yet?"

"*Starving,*" Casey said. "Let's head back."

After finishing off a lunch consisting of roast beef on a hard roll with mayo, turkey, and Swiss cheese with mustard on pumpernickel bread plus Cole slaw and potato salad, Jim and Casey sat close to each other on the plush cushions at the stern of the Chris-Craft sipping Pinot Grigio from chilled glasses.

As they sat in silence enjoying each other's company as well as the relaxing atmosphere Trabinski put his arm around Casey's shoulders caressing her neck and hair with his fingers. He—at that very moment—realized he would be an absolute wreck if for some reason he couldn't be with her. He felt a sudden emptiness in the pit of his stomach as if he hadn't eaten. *I've got to say something. Tell her how I feel and not sound like a bumbling fool doing it.*

He took a sip of wine, cleared his throat, and said nonchalantly, "*Casey?* What do you think about making this a permanent arrangement."

Casey tilted her head so she could see his face. "You mean using the boat like this more often? It would be really nice but how could we possibly do it with our work schedules?"

"*Noo…* I mean us," he said.

Casey abruptly pulled away from his arm and sat straight on the edge of the cushion almost spilling her drink. Her gray eyes went wide with surprise and confusion. She put her hand on his knee and in a voice mixed with suspicion and amusement said, "James Trabinski? *Did you? Just propose to me?*"

He put his hand on top of hers. "*Something like that.*"

Before another word was said the ship to shore radio squawked to life. A few seconds of static then a voice came on.

"Lovely Leah. This is Bayshore marina calling on Marine band channel sixteen at one-five-six megahertz. Do you read?"

Jim gave Casey a puzzled look and stood up. "That's Gary's voice," he said hurrying to the radio on the bridge.

The call repeated itself and Jim grabbed the microphone and pressed the switch. "Bayshore Marina…this is Lovely Leah. Reading you clearly on channel sixteen. Go ahead Gary. Over."

"Hey Jimbo, sorry to barge in on you like this but you remember that Coast Guard VHF radio we installed a couple of years ago? Over."

"Sure do. We picked that one because it had direct connect to all Nassau and Suffolk County precincts. What about it? Over."

"Well, it came to life a few minutes ago. An incoming transmission from a detective Peter Taylor. Says he's from the eighth precinct and needs to talk to you *mucho pronto*. He's holding on channel eighteen. Over."

"Roger that. Switching to channel eighteen."

As he reached over to turn the dial Casey came up beside him and gave him a concerned look as she slipped her shorts on over her bikini bottom.

Another few seconds of static.

"Peter? I'm patched through on the marine band channel eighteen. Do you read? Over."

"Loud and clear Lieutenant. I'm *real* sorry about this. Thought I had a handle on a situation that happened last night, but everything went down the shitter early this morning. Is Lieutenant Talbot nearby? She needs to hear this too. Over."

"She's right here. Go ahead. Over."

A quick click, click of the mic transmit button came through the channel then a brief silence before detective Taylor came back on. "*Jim? Casey?* I don't want to say too much over the radio, but I've got a horrible feeling that the *you know what* is back. Two teenage girls were murdered last night. One in Hillsville the other near Woodbury. The Woodbury victim was brutally murdered according to Second precinct officers at the scene. We have a suspect in custody regarding the girl from Hillsville."

Trabinski broke in interrupting Taylor. "Peter? What makes you think the *you know what* is back if you have a suspect in custody? Over."

"The person we have in lockup, who witnesses said killed the girl, is our young friend... *Tim Ryan.* Over."

CHAPTER 45

July 4th — 10:00 pm.

Lieutenant Detective Cassandra Talbot slapped her steering wheel in anger as she parked her unmarked car in front of the stylish Cape Cod house on Culver Lane. It was adjacent to the one where little Eddie Franks had disappeared. She turned off the Plymouth Fury's engine, clipped her badge on the belt of the gray slacks she was wearing, exited the vehicle and slipped on the matching jacket. She stepped onto the sidewalk and scanned the night sky, roof tops and then the neighborhood for any movement. She thought about the one mother's statement about seeing a shimmer. *Won't see the bitch anyway if she's got her camouflage thing working.*

Casey strode, shoulders back, chin raised, toward the vehicles parked on the street in front of her car; two NCPD cruisers, an unmarked Chevy Belair and a white Forensics' van. She immediately recognized Detective McClosky talking to the forensics attendant along with two patrolmen from her precinct, Callister, and Jones, standing behind him. McCloskey was an up and comer and Casey had picked up vibes from him that he resented her being his superior.

Detective Dan McCloskey saw her approaching. A quick look of annoyed surprise went across his face as he stopped talking to the Forensics man. He acknowledged Casey's presence with a curt nod. "Thought you were away lieutenant?" he said.

Casey stepped closer to him and looking up—he towered over her—said, "I *was*. Bring me up to speed on this." She looked back and forth between McCloskey and the forensics man whom she didn't recognize.

The forensics man spoke first. "We're still doing the cleanup lieutenant. It may take a few days to finish. Haven't seen carnage like this in a long time. Whoever did this was a powerful sadistic psycho with, dare I say it, a cannibalistic appetite."

Casey turned towards the well-lit house. "Show me where it happened."

As they went up the walk to the front door, loud fireworks caused them all to flinch. Instinctively Casey grabbed for her gun nestled in the shoulder holster under her jacket but just as quickly brought her hand back down to her side. She was edgy tonight and couldn't shake it.

"Victim's name?" she asked as McCloskey opened the front door for her.

"Joanne Farber," McCloskey replied. "Sixteen, honor roll student, Girl Scout, Senior level."

McCloskey led the way up the stairs of the cozy tastefully decorated house to the girl's bedroom, Casey behind him and the forensics man following her.

In the hallway at the top of the stairs Casey saw two of her other patrolmen, Haggerty and Reese standing by a brightly lit doorway both holding small notebooks. "*Gentlemen*," she said in a low no nonsense voice. Both officers had somber expressions on their faces and greeted her with a similar tone of voice. "*Lieutenan*t," they said and stepped aside for her to view the room.

She entered the room and gasped involuntarily. Her right hand came up to cover her mouth and her left jammed itself into her pants pocket to keep from shaking. Although the room was being examined and cleaned by the two other forensics agents in the room, the strong coppery smell of blood clung to everything. There were still remnants of it throughout the room; on the walls, the floor near the bed and on the mattress—the sheets had been removed and placed in large plastic bags— as well as a vanity chair and nightstand.

Casey, hand still over her mouth shivered when her eyes landed on the slit window screen. It had been pulled apart wide enough for someone …or something to fit through. Her head spun with déjà vu as she remembered the disappearance of that infant a year ago and a similar split window screen.

She backed out of the room— both hands in her pockets now—and said to no one in particular, "Has cause of death been determined?" Her tone was steady and all business.

The forensics man still standing in the hall talking to McCloskey answered, "Preliminary determination? Cervical fracture at the C1 vertebrae."

Casey looked down at the floor. "Time of death?"

"Again, it's preliminary Lieutenant. There was a lot of blood. Estimated TOD? A little after midnight." The forensics man answered.

She lifted her head and spoke directly to McCloskey. "Give me the play-by-play Dan. Don't leave anything out." She began to pace the hallway.

Detective McCloskey cleared his throat. "It's all in the report Lieutenant. I think…"

"I *want to hear it from you*," Casey snapped.

"Whatever you say, lieutenant," he replied. Casey picked up the sarcasm in his tone and made a mental note to have a little disciplinary heart to heart with him as soon as time allowed.

He pulled a note pad from his jacket pocket and flipped it open to the first pages. "The call came in at seven fifty-five this morning from a hysterical Joseph Farber. Callister and Jones were the closest unit. They arrived at eight fifteen, entered the home and found the victim's mother, Marylyn Farber, sitting on the living room sofa obviously in shock. The father stood next to her with his arm around his younger daughter Melissa. He directed Callister and Jones to the upstairs bedroom where the bloody, mutilated remains of Joanne Farber had been found by her mother.

"I arrived on the scene at eight thirty and joined Callister and Jones. Haggerty and Reese had just arrived. Upon seeing the condition of the body as well as the room we did not enter, and I immediately radioed in for Forensics. I instructed Mr. Farber to fetch a blanket and put it on his catatonic wife, then called for an ambulance. Jones comforted the little girl whose bedroom was on the lower level at the back of the house. She didn't hear a thing. The father, hardly able to speak also claimed to have heard nothing.

"Forensics arrived at nine and I reported the situation to the precinct. Forensics took over and I…"

"Lieutenant? If I may?" the forensics man interrupted. "I can take over from here."

Casey stopped pacing and turned to the skinny, bald man with the black horn-rimmed glasses, wearing a white lab coat. "*Please,*" she said.

The man adjusted the glasses on his face and went to the bedroom door. "What we found when we entered the room could have been a scene from the old Jack the Ripper files. There was so much blood we didn't know what we were seeing at first. The girl's body had been stripped. We found her torn night gown on the floor beside the bed. Her eyes were closed, so most likely she was murdered in her sleep. The odd position of the head on the pillow led us to believe her neck had been broken." He stopped and looked over his shoulder to see the expression on Casey's face. "*Here's* the disturbing part lieutenant. A large percentage of this girl's body was eaten. Our investigation revealed that no meaty tissue areas of the body escaped attack. The flesh had been ripped from her thighs, arms, abdomen, breasts, and rump. Her face, hands and feet were not touched. This attack was so brutal we could have done the autopsy right…"

"Thank you…I get the picture," Casey interrupted. "Any chance a neighbor heard or saw something, Dan?"

"Callister and Jones canvassed the neighborhood but came up with a zero on the witness scale," McCloskey replied.

Casey started down the stairs. "Okay. Let me know immediately if anything else turns up. I'll be at the precinct."

McCloskey, also an astute detective quickly shot a question at Casey before she reached the bottom of the stairs. "Lieutenant? I can tell by the look on your face you have an idea what happened here. Care to *enlighten us?*"

Casey stepped off the last step. "*No!*" she said in a flinty voice. Then she dialed back her tone and said, "*Not yet.*"

Back in her car Casey leaned her head against the steering wheel. *This is so bad. I knew that monster wasn't dead. I have to take action somehow but what the hell can be done. The damn thing is killing teenage girls and is now breaking into their homes to do it. I have to do something! A curfew is a possibility. No, that won't stop the bitch from camouflaged killings during the day.*

She lifted her head off the steering wheel and rubbed the back of her neck. *I need to get this under control quickly or we'll have panic on our hands. Maybe Jim will have some ideas. But right now I have to put something in place, no matter how limited.*

Casey grabbed the mic from the dashboard clip and pressed the transmit button.

"Dispatch? This is unit one…lieutenant Talbot. Come in."

"Go ahead lieutenant…Thought you were away?"

Casey huffed then hit transmit. "I *was.* Now listen carefully. Set up a rotating schedule to have a patrol car cruise Culver Lane and adjoining streets twenty-four- seven until further notice. I'm authorizing a code two on this so please make it happen. I'll be at the precinct shortly. Call me if there are problems. Unit one, out."

***

Eighth Precinct—10:15 pm

Lead detective Lieutenant James Trabinski accompanied by detective Peter Taylor stood in Holding Cell number 2 looking at a forlorn fifteen-year-old boy sitting on the lone bunk in the room. A year had gone by since they last laid eyes on him. Except for a different hair style, he hadn't changed much. He sat on the side of the bed, hunched forward with his hands clasped between his legs. He didn't acknowledge their presence.

"*Hello Tim…* Long time no see," Trabinski said, pulling over the only chair in the room, placing it in front of the boy and sitting so he could see his face when he talked to him. "What kind of mess have you gotten yourself into this time?"

No response.

"Detective Taylor here, tells me you refuse to talk. That won't help. There are people claiming they saw you kill the girl you were with. If this goes to court and they all testify to what they saw you could be sentenced to the Juvenile Detention Center for a long time. So, if you want our help, it would be a good idea to start talking."

Tim Ryan slowly looked up. His eyes were red from crying. "I don't know what happened," he mumbled. "*Honest.*"

Trabinski had noticed a small table against the back wall when he entered the cell. On it was a paper plate with a grilled cheese sandwich, a can of Orange Crush soda and a bag of potato chips. He motioned to Taylor to bring it over.

"You better eat, or you won't have the strength to get out of this situation," Trabinski said.

Taylor carefully placed the items on the bed next to Tim.

Trabinski scooched the chair back a little and crossed his legs. "Tell me what you *do* remember. Start with the girl."

"I didn't know her. She was real cute, so I sang to her." Tim said through a mouth full of sandwich.

"*Sang* to her?" Trabinski asked.

Detective Taylor cut in. "Our boy here is a rock star. Plays guitar in a band called the Dynatones. They were performing at the Teen Club dance last night."

Trabinski put his hands behind his head. "You meet a lot of girls playing in this band?"

"Not a lot," Tim replied with a shrug.

"So, what happened after you sang to this girl?"

Tim took a sip of the Orange Crush. "She came up to me when we took a break. She said she liked the way I sang. She seemed nice so I told her I was getting a coke and heading outside to cool off, did she want to come."

"*Did she?*" Trabinski continued.

Tim nodded. "She didn't hesitate. She said 'sure', and we got our sodas and headed outside."

Trabinski brought his hands down and leaned forward in the chair. "*Then* what happened?"

Detective Taylor was standing behind Trabinski with his arms folded across his chest. He was remembering a rainy night in a junk yard a year ago and a drenched teenage boy wielding a broom handle like a baseball bat.

"I don't know," Tim said shaking his head. "The only thing I remember is me standing on the dance floor, this guy with his arm around my neck and everybody staring at me. I remember feeling like I had been asleep or something."

"Sounds familiar. Doesn't it?" Taylor said softly to Trabinski.

"Sure does." Trabinski stood up. "Tim? Let me see your hands."

Tim wiped them on the napkin that came with the sandwich and held them out palm up to Trabinski.

"Show me your fingernails."

Tim did as he was told and Trabinski and Taylor examined them closely.

They were the nails of someone who either bit them or kept them cut extremely short for some purpose like guitar playing.

Trabinski and Taylor looked at each other thinking the same thing. There was no way the scratches on the dead girl's face came from Tim Ryan's hands.

"Tim? We think you are once again a victim of circumstance. Unfortunately, we can't get you out of here till Monday since it's a holiday weekend. I'll let your parents know you're okay and what to expect from our department and that they can visit you.

"Eat the rest of your sandwich. I'll stop by tomorrow and we'll talk some more." Trabinski said as he left the cell.

Detective Taylor closed the cell door and locked it. When he saw Tim flinch he said, "I'll be right back. Going to hunt up some comic books and possibly games to keep you occupied while you're here. Don't go away…"

Tim had to chuckle at the detective's last remark.

Taylor sat in the comfortable guest chair in front of Trabinski's desk sipping coffee. He had just returned from delivering four comic books, a small, plastic, handheld pinball type baseball game, a car magazine—all of which he retrieved from evidence lock up— and a newspaper with an unfinished crossword puzzle to Tim Ryan.

Trabinski sitting at his desk wanted a cigarette badly. He fought off the need by popping a stick of Beeman's gum into his mouth and chewing vigorously. He hated chomping on gum. It made him feel like a cow chewing its cud.

"Pete? What do you remember about that night last July?"

"Unfortunately, *everything*. I don't think I'll ever forget it."

"Tell me what you recall of Tim Ryan," Trabinski said unconsciously touching the side of his face where the boy had struck him a year ago.

Taylor took another sip of coffee and placed the cup on the desk. "He was standing there in the pouring rain pounding you with a broom handle. You were on the ground and Casey stepped toward you and aimed her pistol at him. When she yelled at him to stop he turned like a stiff legged puppet or a zombie in a trance and swung at her."

Trabinski leaned back in his chair. "I remember Casey telling me that when she encountered him at the junk yard with the dog he seemed

413

to be in a trance. Did you get the impression he was being controlled by the creature?"

"Hard to think otherwise. Suddenly he was a dazed and confused kid sitting in the mud after Casey shot it. *And* …He didn't remember a thing."

"So, your gut's telling you that this…this harpy thing has returned and put him in a trance last night. For what purpose? To lure prey to her?" Trabinski stood and started pacing his office.

"Jim? When I got there last night and saw the same stupefied expression on his face that he had on that night in the junk yard my chest tightened. I knew it was back.

"As for the purpose? I think it's a tactic, a set up. And it worked perfectly until those kids who found the body showed up unexpectedly and apparently scared her off."

Trabinski stopped pacing and put his hands in his back pockets. "Those kids? What did they actually see?"

Taylor pulled a pack of Winstons from his shirt pocket and froze when saw the look on his boss's face. "Uh… sorry Jim," he said and slipped the pack back in place. "After questioning them thoroughly it turns out the only thing they actually saw was the girl's body laying on the sidewalk and Tim walking away. They didn't see Tim kill the girl. They jumped to conclusions."

"Well, that will go in his favor. Did you get any details on Casey's situation?"

"Very little. The girl was killed at home, and it sounded like a blood bath," Taylor replied.

"Okay. We'll need details from her. Two killings in one night tells me this mythological bitch has upped her game. And how the hell are we going to stop her?"

Detective Taylor stood up and rubbed the stubble on his chin. "I think we better shut down the Teen Club dances for a while. Might be a good idea to establish a curfew. What do you think?"

Trabinski, his jaws tired from chewing, spit the spent gum into the wastepaper can on the floor next to his desk. "Definitely close down the dances. The kids will *love us* for that. I doubt if a curfew will work but I'll present it to the captain. He has to initiate that." He looked at his watch. "Is Mickey's Tavern still open?"

"Should be," Taylor replied.

"Let's go find out. I need a drink."

***

Malhela hunkered down in her nest with her wings wrapped around her trying to block out the continuous booming, crackling, and snapping sounds that filled the night. Some reminded her of the popping sounds that came just before the projectiles pierced her body on that cursed night a year ago. Though she felt invincible after gorging herself on the essence of the birthgiver she also felt agitated by the relentless noise. *What is this? Are these pathetic mortals at war with each other? Even the stars in the sky are exploding!*

The exploding stars were the reason she retreated to her nest. She had never experienced such a thing and it brought to mind a legend from the realm about *all* time ending this way. *Perhaps it is the end of **this** realm. So be it. A fitting end to this miserable journey.*

She unfolded her wings and peered out the half open door to her nest. *If I am to be eradicated I will not sit here and wait for it to happen. I will fly till the fade takes me.*

Malhela stepped cautiously out of her nest onto the building's rooftop. She sprang into the clamorous night sky, flying low at first then climbing. She noticed the exploding stars and comet-like streaks in the sky were further away and diminishing. *The fade has begun.*

She spread her wings, gliding in a north easterly direction and realized the night had grown quiet. The assault on her tender ears had ceased. She hovered, listening. There were a few sporadic unremarkable booms and pops in the distance. *They too are fading. How long will it take till there is nothing?*

With no idea where she was going —or caring—she circled and drifted waiting for the end wondering why there were so few mortals on the streets. *Do they not fear the demise of their world?*

As she casually scanned the landscape beneath her, Malhela noticed a black, four wheeled conveyance stop in front of a brightly lit dwelling. She recognized the place immediately. She had dined here not too long ago. The taste of the sweet birthgiver was still on her lips. *At least I will fade with a full belly.*

She watched the conveyance with mild curiosity until the side of it opened and a mortal stepped out. She reared back as if she had been punched. The thought of all time ending instantly disappeared as she hissed hatefully at the figure below. *The elf woman! Now, I will have my revenge! Perhaps I'll even take a bite. I have never tasted elf.*

Malhela swooped down for the attack but veered off when she saw her target approach two male mortals. *They may have those devices that caused my wounds. I will wait for the best moment to strike.*

She soared to the peak of the dwelling's roof, quietly settled down and watched.

Her anger was doing a slow boil and her patience was wearing thin when the red-haired elf woman finally appeared, walking quickly to her conveyance, and entering it before Malhela could make a move. She glared at the vehicle as it made a turn in the narrow street and headed for the main thoroughfare.

Still feeling invigorated from her feast she leapt into the night sky fully camouflaged and followed her enemy. *Let me see if more of my magic has returned. It is time for me to be clever.*

When the elf woman's conveyance turned onto the main thoroughfare and picked up speed, Malhela made her move. She dive bombed the vehicle hitting the top of it with her taloned feet and bouncing off. The top dented and the vehicle swerved momentarily. Then making a quick turn headed directly at the front window of the conveyance. Just when collision seemed inevitable, she did a back flip and splattered the glass with feces. The conveyance again swerved from side-to-side skidding to a stop. Malhela raced ahead of it and abruptly turned, extended her arms straight forward, hands positioned as if holding some invisible object. The conveyance slid to the right, hit the corner of the overpass guard rail and tumbled sideways down the embankment crashing onto the pavement below.

Malhela circled overhead like a buzzard. It was dark but her keen eyes could see the upside-down vehicle's wheels still spinning. Other vehicles were approaching. The light emanating from the front of their metal bodies illuminated the scene as some screeched to a halt. She peered down searching for movement from the overturned vehicle. When nothing stirred after several minutes of circling Malhela smiled. *That will teach you! You Elvin freneza!*

CHAPTER 46

July 5th —Early morning

James Trabinski was about to leave his house for the precinct intending to check on Tim Ryan when his phone rang. It was unusual for him to get a call at home this early in the morning. He stared at it as if trying to see the caller inside. It continued to ring, and it seemed to have an urgency about it. He picked it up and before he could say hello a familiar voice said, "Jim? It's Pete."

He instantly detected the concern in his partner's voice. "I didn't expect a wake-up call. What's going on?"

"It's Casey…"

"*Casey?*"

"She's been in an accident. She's at Central General Emergency. A courtesy call came in this morning from Detective Dan McCloskey at the second precinct. He said he didn't have details on her condition yet. She was unconscious when they brought her in. He thought you should know."

All Trabinski said was, "Thanks" and hung up.

He bolted out his front door, looked between his Impala and his unmarked Ford Galaxy, and though the Impala was a much faster car decided on the Ford and quickly backed out of his driveway.

As he turned onto Plainview Road, he hit the siren and crushed the gas pedal. He would be at Central General in ten minutes.

He skidded his Galaxy to a stop in the Emergency parking lot, shut everything down and ran to the hospital entrance door. He threw it open and hurried to the admitting desk and presented his badge. He struggled to calm down. *You're a cop…not some emotional wimp. Now get it together.* He took a deep breath counted to four and exhaled slowly.

The admitting nurse studied his badge. "May I help you?"

"Lieutenant Trabinski, eighth precinct. A colleague of mine was brought in late last night. Lieutenant Cassandra Talbot," He said with as much authority as he could muster. "I need to know her condition and if I can see her."

"Let me get the attending doctor for you," the nurse said and picked up a phone and dialed.

It seemed like an eternity before the doctor appeared. An attractive woman with short auburn hair, wearing the customary white doctor's coat with a stethoscope stuffed in its pocket approached him. "I'm doctor Clausen," the woman said and shook Trabinski's hand. "You're here inquiring about Cassandra Talbot, lieutenant?"

Trabinski was momentarily surprised to see a woman doctor. Like Casey, she was unique.

"I am," he replied. He didn't like the tone of her voice. "How is she?"

The doctor steered him away from the admitting desk and said in a more conciliatory tone, "She was in a bad car accident last night. She was unconscious when they brought her in, pretty banged up. She sustained a laceration above her left eye and a contusion below the eye plus a distal radius fracture of the left arm."

When she saw the questioning look on his face she immediately said, "A broken wrist. Other than that, she seems to be fine. There were no signs of shock and we're still monitoring her for concussion but so far, we're confident she can be released later today."

Trabinski unconsciously sighed with relief. "Thank you doctor. Can I see her now?"

"Certainly. Follow me. She's in station three."

They proceeded through metal swinging doors and down a long hallway with recuperation nooks on the right side. Each contained a bed, some had medical equipment, and all were divided by heavy gray curtains. A placard attached to an aluminum pole outside each nook indicated the station number. When they arrived at station three the doctor motioned for Trabinski to wait. She partially opened the closed curtain and slipped inside. Trabinski heard her say, "Cassandra? Do you feel up to seeing a visitor?" There was a muffled response and the doctor reappeared. "Okay, you can go in," the doctor said.

Trabinski realized— with the doctor standing there— he had better use police decorum when he first saw Casey. *Going in there and kissing her would certainly raise some eyebrows.*

He slipped through the curtain and there she was sitting up in the hospital bed, wearing a pale blue hospital gown with a small white flower design. There was a bandage above her left eye and a nasty black and blue bruise below it on her cheek bone. Her left arm had a cast at the wrist and her hair was sticking up at the back of her head Woody Woodpecker style.

"*Hi,*" she said with a slight wave of her right hand and a welcoming smile.

"Hey lieutenant," he said feeling like a jerk talking like this. "I came as soon as I got the call. How you doing?"

Trabinski turned to the doctor, sent her a stern look and said in an assertive tone, "I need to speak to the lieutenant in private. Police business. Will you excuse us?"

When the doctor noticed the look on her patient's face as the lieutenant entered, she knew it wasn't police business that needed to be discussed.

"Certainly," the doctor replied. Then in an equally assertive voice said, "You've got twenty minutes, then you're out of here. If she wants to go home today then I want her resting. *Twenty minutes.* Don't make me call security." She chuckled. "Check with me before you leave, and I'll let you know around what time she'll be released." She started to walk away.

"Thank you," Trabinski said.

The doctor looked over her shoulder and with a gleam in her eye said, "I assume you'll be the one taking her home?"

"Uh? Yes." He felt like he had been caught with his hand in the cookie jar. "That obvious, huh?"

"Just a little," the doctor said. "I'll leave you two alone. *Twenty minutes!*"

With the doctor heading down the hall Trabinski came over to Casey, took her right hand and kissed it softly.

"Are you okay? The doctor said you were pretty banged up."

Casey held on to his hand. "I'm fine. Except for the wrist I'm just a little sore. I tried to roll with the punches so to speak and got my arm caught between the steering wheel spokes when the car went over. I know how the clothes must feel in one of those laundromat dryers. The rear-view mirror did this…" She pointed to the bandage over her eye using her thumb sticking out of the cast. "…and the microphone flew off the hook and smacked me in the face. Glad it was under the eye."

Trabinski looked around, saw no chair, and sat on the edge of the bed. "They said you were unconscious when they brought you in," he said.

Casey gently released his hand and rubbed her neck. "I don't remember hitting my head. I remember wondering 'how far am I falling?' as the car kept tumbling downward. I guess I could have been knocked out when the car crashed onto the pavement and slammed me upside down onto the roof."

Trabinski shook his head and looked into her gray eyes. They looked tired. "I'm just so happy to see you sitting here like this. When I got the call, I feared the worst." He checked his watch. He had ten minutes left but decided he should go. She looked like she could sleep. "Okay, that's enough for now. I'm going to let you get some more rest. I'll check with Doctor Clausen and get a check out time."

As he went to stand up Casey grabbed his arm. "*Wait*, I have a lot to tell you."

He gently removed her hand and stood. "Tell me later."

Casey sat forward, flinching, "*No!* Jim? Listen to me. We've got a big, big problem on our hands. After seeing the crime scene last night where the girl was murdered in her home, there is no doubt in my mind…the harpy bitch is back. The forensics examiner said the girl's body had been mutilated, a large portion of it eaten. Cause of death …a broken neck…probably while she slept. *And…*the window screen to the girl's bedroom had been slit and bent open. We know this is her MO. We've seen it before. But, what really scares me is the bitch is more daring than before and more powerful.

"What happened to me was not an accident. I was attacked. My car was literally forced off the road by a powerful gust of wind. I couldn't see her but…I *felt* her."

Trabinski pursed his lips and nodded. "I hate to say it but after seeing Tim Ryan last night there's no doubt in my mind either." He took a quick glance at his watch. "I better go before the warden chases me. Get some rest. I'll be back later, and we'll talk more." He was deeply troubled by the information Casey had just given him but decided to keep it to himself for the time being.

"One more thing," Casey said as she reached with her good hand and retrieved her shoulder bag from the nearby tray stand. She fumbled it open, pulled out the keys to her apartment and handed them to him. "Would you stop by my place and get me some clean clothes before you come get me? Please…"

"Absolutely. It would be a pleasure my lady," he said taking the keys and kissing her hand. "*Sleep!*" He said with a smile and slipped through the curtain just as the doctor appeared.

***

The Bolton residence—Mid morning

After a breakfast of pancakes, eggs and bacon—their mother had returned to doing things like this shortly after the healing elixir had be administered via a cup of Lipton's tea two days ago—Stanley Bolton sat in his room on his unmade bed with the book of spells on his lap. His brother Jonathan sat across from him on the bed that used to be their older brother Artie's, who remained missing and presumed dead somewhere in Guinea, Africa. A year had passed and still no report of his whereabouts.

Stanley was thinking about last night's fiasco at the dance and Jonathan was daydreaming. Suddenly Jonathan said, "Do you think he's dead?"

"Uh? *Who?* Artie? I really don't know, Jonny. I hope not," Stanley replied after being jarred from his thoughts.

Jonathan leaned forward, put his elbows on his knees and clasped his hands in front of his face. "You know? We may be able to find him," he said. "We have the *book.* "

Stanley reached behind him and grabbed a freshly opened pack of Camel's cigarettes, tapped one out and lit it with his lighter. He took a drag and exhaled a smoke ring over his brother's head. "I don't think it's a good idea to be messing with this thing anymore," he said knocking on the book with a knuckle. Jonathan disfigured the smoke ring with the wave of his hand. "Why?"

Stanley squinted at his brother and in a serious tone said, "You have no idea how much trouble can come from using *this*. You got lucky with that healing potion. You could have accidentally conjured up something right out of your worst nightmares."

"I don't have nightmares," Jonathan commented.

"Don't hand me that! You had plenty when you were younger."

"I don't *remember any.*"

"Well, you'd remember this one. It would never go away."

Jonathan folded his arms. "How *would you* know?"

Stanley realized he had said more than he wanted to and was about to dismiss the topic when an idea hit him. *Why not tell him what happened? If he doesn't believe it…fine. If he does, he may be helpful, especially since he claims to be able to read Latin.* He stood up and carried the book to his cluttered worktable in the corner and placed it there. He took a puff on the Camel, blew smoke toward the open window, and turned to his brother. "Since you were the one who got my voice back, I'm gonna tell you something, but you gotta swear to keep your yap shut about it. Understand?"

"Okay, *sure.*"

Stanley began a slow pacing around his room as he filled his little brother in on the events that took place last year. He didn't give a detailed description of the creature they had conjured up, only that it flew and smelled really bad. He went on to tell him that the harpy had stolen his voice, paralyzed him and left him to die right here in this very room. He spoke about it having some weird effect on Tim Ryan. Something he would never talk about.

"…And I never found out for sure, but I always thought the creature was responsible for little kids disappearing and some teenager being killed. And when the police got involved, I knew I was probably right.".

"I know what a harpy is. Read all about them. A mythological creature. All of them had wings of different types. Some had wings like an eagle, others like a hawk and some others had bat wings. They all looked like naked women and had magical powers."

He stopped pacing, surprised at Jonathan's matter of fact comment.

"Wow, you really do read a lot," Stanley said.

"Knowledge is power," Jonathan said with a shrug. "I like to read."

Stanley came over and stood in front of him. "*How old are you?*"

"What's that supposed to mean. You know how old I am."

"If I didn't know better, I'd swear you were a forty-year-old midget the way you talk sometimes."

Jonathan slipped off the bed, walked to the window and looked out at the sunlit street below. "So…," he said over his shoulder. "Why are you telling me all this?"

Stanley came to the window and stood next to his brother. "Because I have an awful feeling in my gut that the damn thing has returned. The police thought they killed it…"

"*Immortal.* Can't be killed," Jonathan interrupted.

"Exactly! So, I need to figure out a way to get rid of this thing and I thought that since you can read Latin you could help me use the book to do that. You game?"

Jonathan stepped away from the window and went to the book on the worktable.

"Sure," he said opening the book of spells. "I know someone who might be more of a help than me."

Stanley still standing at the window, quickly turned toward his brother. "*You* do!?"

"Yes. The person who helped me with the potion. Her name is Phae."

***

Eighth Precinct—Noon

When Lieutenant James Trabinski entered the lock up area to check on Tim Ryan he was surprised to see the boy was not alone. In the cell were Tim's mother and father as well as a portly, balding man with a bushy mustache who looked like he was dressed for the golf course. He was holding a small leather satchel which he unzipped when he saw him approaching. As Trabinski stepped in front of the open cell the man pulled a folded piece of paper from the satchel. "Are you the arresting officer?" he said in a gruff voice.

"Hey Tim. How you holding up?" Trabinski said ignoring the bald man. "Glad to see your parents here." He greeted them cordially and Tim's father introduced William Maddox, the bald man as his attorney who held out the paper and asked again, "Are you the arresting officer?"

Trabinski looked at the man's plump, red cheeked face then at the paper. "I am **not** but… I *do* know him." He despised pomposity and enjoyed disarming those who used it like a sword. "If that's Tim's release I'll be glad to see that he gets it."

The lawyer straightened his shoulders and puffed out his chest as if he was about to give a speech. "And *you are?*"

"Lieutenant James Trabinski, lead detective in charge of homicide for this precinct. And, let me inform you, before you start rambling on with legalese, if you didn't already know, Tim here is considered a person of interest in a recent homicide regardless of being a minor. And since there were witnesses who saw Tim allegedly with the victim we had no choice but to put him here for safekeeping. No charges have been filed, yet. Unless you want this to get ugly."

The expression on the lawyer's face said, 'How dare you?' but his voice said, "*Oh.*" He handed the paper to Trabinski who immediately scanned it then stepped away from the cell. "Okay Tim. You're free to go, but I want you to promise me that you'll call me right away if you remember anything more. Deal?"

Tim looked at his father then at his lawyer. "Sure," he said. Then added, "Tell detective Taylor, thanks for the comics and stuff."

"I certainly will," Trabinski said as he watched them file out of the cell with the fat attorney in the lead. He noticed that Tim walked with a stiffness unusual for a healthy teenage boy. *I don't like the looks of that. He walks like he has braces on his legs. Could he still be under that monster's influence? I hate to do this to the kid but I'm going to have someone keep an eye on him.*

CHAPTER 47

July 5th—Late afternoon

After returning home from the police station, Tim Ryan spent most of his time sulking in his room.

Seeing his guitar and amplifier sitting there, with a note from Jack Murphy, stating his future with the Dynatones looked doubtful, added to his dark mood.

He felt the musical wall he had erected to protect himself from past horrific memories start to crumble; allowing the concealed dread to seep through the cracks like the Blob in that old movie. He hated the flashbacks and what they did to him. *I can't let them in. Not again.*

Tim sat with his elbows on his desk, holding his head. *Why can't I remember anything that happened after I met that girl? Could I really have killed her? Why would I do that? What's wrong with me? Maybe I'm going crazy.*

He reached over and picked up the glass of iced tea he had brought up with him after dinner—his family always ate an early dinner on Sunday—and took a gulp. He started replaying in his head the events of that night that led up to meeting the girl whose name, he had been told, was Marcy Dubrowski. He stopped the replay when he remembered

Stanley and Janey being there. *They had to have seen what happened. They were on the dance floor when I was dragged down the stairs. I have to talk to them.*

Just then he remembered something that could possibly help stop the awful flashbacks and maybe help him recall other things as well. Stanley had the book. He looked at his watch then turned his head and looked out his bedroom window. *Still daylight. He's probably with Janey. I'll call and find out. No time to waste.*

Tim walked at a fast pace up Cabel Street toward Plainview Road. He had learned from Stanley's brother that he was still at Janey's. *No time to waste.* Since his parents and sister were in the back yard—his father and mother talking over the fence to the neighbor while Emily tried to catch fireflies in a jar— he decided to forgo asking permission and slipped out the front door unnoticed. He was in enough trouble already, a little more wouldn't matter.

Crickets and katydids sang to him as he marched along Plainview Road toward Janey's house. He saw Stanley sitting with Janey on her front steps and hurried to them.

Janey looked up in surprise. "*Tim.* Are you okay?"

Stanley jumped off the steps. "Man, am I glad to see you. When the fuzz took you away, I thought you were a goner. What the hell happened?"

"I was hoping you two could tell me. I don't remember a thing after I got a coke for that...the girl."

Janey slipped off the steps and stood next to them. "I saw you singing to her, so I thought you knew her. She sure looked like she was into you. I wish somebody would sing to *me*." She shot Stanley a quick glance.

Stanley looked at her and laughed. "You don't want to hear me sing. Your pretty little ears would bleed."

"What else?" Tim asked.

Stanley scratched his head. "We saw you talking with her then head to the coolers holding her hand. That's why we thought you knew her, so we didn't pay attention after that."

"We went back to our table and the next thing we know the doors crash open and this big oaf...Jerry Lockman to be precise, drags you into the room. Holding you in a headlock," Janey said. "You know him?"

"She knows everybody," Stanley said.

Tim frowned. "Did you know her?"

Janey nodded. "Marcy? I know of her. Kinda ditsy but nice. She was a Pom Pom girl. You know, one of those girls who aren't good enough to be cheerleaders. She had a bad breakup with her boyfriend a few months ago. That's about all I know."

Stanley looked admiringly at his girlfriend and the short sundress she was wearing. "You should be a cheerleader," he said.

"What? You're crazy. With these things?" She pointed to her ample breasts. "I'd kill myself."

Despite his mood Tim allowed himself a quick chuckle at Janey's comment. Then returned to the glum conversation. "Did you know that they thought I killed her?"

They both nodded.

"Well, I didn't. At least I don't think I did. I would never knowingly do anything like that."

Without hesitation they both said, "We believe you."

"Thanks. I appreciate that," Tim said with sincerity in his voice.

"Maybe her ex-boyfriend did it," Stanley said.

Tim looked at Janey then at Stanley. "Stanley, I need to talk to you about something. Something important that I really need to get off my chest. But don't know if Janey should hear it."

Janey feigned being offended and put her hands on her hips. "Oh…Is it about girls?" she said sarcastically, but quickly changed her demeanor when a sudden thought struck her. "Wait a minute," she said in a quiet voice, almost a whisper. "You didn't get some girl knocked up, did you?"

"Look! Don't start spreading that kind of crap around. I'm in enough trouble as it is." Tim snapped.

"Sorry," Janey said.

Stanley put his arm around Janey and pulled her close. "I trust her. She won't blab about whatever it is. You can tell me. Go ahead."

"I don't know," Tim said. "Let me ask you something first. Over here." Tim took several steps away from Janey and stuck his hands in his pockets. Stanley released Janey, shrugged, gave her a puzzled look, and walked over to Tim. Before he could say anything, Tim said in a low conspiratorial voice, *"Does she know about the 'you know what'?"*

Stanley knew instantly what his friend meant. He hadn't shared with her anything about the book and the events that occurred because of it. He kept that dark secret to himself. Telling her anything about it might ruin everything they had going. He justified it by telling himself she didn't need to know.

When Stanley didn't say anything right away Tim knew the answer. "That's what I figured," Tim said. "What I have to tell you involves *that*. Do you want her dragged into this?"

"No. I don't," Stanley replied.

"Drag me into what?" Janey said startling both boys.

Janey Del Grasso tended to be impetuous and hated to be left out of things especially if she thought they were juicy rumors or in Tim's case something mysterious.

"Janey ? Come on love…this is private guys' stuff." Stanley said trying to make it sound like it wouldn't be something that would interest her. But Tim decided to move things along. *No Time to waste.*

Tim looked into her big puppy dog eyes, folded his arms across his chest and asked, " Do you believe in ghosts, Janey?"

Janey laughed. "Of course not."

"How about witches or demons?"

The mirth on her face slipped away with that question. "I've read a lot about witches, so I sorta believe they're real. I'm not sure about demons. What's this all about anyway?"

Stanley realized where Tim was going with this and joined the questioning. "Janey? How do you feel about things like the Loch Ness Monster or Big Foot or things like elves, fairies, and leprechauns? You think they're real?"

Janey squinted her eyes and looked at them. "Are you two goofing on me?

"Answer the question, Janey," Tim said in a serious tone.

She looked down at her sandaled feet and slowly swayed her hips. "I kinda believe they could exist. Nobody's proven otherwise. Now, why the weird questions?"

Tim and Stanley looked at each other, still not certain about telling her.

Stanley broke the awkward silence. " We just wanted to make sure you didn't think we were completely nuts if we told you what we've experienced. And I want to be absolutely sure you don't tell me to get lost after you hear what we have to say."

Janey stopped her wiggling. "Now, you're scaring me. What are you two involved in? Does this have anything to do with what happened Friday night?"

"It might," Tim replied.

Stanley took Janey's hands in his and looked her straight in the eyes. "Before I say another word you have to promise me that things won't change between us."

"Is it that bad?"

"It could be," Tim said.

" I can't promise if I don't know what it is. Stanley, you said you trusted me. So? Trust me. And…you know I love you."

Stanley still felt apprehensive. He looked at Tim for his reaction and when he saw him nod the 'go ahead' he said, "Well, maybe you just won't believe it, and everything will be okay. I have no problem with that. Okay, have a seat." He pointed to the steps.

When Janey was comfortable, he started, " Last year me and Tim…"

Just then the streetlights came on and they all instinctively looked up.

Before Stanley could continue, a voice came from behind them. Janey's mother. *"Streetlights! Janey."*

"Dammit," Janey muttered as she stood up. "I'm almost sixteen and I still have to be in the house when the streetlights come on."

"We'll continue this another time," Stanley said a bit relieved.

Janey kissed him on the cheek. "Call me!" she said and scampered up the steps into the house.

As Tim and Stanley walked back along the dimly lit sidewalk to Cabel Street, Tim said, "I've got a bad feeling about telling Janey."

Stanley lit a cigarette. He seemed to have an endless supply now that he had a job. Tim wondered if someone at the store where Stanley worked—someone eighteen or older— bought them for him.

"Me too," Stanley said as he slipped his lighter back into his pocket. "If she ever learned that I *made out* with that she devil, she'd kill me."

"I'm more worried about putting her in danger. We both know what that thing is capable of."

"You're right. And…I remember thinking when those kids from school got murdered last year that she had done it. I would never be able to live with myself if anything like that happened to Janey."

"Right. Don't forget what she did to you. I think she has some way of controlling us."

Tim recounted his flash backs as well as what he called 'black outs'. "I was told that I hit a policeman with a broom handle last year and knocked him out. I don't remember any of it. But I do remember the weird feeling that came over me the night she entered my room. A feeling that the real me was unconscious somewhere, while another me was doing bad things.

"I never told you this, but after I supposedly hit the policeman, I woke up sitting in the mud, drenched by pouring rain with a dog next to me at a place I've never been in my life. To this day I don't know how I got there. The only thing that makes sense is she somehow put me there."

"So? Do you think she's back?" Stanley asked.

"I *do!* And here's why. I had a similar feeling Friday night."

Stanley tossed the cigarette into the street as they came around the corner onto Cabel Street. "I hate to say it, but I agree with you. Something happened last week, right after you told us that your band was playing at the dance. I caught a whiff of something bad...a familiar bad. I brushed it off as possibly the smell from someone's garbage drifting in the breeze but when I heard a sound like an angry cat hissing, I knew."

"So? What do we do? Now that you have the book back...Can we use it?"

"Possibly. I'm not sure how but get this. Jonathan says he knows someone who might be able to help us."

"Jonathan? Your little brother Jonathan? How?"

They stopped in front of Stanley's house.

"Tell you later," Stanley said and nodded his head toward Tim's house.

There was a silhouette of someone standing behind the screened front storm door. By its size and shape it could be only one person. Tim's father.

"Shit," Tim muttered.

***

Dusk found Malhela, contemplating the fading away of this realm. Somehow it never happened. *What mortals madness was that?*

She now felt emboldened by her success two nights ago, prowling the skies over nearby neighborhoods confidently searching for an opportunity.

Her craving for the sweet taste of birthgiver's flesh and the feeling of strength that poured through her body afterward had grown. It made her feel invincible. She was addicted.

The capture of the birthgiver in her own dwelling on that night was so effortless that Malhela decided to try it again. But how would she do it? Flying from house to house peering in windows seemed absurd, but perhaps if she tuned her keen senses to the sounds and scents of birthgivers in specific dwellings another successful hunt would be accomplished. However, it turned out that process would not be necessary. Fate had delivered her prey.

As the night crept in and the streetlights popped on at various parts of the neighborhood a lone birthgiver casually walked her small dog, enjoying the warm summer evening.

Cindi Boyce, seventeen, hummed along with the Dixie Cups as they sang *Chapel of Love* on her Motorola transistor radio. A thin white wire ran from the radio to the tiny earphone stuck in her ear. She held the device in her right hand while holding the leash for her miniature poodle, Fluffy, in the other.

She had spent the day with friends at Jones Beach and felt pleasantly tired from a day of fun in the sun. She planned to turn in early after taking care of Fluffy.

Cindi had a pretty face, though unfairly marred by acne. Her knockout figure, thirty-six, twenty-four, thirty-five however, compensated for her troubled complexion.

Her sun-streaked blond hair was pulled back in a ponytail tonight and she wore white short-shorts, a revealing flowered tube top and white sandals.

Malhela liked what she saw and flew quietly above her, waiting to see which dwelling the birthgiver would enter. *This is almost too easy.*

When she saw the birthgiver stroll around to the back of a brick faced dwelling Malhela darted to the peak of the roof—fully camouflaged— and stared down. As she folded her wings and leaned forward for a better view of her prey the little white dog went berserk; barking, snarling, baring its teeth, and jumping up as if it was trying to reach her. *The damn thing knows I'm here. This hunt just got a little more difficult.*

Cindi yelled at her dog. "Fluffy! Stop! What's got into you? There's nothing up there."

The dog became more frenzied; barking, yelping, running in circles, tangling itself in the leash and jumping up and down. It was so agitated that it snapped at Cindi when she went to pick her up.

She gently slapped Fluffy's snout. "There'll be no more of that young lady. Bad dog." Cindi carried her shaking pet into the house.

Malhela waited, listening for movement within the dwelling that would tell her where to find the birthgiver. She could hear the dog whining somewhere deep in the house. *I may have to dispose of that annoying thing.*

She scuttled across the rooftop when she heard a window being opened just below her at the side of the dwelling. Quietly she fluttered to the window and peered inside. To her annoyance she couldn't see the birthgiver. This window, though similar in design to the others she had encountered had an opaque type of fabric covering it on the inside. Malhela knew the birthgiver was in the room by her scent. Light from within cast the birthgiver's silhouette on the fabric as she moved about. Her movements were slow and deliberate, which added to Malhela's aggravation. *I can take her now with force or wait till she sleeps.*

She decided to wait so she could make the kill and dine in peace as she had before.

In the meantime, she would take care of the whimpering dog. Its scent told her it was located in some type of cavern beneath the dwelling.

An hour had passed when Malhela returned from silencing Fluffy forever—she had found a small window built into the foundation of the dwelling that allowed access to the cavern where the dog had been placed— and hovered in front of the birthgiver's window. The light was out, and the fabric had been partially raised. Her night vision scanned the interior for the birthgiver and found her sound asleep on a bed crowded with pillows. The bedroom door was closed.

Malhela used her magic to lift the fabric to its highest point, silently slit open the screening, bent it wide as she had learned to do and gingerly stepped inside.

She floated to the foot of the bed and stopped, breathed deeply the birthgiver's fragrance and sighed savoring the moment. But in that instance, her own pungent fragrance gave her away. The birthgiver's eye's blinked open, her nose twitched at the invading odor. She sat up in bed and coughed. "What is that *smell?*" She started to get up but stopped when she thought she saw something move at the foot of her bed. There was nothing there, so she scanned the room and noticed the window. The screen was twisted open, and the shade was fully raised. She reached over and switched on her nightstand lamp. Nothing. The room was empty. Then she heard a sound like someone folding a road map and turned toward it. Fear took over when she saw a shimmering ghost-like shape near her bed. She screamed, "*Dad!*"

Malhela pounced and silenced Cindi Boyce with a quick twist of her head. She had to move fast. There would be no relaxed dining this evening. She stripped the birthgiver from the waist down and sunk her teeth into the tender meat of the inner thigh. She ate quickly like a hungry savage, but alert to the sounds and scents of a mortal approaching. The flesh of this birthgiver was deliciously sweet and Malhela could feel the female's essence flowing through her. She needed more regardless of being discovered and tore into the other thigh like a ravenous animal.

She was licking blood from her lips when she heard footsteps on the stairs outside the room. Then a soft knock on the door and a male voice said, "Cindi? Did you call me?" The door opened slightly, and a man's head appeared. "Cindi?"

Malhela's head was spinning with euphoria from ingesting this particular birthgiver's substance and she acted without thinking. She slit the man's throat and grinned as she watched him slump to the floor. *Never interrupt me when I'm eating.*

She went back to her entrée, rolled the body over on its stomach and ran a hand over the firm rump. *One more bite before I go.*

CHAPTER 48

July 6th—Dawn

"In all my years on the police force I've never seen anything like this," Trabinski said as he left the crime scene at the Boyce residence, detective Pete Taylor at his side. "Now…young women aren't even safe in their own homes."

"Looks that way," Taylor said. "And those guys up in Boston think they have problems with that *Silk Stocking* strangler. We've got a real shit storm on our hands here and though we have a pretty good idea who the killer is, we're still in a quandary about stopping it."

Trabinski came up to his car, parked at the curb in front of the Boyce house, stopped and patted his pockets for a pack of cigarettes. A creature of habit. "Dammit!"

"Lose your pack of gum Jim?"

"No…No I *didn't*. It's right here," Trabinski said sarcastically as he pulled a sleeve of Beeman's from his inside jacket pocket and waved it at Taylor. "I picked a bad time to quit smoking."

Trabinski popped a piece into his mouth as he watched Taylor scanning the area around them. Sometimes staring off into the distance.

He was about to question him, but Taylor beat him to the punch with a question of his own.

"Have you given any thought to the location of this crime?"

"Not really, why?"

Taylor leaned on the car. "I may be all wet but think about this. We're on Meadow Lane right now. Before it was demolished, that junkyard where we had our little rumble with the creature, was about two miles from here."

Trabinski folded his arms. "Go on."

Taylor stepped away from the car and started pacing the sidewalk.

"Well, I was thinking. What if this thing did survive? She would probably come back looking for her old nest. Right? Can't find it so, she builds another one…maybe near the same spot."

Trabinski nodded.

"We already know that she likes her nests secluded and above ground. First nest was the Ryan's garage attic and the second high up on that mountain of junk."

"Hold up," Trabinski said raising his hand as if stopping traffic. "So, you're thinking these killings are in the radius of her new nest."

Taylor stopped pacing. "Precisely."

"Okay and how does that help us?"

"Find the nest. Stop her, stop the atrocities."

"Easier said than done. We don't have the time for an extensive search."

Taylor grinned. "I was thinking about that too. We get Traffic Control to lend us a whirlybird and we find the damn nest from the air. I bet it wouldn't take long."

Now it was Trabinski's turn to pace. "Okay. Let's say we find the nest... Then what?"

"I've been thinking about that too..."

"You've been doing a lot of thinking, *lately*," Trabinski interrupted.

"That's what I do when I can't sleep. So, the other night an idea struck me while I was watching a movie on the Late Late Show. It was that old Howard Hawks film, The Thing From Another World. Ever see it?"

"That the one takes place at the North Pole?"

"That's the one. So, when it came to the scene where they douse the creature with gasoline and set it on fire I thought, that's it. We'll fry the bitch."

"If I remember correctly that didn't work out too well," Trabinski commented dryly.

It turns out that Taylor wasn't too far off with his idea. A harpy, according to lore, could be destroyed by fire but there was a catch. The ashes had to be separated and dispersed in four directions; north, south, east, and west to prevent them from being magically reassembled.

"We've got to try *something*. *Do* something before it kills again." Taylor said as he opened the car's passenger door.

"I agree. Let's go get us a helicopter."

***

Eighth Precinct—9 o'clock am

"I'm telling you Ted, that's all I can give you," said Captain Walter Philbrick as he folded his arms and leaned back in his high back leather desk chair. He was addressing Ted Newman, the top reporter for the *Long Island Daily Press,* who was seated across the desk from him in a comfortable leather guest chair.

Newman was a forty-five-year-old veteran of the newspaper industry. He was five foot seven with a slender build. He had red hair on both sides of his head, nothing on top. His face harbored a pink bulbous nose which separated two alert blue eyes. The lines on his forehead always made him seem to be frowning.

Today he was wearing a tan, light weight suit, a bit wrinkled, a white shirt, open at the neck, a loosened dark brown tie and a white straw fedora.

"Come on Walter. You gave me nothing. Big deal. You gave me the girl's name who was murdered at the dance. I already knew that. You said you have a suspect. Give me a name. Details."

Philbrick closed his eyes for a moment then opened them and said, "Can't do that either. Just be happy that I told you about the suspect."

Newman leaned forward, notepad and pencil in hand. "Okay. Then give me a break on the Valenti case. You've been stonewalling me for a year about that poor kid's murder. She was one of my best cub reporters. She could have been a star one day. Her family deserves closure and so do I."

Philbrick shook his head. "It's a complicated case and still under investigation. I promise, you'll be the first to know if something can be released."

"Still stonewalling Philbrick. I'm going to write a real nice article about how cooperative you are," Newman said sarcastically.

At that moment Trabinski and Taylor appeared at the captain's office door. Seeing that the captain had company Trabinski said, "We'll come back."

Philbrick stood up. "He was just leaving."

Newman slowly got up from the chair and wagged a finger at Philbrick. "You asked for it."

As he exited the office, Trabinski, overhearing some of the conversation, grabbed Newman's arm and stopped him. In a tone of voice that equaled Newman's sarcasm he said, "Just remember, freedom of speech or not, it's a felony if you interfere with an ongoing police investigation."

Newman pulled his arm away from Trabinski. "Well, maybe it should be a felony for cops to be goofing off. You flatfoots never solved the disappearance of that little boy from the playground a year ago. Did you? Oh, I know, I know it's still under investigation. Just a bullshit excuse, if you ask me, for incompetence. Have a nice day, gentlemen," Newman said as he strutted down the hall towards the precinct exit.

Taylor watched him leave. "What an asshole."

Trabinski and Taylor gave the captain a full report on the latest killing. They reluctantly told him the MO of the last four events—which included the two being investigated by Lieutenant Talbot's team—matched that of the mysterious creature they thought they had killed

a year ago. They concluded with certainty that the creature had somehow returned and was more dangerous than before.

Philbrick had listened silently during their report, sitting at his
desk with his fingers steepled in front of his face. Now he stood and
walked towards the window at the back of his office. He stared out the
window with his hands behind his back at the shrubs that stylishly
edged the parking lot.

"Ideas?" He asked.

Trabinski mentioned Taylor's plan to locate the nest and hopefully
destroy the beast with fire.

Philbrick returned to his desk but remained standing. He ran a
hand through his close-cropped hair. "I'm going to initiate a level four
to establish a task force, then advise the chief and the mayor to autho-
rize a curfew for the towns affected by these killings. They'll of course
want to know why so I'll have to go with the serial killer scenario. With
the news about what's going on in Boston, I'm sure they'll take action
immediately. In the meantime, I'll secure you a chopper."

"Captain? This thing is breaking into homes and killing young
women while they sleep. A curfew is a start, but I'm not sure it will do
any good.

"One of the cases Lieutenant Talbot is working on involves a
child being abducted from its backyard in broad daylight in front
of witnesses. They claim to have seen what they called a 'shimmer'.
Nothing else. The boy just disappeared. Exactly like the kid at the playground last year. This damn thing has the ability to be almost invisible.
How do we protect the community from that?"

Philbrick finally sat down.

"Somehow we have to make the public aware of what's going on," Taylor said. "Keep them on their toes so to speak. Watch the skies, that type of thing. Without causing a panic of course."

The expression that appeared on Philbrick's face was that of a person about to make a distasteful decision.

"Get Newman back in here."

***

Stanley Bolton had the day off and immediately called his girlfriend after he finished breakfast to see if she had plans for the day. After a cheery hello, Janey said, "You didn't call me last night. I waited and waited."

"Sorry love. By the time my mother got off the phone I figured it was too late." Stanley had picked up on the way the guys in these new British bands, especially the Beatles, talked to girls. They seemed to always use the word "love" when they spoke to an attractive young lady. Stanley liked the way that sounded, and it became his term of endearment for Janey.

"It's alright, "Janey said sweetly. "My mother wouldn't have let me talk long anyway last night.

"So, are you going to give me the scoop on this mystery you and Tim are involved in?"

"Yes, but I want Tim with us when I do. I was thinking about meeting him on his paper route. That way there'll be no unwanted ears around. You know what I mean?"

"Sure," Janey replied.

"So, can you go with me?"

"Hold on…" Stanley heard the phone being put down.

Janey came back after a couple of minutes. "Yep, I can go. I'll get my bike out and meet you in front of my house. What time?"

"Great. I'll call Tim to find out and let you know. Sit tight. Bye."

Stanley made the call to his friend and finally got him on the phone after debating with Tim's sister Emily, who acted like she had appointed herself to screen all calls involving her brother. When Tim answered he sounded out of it and a bit sad.

"Did you just wake up?" Stanley asked.

Tim mumbled, "No…What's going on?"

"What time are you delivering your papers today?"

"I'll probably pick them up at the Newsday office at twelve thirty. That way I can finish up early and get home. Why?"

Stanley lowered his voice. "You and I need to talk about Jonathan's new friend and Janey still wants to know about our mystery, so I thought we could kill two birds with one stone while delivering your papers. There'll be no one around to eaves drop. Okay with you?"

"Well, I'm not so sure about the eaves dropping part," Tim said, still sounding like he had no strength to move his lips.

"What do you mean?"

There were a few minutes of silence and Stanley thought they had been disconnected but Tim came back on. "When we got home from the police station yesterday detective Taylor called to advise my parents that I would be under observation by the police department since I'm still considered a person of interest. I guess they're afraid I'll run away or something. He said they have to do this since I'm a minor.

"This morning I noticed a black car parked two doors down from us. Looks like the observing has begun."

"Who cares?" This sounded like the old Stanley. "Let them watch. You're not doing anything wrong. I doubt they'll be interested in us talking while you deliver papers anyway. Me and Janey will meet you on your route between twelve thirty and one o'clock. See you there."

Stanley hung up and went to find Jonathan. He wanted to know more about this Phaedra person.

Kraemer Street—12:45 pm

Stanley, Janey, and Tim joined up on the corner of East Marie Street and Kraemer and began walking their bikes to Tim's first customer. Keeping his head down as he walked Tim said, "Don't look, but we're ...*I'm* being followed. I guess it's part of being observed."

A black, no frills 1961 Mercury Meteor cruised slowly by and parked up the street at the corner of Kraemer and Clinton.

"A little creepy if you ask me," Janey said.

Stanley turned his head and gave her a questioning, concerned look. "Speaking of creepy. Are you sure you want to hear about our dilemma?"

Janey nodded. "That's why I'm here. Just waiting on you to start."

Stanley gave Janey a full account of the conjuring events that took place last year— He had strategically left out certain details that he felt she didn't need to know—and waited for her reaction.

A doubtful look crossed her face. "Wow! That's some story. Sounds like one of those bad horror movies."

451

"It's all true," Tim added. "And I haven't even told you about what happened to me."

Janey looked at Stanley then back at Tim. "Well, I don't know what to think about you two blockheads. Not very smart to be fooling around with stuff you know nothing about. It almost got *you* killed Stanley. I'm surprised at you Tim. Don't they teach you about staying away from that kind of thing in your Catholic high school?"

Tim said nothing and delivered another paper.

"You really think this harpy thing killed those two kids from our school last year?" Janey said to Stanley.

"I do."

"And I'm pretty certain it killed that kid Danny too," Tim said returning to his bike for another paper.

"You mean Danny Sanfield? The punk that Paulette went out with? I wondered what happened to him. I heard the police were looking for him."

"That's him."

"So, you think this creature has returned and may have murdered Marcy Dubrowski?"

"I feel her presence," Tim said. "And I think she's targeting teen-age girls."

Janey stopped walking her bike. "Oh!"

As they continued on, Stanley told them what he had learned from Jonathan. Apparently, a young woman named Phaedra had helped him use the book to make the potion that healed Stanley and his mother. According to Jonathan she knows what the book can do and may be able to come up with a way to end this nightmare. She is either the owner or manager of the Apothecary store located on Broadway. Jonathan said she was nice. When he was finished, he said to Tim, "What do you think? Shall we pay her a visit?"

***

Casey Talbot's apartment—6:00 pm

Casey dug into her shrimp lo mein with a fork after several failed attempts to use the chop sticks that came with the takeout. She was ambidextrous and used her left hand to eat but the cast on her wrist made the chop sticks unwieldly.

She sat across from Trabinski at her dining room table watching him cut his General Tsao chicken into bite sized pieces on the plate she had provided for him. Though being together like this felt good, the mood was somber.

"The eye looks better," He said.

"It's getting there. I'll have to use a lot of makeup when I go in tomorrow."

Trabinski took a sip of coffee. "I thought the doctor told you to take a couple of days off."

Casey twirled some noodles on her fork. "You know I can't do that. I already feel like a slacker. There's too much going on. I'll be fine.

"Taylor told me about the Meadow Lane killings. He said he thought I should know since we're all involved with this harpy fiasco and that you had a plan. Don't be angry with him for calling me. He's just concerned about our safety."

"I'm glad he did. Forcing your car off the road tells me the bitch is targeting you. I don't like you recuperating here by yourself. As you said, it's becoming more daring. The damn thing may be watching us right now. I want you to stay at my place."

Casey's gray eyes sparkled for a moment and with a winsome smile she said, "Soon, but not yet." She quickly changed the subject. "What's this plan Taylor spoke about?"

Trabinski paused a moment to reflect on Casey's comment then proceeded with the information. He gave Taylor credit for the plan and told Casey about the aerial search for the nest and the idea of burning the harpy when they found it.

Casey took a taste of her Chinese green tea and gingerly placed the cup back on the table. "Not a bad idea. Let's hope it doesn't take too long to find the nest."

"I agree," Trabinski continued. "In the meantime, the captain is getting authorization for a curfew from the chief and the mayor."

Casey frowned. "What good will that do? We know this monster has no time schedule. And…it's breaking into homes now."

Trabinski absent mindedly reached for a cigarette and rolled his eyes when he found the pack of gum instead.

"I know. The captain is going to enlist the press to diplomatically alert the public about the situation."

"He's not afraid it will cause a panic?" Casey said.

Trabinski finished off his coffee.

"It's a fifty-fifty chance. I think he's hoping to make people more alert to what's going on around them. Maybe prevent further attacks. We'll have to wait and see how the press handles it."

Casey slid the flat end of an unused chopstick under the cast and started scratching with it. "Starting to itch already. This is going to drive me crazy.

"I'm curious about this aerial search. Will a fixed wing aircraft be used or helicopter?"

"Helicopter. The captain's tapping Traffic Control for it. They said it will be available tomorrow."

Casey stopped scratching and slid her chair back from the table.

"Good," she said. "What time do we take off?"

CHAPTER 49

July 7th—Mid – morning

It was a perfect day for flying as well as nest hunting. Visibility was unlimited.

The Bell 47J Ranger Traffic Control helicopter moved through the clear blue-white sky at a casual sixty miles per hour at an altitude of eight hundred feet. Casey and Detective Pete Taylor sat in the rear of the four-passenger aircraft—Trabinski assigned by Captain Philbrick to assist with organizing the task force had to unhappily resign from this search party. The pilot, Sergeant Lou Tucker sat front and center with the best view out of the one hundred eighty-degree Lexan "bubble" windscreen.

"Where we headed Lieutenant?" Tucker asked through the mic attached to his headset.

Casey adjusted her headset to a more comfortable position over her ears. "Do you know where Rocco's Junk Emporium was located… off New South Road?"

"I do. I used to buy parts from him for my pickup truck."

The steady *wup wup* of the overhead blades made communication, even through headphones, tedious.

"Sorry? Say again. You *do* or you *don't* know the location?" Casey asked.

"I know where it is," Tucker replied then gave her a thumbs up over his shoulder.

"Okay, take us there. We'll use that location as the axis for a ten-to-fifteen-mile radius sweep of the surrounding areas. Copy?"

"Roger that. Rocco's junkyard. ETA ten minutes."

As the helicopter cast a bug-like shadow on the dirt packed grounds of the junkyard it slowed to a hover. "Anything in particular you're looking for lieutenant?" Tucker asked.

Detective Taylor answered. "We're after a killer who likes to hide out in high places. Seems to return to that lair after each killing. We chose this location because the killer's last hide out was here. We think there may be a pattern since the recent murders were in this area."

"So? What are you thinking? Water towers? Silos? That kind of thing?"

"Perhaps," Casey replied. "Whatever the structure there will be something unusual about it. It may look like the digs of a homeless person or something like a nest."

Casey held her hand over the mic and turned to Taylor and gestured for him to do the same. She pointed to Tucker. "It doesn't seem like he knows the details of this search. We better keep our conversations vague. It probably wouldn't happen, but I can't risk him going all flakey if he hears we're searching for a monster. Especially while he's flying. Agreed?"

"Agreed," said Taylor.

"Sergeant? Please proceed north along New South Road. Previous rate of speed will suffice. I think this altitude will work for a while. At the ten-mile indicator begin your radius sweep eastward another ten miles. Copy?"

"Copy that…"

The Ranger's nose tilted down as Tucker took it out of hover and accelerated northward.

Miniature houses lined up in neat rows, along meandering streets, passed beneath the helicopter. From this altitude they all looked the same. Sergeant Lou Tucker concentrated his flight path away from these neighborhoods since they were all low-lying areas. He flew the Ranger to specific areas where he knew high structures existed, but after an hour of this exercise nothing had been found that caught his passengers' attention.

"Lieutenant? We've got enough fuel in the tanks for one more sweep. Then we'll have to call it a day. Do you want to go around again?" Tucker asked. His voice sounded tinny through the headset.

Casey gave a quick glance at detective Taylor who was rubbing the back of his neck but still scanning the area below with his binoculars. Her neck was also feeling a bit stiff from craning for a better view. She felt disappointed that the search was looking more and more like a waste of time.

"What's our present location, sergeant?"

There was a momentary pause as Tucker checked his bearings. "Coming up on Massapequa with our westerly flight path adjustment just ahead. Shall I proceed?"

Probably should wrap this up, Casey thought, but something in the back of her mind was scratching at her memory door to be let out. She closed her eyes and leaned her head against the seat back and absent mindedly rubbed the side of her nose with her good hand. Thinking.

"Lieutenant? What's the plan? You copy?"

Pete Taylor looked over his shoulder at Casey and was surprised to see her sitting with her eyes closed. The movement of her right hand slowly rubbing her nose told him she wasn't sleeping.

Casey, with her eyes still closed said, "Sergeant? Please return to our axis point at the junkyard. Slow approach if you will. Thanks."

"Roger. Returning to axis point. Slow approach."

Taylor continued to look at Casey. "What's on your mind?" he said.

Casey leaned forward, looking passed Tucker's right shoulder out the from windscreen at the panoramic view in front of her.

"I'm not sure, but I've got this feeling that we overlooked something. Something right under our noses."

In less than fifteen minutes Tucker announced they were over the junkyard. Casey asked him to hover in place.

Casey and Taylor, binoculars in hand, searched the area below; both tilting their heads this way and that for better views out the square windows. Then she saw it.

She gently banged Taylor's arm with her cast then pointed with her right hand. "There!"

Taylor undid his seat belt and slid across the bench seat next to her.

"You may be right," he muttered.

"Sergeant? See that abandoned warehouse building off to the right. Can you position us just above it?"

"Sure can," Tucker replied.

Taylor slid back to his original position and fastened his seat belt just as the helicopter banked towards the building.

The abandoned warehouse, once thought to be the ideal stake-out location by police a year ago, stood unkept across the street from where Rocco's Auto Wreckers and Junk Emporium once did business. Vegetation had seized control of the property and even climbed the walls of the structure, some protruding through the broken lower-level windows.

All manner of foliage crowded the building, preventing access through the ground level doors. The walls, once gray, had now taken on the hues of the encroaching flora. The pungent, earthy odor of mold drifted everywhere.

As they came over the building and Tucker put the Ranger in hover mode Casey caught sight of a shed-like structure on the flat roof of the building. "What do you think that is?" she asked Taylor, who had once again slid next to her.

Taylor raised his binoculars. "Could be a maintenance hut. Probably housed water and steam valves, things like that, for the warehouse.

"Take a look at the door," he said pointing.

Casey adjusted her field glasses and focused on the shed. "Looks like it was pried open."

"A good place for someone to hide out," Taylor said for Tucker's benefit.

Or something, Casey thought.

Then she heard Taylor say something incredibly crazy.

"Sergeant? Can you put this whirlybird down on that flat roof? I want to take a look inside that shed."

Tucker looked out the front windscreen scrutinizing the roof for a few moments. "Looks like it will hold us, but I suggest doing a hit and run just to be safe."

"Hit and run?" Taylor asked.

"I'll maneuver in low and hover, allowing you to jump out. Then I'll lift off until you're ready to come back."

"Fine," Taylor said.

"*Wait a minute!*" Casey shouted. "You'll do no such thing detective. This is a search and discovery mission only."

Taylor didn't want to get on her bad side especially since her relationship with his boss had apparently become serious, but this had to be done. Someone needed to make certain, one way or the other, this was the nest or not. In a calm voice he said, "We have to make sure before we call in the cavalry. What if it turns out to be nothing? We'll look like a couple of rookies."

"And…What if it turns out to be… *something*?" Casey inquired.

Taylor shrugged. "This was my idea remember. I'll take my chances."

"I don't like it," Casey said.

"Me neither. Take us in, sergeant."

"Roger that…"

Casey rested her cast on the pilot's shoulder. "Before you do that, sergeant, radio in that a possible site of interest has been located and a member of the search party is going in to investigate. Details to follow. Thanks."

"No problem lieutenant."

Taylor jumped from the Ranger and hurried away from the wash of the rotors. As he approached the shed, he pulled his Colt .38 Special snub-nose revolver from his shoulder holster, and with a slight crouch walked cautiously toward the door.

He paused when he thought he heard a hissing sound. *Man...I hope it's not full of snakes. I hate those suckers.* He readied his revolver and was about to take a step forward when the smell hit him. With his left hand he pulled a handkerchief from his jacket pocket and held it over his nose. *Whew. Something definitely rotting in there.* He suddenly took a shooter's stance, dropping the handkerchief and gripping his pistol with both hands as a figure slinked through the space in the open door.

Though Taylor knew the possibility of finding the harpy at this location was a fifty-fifty proposition he was still stunned when she actually appeared. He couldn't take his eyes of this beautiful yet bizarre woman standing naked in front of him. She had the body of a well-trained athlete with the face of a gorgeous movie star. Her bat-like wings were folded back, and she stood with her feet— from which dangerous looking talons protruded—spread apart. Her hands were on her hips.

Taylor almost dropped his pistol when she said in a seductive voice, "May I help you?"

From above, Casey could see the whole scene unfold. "*Shit!*" she said.

Tucker, surprised to hear a word like that come from such an attractive woman almost choked on his own words. "What in God's name is that? Is that a woman?

"Get him out of there sergeant…now!" Then as the aircraft made a turn to descend Casey saw Taylor tumbling from the roof top. "No!" she screamed.

"Get down there…get down there!" Casey ordered.

Tucker was already on the radio. "This is Traffic helo, bravo 124. We have a 10-13. Officer down. Repeat code 10-13, officer down." He gave the location then proceeded to put the Ranger down in the dirt lot of the extinct junkyard.

***

Malhela had been lounging in the afterglow of the previous evening's successful hunt when her keen ears picked up a rapid thumping sound high above her. Though she was in the middle of concocting a new hunt—She didn't want the wonderful feeling she obtained from the essence of the birthgiver to end or even diminish a little—her curiosity got the better of her. She peered from the shadows of her nest as the sound grew louder and closer. When she looked up, she was astounded to see what appeared to be a giant insect. *A libelo here?* Malhela crouched behind the door and watched as the giant dragonfly approached. The realm had insects like this but not as big. She realized as she studied the bulbous head of the creature there were mortals seated inside. *This is no insect! More trickery from these wretched mortals.* She was about to reach out with her newly enhanced magic and destroy the mechanical bug when a mortal jumped out from its side. Malhela silently watched the male mortal approach but instinctively looked up as the flying machine began to rise. She could see the two other mortals looking out through the clear bubble that she had thought was the insect's head. She hissed angrily when she recognized the female mortal. *That damn elf woman survived! Perhaps she has magic of her own.*

The male in front of her stopped and took a peculiar stance. Both his hands gripped an object she had seen before. She remembered it fired those magic painful projectiles.

Having confidence in her power she decided to be coy with this male. Maybe play with him a little. So, she shimmied seductively from behind her nest's door into the bright daylight and placed her hands on her hips. She tilted her head coquettishly and said sweetly, "May I help you?"

When she saw the male almost drop the weapon in his hand she wondered if she could seduce him into serving her. *It may be useful to have a slave who can use that device.* She smiled and gestured with a finger for him to come closer but quickly stopped when she heard a click from the weapon in the mortal's, now steady hand. Instantly remembering the pain caused by the magic projectiles she thrust out her arms, invoked her magic and tossed the mortal off the building.

Malhela went to camouflage and stood near the entrance to her nest watching the bug machine head away from her. She grinned. *Now, back to planning my next hunt.*

***

July 7th—Dusk

The old Whitticker place, located on the corner of Plainview Road and Cliff Drive, had been abandoned for many years after the disappearance of Charles Lovecraft Whitticker. It sat back seventy feet from the road. Ancient Elm trees and unruly Maples shrouded the 1933 structure. The bushes planted ages ago adjacent to the sides of the house were overgrown and unsightly. The lawn had evolved into a field of tall grass and weeds while moss conquered the pitched roof's scalloped shingles.

A buckled concrete walkway weaved its way from the Plainview Road sidewalk to the weathered, rickety front porch. Numerous faded and decaying newspapers had accumulated on the steps. There was no mailbox.

Strange as it may seem, there was only one broken window on the ground floor which someone—maybe the police— had boarded up.

Behind the three story pseudo-Victorian house, a large, dilapidated barn-like structure languished through the years. A rutted dirt path served as a driveway onto Cliff Drive.

Overall, the property maintained a gloomy, haunted atmosphere.

No one ever knew what happened to Whitticker. There were rumors aplenty and the police grew tired of checking out the place for squatters and ghosts. Keep Out signs had been posted. It had become a favorite place for Halloween trick or treaters daring each other to go there for candy. Few ever took that dare.

Neighbors wondered why the house or at least the land had not been put up for sale. Here too, rumors flew. One such claimed the property was a protected historical site governed by the Masons or some obscure religious group. Nothing was ever proven.

Now, after all these years something was going on there. Little by little, changes were occurring. The barn-like structure at the rear of the property seemed to be the main focus. The sounds of hammering and sawing could be heard coming from there, mostly at night. There were reports of two dark figures moving about the building. Coming and going at all hours.

Lights were now on inside the main house and silhouettes could be seen moving about behind pulled shades.

Who was the new owner? This was the primary gossip inquiry up and down the street. The answer surprised some and made others suspicious.

The Old Whitticker place now belonged to a beautiful young woman named Phaedra Colefax.

CHAPTER 50

July 8th—Central General Hospital—Morning

The scene in the recovery room had a déjà vu feel about it, only this time it was Detective Pete Taylor in the hospital bed.

Lieutenant James Trabinski stood at the foot of the bed taking in his partner's appearance. "You are one lucky son of a gun my friend," he said.

Taylor, finally coming around after surgery for a broken right collarbone said with a forced smile, "Don't I know it!"

"All that jungle around the warehouse cushioned your fall," Trabinski said.

"Yeah, after I bounced off the damn tree and busted this up," Taylor said tapping the sling holding his right arm in suspension.

Lieutenant Casey Talbot sat in a semi-comfortable visitor's chair at the left side of the bed; her left arm, sporting the cast rested in her lap. "With all the scratches and cuts on your face and the bruises on mine, people will think we were fighting *each* other," Casey commented.

Taylor gave a quick laugh.

The branches, shoots, and stems of the overgrown flora, punctured and sliced parts of his face as he landed headfirst into them. He was equally lucky that his eyes weren't injured at all.

With a grunt Taylor made himself more comfortable. Casey helped him adjust the pillows behind his back. "Did Casey tell you we found the nest?"

Trabinski nodded. "She did. Another stroke of luck if you ask me."

"Now the question is what to do about it," Casey said.

"Like I was telling Jim the other day…torch it."

Casey looked over at Trabinski, "Torch it? How? With what?"

"Flamethrowers," Taylor said. "That's how they did away with those giant ants in the movie, *Them*."

A smirk crossed Casey's face. "I think you may have hit your head a little harder than they thought. We're not dealing with ants of any size. We have a devious, cunning and dare I say intelligent predator on our hands."

"It's not a totally bad idea," Trabinski interjected. "If we put together a covert operation, we may be able to set the nest on fire trapping the bitch inside."

Casey blinked at Trabinski. "*Flamethrowers?*"

"Why not? I believe the National Guard still has some functioning units."

Casey started rubbing the side of her nose. "I may have contacts there. But how do we get them to sign on to *this*?"

Trabinski went to his jacket hanging on the back of the door and pulled a folded newspaper from it.

"Might not be that difficult," he said, opening to the front-page headlines of the day's Long Island Daily Press and holding the paper up for them to read.

POLICE ENFORCE CURFEW IN ATTEMPT TO END KILLING SPREE.

"The press is warning residents, especially young girls to obey the curfew and if possible, travel in groups during the day," Trabinski continued. "They are also telling people to close and lock their windows at night and to purchase fans if they don't have air conditioners mounted in them.

"The article goes on to advise people to contact the police or the newspaper immediately if they see anything strange, weird, or unusual regardless of the time of day.

"Hopefully, that will keep people on the alert day and night."

Casey asked to see the paper before Trabinski put it away. She scanned the article. "Well, it's poignant enough that the Guard may offer assistance. I'll reach out to the people I know and see what they say."

"Did *Newman* write that?" Taylor asked.

Trabinski nodded. "Yep."

Casey looked up. "Whose Newman? Should I know him?"

"Head reporter for the paper. Been on our backs for a year touting our incompetence in crime solving. The young female reporter who was murdered last year was his protégé," Trabinski said.

"Oh…," Casey said. "Now I understand the tone of the article." She handed the paper back to Trabinski and looked over at Taylor. "I have a question if you're up to answering it."

"Let's hear it," Taylor said.

Casey scratched her arm at the base of her wrist cast. "Why didn't you shoot the damn thing when you had the chance? From my view, it looked like you had your .38 pointed right at her head."

Taylor closed his eyes for a moment and sighed. "That's a good question. That was my intent. Shoot first, ask questions later. But, when she didn't attack I hesitated and that was a mistake. She just stood there with her hands on her hips staring at me. Her face was captivating and *her eyes*…like those of a big cat, a tiger or leopard, were hypnotic. Then she spoke to me in such a sweet seductive voice that right at that very moment I would have done anything for her."

Trabinski reached into his shirt pocket for a stick of gum. "Do you remember what she said?"

" 'May I help you?'" That was all she said. Don't ask me how or why but despite that desire I thought of Tim Ryan and prepared to fire. That's when I suddenly found myself airborne without the chopper.

"Jim? That she demon has the ability to put you in a trance. I am absolutely certain that's what happened to Tim Ryan. She controlled him."

"Still going to be hard to prove," Trabinski said, gently slapping the rolled-up newspaper into his left hand. "You know? Somebody better get a picture of this deadly beauty. I still haven't seen what she looks like."

Casey's eyes narrowed as she slowly glanced up at Trabinski. "You don't *need* to see what she looks like," she muttered.

***

Stanley and Jonathan Bolton stood holding their bikes waiting for Tim Ryan at the corner of Cabel Street and Plainview Road. They would rendezvous with Janey as soon as Tim arrived.

A friend of Stanley's at Penn Fruit had agreed to switch days with him. This way he could carry out the plan to visit Jonathan's friend, Phae.

The idea was to help Tim finish delivering his papers early then head into town to the Apothecary establishment. Jonathan carried the book—safely nestled in the old school bag he had used on his previous visit—in a rear side basket of his Huffy.

"I still have that cop following me," Tim said as he rolled his bike to a stop next to his partners in crime. "I don't think I'm going to be able to go into that store with you. I may have to wait outside."

We'll figure something out. You've got to be there. Let's get Janey," Stanley said.

On their way into town, after they finished delivering Tim's newspapers, Janey came up with a way to illude Tim's police shadow. Tim hoped it was something that would throw his observer off the trail. Especially with Janey standing out like a radiant flower between three weeds.

She wore a snow-white bib-overall shorts outfit over a lavender top, white anklet socks and tennis shoes. While the three of them wore drab clothes that wouldn't attract attention.

Janey had asked Jonathan the location of the Apothecary store then laid out her plan.

"It sounds like the Apothecary is two stores down from Hurley's. This is good. Behind Hurley's is an alleyway that runs along the rear of those buildings. Probably right to the back of where we want to go. We'll go into Hurley's like we're getting ice cream or something after a hard day of delivering papers and then slip out the back unnoticed by Tim's tail. Easy peasy...Right?"

Sounds good to me," Stanley said.

Tim looked doubtful. "I don't know..."

Jonathan grinned. "Let's get some ice cream," he said as he quickly pedaled down East Marie Street and turned left onto Broadway.

They secured their bikes in the rusted metal bike rack in front of Hurley's Ice Cream Parlor. Tim, keeping his head down, saw the black Mercury make a slow turn onto Broadway and park across the street from Hurley's. *This may work.* He thought. *As long as he doesn't decide to come in for something.* He turned and nonchalantly followed the others inside. Jonathan walked ahead of Stanley holding the precious schoolbag at his side.

The walls of the popular hangout were brightly painted in alternating white- and cream-colored panels. Dark red booths with white tables ran along the wall to the left of the entrance. A gleaming black counter with protruding fountain handles occupied a space to the right, in front of a wall of shelves filled with glistening glassware, dishes, and bowls. It was surrounded by chrome stools with dark red vinyl tops. There were a few customers: An elderly couple seated in a back booth, two teenage couples in the center booth and a couple of girls seated at the counter flirting with the young man working there.

Janey, in the lead, made her way over to the end of the counter. "Hi Tommy," she said offering up a cheery dimpled smile to the kid pulling on a fountain handle. "I didn't know you worked here."

"Started right after school let out," he said. "Good job for the summer. What can I get you?"

"Um? I just need a little favor," Janey replied.

"For you? Sure. What do you need?"

Tim looked sideways at Stanley and whispered, "Who's this guy? She seems pretty chummy with him."

Stanley shrugged. "I told you, she knows everybody." But the tone of their conversation was irking him. A little too friendly he thought as he stepped next to Janey and put his hand on her shoulder. He didn't say anything, just smiled at the soda jerk.

Janey made up a story about playing a trick on someone and they needed to sneak out the back door. She promised Tommy nothing would take place in the store.

Tommy adjusted the white paper hat that he wore. "Okay, but you have to buy something first."

They stepped out the rear door of Hurley's into the shaded alleyway. Janey spooned a bit of vanilla and strawberry ice cream from a small paper cup into her mouth, Stanley, and Tim slurped chocolate shakes through straws while Jonathan struggled to keep from dropping his Nutty Buddy ice cream cone on the ground. Stanley, seeing his brother's dilemma quickly took the schoolbag from his hand.

As they hurried along, the alleyway widened behind one of the stores.

"This is it," said Jonathan pointing to a sign that read Apothecary Deliveries. "Follow me," he said and proceeded up a narrow walkway between the buildings. They marched behind him, single file to the Broadway sidewalk but halted when Tim told them to hold up. He surreptitiously poked his head around the corner of the building to the right of the Apothecary, scanning for the Mercury. It was still parked across from the ice cream parlor.

"We're okay. Let's go," he said quietly.

Jonathan led his brother, Janey, and Tim into the store. The tiny brass bell over the door announced them. He was excited to see Phaedra again and couldn't help but smile when he noticed her at the counter.

She was wearing the same style dress she had worn when he saw her last, only this one was a dark indigo. Her paisley headband matched the color. She looked beautiful as usual.

An older, heavy-set man with a bright pink face stood at the counter ogling her decolletage. His transaction obviously complete but in no hurry to leave.

Stanley held Janey's hand as they scanned the store's contents. "What is all this stuff?" Janey asked then suddenly sneezed as the ceiling fan circulated the mixed fragrances of cinnamon, jasmine, sandalwood, and tobacco her way. "Sorry," she whispered as if she was in the library.

Phaedra looked past the man's broad shoulder and saw the troop of teens with a familiar young boy standing by the front door. "Excuse me, sir. I have customers. Thank you for the purchase and please come again soon."

The man left without saying a word but shot the young foursome an annoyed puzzled look as he passed them.

"Jonathan! How good to see you again!" Phaedra said as she sashayed from behind the counter. "And who are your friends?"

Jonathan made the introductions and was about to say something more when Phaedra interrupted him. "Stanley, so nice to finally meet you. Jonathan has told me of your experience with the book."

Stanley...and Tim just stood there with dumb looks on their faces. This young woman had taken their breath away. Stanley's eyes flicked between her face and cleavage until Janey punched him in the arm. "Huh? Oh yeah. Nice to meet you too. The book is why we're here." He pointed to Tim. "We need your help."

Phaedra turned to Tim, whose cheeks had a rosy coloring, and smiled. "It depends on what it is you need my help *with*."

Tim broke out of his stupor and said, "This is not a joke. What we have to tell you is all true. If you don't believe us, we're in serious trouble. And...people are dying."

The smile faded from Phaedra's face, replaced by a look of concern. "People are dying? Are the police involved?"

"Yes," said Tim.

"One moment," Phaedra said holding up a finger.

She strutted to the front door, locked it, and turned the sign over so it now read CLOSED. Then she faced the group with her arms folded across her chest. "Tell me what you did," she said in a voice that sounded very much like a parent about to scold their child.

As Stanley began his tale, Janey stood with her arms crossed as well, scrutinizing—with a touch of envy, but more curiosity— the woman who had the boys enthralled. There was something that didn't seem right. Yes, she looked like a beautiful young woman in her twenties, but her demeanor came across as that of someone older. The way she spoke, the sound of her voice and the way she moved, Janey felt, belonged to a mature adult who knew how to handle people, and this made her feel uncomfortable. What had she gotten herself into?

Janey's intuition was correct.

Phaedra Colefax was born Priscilla Anne Colefax on August 1st, 1921; the only child of wealthy Boston businessman Edward Colefax.

While attending Boston College she met and fell in love with Charles Whitticker. They were both literature majors and found that they both had deep interest in the occult. Charles, totally impressed by her intelligence and wit, let alone her beauty, had taken to calling her Phaedra—the name of the Cretan Princess in Greek mythology—which meant 'bright'. She, of course, was flattered and began calling herself by that name.

In their senior year Charles became obsessed with the writings of a relative who had proposed that a race of ancient beings dwelled in a realm of another dimension. At first, Charles thought the stories purely fiction, but research led him to believe they may be true.

After graduation, he and Phaedra spent the summer on a quest for facts and stumbled upon a book of spells that his relative had supposedly obtained from the mysterious realm. Through the next two years as they pursued their Masters in literature, Charles and Phaedra dabbled with spells from the book to test the legitimacy of the content. There were minor successes which urged them to try more. Then on Phaedra's 25th birthday, Charles playfully cast a spell on her that would prevent the love of his life from ever growing old. They both had laughed at the absurdity of it, saying, "How will we know it worked?"

They had talked about marriage after obtaining their degrees but that never happened. Charles had used the book to find a way into the realm, leaving a frightened Phaedra behind. When he returned a week later, he was different; furtive, anxious, and clingy as if he was afraid he might lose her. He spoke to her with urgency about establishing a church of the Old Ones and how they needed to recruit disciples immediately. Phaedra went along with the idea without question. She was relieved that he was safely back and relished the childlike affection he heaped on her. He had even brought back a piece of brightly polished gold jewelry for her. It was meticulously engraved with bizarre symbols and resembled an Egyptian cartouche. He had asked her to consider this a temporary engagement symbol until they had the time to select a proper ring for her. She accepted the gift and wore it on a thin gold chain around her neck every day.

Unfortunately, they found themselves subject to intense ridicule during the final days of their graduate studies. They were forced to leave.

Charles had become more anxious and paranoid with every passing day. He insisted the church had to be established somewhere else and begged her to come with him. He told her that things would be fine once the church was established, and they could be married. He closed the conversation by saying he had found a house on Long Island where they could live and work unhindered by closed minds.

They both tapped into their lucrative trust funds and purchased the house. Charles took a job at a place with a printing press, where he would secretly make copies of the book of spells. It was to be the church's bible. Phaedra worked in the library. The year was 1947.

This lifestyle went on for several years, until one day she had come home from work and found a note from Charles. Confusion overtook her curiosity as she read:

I've been called. Must go. I have no choice. You must continue with the church while I'm gone. I'll be back as soon as I am able.

I love you dearly,

Charles

After a year of waiting, the loneliness of the big house along with the increasing doubt of his ever returning, forced her to move out. She left the house untouched in the hope he would return to familiar surroundings and took up residency in a spacious apartment above an empty store front in the heart of town.

It was around this time that a question asked years ago was answered.

The librarian, Mrs. Galore, a stout woman in her late fifties, had hired Phaedra back in '47. During the interview she had commented that Phaedra, with her good looks should be a model not a library clerk withering away behind stacks of books.

On this particular day, when she saw Phaedra enter the library she was struck by her appearance. She waited till the girl had taken her place behind the counter and said in a friendly tone, "Phaedra? How *do* you *do* it? You look exactly like you did when I first hired you. Have you discovered the fountain of youth my dear?"

No, not the fountain of youth Mrs. Galore.

Phaedra paced the floor in front of Stanley and Tim silently digesting what she had been told. Her short dress swished with every stride. Jonathan with eyes wide, watched and waited for her response. Janey broke the awkward silence with another sneeze. She would have to get outside soon.

Phaedra stopped her pacing and looked at Jonathan. "Were you involved in this foolishness too?"

He stuck out his chest and said proudly, "No I wasn't. I just borrowed the book from My brother. That's all."

"And…What's your role in all this?" Phaedra said to Janey.

Janey stepped closer to Stanley and took his hand. " I just want to help Stanley get rid of this thing. It almost killed him."

Phaedra nodded. "Very courageous…I guess. My recommendation to you is distance yourself from this situation without hesitation. These two…," she gestured toward Stanley and Tim. "…have started a deadly game and there may be consequences that include you."

Janey squeezed Stanley's hand. "I'll stay. I'm not afraid."

"You should be," Phaedra said to her.

Stanley gave Janey a troubled smile and released her hand. He picked up the schoolbag with the book inside and held it in front of him. "Will you help us? *Can* you help us?"

Phaedra rubbed the gold cartouche pendant, hanging from her slender neck, between her thumb and forefinger. "I will try to help, but no promises. I have an idea that might work. The only problem is we can't attempt anything here. For it to have any chance of working, we'll need to meet at my church."

Stanley, Janey, and Tim all shared puzzled looks with each other.

"Church?" Stanley said.

"You have a *church*?" Jonathan asked.

Phaedra held out the pendant. "Yes Jonathan, don't you remember I told you I was a priestess."

"Oh, *yeah*," said Jonathan.

"If you want to do this, we must all meet as soon as possible." Phaedra moved to the counter, tore a page from a receipt pad and wrote down the address of her church. "Perhaps tomorrow evening?" she said, handing the paper to Stanley.

Stanley silently questioned his brother and friends with just a look. Go or no go?

Tim cracked his knuckles, took a deep breath, and said, "No time to waste. It may be our only chance."

The others nodded.

Phaedra led them to the store's back entrance. Before unlocking, it she said, "Then it's agreed. I'll see you all tomorrow night. You pick a time that works for you. I'll be there waiting."

With that said she pushed open the door and ushered them out into the alleyway.

CHAPTER 51

July 9th —Central General Hospital—morning

"You're looking better," Lieutenant James Trabinski said as he entered Detective Pete Taylor's hospital room with Lieutenant Casey Talbot at his side.

Taylor had a breakfast tray in front of him with empty dishes, an untouched glass of apple juice and half a mug of black coffee. "Morning. I feel fine. Can't wait to get out of here. Though, there is an angel of mercy that checks in on me once in a while. Real cute… jet black hair and single, she could make me want to stay a bit longer." He said with a chuckle.

Casey smiled and said to Trabinski, "He's definitely feeling better."

Taylor put the morning paper he had been reading on the tray stand, picked up the mug of coffee and took a taste. Then nodding at the paper said, "Looks like the curfew has stirred things up. What's happening on our end?"

"That's one of the reasons we're here," Trabinski said as he pushed over a visitor chair for Casey to sit. "We wanted to fill you in since it doesn't look like you'll be attending our little monster bash."

Taylor's face expressed disappointment, but he nodded in agreement.

"We've been authorized to strike the nest...,"Casey said.

Trabinski moved to one side of the bed. "We were able to contact the people who own the building. It's scheduled for demolition by the end of the year. They don't care what we do to it. So, we're off the hook as far as that goes. However...," he looked over at Casey.

"I checked with the people I know at the National Guard base in Jamaica...no flamethrowers. Sorry, but here's the thing. As you well know, that shed or hut or whatever you want to call it, is fabricated metal. Even if we had the units, they would only bake it, not destroy it the way we need."

Taylor grunted. "Okay? How about a bazooka then?"

"Too risky," Casey answered. "The rocket may punch threw it and explode in somebody's back yard. We'd all be in deep manure if that happened."

"Then what? Dynamite?" Taylor continued.

Casey leaned back in the vinyl cushioned chair and crossed her legs. "Too much fuss with the fuses, plus... How would we plant the sticks without the bitch catching us in the act?"

Taylor finished off the mug of coffee. "Why don't we just do the owners a favor and demo the entire building for them? That should do the trick."

"We need to trap her inside the nest. She'd fly away as soon as she realized what was happening," Casey replied.

Taylor raised his good hand in a gesture of frustration. "I give up. What do we use then?"

Trabinski answered in a serious tone, "Pineapples."

"*Pineapples!?* Very funny lieutenant, but I don't get the joke."

Casey chimed in. "The Guard gave us two cases of MK2's. Hand grenades. In the army we called them *pineapples.*"

"Hand grenades. Why didn't I think of that? How do you plan to deliver *these* pineapples? It would be nuts to stand there and throw them. Our friend would definitely see you coming." Taylor said.

"We won't be doing that," Trabinski added.

Casey uncrossed her legs and leaned forward toward Taylor. "Do you remember seeing that small narrow structure at the other end of the roof, when we flew over it the other day? It had a door."

Taylor shook his head. "Don't think I saw it."

"Well, we found out…actually Jim found out from the owners, that there's a inside stairway that goes up to the roof. It ends at that door. That will be our vantage point.

"The plan is to use a grenade launcher from that doorway. I happen to have two M1 Garand rifles that I smuggled back from Korea. One has an attachment for launching grenades. Jim and I will quietly set up, at that position, and I'll blow the bitch up with a couple of grenades from my rifle. A little retribution from yours truly."

Taylor put his good arm behind his head. "Not as cool as flame-throwers…but I like it. So…Two questions. How will you know she's in there and when do the fireworks begin?"

Trabinski scratched the back of his head. "It's a fifty-fifty chance she'll be in there but based on her MO of killing the teenage girls at night we're confident she'll be resting during the daylight hours. So, with that in mind we'll make our move today, at noon." He glanced at his watch, then at Casey. "In fact, we should be going."

Taylor reached out and did an awkward left-handed shake of Trabinski's hand, then gently held the tips of Casey's fingers. "Good luck you two. Send my love to that she demon along with one of those pineapples."

***

The abandoned warehouse—Noon

In an effort to be discreet in their movements, Trabinski had borrowed a used mail truck and parked it in the weeds growing through the cracked driveway in front of the warehouse. The hope was this vehicle would not attract unwanted attention from above.

Casey— dressed in a dark green army T-shirt, khaki tactical trousers and black combat boots—sat in the back of the truck prepping the M1 Garand grenade launcher. Six grenades had been carefully packed in a heavy canvas army duffle bag. Trabinski would carry this to the roof top.

While assured by the owners of the warehouse that nothing flammable or explosive currently existed in the building, Trabinski recruited the Bethpage fire department to have a truck standing by. It was parked a block away from the building. Using a Walkie-Talkie, he alerted them that they were about to proceed, then handed it to Casey.

She contacted Haggerty and Reese who sat in an unmarked car across the street from the fire truck. "Gentlemen, we are heading into the building now. Stay put till I give you the all clear. If you don't hear from me shortly after the explosions...come a running. Ten-four?"

"Ten-four lieutenant," Haggerty said.

Trabinski— wearing a black t-shirt, blue jeans, and Herman's Survivor work boots—slid out the driver's side of the truck and hurried around to the rear door and opened it. "You ready?" he said to Casey. He was a bit worried about her being able to fire this weapon with her wrist still in a cast.

"Show time. Let's go!"

Trabinski, remembering the jungle that surrounded the building and its entrance, brought with him the fifteen inch Bowie knife Gary Ojika had given him as a Christmas gift.

During their Coast Guard days Gary had called him Jim Bowie because of his obsession with the history of the Alamo. So he thought the knife with the carved bone handle would be an appropriate gift. Trabinski treasured it and always kept the blade sharp.

After cutting through the thick vegetation that hampered their approach, Trabinski carefully unlocked the main door with the key he had obtained from the warehouse owner. They stepped into a vast empty space and walked softly to prevent their foot falls from echoing as they approached the metal stairway.

At the top of the stairs Trabinski gently placed the duffle bag on the landing and slowly disengaged the door's deadbolt.

Casey, carrying her rifle, came up behind him. "Sure hope that miserable bitch is in there," she said sotto voce.

"Me too," Trabinski said as he gingerly opened the door part way, trying to keep the squeak of the rusty hinges at a minimum. Bright July sunshine spilled in, temporarily blinding them. Casey quickly pulled a pair of sunglasses from one of the many pockets in her trousers and put them on. "Open the door a little more so I can center this thing."

Trabinski did as he was told and was surprised to see her position the rifle with its stock touching the floor of the landing with the barrel facing up and out. He had pictured her holding it in a conventional manner, firing from the shoulder position.

"Okay. Hand me a pineapple and let's make fruit salad of this monstrosity."

She took the grenade from Trabinski and secured it in place. "When I fire this…give me another right away. I'm going to try and put this love note directly into the nest through that slightly opened door."

"Got It."

Casey took a deep breath, let it out slowly and squeezed the trigger. There was a loud pop as the grenade sailed across the rooftop arcing between the twisted door and the shed frame. The door exploded into the air and the frame buckled. Casey quickly launched a second grenade and it sailed swiftly into the nest entrance. A thunderous explosion blew the roof off. Pieces of metal and debris shot skyward. A large wheeled valve still attached to piping plummeted to the rooftop.

"One more!" Casey shouted. She reached out and Trabinski carefully placed the third grenade in her hand. Though slightly hampered by the cast she adroitly fixed the ordinance to the Garand and fired. The grenade fell in the center of the smoking remains of the shed and blew the walls out in three directions.

As the smoke began to clear they could see another wheeled valve of some sort protruding from what was once the floor of the shed. Rubble lay scattered across the roof. There was nothing left of the nest.

Casey and Trabinski stood up and stepped out onto the roof. She reached over and unclipped the Walkie-Talkie from his belt and gave the all clear to Haggerty and asked him to advise the firemen that their services wouldn't be needed. And, thanks for the help. She looked up at Trabinski who was standing there with his hands on his hips. "What's up?"

He took the Walkie-Talkie from her and said, "Let's go check out your handy work."

They strode toward the ruins, carefully stepping over fragments of twisted metal until they came to the smoldering hole in the roof. Scattered around it were small white fragments that appeared to be bone as well as pieces of cloth. Nothing that looked like the remains of the harpy.

"What do you think?" Trabinski asked.

Casey took off her sunglasses and peered into the hole, hoping to see the twisted bat winged shape of the dead harpy somewhere below. She saw only debris and dusty smoke. " I don't know," she said stepping back from the hole. " We should have seen something. Heard something. Some indication she was in there and injured. I hate to say it, but I think we missed her."

"I think you're right."

As Trabinski scanned the detritus laying on the roof around him for anything they may have overlooked, Casey knelt down to examine the white chunks of matter scattered before her. She used a small piece of jagged metal from the shed to pick up a shredded piece of cloth. A quick, soft moan escaped her lips.

Trabinski turned his head. "Casey? What is it?"

She stood, still holding the piece of metal with the cloth hanging from the tip. "This looks like bathing suit material," she said pointing to the strip of fabric. "I think we found Eddie Franks."

Trabinski pulled the walkie talkie from his belt. "I'll tell Haggerty to call forensics."

Casey put the piece of cloth back where she found it and looked up at Trabinski. "This is the part of my job I hate. I've been told you get numb to it. I don't think I ever will."

"You won't," said Trabinski. "Unless, you're not human."

They strode back to the stairway.

"Okay, so we missed the damn thing," Trabinski said. "But maybe she'll be too busy finding a new nest to hunt down anymore young girls."

"And after she finds one…What the hell do we do?" Casey said trying to control her frustration.

"Let's see what her next move is. The task force basically has a drag-net out for her. We have cruisers patrolling everywhere. And if people are paying attention to the ten o'clock curfew as well as the press, she has to be feeling the pinch. Maybe she'll make a mistake, do something stupid."

"Hmmm…I hope you're right. Let's go file our report and face the music," Casey said.

***

Malhela was feeling frustrated as well. She had spent the morning doing recon on the places where she had seen birthgivers before and was feeling vexed by not finding any. Even the yards with the ponds were without swimmers of any age.

The birthgivers she encountered were all in groups, most accompanied by males. She sensed a sort of uneasiness radiating from them. *What was going on here?*

To add to her frustration, she saw the four wheeled conveyances used by the police mortals everywhere she went. This coupled with the locked birthgiver windows she had experienced the night before, led her to believe there was a conspiracy afoot.

A feeling of desperation started to creep up on her. She needed a replenishment of birthgiver essence soon. Her body was starting to ache for it. She may have to take drastic measures.

As she headed back towards her nest to think things over, she heard a *boom,* then another and another. She saw smoke billowing in the distance, directly in her flight path. She recalled the night of the exploding stars. *What could these maddening mortals be up to now?* Malhela never thought it could be her nest and continued on. Suddenly she saw the ruins of her onetime refuge through the dissipating smoke. She couldn't believe her eyes. She looked around, confused, thinking she was someplace else. But realization settled in. Her nest was gone. And she knew who was responsible. This was an attack by the elf woman and her mechanical dragon fly.

Her hatred for the elf woman came to a boil in her head building to an explosive pressure that suddenly sent a sharp stabbing pain to the base of her skull; so excruciating that for a moment she literally could not see. She let out a screech that would have made the sound of finger-nails on a blackboard seem like a lullaby. Rage followed close behind.

With her hands on both sides of her head, Malhela thrashed and spun upward through the cloud dappled sky, until finally the pain subsided. The rage, however, took over. Her blurred vision caused her to fly in an erratic pattern. She closed her eyes and rode the updrafts for a while trying to calm the rage. When she finally opened them, she could once again see clearly, despite the dull throbbing behind her eyes. In the distance she could make out a dark spire jutting out above a dense tree line. Perhaps an adequate place for a nest. She darted towards it.

CHAPTER 52

July 9th—Late afternoon

Patches of fading afternoon sunlight, broke through the Elm trees that lined Plainview Road as three teenagers and one young boy walked furtively along the sidewalk.

The teenagers had told their parents they were going to see the new Walt Disney movie *The Moon Spinners* at the Clearview Cinema on South Oyster Bay Road. The young boy insisted he wanted to see that movie too. They would take the bus to and from. They promised to be home before curfew.

What they failed to tell their parents was, they were going to see the movie someday, but not tonight.

Tim Ryan, Stanley Bolton, and Jonathan Bolton met Janey Del Grasso on the corner and proceeded toward the address given to them by Phaedra Colefax. She had told them the book was not needed so Stanley had left it stashed underneath his bed at home.

"Any problems with your parents letting you out?" Stanley asked Tim.

Tim gave a quick laugh. "You won't believe this. They actually thought it was a good idea. I think they felt sorry for me, or it may have been due to my father's lawyer calling to say the police no longer considered me a suspect. I'm no longer under observation. So, that works out great for our plan. We don't have to worry about somebody following me."

"Very cool," said Stanley.

Jonathan looked at the paper with the address of the meeting place written on it. He glanced across the street and quickly scanned the numbers on the mailboxes. "Hey, this place isn't far. It should be right over there." He pointed to a corner house on the other side of the road.

Janey stopped walking. "Wait. *That's* where we're going?"

"Looks like it," Tim said.

"I don't know about this," Janey said, suddenly looking frightened. "That's the old Whitticker place. It's supposed to be haunted."

Stanley put his arm around her. "I thought you didn't *believe* in ghosts?"

"Well…A girl can change her mind. That place always gives me the creeps."

Jonathan looked both ways for cars then said as he darted across the street, "Come on. It's fine. There's lights on and everything."

Feeling nervous and excited at the same time, Jonathan went up the repaired porch steps to the front door. A sign taped there, read, GO AROUND BACK.

The foursome followed a broken and crumbling walkway around the right side of the house and spotted a barn-like structure. It was obviously being renovated. The front wood panels were unpainted and looked new as did the large double doors. A temporary light fixture had been placed above the door; its naked bulb surrounded by flying insects cast a speckled glow over the entrance.

Ladders rested against a side wall, leading up to a makeshift scaffolding on the roof. A stack of shingles as well as strips of plywood lay on the ground nearby.

As they came closer, they noticed an odd-looking black car parked on the grass behind the house.

"What kind of car is that?" Janey asked Stanley.

Jonathan answered for him. "Looks like a 1963 Studebaker Avanti."

"Nice," Tim commented. "Expensive."

While they were admiring the automobile, Jonathan caught movement out of the corner of his eye. He turned and watched as the double doors opened. "Guys? Time to go." He pointed to the barn.

Phaedra Colefax beckoned to them from the entrance. "Come in, come in," she called. She was wearing a black, hooded silk gown with a plunging neckline adorned with the glistening gold pendant.

Witch, Janey thought with a shiver.

The movie *Black Sabbath,* immediately came to Tim's mind.

Hmmm… Thought Stanley.

"She's so *beautiful,*" Jonathan whispered.

Phaedra ushered them inside. "Welcome to the church of the Ancient Realm," she said with a flourish. "As you can see, I'm doing some remodeling."

The interior of the building had the tangy sweet smell of cut pine. Everything appeared new, including the ceiling rafters and beams;

rectangular pewter box lamps attached to long black chains hung from them, casting brilliant light throughout the nave.

Two short rows of pews on either side of the hard wood aisle were in the process of being sanded while others behind them were in varying stages of construction. Miscellaneous tools—Hammers, chisels, screwdrivers, files, and hand sanders— were strewn haphazardly around the work area.

The only item that did not look new was the altar situated on a raised oak platform in the sanctuary.

Its base, a large chiseled hunk of weathered granite, displayed a large replica of the cartouche worn by Phaedra at its center. On top rested a flat, rectangular slab of marbled stone. Pewter candelabras sat at each end of the slab with unlit candles. A large book had been placed between them.

The foursome examined their surroundings in silence. They were alone with Phaedra in this echoing hall.

"It will be a beautiful place of worship when completed," Phaedra said. "Shall we attempt to reverse the spell you wrought?"

She led them to the altar, asked Stanley to light the candles on one candelabra and Tim the other, then opened the book with reverence. She took the matches from Tim and lit the leafy contents of an ornate clay bowl which had been placed on a small, scalloped pedestal near the book. A thin column of smoke snaked upward releasing a heady fragrance of incense and sandalwood.

Jonathan, though engrossed in Phaedra's every move still noticed that this book was much larger than the one they had. *This must have all the spells and anti-spells,* he thought.

Phaedra gently placed a hand on Stanley's shoulder and said in a soft voice, "Tell me again the name of the entity you summoned."

Stanley hesitated. Even though he had given the name to Phaedra at her store, he felt nervous about saying it aloud again.

Phaedra squeezed his shoulder. " Go ahead. Tell me."

Stanley looked into her hypnotic green eyes. *This is why we're here. Can't wimp out now.*

"Malhela," he said in a voice just above a whisper.

She looked over at Tim. "Say her name."

Tim steadied himself. He was feeling a bit lightheaded. "Malhela," he muttered.

Phaedra took a step back from the boys. "Please stand below in front of the altar facing me."

When Tim and Stanley were in position she said in a matter-of-fact tone, " I can't promise this will work. I've had success before with reversing spells but never involving a being of this nature." She flipped a couple of pages in the book. " This Malhela is a powerful, magical creature and quite deadly. I'm not sure what to expect when I call her. I will apply the knowledge I have of the realm to hopefully send her back. Shall I proceed?"

Four pairs of wide eyes looked up at her.

"Um? Stanley?" Janey whimpered. "I don't like this. I think I'll wait outside."

Before Stanley could answer, Tim said, " Janey? That's *not* a good idea. Did you forget about what happened at the dance?"

The look on her face said she understood but she didn't say anything more.

Stanley stepped away from the altar, took Janey's hand and led her to one of the finished pews. " I won't let anything happen to you. Just sit here. You'll be okay," he said giving her a quick peck on the lips.

Back at the altar, Stanley glanced at Tim. "Ready?"

Tim nodded. "Let's finish this."

Stanley looked up at Phaedra. " Go ahead."

Jonathan stood behind Tim. He had his hands in his pockets and swayed side to side. He waited in expectation of something mysterious and magical happening. He looked at his brother who stood like he was at attention. Then at Tim who was cracking his knuckles. Then at Janey whose face was as white as her blouse. He suddenly realized he was holding his breath and exhaled.

At that moment he thought Phaedra was leaving. She stepped away from the altar and headed for the side door. All four heads turned, eyes following her as she opened the door to the yard outside. But, to their relief she returned to the altar without a word.

"Let us begin," she said, as she pulled the gown's hood up over her head. She picked up the fragrant clay bowl and waved it over the book a few times.

"Malhela, Malhela! Veni nunc ad me!" she chanted. "In nomine Cytizuz, summus dominus regni. Praecipio tibi videri."

Phaedra set down the bowl, raised her hands and commanded Malhela again to appear in the name of Cytizuz, high lord of the realm. She waited. Nothing happened. She flipped another page and clutched the gold pendant hanging around her neck. "Malhela, Malhela! Appear and be released!" she said in Latin.

A *whoosh, whoosh* sound came from outside, then the door rattled as if caught by a gust of wind and a dark figure entered the light.

After enduring the day's failure with the nest and a demeaning session with Captain Philbrick, James Trabinski and Casey Talbot felt they deserved at least a good dinner. So, they went home, changed and were now on the way to their favorite restaurant, The Broadway Café.

Trabinski had picked up Casey at her apartment, cruised down South Oyster Bay Road and turned onto Plainview Road. They had driven about a quarter mile in companionable silence when Casey suddenly said, " Unless I'm delirious from fatigue, I just saw Tim Ryan and Stanley Bolton at that house back there."

"What house?" Trabinski asked as he slowed his car.

"On the corner we just passed. A creepy looking place. They were with a girl and a little boy. I thought Ryan was a suspect under observation?"

Trabinski made a U-turn. "Based on what we now know about the harpy, we cut him loose. Waste of manpower tailing him when the task force needed all hands on deck."

"Makes sense," Casey said. "I wonder what they're doing there?"

" That's the old Whitticker place. It's been abandoned for a long time. People claimed it was haunted. Maybe they're on a trick or treat recon," he laughed.

" Halloween's a ways off. They all look nervous, like they're up to something. Can you pull over?"

Trabinski parked at the curb and turned off the engine. "They're going around to the back of the house," he said.

Casey shivered, even though the evening was a balmy seventy- five degrees. "Jim? I think we better check this out. I'm getting a feeling that something's not right here."

"Strong feeling or a hunch?"

"Not a hunch," Casey replied.

Trabinski leaned over, opened the glove compartment, and removed a Colt .45 Government model 1911 classic pistol. He handed it to Casey, then reached under the front seat and grabbed his .38 Special.

They exited the vehicle, tucked the weapons behind them in their waist bands and strode across the street.

Trabinski went up the front steps to the door of the old house and read the sign taped there. " 'Go around back' is all it says. Let's go have a look," he said to Casey.

They cautiously followed the crumbling walkway to the back of the building and stopped at its corner perusing the area in front of them.

"Looks like someone's rebuilding that barn," Casey said pointing to the structure at the back of the property. "Why would the kids have anything to do with that?"

"Maybe it's something innocent? Like a square dance or some-thing of that nature. But whoever is running this show has money," he said and gestured toward the black Avanti. "You don't see too many of those."

"Doesn't feel innocent to me," Casey said.

They stood there in silence, listening. "Too quiet," Casey said softly. "No crickets or katydids."

Then they heard a scream.

Janey jumped up and screamed at the sight of the creature before her. Stanley rushed to her side but was instantly knocked to the floor by an invisible force.

Malhela stood in a hunched fighter's stance with her arms slightly out stretched from her sides. She glared at the healthy birthgiver standing there screaming. The craving for the female's essence fogged her thinking. Malhela needed to taste that flesh, *now.*

Tim Ryan stood frozen in place. Memories of that night in his room came flooding back to him. The flashbacks instantly fired in succession. He wanted to run but couldn't get his feet to move. He saw Stanley on the floor, struggling to get up. *We're all gonna die*, he thought. Then Phaedra stepped down from the altar and confronted the harpy.

Malhela, let her approach and scrutinized her appearance. She noticed the symbol of Cytizuz hanging around her neck and fought back the craving. She tilted her head and said in a menacing tone, "And...*who are you?*"

Phaedra stepped in front of Malhela and held up the gold cartouche. " I am Phaedra, high priestess of the church of the Ancient Realm. Keeper of the word of Cytizuz. I…"

" Nonsense!" Malhela shouted as she tossed Phaedra up the aisle like a rag doll.

Jonathan, who had been watching the scene unfold with frightened interest, ran when he saw Phaedra go down.

Without warning the front entrance doors to the barn crashed open. Trabinski fired two shots into the air. "Stop right there," he said to Malhela as he slowly moved up the aisle.

Casey did a flanking maneuver to the right. Her pistol aimed at the harpy.

Malhela instantly recognized Casey and let loose an ungodly screech that caused them all to cringe. Then with a hiss and wave of the hand sent Casey flying into a stack of two by fours staged for construction near the entrance. Her pistol skittered across the floor.

Trabinski went to fire but held up when the creature grabbed the girl. Suddenly, his gun flew from his hand, and he found himself sprawled out on the dusty floor.

Malhela brought her arm around the birthgiver's throat and began frantically tearing off the clothes she wore with her other hand. The birthgiver was struggling and screaming.

In the throes of this feeding frenzy, Malhela ceased removing the clothing and positioned her hand on the birthgiver's head preparing to break her neck and silence her, but she abruptly stopped.

Malhela's head snapped back, and her arms shook, releasing the birthgiver. A sharp pain pierced her back between her wings. She hissed and bared her teeth in a hideous grimace. She felt the pain go deeper paralyzing her where she stood.

Jonathan Bolton, fueled by pure adrenaline, drove the twelve-inch shank screw- driver he had found among the scattered tools, deep into the harpy's back. He remembered reading that doing this would immobilize the creature as long as it wasn't removed. He gave the handle a final shove and hurried away to help Phaedra.

Trabinski helped Casey get to her feet then retrieved their weapons as Stanley went to a shaking Janey—who was desperately trying to cover herself with the remains of her tattered blouse.

Tim Ryan, still standing in the same spot stared at the stricken Malhela. *What do we do now?* From the corner of his eye, he saw Phaedra limping up the aisle with Jonathan at her side.

Lieutenant James Trabinski was wondering the same thing. He scanned the construction materials for a rope or wire. Something to tie up this weird beauty. But found nothing useful.

Casey wondered who this woman Phaedra was, and what role she played in all this, as she watched her go to the altar and flip some pages of a large book that had been placed between two lit candelabras.

The room was as quiet as a tomb. Even Janey's sniffling had died away. Malhela stood like a shivering statue.

Phaedra raised her arms and chanted in Latin, "Malhela, in the name of Cytizuz, lord of the ancient realm, I open the gates for you. In the name of Cytizuz, I, high priestess of this holy church dissolve the conjuring that summoned you. In the name of Cytizuz, I say the words. You, Malhela, are released from this task. Leave us!"

They all watched in awe as a spiraling vertical cloud appeared around the harpy like a fluorescent halo. Slowly it changed to a swirling, blue gray shroud around her. There were tiny flashes of light from within. Then, as quickly as it had come, it was gone, taking the harpy with it.

Jonathan's screwdriver fell to the floor.

For a moment Stanley and Tim's eyes met. A profound understanding passed between them.

Trabinski turned to Casey, who was staring at the spot where the harpy had been, and said, "You okay?"

Casey blinked. "I'm fine. Trying to understand what just happened here."

"I know what you mean," Trabinski said. "At least we can finally put this case in the *closed* file."

Casey took his hand. "I hope so."

***

The vertical cloud irised open spilling Malhela onto the cinereous landscape of the realm. It took a moment for the dizziness to subside and her eyes to adjust to the gloom, but one quick glance through the amber haze told her she was home.

Just as she heaved a sigh of relief she felt strong hands seize both her arms. She immediately struggled to free herself but gave up when she heard a wet snort and caught the pungent scent of Cityzuz's guards.

Two Gratherx—three eyed, hog-like beings—stood on either side of her. She knew there was no way of breaking free of these powerful creatures, so she remained still, thinking.

As Malhela was about to protest this type of treatment as a citizen of the realm a familiar voice said, "Welcome home sister. The Lord wants to see you."

EPILOGUE

The days following the harpy's demise had a relaxed feel to them. The curfew had been lifted. The tension in the air abated. And life in Hillsville along with the surrounding neighborhoods appeared to be getting back to normal, especially after the *Long Island Daily Press* headline hit the streets.

COUNTY COPS TAKE DOWN DEADLY KILLER IN ABANDONDED WAREHOUSE.

Though this was based on a spin statement released by Captain Philbrick, it answered all the pertinent questions and neatly avoided the sticky ones. It put people's minds at ease.

Tim Ryan looked forward to spending the remaining weeks of summer as a new member of a band known as the *Interludes*, playing lead guitar for them. It didn't matter that their repertoire was geared toward the songs of the Rolling Stones and Motown; music was back in his life.

Janey Del Grasso spent the days after being attacked trying to get herself back together emotionally. For a few days she blamed Stanley for what had happened but soon realized she was being unfair, especially since she had been given the opportunity to not be involved. Stanley had apologized and asked her forgiveness —which she quickly gave.

To confirm his true feelings he presented her with a sparkling, pink crystal ring and formally asked her to go steady. He had no pin to give her and couldn't afford a High School ring, but Janey lovingly accepted the ring as if it was a real diamond. The thoughts of summer lovin' and hot August days at the beach pushed the lingering darkness away.

Jonathan Bolton had other plans for the rest of the summer. His curiosity about the mysteries of the occult had grown stronger and so he took possession of the book of spells— the thought of using it to find his brother Artie still engrossed him. He defused Stanley's protest by saying, "Don't worry. I'll be careful. I can always ask Phae for help."

Now that he knew she lived nearby, he spent as much time with her as possible, learning everything he could about the Church of the Ancient Realm. He was intrigued by it all, and she never discouraged him.

Phaedra, during these days and weeks had met with a series of roadblocks that slowed her progress with the church: She had failed to file the proper documents to establish a legal house of worship, had not obtained township permits to do the construction on the property and had received notices from township officials questioning her intent.

Adding to her frustration, the police wanted to confiscate the book of spells, claiming it remained a possible threat to the safety of the public. To appease them she promised to destroy the book.

Captain Philbrick demanded there be witnesses to make certain the dangerous instrument was indeed eliminated.

Lieutenant Trabinski assigned the task to the still recuperating Detective Pete Taylor since he was not able to do anything more rigorous than watch and do paperwork.

Phaedra cunningly burned a book—one of the many copies she had stored at the Apothecary—in a brief ceremony at the church while Taylor and his new girlfriend, Nurse Linda Marantz watched the proceedings. The original book of spells had been secretly locked away in an old desk inside her house.

On the afternoon of Friday, July 31st, Jim Trabinski had taken Casey to have her cast finally removed. The doctor gave her a clean bill of health plus some exercises and sent her on her way.

They sat in Trabinski's Impala waiting for traffic to clear so they could leave the doctor's parking lot when Casey said, "Remember that restaurant you took me to on our first date?"

"Sure, the Blue Grotto. What about it?"

"Let's have dinner there," she said romantically as she leaned her head on his shoulder.

In the dim blue light of the restaurant, Casey and Jim sat at a table adjacent to a wall of aquariums, waiting for their drinks to arrive. Casey stared at the numerous multicolored tropical fish that glided through the tanks.

Trabinski noticed a look on her face that he had not seen before. It could only be described as *dreamy*. He was about to say something when she turned her head and smiled at him. To him it looked like the smile of a person who had made a happy decision.

The drinks were served; Chablis for her, Jack Daniels on the rocks for him. They toasted each other and each took a sip. Casey looked at her left hand as if examining it. Then wiggled her fingers.

"Stiff?" Trabinski asked, thinking about her hand being immobile in the cast all these weeks.

She answered with a question. "Remember our boat trip that was so rudely interrupted?"

" I'll never forget it," Trabinski replied.

"Do you remember what you asked me?"

Trabinski grinned.

Casey put her left hand out, palm down and wiggled her fingers playfully in front of him. With her pixie hair style and twinkling gray eyes she looked like a little girl at Christmas time.

"I'm ready," she said with a giggle. "Let's pick a date."

The day after Stanley had given Janey the ring, he felt compelled to make amends with the other important person in his life.

He and Janey found Tim just finishing up his newspaper deliveries. Quick hellos were exchanged followed by an awkward silence as Tim and Stanley stood looking at each other. Janey held Stanley's hand wondering what was about to happen.

Tim finally broke the silence. "So? I guess we can finally breathe easy. The nightmare is over."

Stanley nodded, took a deep breath, exhaled slowly, and said, "Look Tim," he hesitated a moment then continued. "I'm really sorry about everything that happened. I swear. No...I promise I'll never mess around with anything involving the occult again no matter how bored I get."

Tim reached out and shook Stanley's hand. "That goes for me too. What do you say we hit Hurley's and close the deal?"

Stanley smiled. "You buying?"

ABOUT THE AUTHOR

P.A.Russell is a fiction writer and professional musician. He is a Sci-Fi film and television aficionado and co-author of *The Amazing Science Fiction and Horror Trivia Game*.

Authors Michael Crichton, Clive Cussler, Douglas Preston and Lincoln Child have had a strong influence on his writing.

After attending numerous writer's workshops and courses to hone his story telling skills he is excited to present his debut novel *A Call to Evil*.

He is a graduate of Fairleigh Dickinson University and resides with his wife in Roxbury Township, New Jersey.

The author welcomes your comments. Please send via email to pruss44697@aol.com.